THE LOST GIRLS OF ST ANN'S

An utterly heartbreaking and gripping family saga

CATH STAINCLIFFE

Originally published as *Trio*

JOFFE BOOKS

Revised edition 2024
Joffe Books, London
www.joffebooks.com

First published by Severn House Publishers Ltd
in 2002 as *Trio*

This paperback edition was first published
in Great Britain in 2024

Cover art by Jarmila Takač

ISBN: 978-1-83526-387-7

AUTHOR'S NOTE

I was adopted as a baby and in the last few years I have been re-united with my Irish birth family, including seven full brothers and sisters. Of course, I have drawn on my own experience of adoption and that of my families and friends in writing the book, as well as using anecdotes, stories and accounts I have come across over the years — it would be impossible not to. But *The Lost Girls of St Ann's* is not my story: it is fiction not fact, the characters here are invented and their adventures imagined.

In 1960, thousands of babies were placed for adoption in the UK. This is the story of three of them . . .

ACKNOWLEDGEMENTS

This book is dedicated with love to my parents: Evelyn and M.J. and Margaret and David. And with thanks to After Adoption in Manchester and NORCAP, who do so much to support people involved with adoption.

PRINCIPLE CHARACTERS

Theresa: Adoptee
Kay & Adam: Adoptive parents of Theresa (also Dominic, Martin and Michael)
Caroline: Birth mother of Theresa
Paul: Caroline's husband
Davey & Sean: Caroline and Paul's children

* * *

Pamela: Adoptee
Lilian & Peter: Adoptive parents of Pamela
Joan: Birth mother of Pamela
Penny: Joan's partner

* * *

Nina: Adoptee
Marjorie & Robert: Adoptive parents of Nina and Stephen
Megan & Brendan: Birth parents of Nina (also Francine, Aidan and Chris)

PROLOGUE

'Stop your noise,' the nurse said. 'Remember your dignity.'

She felt like laughing at the reprimand. Dignity? How could this ever be dignified. Lying here with her legs apart and everything leaking and she'd even dirtied the bed. She had been mortified, the smell alerting her to what she'd done. She felt nothing beyond the fist of pain that kept squeezing at her, pulling at her insides, sticking its nails like knives into her spine and bruising her bowels. Making her scream to her God, to her mother. Why have you abandoned me?

The baby inched a little further down the birth canal with the next contraction. One fist was pressed between shoulder and ear, the other tucked under the chin. The ripples of muscle shifted the baby, twisting it a little, squeezing the head, which was cone-shaped from the pressure and from the last couple of weeks spent lodged tight in the cup of bones. As it moved forward the plates of the baby's skull slid together, reducing the circumference. The baby could still hear the familiar drumbeat that had marked its time in the womb and feel the vibrations that rocked its world. Though the sloshing and roaring of the placenta was more distant now and there were new sounds, fast and high-pitched, that quickened the baby's heartbeat.

'Give a good push,' the nurse said. 'Push from your bottom.'

She didn't want to push. She wanted to die instead. To be anywhere or nowhere. Not to be here. If she pushed she would split wide open, bleed to death. She'd rather die before the push than after it. Spare herself more agony. The ring of pain sickened her and she tried to swallow.

'No,' she managed.

The nurse tutted at her loudly, cast a look of contempt.

'It hurts,' she whimpered. Wanting her mother, wanting a cuddle, someone to gather her close and make it all better.

'You should have thought of that, shouldn't you?' The nurse snapped. 'I've other girls to see to. I can't spend all night with you. The baby won't be born by itself; you'll have to push.'

She lay back as the contraction faded, weak, her limbs trembling, eyes closed.

'I'll be back in a few minutes. You're not the only one having a baby, you know. All that fuss.'

She heard the door close. Gave in to sudden hot tears.

Please God, she prayed, help me — please, please help me. She was cold now. Shivering and too weak to reach the blanket folded just so at the bottom of the bed. She felt a roll of nausea, a sour wash in her mouth and throat but nothing came.

I hate you, she cursed the nurse. She was too young for this, barely a woman. She wanted her childhood back. To run home to her mother and show her the pain. Help me.

A fierce contraction tore through her thoughts, catapulting her upright. She tried to press her fingers deep into the flat bones at the base of her back, trying to match the pain with more of her own, but it didn't help, she couldn't push deep enough. She would move when the pain stopped. She moaned, her mouth apart, her lips cracked, a long, slow, deep sound. The pain ebbed away. Shakily she pitched forward, shuffling to get where she wanted. Simple movements demanded such concentration, as though nothing was working right anymore. She managed to get on to her hands and knees, facing the end of the bed.

The baby hiccupped twice, its head only a couple of centimetres from the opening. The roaring sound was fading, the drumbeat went on. The baby's heartbeat speeded up.

Then it came. Relentless, like a log rolling through her, an overwhelming compulsion to push. She was amazed at the power of it. She hadn't wanted to before, didn't even know what she was supposed to do, though some of the girls had said you just pretended you were bunged up and going to the toilet, but now it was all happening. Her body knew exactly what to do. She closed her eyes, aware how her breathing had changed; she was panting now like a dog in the sun. Appalled and energised by the sensation, she began to make a curious growling sound deep in her throat. Like a wolf, for heaven's sake. She felt herself stretching, opening, the unstoppable force bearing down through her and on and on. Then it receded and she hung, quiet, hearing only the harsh stuttering of her breath.

It came again, before she was ready — faster, wilder. She made the noise in her throat, shifted her knees a little further apart, gripped the sheet and wound it tight in her hands. Stretching wider, feeling her mouth stretching too to let the howling out. Feeling the hard, round, solid lump forced through her vagina, gristle against gristle, bone on bone. A stabbing, stinging pain in the midst of it all.

As the baby's head was born, the upper torso swivelled so that one shoulder presented itself for the next push.

She lowered her head to rest between her arms on the bed. She gazed back but could not see anything beyond the swell of her belly and behind that her knees. Summoning all her strength she pushed herself back up, kneeled higher, steadying herself with one arm she reached back between her legs with the other hand. She felt a thrill of shock as she felt the hot, slippery hair of the baby's head, the scalp loose and wrinkled under her fingers.

'Oh God,' she gasped. 'Oh, God.'

The next contraction rolled in. She shuffled forward before it built, and clutched at the metal bed frame for leverage. Pushing it to counteract the force. She felt the new friction of the mass forcing its way from her, stretching her body, bursting her open.

The roar she made grew louder and culminated in a gasp as the weight slithered from her with a sucking sound. She knelt, her muscles twitching with spasms, and looked beneath the bridge of her body to where the baby lay. A coil of life, shock of black hair, red skin streaked white, as though it had been dipped in dripping, eyes, nose, mouth. One fist tucked under an ear, as if it was considering something. The other fist moving, waving to and fro. Long, curving cord like something from the abattoir, snaking from its belly.

She looked at the baby.

The baby looked back.

The door swung open.

'Lie down,' barked the nurse, 'you'll fall, you silly . . .' She faltered as she neared the bed and saw the infant. 'You could have crushed it,' she scolded. 'What on earth were you thinking of? Turn this way, carefully.' She issued instructions until the woman was lying on her back again. She raised the baby and slapped it on the bottom. A thin wail cut the air. The woman wanted to cry too. The nurse proceeded to cut and clamp the umbilical cord, wipe the mucus from the baby's face and wrap the baby in a cloth.

A second nurse came in. A younger one, who had been more sympathetic when she had been admitted. She looked at the baby. 'A girl,' she observed. 'Bless her. Have you got a name?'

'She's for adoption,' the other interrupted.

'Can I see her?' the mother asked.

'You're not finished yet. You've still to deliver the afterbirth. Then you'll need examining and see if there's any stitches required. You probably tore yourself leaping around on the bed like that. You'll need cleaning up and Baby needs to be checked and weighed. Sister will take her to the nursery.'

'I have a shawl,' she said, hating the tears in her voice.

'I'll take it with her, shall I?' The younger nurse offered. The simple kindness robbed her of speech. She nodded quickly.

'In your bag, is it?' Another nod.

The nurse took the wool-and-silk shawl and the baby and left.

She felt a fresh contraction, leaned her head back against the metal bars of the bed, eyes squeezed tight shut, lips compressed. A ring of grief swelling in her throat, choking her. Theresa, she thought, remembering the black pools of the baby's eyes. That's her name, Theresa . . .

* * *

. . . Outside the door, poised for flight. Her heart was bumping too fast in her chest, fingers clenched. She could just go. Turn and walk away. Cruel, yes, but not impossible. This side of the door there was still room for fantasies, for dreams of what she might be like, for scenes of happy ever after, of coming home, of finding peace. But in there, once across the threshold, there would only ever be reality: stark, unrelenting, unchangeable. No going back. No escape. Her ears were buzzing and her skull and back felt tight with tension. She couldn't breathe properly.

She closed her eyes momentarily, fighting the rising panic. Don't think. Just open the door.

She put her hand out and grasped the handle. Turned and pushed. Stepped into the room. Saw the woman on the couch rise unsteadily to her feet. Smiling. Moving towards her, mouth working with emotion. Little exclamations popping softly, *hello, oh, hello*. Arms opening, eyes drinking her in.

The two women embrace.

The younger started to cry, noisy sobs and sucking sounds.

'Twenty-eight years,' the other said, her voice muffled with emotion. 'I never thought I'd see you again. Come on.'

She led her daughter to the couch and sat with one arm around her, listening to her weep. She smelled her hair and felt the smooth skin of her fingers and waited for the crying to gentle and cease. There was no hurry after all. Years lost; but now they had all the time in the world. Forever.

And the daughter in her hot, damp sea of tears, felt them emptying out of her, on and on like when they change the lock gates on the canals. Made no effort to control them. Holding the hand, strong and bony like her own, hearing the drumbeat in her ears. Till she is all cried out. Feeling the wheel turn. Finding herself in a new place. Tender and bewildered and brave.

PART ONE: BIRTH

CAROLINE/JOAN/MEGAN

'It's not just morning sickness,' Megan complained, 'it's morning, noon and night sickness.'

'You look like you're wasting away,' Joan remarked drily.

'G'wan.' Megan was pleased with their new roommate: older, more sophisticated, shorthand typist no less. She had more about her than Caroline, who was kind but really shy and desperately unhappy.

'And you should put your legs up,' Joan instructed Caroline.

Caroline kicked off her shoes and carefully swung her legs round and on to the bed. There was little definition of the ankles left, the flesh was puffy and mottled red from calf to toe.

'Does it hurt?' Joan asked.

Caroline nodded. She looked tired, dark circles under her rich brown eyes. She had a wide face, a sallow complexion and wore her shiny dark-brown hair pulled back and tied in a ponytail.

Megan was brushing her hair. It had grown and she liked it long and bushy, springy red curls like Rita Hayworth. The brush wasn't much good though, the soft bristles created more static electricity than anything else. Joan wore her black hair in a beehive, but hers was straight to begin with. She backcombed it and used sugar and water to set it. Joan was tall anyway, but with her hair up like that she looked even leggier, like some film star.

'You should tell Matron,' Megan said to Caroline.

'I did.'

'But it looks worse today.' Megan told her. 'They shouldn't still have you doing the laundry, with feet fit to burst.'

'Megan!' Joan's inky blue eyes narrowed in warning.

Megan shrugged and put her brush down. 'Suppose it's better than the kitchen though,' she added. She foraged in her cupboard and came out with a knitting pattern and a pair of needles stuck into a ball of soft white wool. She rubbed the wool against her cheek. It was so soft. They'd lots of new stuff like this coming in, a million miles away from the scratchy wire that Mammy had used to knit all their stuff.

'At least you can sit down to peel the vegetables,' said Caroline. 'I'm standing all the time in the laundry.'

Megan waved her needle at her. 'If you've morning, noon and night sickness, the odour of cheese pie and liver stew tips the balance. And that's not all that tips.'

The girls smiled.

'What are you knitting?' Joan asked.

'The layette.' Megan passed her the pattern. Black-and-white photographs of babies wearing the various outfits adorned the front cover. 'White, of course, to suit a boy or girl and I'm doing the longer coat.'

'I can't knit,' said Joan.

'G'wan,' said Megan, 'everyone can knit. You can knit, can't you, Caroline?'

'A bit.'

'It's easy,' said Megan. 'How come your mammy never showed you?'

'Oh, she did. I was always dropping stitches or getting the wool so tight I couldn't budge it.'

'Tell us about being a secretary. Was it hard at secretarial school?'

'The shorthand's the worst. And the teachers.'

'Does it cost a lot?'

When Joan told her, Megan thought she was kidding her for a moment. 'Flippin' 'eck,' she said, 'you can count me out.' Then she had a thought. 'Tell you what, I'll teach you to knit and you teach me shorthand.'

'What about the typing?' Joan laughed. 'I don't want to learn knitting anyway.'

'Suit yourself!' Megan tossed back her hair, pretended to be offended. She began to knit, the needles clicking in a steady rhythm. 'I'll just have to go back to the factory.'

'But you said you were getting married,' Caroline said.

'I am, as soon as I'm old enough. Daddy won't give his permission. Anyway, Brendan's got to do his apprenticeship and he's not meant to get wed till he's done. We wanted to,' she said to Joan, 'we wanted to get married and keep the baby.' Her hands stopped moving. She gripped the needles.

'That's not fair,' said Joan.

Megan could feel Joan's eyes on her but didn't want to catch them. There were tears stinging in her head but she would not cry. 'No,' she said abruptly. 'Who said life was fair? They had that wrong. Still—' she forced practicality back into her voice, carefully wound the wool round the needle — 'there's no budging them and I can't run off to Gretna Green the state I'm in, so it's the best of a bad job.' She slid the stitch over, drew the wool around for the next.

'Lights out in ten minutes,' a voice called, knuckles rapped on the door.

'Are you going to see Matron?' Joan asked Caroline.

'I'll see how it is in the morning, it's usually better after a lie down.'

She was so young, Joan thought, just sixteen. A dark horse. Not like Megan, who chattered day and night. The two girls were the same age but Megan's bright personality and her bubbly confidence made her seem older than Caroline.

It was Caroline who had first shown her round, leading her upstairs and into the bedroom. 'That's yours.' Caroline had pointed to the bed at the end of the row. There were three in the room and a small cupboard at the side of each. In the furthest corner, in an alcove to the side of the window, there was a wardrobe.

'How long have you been here?' Joan had asked her.

'A month.'

'What's it like?'

The girl shrugged. 'Bit strict. It's all right if you remember the rules.'

'Who else shares?'

'Megan, she's at the end. She came last week.'

'There's not just three of us?'

'No. There's four rooms like this and a big dorm downstairs next to the nursery. You go down there after.'

The girl seemed shy, jiggling one leg as she talked, unable to look at Joan for long without glancing away. She was bonny, a big-boned girl with a broad face and large, chocolate-brown eyes that made you think of an animal; something trusting like a dog or calf.

'I'll unpack then.' She was probably not expected to stop and natter.

The girl nodded. 'Tea's at half past.' She slipped out of the door.

Joan sat heavily on the edge of her bed and took a deep breath. She would be here until May, maybe June. The room had cream wallpaper with pink roses on, quite nice. At the doorway there was a holy-water holder, the cup of water at the feet of a small statuette of Our Lady. On the wall opposite the beds, a picture of Christ the Redeemer, arms flung wide in welcome.

With a sigh Joan turned and lifted her case on to the bed.

She put her underwear and nightdress in the small drawer in the bedside table and hung her second-best suit and two maternity frocks in the wardrobe. It smelt musty and she wondered how clean the other clothes were, a shabby dress and coat and a pinafore dress. She had a small vanity case with her as well as writing paper, stamps and envelopes, a prayer book and a rosary.

The three of them had been thrown together and in the days that followed she had come to enjoy Megan's irrepressible spirit and to feel protective towards Caroline, who was so patently unhappy. Now they tended to sit upstairs even though they could have joined the other girls in the sitting room, where there was a fire and the wireless to listen to for an hour in the evening. As long as the sisters regarded the programmes broadcast as acceptable for their charges.

They were all so different but here they were, hidden away in St Ann's; good Catholic girls gone bad. She got her nightdress out and changed quickly. There was no heating in the bedroom and it was a cold March night. Two more months, Joan told herself, and it will all be over.

* * *

Caroline

Her mother had brought her here. Getting the bus into Manchester and then out again south to the home. There was a place nearer them — St Monica's — but her mam argued that it was too close.

'Tongues'll be tittle-tattling,' she said. 'This way no one will set eyes on you. We'll say you're visiting Dulcie in Sheffield, helping with the twins.'

Twins. Ran in families. Could she be having twins? Not one baby but two? It was all done and dusted according to her mam. After the first awful shock, when she'd seen Mam's face go white as fish, her eyes hollow out with dismay.

'Oh, Caroline,' she'd said, and the gentle reproach was harder to bear than the harsh words that followed.

All the *how could you's* and *this family's*, the *respectables* and *let us downs*, the ruin and calamity. And she fancied after that that when her mam looked at her she saw dirt, a soiled creature. A disappointment. Her dad was told and when he came home and found her in the scullery he left the house. After that he ignored her most of the time and if he did have to speak it was with a cold sting in his words. She had lost his love overnight.

Caroline had wept to her mam and begged forgiveness but when talk turned practical and her mam started to organise her stay at St Ann's, then a small fierce voice had winkled its way out.

'I want to keep the baby,' she cried.

'Caroline, you can't,' her mam cried in horror, wheeling round from the lowered wooden creel where she was hanging the washing to dry. She seemed more shocked at this suggestion than she had been at the pregnancy in the first place.

'Have you any idea . . .' Mam broke off, speechless at her daughter's folly, slapping the wet shirt in her hands on the table in frustration. 'Where would you live? You couldn't live here. Oh, no—' she shook her head fiercely — 'you can throw your own life away, you can condemn your baby to the most miserable existence, but you'll not drag us down with you.'

'I could get a room.'

'Not with a baby,' her mother snorted. 'No one would have you. You'd end up beggin' on the streets, or worse.'

'I could work,' she retorted.

'And who would care for the baby?'

'Well . . .' She struggled for solutions. Was it so impossible?

She tugged at her nail, thinking desperately, tears soaking her cheeks.

'Think of the child,' her mam urged, 'growing up a bastard.' The word like a slap. 'Is that what you want?'

'Caroline—' she put down the shirt, moved to put her hands on her daughter's shoulders — 'if you care for this baby you'll want the best for it, a good home, a happy family. A future. You can't give it that. There are people out there desperate for a little one. Good people. It's the only way.'

She pulled away then, devastated. She didn't go to her room but ran out the back and walked up the ridge that ran behind the house. She relished the cold wind that stung her eyes. Digging her nails deep into her palms she strode half-seeing, her nose running so she had to wipe at it every few yards. She went as far as the first outcrop of rocks, Little Craven, and sat in the dip in the weathered stone that the children called the armchair. Facing away from the hamlet and the city in the distance she let her eyes roam across the moors to the peaks beyond. The first snows had reached the tops and she fancied she could smell snow in the air in among the bitter tang of the heather. She sat there until dusk drifted down while the chimneys behind were all smoking and the sheep bleated more loudly. She watched the clouds darken to purple and heard the clatter of the train in the next valley.

She felt blank, empty. A slate wiped clean. Except she wasn't clean. She was mucky. And no amount of scrubbing or soap or prayer or pleading would put things right.

She didn't argue again and, when the time was right, before she started to show, her mam brought her to St Ann's. She had to answer all the questions for the form and she never let on then that there was any other thought in her head but having the child adopted.

* * *

Joan

When Joan realised she was pregnant, her first thought was that now Duncan would have to leave his wife. But, of course, he could never divorce her, being Catholic, so he could never marry Joan. They would have to move away, go to London. There was always work in London. They could buy a ring, tell people they were married. Who was to know the difference? Unless they spotted the 'Miss' on her Family Allowance book. Would they even give her a book if she was an unmarried mother?

She finished her Blue Riband, put the paper in the tin that she brought her lunch in and leaned back against the park bench, letting her eyes roam around the empty pathways. Only a few stolid dog-walkers passed her. The wind gusted and caught at her eyes, a cold wind from the east. There was talk of snow. Not many chose to eat by the boating lake at this time of year. That's why she'd come here. He'd never do it. There wasn't even any point in telling him about it. Damn! She swore, it was all so sordid. Snatched hours driving up on the moors with a picnic rug in the back or after work when he'd ask her to stay behind to finish some letters and they'd wait until Betty had tidied up the petty cash and washed the cups and put her hat and coat on and said 'toodle-oo then' as she invariably did.

Listening as Betty click-clacked down the steep staircase, waiting for the thud of the front door. Joan's mouth would go dry and her skin tighten as her fingers rested on the typewriter keys.

Then Duncan would come and stand behind her at her desk. Run his hands across her shoulders, down the front of her blouse, circling her breasts and she would feel weak and wicked and she would do anything then.

There was a steady wind riffling the surface of the boating lake. The boats had gone now. The season over, they were stacked in the boathouse until the spring. Ducks paddled lazily about, oblivious to the cold. Joan sniffed, fished in her coat for her hanky.

He always had to go, so soon. Too soon. Home to his tea, his wife, and *I Love Lucy* on the television. So their sex was always frantic. They were always half-dressed. It was never enough for her. He didn't seem to mind but she wanted more time, time to linger, to revel in it, to flaunt herself, tease him, be teased. But no. As soon as Duncan was done he was off, home to Scotch on the rocks and bloody Canasta, and Joan would gather the mail and post it on her way back, her limbs still fluid with desire, her nipples hard, the simple act of walking maintaining her excitement. Still swollen with sex.

'I'm back,' she would call to her mother then climb the stairs to her room, where it was her habit to change out of her office clothes. On the nights when he had left her flushed and dizzy she would sit by her dressing table, looking in the mirror, running her hands over her brassiere as he had done, then down between her legs. Stroking herself fast and light she imagined him with her, in her or watching, and closed her eyes, feeling the waves gather inside her then break over her in quick succession.

It was probably a sin, impure deeds, just like seeing Duncan was a sin, but she mentioned neither at her regular confession. Father McRory would have a dickie-fit, she thought. It had never happened with Duncan, her climax, it never would. So many things were out of the question with Duncan.

She stood up abruptly from the park bench. Time to get back to the office. Her fingers were numb at the tips and her back felt chilled. Joan took the path to Wilmslow Road, along past the rose gardens. The bushes had been pruned back hard, only stumpy stalks remained, looking ugly and barren; such a contrast to the rich sea of blooms in summer.

She never fell asleep in his arms, in his bed. Never went out to a cafe or a restaurant with him. She couldn't give him a Christmas present or hold his hand on the street. His wife had all that. Everything. Except she hadn't been able to give him a baby. And Joan could — except she wouldn't, it wasn't allowed. Like some awful practical joke.

The doctor had confirmed her suspicions and advised her about the mother and baby home. 'It's not the end of the world,' he said. 'There's no need to do anything silly. A year from now and you'll be able to put it all behind you.'

She pictured herself on someone's kitchen table, a wire coat hanger making her bleed. Or buying Penny Royal from a chemist's on the other side of town. Or was the doctor thinking of her hurting herself, putting her head in the oven or throwing herself into the Mersey? Well, he needn't worry.

She crossed Wilmslow Road and walked past the shops to the corner building where the office was. She wouldn't tell him. Things would go on as normal for the next few weeks and then she'd give her notice. She would think up a reason, a better position or something. She'd go to the Home, have the baby. Give it up.

She went in and up the stairs.

'Bit parky out there,' Betty commented as Joan hung her scarf on the rack. 'You know what you get, sitting in the cold?'

Frozen, thought Joan. She could see Duncan through the open door to his office at the end of the larger room, pretending to read, but she could tell from the set of his back that he was eavesdropping.

'Piles,' said Betty.

'That's from stones,' she couldn't help smiling, 'not benches.'

Betty grunted and returned to her ledger.

'Joan,' he called.

She walked to the doorway.

'Any chance of staying on a bit today? I've a whole heap of these to get done.'

'Yes,' she said simply.

* * *

Megan

Soulmates they were, her and Brendan. Made for each other. She watched him at the counter, waiting for the girl to get the coffees from the big machine. Even looked alike, same flame-red hair and bright-blue eyes. She'd more freckles though. She knew they'd get married. Everyone kept on about how young they were but that was daft. They were both in work, what else was there to wait for? They'd need to save a bit, of course, they'd have to stay at her mammy's till they got on the housing list.

She'd seen a lovely ring, white gold, quite plain.

He brought back the drinks.

'You'd make a good waiter,' she teased.

'Go on. Dying breed with all the self-service.'

'They won't bring it in everywhere,' she said scornfully. 'Restaurants and that'll still have service.'

The grocers on Mount Street had put out fruit and veg and a sign saying pick your own.

'I don't fancy that,' her mammy had pronounced, 'everyone handling the fruit. Silly notion.'

Mammy was still stuck back in the old country. She didn't like modern stuff. Megan did.

Even their names practically rhymed — Megan, Brendan.

She poured sugar in her drink and stirred at the froth, watched the gaggle of lads and lasses piling in from the pictures. Waved hello to those she knew.

When she turned back Brendan was pulling a daft face; sucking his spoon so hard that his nose was pinched and white.

'Give over,' she laughed.

He crossed his eyes.

'Eejit. Put 'Living Doll' on . . . and 'Dream Lover'.'

He waggled his eyebrows at her and licked his lips.

'Go on.'

He went over to the jukebox and put his money in, pressed the buttons. Megan watched the records move round and the black disc selected and lowered to the turntable. She joined in the song.

'Fancy a walk?' Brendan asked.

'I'd better get back, they've left Kitty in charge and they'll all be swinging from the chandeliers.'

He frowned.

'I told you,' she shoved his arm. 'They've gone to see *Some Like It Hot*.'

'Ten minutes,' he bartered.

'It's flippin' freezing out there.' She knew exactly what Brendan's ten-minute walk would involve.

'I'll keep you warm.' He did his John Wayne voice, making his eyes go sleepy looking.

'I know your sort of warm,' she said primly.

His eyes flew open and he looked shocked. She snorted, got a load of bubbles up her nose. Wiped at her face. 'Come on, take me home,' she drained her cup.

'Kathleen,' he joked. 'What mass are you going to?' He wouldn't give up.

She caught her lip between her teeth, teasing him a moment. 'Early, I think.'

He winked and caught her hand.

She smiled.

The rest of the family went to the eleven o'clock. It gave Brendan and Megan the run of the place for a whole hour, though the last ten minutes were always spent setting the table and getting the veg on so it looked like they'd been making themselves handy.

Very handy.

She smiled again and pulled away. Outside, they linked arms. It was bitterly cold for September. The sudden frosts had caused most of the trees to drop early and the smell of rotting leaves mingled with the smoke from coal fires and the stink of dye factories along the canal.

She pulled her muffler up to cover her nose and pulled him closer.

* * *

Caroline

Caroline just couldn't believe that you could get pregnant on your first time. Her understanding of it was a bit hazy, though she knew something from seeing the animals on the farm where she helped out and from the local wildlife to have a rough idea of the way of the world.

It was when she tried to apply it to her own experience that things got all mixed up. For example, they had to keep Bess, the dog, inside when she was on heat or there'd have been pups. But Caroline's mam had told her that her own monthlies were a clearing-out, so how did that work?

She turned over in bed. The room was bitter now and although she had heaped extra blankets on and wore her socks her toes were like ice and she knew she wouldn't sleep until they were warm. She reached down, her head under the covers, to rub at her feet.

If she'd only known, if she'd had an inkling. It had all been so quick. Five minutes. If only she could take that five minutes back.

A barn dance to mark the end of harvest. Jim Colby, chuffed at the amount of hay baled in his barns and the promise of a good fruit crop to follow. A hot summer had blessed them.

Caroline liked Roy, Jim's middle son. A quiet, hard-working boy with sulky, film-star looks like Montgomery Clift. Roy had no steady girl and despite his looks no bad reputation. He was shy and didn't mix much.

She'd worked alongside him at the farm for the harvest. Hot, thirsty work, following the tractor or the baler, stacking the bales, chaff and dust in her throat and her eyes and her ears.

Any talking was snatched, desultory. Breath was too precious and there was nothing the flies liked better than an open mouth.

She'd been hoping he'd dance with her at the hoedown and he had, several times, till it seemed they were matched for the evening. They'd done Strip the Willow and Maid's Morris, ending up breathless from the pace and the hilarity that erupted when some lummock with two left feet had the set in disarray. She'd worn a new dirndl skirt, red and black, and a white bodice blouse. The skirt flew out when he spun her round, just right for the swings. In-between the demanding dances they gulped down cupfuls of dry cider.

'I need some fresh air,' she said after an hour of this, and he followed her out of the barn and round to the little orchard at the back. She sat herself down and lay back on the ground, sighing aloud. 'I'm jiggered,' she said, then giggled.

He was quiet. He sat beside her. She opened her eyes and looked through the boughs of the apple tree to the sky with its frosting of stars flung between wisps of cloud. She turned to look at him and he lowered his face to hers. Excitement prickled her skin, mimicking the tickle of grass beneath her bare arms and legs.

His lips were firm and dry and warm. She wondered whether she should move but she was fearful of breaking the embrace. She lay still and felt him shift about, his lips still moving slowly on hers.

He lay alongside her, then she felt one of his arms across her knees, then his fingers stroking along the side of her leg, under the edge of her skirt. It tickled and she squirmed, stifling a giggle, making a tiny mew in her throat. Roy wriggled against her, she felt his hand again, grazing her thigh, the inside, moving up. Her stomach lurched, it felt so good. Like the swing boats at the fair or the waltzers, a tingling, dizzy feeling. But she shouldn't let him. She twisted away from his kiss.

'Roy,' she whispered. 'Don't.'

'I won't hurt you,' he said. His voice sounded strange. 'Please.'

He didn't wait for an answer. His mouth found hers again, damp now, and his hands moved, he was touching her down there, edging his fingers inside her knickers. What did it feel like to him? Another hand on her breast. She felt giddy, like she was melting. She must stop him. But it didn't hurt, it was so nice. Oh, golly it was so nice. He eased the tip of a finger inside her and she felt her thighs tighten and everywhere glowing. He moaned. She swallowed hard. He kissed her, moaned again as if he was hurting. He kissed her neck, moved until he was above her, bracing his weight on one arm, breathing fast. He said her name. Kissed her, slid his finger further in and wiggled it about. She could just make out his face in the dark, the whites of his eyes. 'Please,' he said again.

She closed her eyes, heard her own breath sighing. Then the band started up again, a waltz. She felt the pressure between her legs, a sudden change as he took his finger out and there was pushing. She realised with a rush of horror what he was doing. 'Roy! No.' Her words sharp, she tried to get out from under him but his weight was too much for her. 'No.' She pushed at his face with her hands.

He gave a shudder and yelped, rolled off her.

'You shouldn't,' she yelled, 'you shouldn't!'

'I'm sorry.' He sounded upset too. 'I thought you wanted . . .' And then, stupidly. 'I do like you, Caroline.'

She felt sticky and uncomfortable. The giddy mood from cider and whirling about was replaced by a heavy sense of guilt and worry. A burst of clapping rang out from the barn.

'We better go back in,' she said in a small voice.

'I'm sorry.'

'It's all right,' she said gruffly. 'I'm not that sort of girl.' She didn't like to think about how nice the stroking had been.

'I know. I never meant . . .' He stuttered to a stop. 'Oh, God.'

She scrambled to her feet, arranging her dress, brushing bits of grass and fragments of apple bark from her hair.

She didn't dance again and left before the end of the evening too uncomfortable with the glances from Roy, who sat with his brothers across the other side of the hall.

The cloud was clearing as she walked back, more stars were visible, silver sparkles in an indigo sky. She saw a falling star and wished, wished that it would be all right. Though she couldn't have explained what she was so worried about, not having any notion then that what Roy had done was go all the way and that you could get caught first time.

* * *

Megan

'I'll bloody swing for him! I'll knock his ruddy block off! The weaselly fucking bastard!'

'Daddy, no!' Megan cried.

'Anthony,' her mammy admonished, hating his lapse into coarse language.

'What were you thinking of?' He rounded on his daughter, fists balled with frustration. 'You silly, little eejit.'

Megan gulped, tried to stop crying. 'He wants to marry me.'

'Oh, no,' Anthony Driscoll announced. 'Over my dead body.'

'Mammy, tell him,' Megan pleaded.

But her mammy blinked. 'Yer awful young.'

'You were my age when you had me.'

'That was different,' her daddy announced.

'Why was it? Mammy was pregnant when she married you. I can do my sums, you know. I wasn't born three months premature, was I?'

He lurched towards her, anger furrowing the muscles in his face, his arm swinging back.

'Anthony!' her mammy barked. He had never hit them, none of them. It was something he prided himself on. But this was taking him to the limit.

'Jesus wept!' he railed and slammed his hand on the table. 'You'll not marry him, I'll not give my permission.'

'Why?'

'He's a clown. He's got no prospects, no land. Nothing.'

'We're not back home now,' she retorted. 'I'm not after a farmer. He's apprenticed. He'll learn a trade. He'll be a printer. We won't need to wait half our lives for an itty-bitty strip of boggy land that won't grow any bloody thing.'

'Megan!' Mammy snapped.

'It's not fair!' she yelled.

'When you're twenty-one you can marry who you like, but until then you live in my house and you marry who I say.'

Six years! He was touched in the head. 'It's your grandchild,' she protested. 'It's a bastard and you don't want it, but I do and it needn't be like that.'

Her mammy started at the sentiment. Megan knew if it was only her there might be some chance, but her daddy was the stubbornest man in the world.

'I want it, Daddy.'

'Oh, now you do.'

'And Brendan does.'

'I have no more to say on the matter.' He clenched his jaw shut.

'Mammy,' she appealed for help.

'You're not the first, Megan, and you won't be the last. I tried to raise you good, teach you right from wrong. If Brendan had an ounce of respect . . . You've gone to the bad and it must be put right. We'll talk to the Catholic Rescue.'

'I don't want to!' Her voice was high and childlike. She began to cry again. Her mother put her hand on Megan's head. 'It's the best way,' she cajoled.

'Please, Daddy.'

'Enough,' he said shortly and she watched the feeling drain from his eyes and his look turn, the bright pain replaced by a dull grey stare, dead as stones. She couldn't win. Another day, a different moment, perhaps he'd have said yes, hesitated in his decision long enough to hear her pleas and see the sense of it. But now, once he'd said it, that was it. No matter how wrong he might be, or what harm might result, he would be unmoving. She hated him for it. She would never forgive him, she told herself, never, never, not until they put pennies on her eyes.

* * *

Joan

'I've got a new job,' Joan announced to her family during their evening meal. Her stomach rippled with tension. 'Down in London. Frances told me about it. And I wrote to apply and they've offered me it.'

She held up the letter. She had typed it herself earlier that day. Betty had gone to the post office for stamps and Duncan was out seeing a customer. It was the first chance she'd had. She'd invented an address in London. She'd never been there but had heard of Shepherd's Bush. It was easy enough to come up with 16 Market Street, Shepherd's Bush. Her fingers flew over the keys, offering herself the position of secretary. She had signed it with a flourish. Arthur Bell Esquire. She found a used envelope with an illegible postmark and inserted the letter.

'Good grief!' Her mother froze in the process of dishing up the treacle tart. 'It's all a bit sudden, isn't it? You never said a word.'

Her younger brother Tommy gawped, her father looked stunned. 'What's brought all this on?' he asked her. 'What sort of position?' He held his hand out for the letter.

Her mother resumed sharing out the sweet, one eye on Joan.

'Secretarial, small firm. You know I've been wanting to go for ages. Frances says it's super there. Very lively. There's a room coming up at her lodgings, so I won't even need to find a place.'

'And you're leaving Harrison's just like that?' He frowned at the letter.

'Daddy, I'll work my notice and they'll find someone else easy enough. I don't want to work in the same office all my life.'

'Don't know you're born,' he muttered. 'Pass the Carnation.'

Joan handed him the jug of evaporated milk. He held the letter out to her mother.

'It's a bit of a shock, Joan,' her mother managed. 'I wish you'd said something.'

'I was going to but it's all happened so quickly. This job at Bell's is vacant now and if I don't jump at it they'll take someone else. Manchester is so stuffy,' she said. 'I want to see what London's like.'

'When's all this going to happen?' Her father said. 'How long's your notice?'

'A week. I thought I could get the coach next Saturday.'

'You'll miss Grandad's birthday,' her mother complained.

'Grandad won't mind.'

There was a pause. Joan listened to the clock ticking, to her father's huffs and puffs as he ate.

'Your mother's right,' he said. 'You could have given the family a bit more consideration, springing it on us like this.'

She sighed. 'I want you to be pleased for me,' Joan tried. 'It's so exciting.'

'We are, Joan.' Her mother smiled. 'It's just so fast. But we are. Aren't we, Ted?'

He raised his eyebrows and nodded, making it clear that any pleasure was tempered by reservations at how Joan had behaved.

'You'll need something to manage on until your first wages come through,' her mother said.

'I've got a bit in my savings.'

'You're dipping into your savings for this?' Her father looked disapproving. Joan felt a wave of irritation which she fought to hide. The last thing she wanted was to lose her temper now. 'It's a week in hand,' she lied. 'I won't need much.'

'Things are dearer in London,' her mother put in.

'Frances will help me out, too. It'll be fine.' Joan wiped the sweat from her palms on her slacks and resumed eating. Lies all told. Relief lapping at the edges of her skull. Better than the truth. Why hurt them? They'd be disgusted, ashamed of her. They'd demand to know who the father was. There'd be scene after scene. She couldn't do that. The tart was sweet and cloying in her mouth, the Carnation milk silky. She was ravenous and nauseous all at once. She wanted more. She'd go for chips later.

'I'll see the Tower of London,' she said to Tommy, feeling a little giddy now it was done, 'and Buckingham Palace.'

'They're changing guards at Buckingham Palace,' he sang, his eyes dancing, 'Christopher Robin went down with Alice . . . Can I come and see it, too?'

'One day,' she told him, 'when you're bigger. London's a long way away, hundreds of miles.'

Not a place any of them would visit on spec. No chance of them ever finding out that she wasn't there.

* * *

Megan

The place gave her the heebie-jeebies. It looked like some old house out of a Dracula film with turrets at the corners and ivy all over it. Jesus, there were even gargoyles on the corners of the roof. She half-expected Christopher Lee to answer the door, or Peter Cushing.

She'd seen it at its worst when they'd arrived, her mammy clutching her elbow and Megan holding a small, brown, boxy suitcase that had been a wedding gift to her parents. It had her daddy's initials on, A.C.D. — Anthony Christopher Driscoll. If everyone had their own, hers would have read M.A.D. — *MAD*. Megan Agnes Driscoll. Great, that. Hadn't they thought of that when they picked the names? The kids had ribbed her endlessly at school, 'Megan's mad, just like her dad.' Could have been worse. Think of being P.I.G. or S.O.W. Whatever she called the baby, she would be very careful about the initials. Brendan's were B.J.C. — Brendan Joseph Conroy. So her married name would be Megan Agnes Conroy. She wouldn't be *MAD* then. One fella in Brendan's school, the school in Donegal he was at before they came over, he was Terence Gough — T.G. — which everyone used as shorthand for Thank God. Thank God for Terence Gough. Excepting Brendan said he was a poor wee runt of a boy, cack-handed, and he stank, and no one would want to thank anybody for him.

Mammy rang the bell. There was a thick fog that afternoon. It was only four o'clock and already it was pitch black. Megan could taste the soot in the air, the flavour of bad eggs and the feel of chalk on her tongue. There were tall trees round the house, bare most of them in late February. She tried to imagine it in spring with sunshine, in May when the baby would come. And failed. The place seemed built for winter.

The nun who answered the door bore no resemblance to Peter Cushing or Christopher Lee and she was quite cheerful in spite of her surroundings.

'Come in, come in,' she chirruped when Mammy said their names. 'I'm Sister Giuseppe. Matron's expecting you.'

Megan wondered what on earth possessed her to take Giuseppe for her name? Sounded like the old woodcarver in Pinocchio, though his was a bit different, Giuppetty, was it? And she'd a thought that one of the uncles at Granelli's ice-cream parlour was a Giuseppe. But when you could be a Lucia or a Carmel or something pretty why go for a whiskery old man's name? Maybe you couldn't choose for yourself?

Sister Giuseppe showed them where to sit. There were three wooden chairs along the wall in the entrance hall. There was a side table beyond with a holy-water dispenser above it. Our Lady. An old-fashioned one, the paint dull on the plaster. You could get them that glowed in the dark now, crucifixes and all, made of some new plastic stuff.

Megan settled the box case on her knee. The entrance hall had a parquet wood floor with tiles all around the edge in a zigzag pattern. The walls were very plain, green below the dado and cream above. Bit like a hospital. The place was enormous. There was a staircase down the hall, like something from *Gone With The Wind*, splitting into two on the landing, a huge picture hung up there in a thick gilt frame, a picture of St Joan of Arc, seated on a horse, with temples and hills behind her. The place smelt of beeswax and coal. Megan wondered where all the girls were, the fallen women. She didn't feel like a fallen woman. She felt very small and scared and she wished they could just go now. Take the box and go back home and have the baby and marry Brendan and make everything right.

'Mrs Driscoll?' Another nun. Older this time, with grey curls peeping from the edge of her wimple. Thick glasses and a rough, red complexion. 'Good afternoon. I'm Matron. Sister Monica.'

'Yes, Sister. You wrote.'

'That's right. You're up in Collyhurst?'

'Just beyond.'

'St Malachy's?'

'Yes, Sister.'

'I knew Father Gilmartin from Salford, we were both at St Claire's for a while.'

Connections established, they followed Sister Monica into a generous-sized room which held a desk and several upright chairs, a filing cabinet and some easy chairs around the fireplace. Above the mantelpiece was a picture of Our Lady of Perpetual Succour and behind Sister Monica's desk one of the Sacred Heart. A tea tray with cups for three sat on the desk.

'You'll have some tea before your journey back?' Sister addressed Mammy. Megan felt a rush of heat inside. She wasn't going back, she had to stay. She could see pink wafers on the tray. Her favourite. Peak Freans.

'We'll do that then and have a little chat, and then I can show Megan around the place. Tea is at five thirty, so we've plenty of time. When's your bus?'

'They're every twenty minutes back to town, so I'll be fine, thank you, Sister.'

Sister poured tea and Megan got a cup and a biscuit. Sister Monica established Mrs Driscoll's home town in Eire and the two regaled each other with families they knew, priests and schools and seminaries and churches. Megan let the chat bubble round her. She felt tired and cranky. Oh, Brendan. She missed Brendan. He had been banned from the house and she from seeing him. She had sent him a couple of notes to work, getting her sister Kitty to take them on her way to the factory. She knew he still cared. She saw him at Mass, his family all stuck to him like sticky burrs and no chance to talk.

'Now, Mrs Driscoll.' The tone changed and Megan paid attention again. 'Do you have any questions?'

'No.'

'And we think the baby is due in the middle of May?'

'Think so.'

'Father Quinlan does the purification ceremony here and then Megan will be able to make a clean start of it all. Yes?'

'Yes, Sister.' She didn't want her mammy to go. She didn't want to be left here. She felt herself getting hot, like a burn travelling up her back, along the sides of her arms and her neck.

'The baby will be placed and Megan will need to give her consent for the formal hearing. It's only a couple of minutes and the parties never meet. You won't see the parents. Just a formality.'

She felt a flare of resentment. She and Brendan were the parents, the real parents. If they'd been a few years older they could have got married and no one could have stopped them.

'I'll be on my way.' Her mammy rose and Megan took in the shabby green tweed coat, the ill-matched hat, the determined face her mother had put on.

She stood for a hug, suddenly panicky, no air in the place, fevered, her eyes hot. Mammy's touch was swift, almost brusque, not giving either of them the chance for a show of emotion.

'Ta-ta, now. Thank you, Sister.'

'Mammy.' Megan tried to slow her down, no idea what to say.

The door opened and Sister Giuseppe was there. Like Igor, Megan thought. There'd been no signal. 'Mammy.'

'Sister will see you out, Mrs Driscoll.'

Her mother practically ran from the room and the door closed on them.

Megan stood, her throat parched, her heart fluttering in her throat.

'Sit down, Megan,' Sister said quietly, but there was no warmth in the voice. 'Let me check your notes.'

* * *

'Father's name?'

Joan shook her head. 'He doesn't know.'

'You couldn't tell him?'

'He isn't free.'

She could sense the disapproval from the other side of the desk like a fret of distaste settling about her. She hadn't just been careless, she had led a married man astray. Home wrecker, scarlet woman.

'Can you leave it blank?' She fought to sound calm and contained. Inside, her heart was whipping about and her nerves singing like piano wires.

The nun blinked and gave a curt nod.

'Your occupation?'

'Secretary.'

'Nearest relatives?'

'Mr and Mrs Hawes.'

'Parents?'

She nodded.

'Any brothers and sisters?'

Joan told her about Tommy.

'When's the baby due?'

'Early June, I think.'

The nun unfolded a small slip of paper and glanced at it. 'You've seen the doctor,' she confirmed.

'Yes.'

Duncan had gone white when he'd opened her letter giving notice. She'd worded it in the usual formal style.

Dear Sir,

I am writing to inform you of my intention to leave my position of Secretary on February 25th, two weeks from today.

Yours faithfully,

Joan Hawes

No reason. No warning.

She had watched him open it from her own desk, her knees clenched together, toes pressing into the floor.

'Joan?'

Betty looked up too at the unusual urgency in his tone.

'Yes, Mr Harrison?'

'Can you come through?'

He nodded for her to shut the door behind her.

'What's this?' He flung the letter down, angry, a muscle by his mouth twitching.

'I'm going to London.'

'Why?' Like it was the moon. 'Why, Joan?'

She bit her lip, steadying herself. The less she said the better.

'Reconsider.'

'Mind's made up.'

'I thought, you and me . . .'

What you and me? 'You have a wife.'

'Oh, Joan.' He looked at her pained, as if to say it wasn't his fault that he was married, as if she was being unfair.

'I don't want you to go,' he said.

She didn't reply, wrapped her arms tighter round herself.

'You could have told me. Not like this,' he pushed at the letter with his fingers.

She waited.

'So this is it? All you have to say?'

'I'll work my notice,' she said. 'But I won't be able to stay late.'

He bristled then, his lips crimping together, his colour darkening. Would he spit at her? Curse her? She avoided his eyes. The shrill bell of the phone burst through the silence, making her start, the prickle of sweat everywhere.

'Go,' he nodded towards the door, leaning forward to pick up the letter with one hand and the phone with the other.

* * *

'While you're here,' the nun was saying, 'you'll be expected to help in the running of the Home. Sister Vincent oversees the housekeeping and she'll let you know what you have to do. Girls work in the laundry and the kitchens and the nursery. The society has granted you a place here on the understanding that you are truly sorry for what you have done and wish to redeem yourself. You will observe the laws of the Home and God's laws and act with proper modesty at all times. You understand?'

'Yes, Sister.'

'You'll pay an allowance for your keep and for the child, based on a daily rate. If there's any problem settling the amount you must confide in me immediately. Is that clear?'

'Yes, Sister.'

'People in the parish are very supportive of the work the society does and, of course, they know St Ann's is a mother and baby home but this is a good area and we do not antagonise our neighbours by parading about in the streets. You'll be encouraged to remain in the Home unless you are specifically sent on an errand by one of the sisters. There's a garden at the back and we have a chapel and a small library, so there is really no need to go elsewhere for anything. If you wish to write home, letters can be given to Sister Giuseppe. And any visits here must be arranged in advance.'

Joan wouldn't be having any visitors.

'When your time comes you'll go over to the maternity hospital in Withington. On return here you will help care for the child until a placement is made. The father's not a darkie is he?' She glanced at Joan, suspiciously.

'No.'

'You're sure?'

'Yes.'

'Because we can't place them for love nor money. They end up at Barnardo's, most of them, or St Francis's — they take the boys.'

She needed a cigarette even though she'd smoked her tongue to gravel on the way here.

'You've got your bag?'

'Yes, Sister.'

The nun left the room briefly and returned with another girl, large with child. A big-boned girl, dark hair in a pony-tail, a young face. Fifteen or so, Joan guessed.

'Caroline, show Joan up to the room. She's in with you and Megan.'

Joan smiled at the girl, who gave a ghost of a smile back, but her brown eyes were dark, sad, and she glanced quickly away.

* * *

Megan

It was Brendan's dad who told Brendan about Megan's condition.

Mrs Driscoll had heard Megan throwing up three mornings in a row. Megan's baloney about a funny custard from the cake shop wouldn't wash.

'You're pregnant!' Maggie Driscoll shrieked.

'I'm not.'

'And black is white, I suppose.'

'Mammy . . .'

'Megan, I've had nine children.'

Megan slumped into her seat, covered her face. 'I can't be,' she insisted.

'Is it Brendan?'

Silence.

'Well, it's not the immaculate conception, is it? It'll kill your father.'

She fetched her coat, pulled on gloves and a headscarf, knotting it tight under her chin.

'Where are you going?'

'Out. You stay here. Mind the others. Bernadette will want feeding in half an hour.'

Megan nodded.

'And bring that washing in if it turns wet.' She slammed the back door behind her.

Megan rose. She was cold, her ankles like pipes of cold metal, she put some more coal on the fire. It couldn't be true. Please God, let it be collywobbles. Or the flu. But she knew her mammy's diagnosis was right. And now it was spoken, out in the open, a great clonking mistake. She broke the embers of the fire apart, exposing the fierce orange glow, and hefted the brass coal scuttle once and then twice. Shiny lumps and bits blanketed the fire, a wall of tarry smoke rose up the chimney, the fire spat and hissed as it ate the gritty coal dust. It would be some minutes before the heat returned. She busied herself drying the breakfast dishes.

* * *

'Maggie, come in.'

'Kate.'

The women knew each other from the Union of Catholic Mothers. But those get-togethers were their only social contact. They were not close friends and for one to turn up on the doorstep of the other was an extraordinary occurrence.

Aware of this, Kate Conroy led Maggie Driscoll into the front room, reserved for formal occasions and out-of-bounds for much of the time, even though the house was overcrowded.

Kate had a utility suite. A green covered sofa and two chairs. The only thing you could get after the war. A piano and sideboard were thick with studio photos of the family and their relatives. A picture of Pope John XXlll took pride of place over the mantelpiece. There was no fire in the grate and the room was chilly and unwelcoming. Mrs Driscoll kept her outdoor clothes on.

'I'll not beat about the bush, Kate. It's about our Megan and Brendan. She's expecting.'

'Oh, Lord!' Kate's hands flew to her mouth and her eyes swam. 'Oh, no!' she moaned.

'It's a terrible thing but they've only themselves to blame.'

Kate shook her head again. Closed her eyes. Weary. You worked so hard, unremittingly, feeding them, keeping them clean and safe and clothing them. Day after day and at the end of it this was how they rewarded you.

Maggie Driscoll spoke again. 'I think we should keep it quiet until it's clear what they are going to do.'

'How old is she?'

'Fifteen.'

'Barely grown.'

'Too young to know what's best. I haven't spoken to Mr Driscoll yet, but I wouldn't want to push them into an early marriage and then it all go bad. St Ann's may be the best solution.'

'Aye. But Brendan, we won't let him shirk his duties if you decide . . .'

'Yes, yes, I know.'

There was little else to say and after a pause Maggie Driscoll rose. 'I'll be getting back.'

'I'm sorry,' Kate said, 'I'd no idea.'

'I know.'

Brendan's father returned from the market where he had a pots and pans stall to find his wife red-eyed and woebegone. She told him the situation. When Brendan got in from the print shop a little later his father knocked him into the middle of next week.

That's how he heard about the baby.

* * *

Joan

She had worked the remainder of her notice out in an icy atmosphere. She made sure that she and Duncan were never alone.

'What's wrong with his Lordship?' Betty had asked her.

'He thinks I'm letting the firm down,' she said, 'handing in my notice.'

Betty raised her eyebrows. Whether she believed this explanation was hard to tell. It wasn't difficult for Duncan to replace Joan. There were plenty of youngsters coming out of secretarial college and several had applied for the post. Duncan selected two for interview and silently passed her a letter for typing and sending. She felt quite immune to the whole business until the girls arrived in the Thursday afternoon. Jenny and Rosemary. Jenny was very pretty and, with a pang, Joan imagined Duncan seducing her. The thought sickened her and she had to go and sit in the toilet until she'd collected herself.

On the Wednesday morning of her final week Duncan came into the office in a foul temper. He roared for Betty to bring him in the salaries file and then sent her out for a new ledger. As soon as she'd gone he came through.

'Are you expecting?'

'What?' She feigned surprise.

'You heard me. Are you pregnant?'

She stared at him coolly while her insides twisted with tension. She forced the edge of a smile to curl her lip.

'Why else?' he said when she didn't reply. 'Why suddenly up sticks and go to London? No warning, nothing.'

'It's an ambition of mine,' she said crisply. Not that he'd have known, never asked her about her dreams, her passions.

'If you were, Joan, I could help. We could help. Catherine and I, we've been considering adoption.'

She couldn't believe it. Rage sluiced through her. How dare he. What did he imagine, a private arrangement? His wife kept in the dark about the exact parentage of the child. 'Girl at work, darling, got herself in a bit of a mess, nice family, thought we could help, baby'll need a home . . .' She loathed him for this. And how could he imagine that she could live knowing who had her child, where it was, what Daddy was up to when he worked late at the office? She would give up the child. She would know nothing of its future. She wouldn't see it again. End of story.

'I'm not pregnant, Duncan.' She funnelled the words through tightly held teeth. 'I could have been but nothing happened. Just like Catherine. Looks like the problem lies with you.' She saw the remark meet its target, piercing his self-esteem and rocking all that superior certainty. He pressed his lips together and turned away. She felt cheap and mean but it was his own fault. She blinked several times and resumed typing. Hitting the keys and banging the carriage return far too hard, the stinging in her hands a welcome distraction from the coil of fury breaking around her heart.

* * *

Caroline

She bent to pull the sheet from the bed, adding it to the pile in the cart. The effort made her grunt. She was big now, enormous. She felt like a clumsy giant. The skin of her belly was all stretched and you could see the veins like blue threads criss-crossing it. Nearly lunchtime and her feet were already aching. She could feel her bones pressing against the floor, her ankles swollen and hot.

'What will you do after?' Megan had been put on to laundry with her. Cook wouldn't put up with her rushing out to be sick every half hour. Megan worked quickly. She was like a bird, Caroline thought, small and swift and she had those alert bright-blue eyes.

'Go home.'

'Have you finished with school?'

Caroline nodded. She had not been able to complete her final year and get her certificate. She'd be too old now, no one ever went back to school. She liked the idea of farming but the only way to do that was to marry a farmer and even thinking of Roy and the farm made her belly turn over and her mouth dry up. She liked to grow things. She'd helped Grandma on her allotment since she was a tiny child and had absorbed all her tips and sayings and become familiar with the cycle of the year. Last year she'd grown enough vegetables on her own patch to be able to feed the family and give stuff away. There wouldn't be anything this year. The weeds would be waist high. By the time she went home it would be too late to sow anything. *If* she went home . . .

She was making a plan. Not something she could share with anyone. Especially not Megan, who was always up to the minute on the latest rumours. So Caroline kept pretending that she was going to behave just like all the others. Give in, give her baby up.

Between them they dragged the cart to the next beds.

One of the worst things about being in the home was not being able to go out. She couldn't just go off for a walk, not that her ankles would let her go far, but even trips to the park were discouraged. As if the girls were contagious. She felt cooped up. She wanted to be up on the ridge or down at Shudder's Force, where the water cascaded from the limestone cliff into the pool at the bottom; see the drops spraying on to the ferns and reeds that ringed the pool, spy the deadly nightshade. Drink in the smell of wet stone and drown in the roar from the falls.

She wrestled with a pillowcase. 'I don't know what I'll do. Look for a position in Bolton. There's not much out our way.'

'Factories pay well, they're always taking people on.'

Caroline nodded. She might have to do that but the thought of being stuck in a shed all day amid the clamour and commotion and the gangs of girls with their flashy make-up and endless joking made her skin clammy. She was a country girl, not like Megan and Joan, who had lived in the city all their lives; who were used to the bustle and the noise and the hard edge everything had.

'Will you go back to the same place?' Caroline asked Megan.

'If they'll have me. It's only five minutes down the road and they're a great bunch. We all go down the Mecca Ballroom of a Friday.' Megan stretched her hands out and began to dance, rolling her big stomach from side to side and clicking her fingers.

Caroline laughed. 'Give over.'

'Something funny?' Sister Vincent swept into the room, acid on her tongue.

'No, Sister.' They both replied.

'No. I don't think there's much to laugh at, is there? Your time would be better spent meditating on your transgression and begging Our Lady to intercede for you.' Her eyes were steely, her lips pursed with dislike.

'Yes, Sister.'

'When you've done this, fetch the laundry from the nursery too.'

'Yes, Sister.'

Caroline listened to the rustle of long skirts and the clap-clap of her shoes as the nun withdrew. Megan pulled a face but neither of them spoke.

Caroline didn't like going down to the nursery. All the cots and the babies bundled in them. She didn't like to see that, it made her think of her baby destined for one of those cots, bound for another life, and how she must stop that happening. As she bent to fold the blanket, she felt the baby turn and butt up against her ribs. She stopped and put her hand there.

'You OK?'

'Kicked.'

'Mine's at it a lot. Reckon I've got the next Jimmy Greaves in here. It's either a footballer or a clog dancer.'

But you'll never know, Caroline thought. We'll never know anything of what becomes of them — who they are — if we leave them. And the heavy dread settled on her like a rock.

* * *

Joan

There was only one person who knew that Joan had not gone to London; her friend Frances whose rooming house Joan was supposedly living in. Joan wrote to Frances explaining her situation, begging her not to let her down and asking if she would forward letters from Joan to her family.

I couldn't bear to see them hurt because of my own dreadful mistake. It would be hateful for them to lose their reputation too. Please say you'll help?

'Of course I'll help,' her friend replied by return of post.

It's not my place to judge you and you're right, why should everyone else suffer? What does the man say? Hasn't he offered to marry you? It was such a shock to hear your news. Perhaps you could come to London after all when it is all over. It is so thrilling Joan, you should see Oxford Street and Carnaby Street and all the new styles. I've just treated myself to a new spring coat. Bright pink and utterly gorgeous. I've also been out several times with a boy from work called Harold. We go to the Palais jiving, it reminds me of the Plaza back home — we had some wonderful lunchtimes there, didn't we? Not sure what I think of Harold yet but he has dishy eyes and he's very keen. That's enough about me. I hope you don't feel too wretched and that time passes quickly.
Your friend always,
Frances.

Joan lay in the dark and thought about Frances. What would she have done without her? She couldn't sleep. Someone had said it was preparation for when the baby came, so they would be used to broken nights. Joan had heartburn, ghastly and constant, she had to sleep virtually upright. She would hear Caroline snoring softly and Megan coughing.

They never really talked about it, Joan thought. Here they were, all in the same boat and plain as the nose on your face, but it was alluded to almost as if it was happening to someone else. They were all stand-ins, she thought. She felt the baby swivel, moved her hand across her stomach and felt a hard lump through her belly. The lump moved, she took her hand away.

How could she do this? She didn't want this child moving inside her, she didn't want a baby. She was fearful of the labour. Women died, some of them, their life bleeding away. The panic gripped her and the acid reflux rose in her throat. She shuffled further upright, rubbed at her chest with one hand, trying to soothe the burning pain. There was no way back. It was like Hansel and Gretel without the white stones or the kindly white bird. She closed her eyes and made a simple prayer. Please God, let it be all right. Let it be over soon. Don't let me die. They thought she was so poised, Megan and Caroline, she could see it in their glances and hear it in their questions. They were little more than children themselves, too young for all this, and she . . . If they only knew, she felt as lost as they did, but because she was older they expected her to be measured and grown-up about it all, like a big sister they could rely on.

She shivered — the covers kept slipping down. Megan had made her a bed-jacket. A ghastly, fluffy blue cape, but she appreciated it now. They must have been designed for women with heartburn. She pulled it from under her pillow and worked it round her shoulders. She sat back. The baby kicked again, unexpectedly. Making her want the toilet. Go to sleep, she thought. Outside, the first steel grey light edged along the top of the curtains. She felt relief. It would be easier now. It was the dark that was the worst time. She hated the dark.

* * *

Caroline

The days dragged by in a sort of a dream. They were kept busy with endless, backbreaking chores and fell into bed desperate to rest. Time to talk, write letters, read, knit and brood was strictly limited. Only in their final month were the girls allowed less onerous duties — dusting, mending, sewing.

Caroline began to spend every free moment in the garden. There was a terrace behind the house where the babies were put out in their prams every morning. Beyond that there was a lawn and borders. To the side of the house there was a rose garden and a herb garden with crazy paving and bowers and, at the end of it, in amongst a shrubbery and beside an old elm tree, was Caroline's favourite spot. Even back in February, when everything else was bare and broken-looking, the holly and rhododendrons were glossy green. And there was a little witch hazel with a sprinkling of small, frilled yellow flowers. They looked like someone had made them from strips of crinkled paper, and their rich, sweet scent was powerful in the cold winter air.

Bluebell bulbs were coming up now beneath the elm and she could see the clusters of flowers ready to turn lilac-blue and fall open. A blackbird had a nest in the tree and serenaded them from the middle of the night through most of the day.

Her mother had visited twice, bringing her a new nightdress large enough for the last weeks and special underwear and a shawl, a proper wool-and-silk shawl, that Caroline had written and asked her to get. They barely referred to the baby and Caroline imagined how different it would have been if she was married and expecting. Then, surely, Mam would have been full of interest and advice, Grandma too. They'd have sat and had coffee and biscuits and swopped stories and Caroline the centre of it all. Instead now there was an awkward tiptoeing around it all.

'Be brave,' Mam said the last time she came. 'I'll pray for you.' And Caroline had gone to hug her but Mam had just grabbed at her hand. Caroline was hurt. Her mother couldn't bear to touch her, the bump between them a huge accusation. Later, though, she recalled her mam's face. Close to tears. A hug would have set her off perhaps and she was being brave in her own way, wanting to be strong and resolute as an example for Caroline.

* * *

Megan

Megan had finished her layette. She'd done the matinee jacket, hat, gloves, rompers and bootees. She had carefully cut and sewn a nightie and embroidered a pattern of yellow ducks along the yoke. She had also knitted a matinee jacket for Joan's baby, seeing as Joan was sticking to her story of not being a knitter.

'They've plenty of clothes here,' Joan had said.

'It's nice to give them something new though, isn't it? Something to remember us by. Unless you don't want to,' she added quickly, realising that she might have upset the apple cart. Mouth like the Mersey Tunnel. Always putting her big foot in it.

'No, thank you, it's lovely,' Joan took the tiny garment.

'And they won't get mixed up because mine's the pearly buttons and yours the clear.'

Caroline had done her own knitting, so Megan didn't need to do anything for her. But in the last two weeks Megan's baby had dropped and was sitting on some nerve and she could barely move without the pain so sharp she fair passed out. So they let her sit and sew and knit for anyone who wanted. One girl was having twins and she did them lovely woollen sailor suits. Very small because they usually weighed less.

She was longing to see Brendan. She'd had a terrible dream one night where she'd gone home and Brendan was there with a new girl. All lovey-dovey. And when she asked him what his game was he laughed at her and in the dream she saw she had no clothes on and everyone was looking and pointing. After that she wanted to write to him but she didn't dare. Her father had threatened that if there was any communication between them he would have Brendan for improper relations with a minor and that would be the end of his apprenticeship.

Megan cast off the stitches on the mitten she was doing and cut the wool. Outside, it was a blustery day, real April showers and the wind sending the clouds scurrying here and there. The girls were in and out every ten minutes to the clothes lines.

Sister Giuseppe came in then, the most placid of the nuns. Her brow creased. 'Have you see Caroline?'

'No, Sister. She might be in the garden.'

'In this?'

Megan shrugged. Caroline spent more and more time outside. Not doing much but just brooding as far as Megan could tell. As the time went on she was becoming quieter than anything. Thank heaven they had Joan in with them, at least you could hold a conversation with Joan and have a bit of fun. Caroline went around with a face like a wet weekend. Of course, she was a bit low. Bound to be, but it didn't help anyone to dwell on it so. Megan had said as much to Joan one day but Joan had smiled at her. 'She's very young, Megan.'

'So am I.'

'But you've got something to look forward to.'

'You mean me and Brendan?'

Joan nodded.

Maybe she was right. Maybe something truly awful had brought Caroline here. She could have been forced or something. She never said anything, never referred to the father, nor did Joan to hers. Megan seemed to be the only person in the whole place who could.

Sister Giuseppe had gone off looking for Caroline, and Megan finished the mitten off. He'd know to wait for her, wouldn't he? If he had so much as sniffed at another girl while she was here, going through this, she'd kill him. Chop him into bits and chuck the pieces in the canal. She would. So he best be behaving himself. And then one day, they'd show them all, especially her daddy. They'd have a dirty great wedding and dance till the morning and they could all go jump.

* * *

Joan

Joan was assigned to the kitchen at St Ann's. She had to get up at six to help light the fires and start breakfast. Porridge had been cooking all night in a huge double porridge pot. They used Quaker Oats at home, ready in ten minutes. Why on earth they couldn't do it here she didn't know, but everything here was done the old way and the most difficult one too, she reckoned.

The ashes from the fire went into the ashcan and the grates were swept then the new fire built. It was the coldest time of all and Joan could see her breath as she folded paper like crackerjacks for firelighters and then built the pyramid of kindling and coals. The fire in the kitchen didn't always draw well and Joan had to stretch a sheet of newspaper across to encourage the flames to leap for air. Once the fire had hold she helped the other girls lay the tables and prepare bread and margarine and jam to follow the porridge.

Cook would be busy already sorting out the ingredients for dinner and tea.

At seven thirty the rest of the house was expected to be ready in the dining room and Matron would start the day off with prayers. By nine the pots were washed, dried and put away, the great porridge pan scrubbed clean, the clots of porridge removed from the sink. The surfaces wiped down and clear.

Joan had ten minutes tea break. She went upstairs and got out her stationery.

Dear Mummy, Daddy and Tommy,

London is very big and very noisy. There are pigeons everywhere and starlings just like we have in Piccadilly Gardens but even more of them. The traffic is busy and doesn't stop even in the middle of the night.

I am settling in fine and Mr Bell is very happy with my speed and accuracy. I have to get the Underground home from work. I haven't been to Buckingham Palace yet. Has Tommy finished his go-kart? Say happy birthday to Grandad for me. I'm sending him a card, too.

Cheerio,

Joan

She folded the paper and slipped it into a matching envelope, took a stamp from her purse and licked it. She wrote the card to her grandfather, stamped and addressed it and put both envelopes into a larger one with a quick note to Frances.

Thanks so much for this. Just pop them straight in the post. Feel very cut off from everything here. No television and the radio is usually limited to Sing Something Simple and the like so we never hear the Goons or even Two Way Family Favourites. I have a go on the old piano now and then but they don't approve of anything too modern. I'm keeping well. I am going to come to London! Might there be any rooms near you? Your coat sounds lovely. Where did you buy it?

Time to go back down. And begin making dinner.

* * *

Caroline

'Yes, Sister?' Caroline turned from the sheet she was sewing end-to-middle.

'Sister Monica wants to see you.'

'Yes, Sister.'

Caroline had not been inside the Matron's office since her admission. Anxiety rippled through her and she felt her heart falter. Had she done something wrong? She made her way as quickly as she could to the office and knocked on the door.

'Come in.'

Sister Monica sat at her desk and motioned for Caroline to sit opposite her.

'There's been a telegram, Caroline. I'm afraid your grandmother has passed on.'

Caroline stared at her uncomprehendingly. Shaking her head even as she tried to decipher the words. 'Grandma?'

'Yes.'

Her throat felt dry, she sucked at her cheeks, trying to find saliva. Her vision blurred and she blinked her brown eyes fiercely. Grandma. Beating rugs with a huge, cane beater, her hair covered in a twist of coloured scarves; Grandma making lace, her face screwed up like an old apple, her mouth a row of pins, reciting dialect poems and singing all the songs she knew. A fierce, funny woman, incredibly tall. Who called Caroline 'Mouse' on account of her quiet nature and made enough noise for the two of them when they were together.

'We'll ask Father Quinlan to include her in prayers.'

'The funeral . . .' Caroline began.

'You have to stay here,' Sister Monica said firmly. 'You can't go.'

Caroline stared at her in amazement. Not go? 'But, Sister . . .'

'It would not be appropriate, Caroline. It would be a dishonour.'

She was dirty.

'Whose is it?' Mam had said. Cheeks drained of colour, eyes boring into her.

'Mam, I . . .'

'Who?'

'Roy Colby.'

'Good God. And how long has this been going on?'

'Nothing's going on.'

'Something must have.'

'It was just one time. It was an accident.'

'Oh, yes. An accident. He accidentally got you in this mess. Have you no decency, no pride?'

'Mam, I'm sorry,' she bawled, unhinged by the look on Mam's face.

'Do you want to marry him?'

'No.'

'I'll not ask you again.'

'No. I don't want to marry anyone.'

'Right. The Colbys need never know. Nor anyone else.'

And so her mother had sorted it all out and told everyone that Caroline was helping with the twins in Sheffield. Now what would she tell them? When there was no Caroline at Grandma's funeral? Another lie?

She bit on to the flesh of her cheek and sniffed hard.

'It's sad news but remember she is with Our Heavenly Father now. She's at peace. Our blessed Lord has called her to him and has rewarded her.'

She would call the baby after Grandma if it was a girl, a way of remembering her. And she would tell him, or her, all about Grandma.

* * *

Joan

Joan dreaded the labour. How could something so large get out of her body without killing her? There was no one she could ask about it. The other girls were just like her, their ideas a mishmash of fact and fantasy. Matron never spoke about it, even though she would sit in on the medical checks when the doctor came.

She put the duster down and sat on the chair. The library. Fat lot to read in here. Religious texts ad nauseam and uplifting novels that were on the approved list from the Vatican. No romances and certainly nothing stronger. Out there in the real world they were selling *Lady Chatterley's Lover* and you had naked people leaping around in the theatre. Four letter words and all. Elvis swivelling his hips in no uncertain way. Things were changing. The world was changing. But not here. Here it was ancient. She let her hand rest on her stomach, on the ledge at the top of her bump. The baby moved a lot now but when she tried to imagine it, to think of seeing it, of what sex it was, she failed completely. Maybe it would die, perhaps it was a sign. She didn't even have a name. She knew she should think of something, but whatever she chose would be changed anyway. It felt hypocritical to pick a family name; her mother was Elizabeth, her father Edward after his father, grandmothers Irene and Patricia, her other grandfather John. But the child would never know them and they would never know of its existence. She wished it were all over and done with.

She hated the way her body had changed. She was like an elephant. Her belly button stuck out now, her breasts had ballooned, the discs around her nipples had gone a startling dark colour. Even her hair felt different, thicker and greasier. The endless heartburn kept her from sleep. She'd been invaded by this creature and she wanted rid. A stabbing pain forced her to her feet. She was running to the toilet every five minutes, too. After she'd been to empty her bladder she went to her room. Caroline was there, curled on her bed, crying.

'What's wrong?' Joan sat beside her.

'Everything,' she wailed. 'My grandma's died and they won't even . . . I can't go . . .'

'Oh, Caroline. I am sorry.' She let her hand rest on the other girl's shoulder. On top of everything else, thought Joan. I'm three years older and I feel so lost she must be . . . She let her cry, listening to the gruff sobs, and when the sounds tailed off Joan fetched her a fresh hanky.

'I've got one somewhere,' Caroline said, her voice thick.

'Don't be silly, use this.'

'I'll make sure you get it back.'

'Beware the laundry thief,' Joan joked gently. Small items inevitably went missing with the sheer amount of laundry each day and were not always recovered. Caroline gave a small smile, wiped her eyes and blew her nose. Her face was shiny from crying, her nose and lips red and puffy.

'Tell me about your grandma,' said Joan. 'Unless you'd rather not.'

'It's OK,' said Caroline. 'She was a bit odd really. Eccentric. Always bursting into song and quoting from poems and plays and things. She read the library wall-to-wall and she would make up stories—' Caroline's eyes filled again — 'adventures; and there was always a little girl . . .' Her voice squeaked to a halt. She sniffed hard. 'She'd been to lots of places. All over the world. She was an entertainer on the cruise liners, until she met Grandpa. She settled down with him.'

'She sounds fabulous,' said Joan.

'I feel so rotten, not going.'

'You haven't got a choice,' Joan said gently.

The bell for lunch rang through the hallways.

'Are you coming down?'

'I don't want any.'

'I'll bring you a cup of tea.'

'I'm not allowed, am I?'

'Oh, bother that,' Joan said. Though when she did bring the tea upstairs she made sure that none of the sisters saw her.

* * *

Megan

'Aaah!' Megan gasped and clutched the table top, her ginger curls falling over her face. 'Oh, god that hurts.'

'Megan?' Sister Giuseppe came over and placed a palm on Megan's stomach, her lips moving as she counted. 'Here, sit down.' She moved the chair and Megan lowered herself on to it gingerly. 'Aah,' she gasped again.

'I think it's time. Is your bag ready?'

Megan nodded. She was scared.

'I'll get it, Sister,' Joan called from the doorway.

Megan was taken by taxi to the maternity hospital. She was still in labour eighteen hours later when the girls at St Ann's were having breakfast.

Joan was reaching for toast when her waters broke, drenching her clothes and soaking her shoes. The liquid pooled on the linoleum of the dining-room floor.

It was unheard of for three of the girls at St Ann's to give birth on the same day but, when Caroline was brought in at four o'clock that afternoon, she was already fully dilated.

By midnight three babies were born. Three baby girls.

PART TWO: ADOPTION

JOAN/LILIAN/PAMELA

Lilian

After the third miscarriage the doctors had advised against trying for any more babies. Lilian Gough had to see Mr Russell at St Mary's. He was very nice but they didn't really know why some women had her problem and couldn't carry to full term. But he was clear that there was little hope of the situation improving. She had expected him to say that. Well, more or less, but she had hidden a tiny ray of hope that she would be proved wrong.

There was also the vexed question of sex. Blushing like a beetroot, she had tried to broach the subject. 'But my husband, that side of things . . .' Wanting the ground to swallow her up. Pushing her tortoiseshell glasses back up her nose.

'There are devices . . .'

'We're Catholic,' she said in a rush.

'Ah!'

'And the rhythm method, well, we got caught out like that the first time.' Her cheeks blazed. She fiddled with the strap of her bag. She wished she'd left her long, light-brown hair down instead of putting it up in a chignon, then she'd have been able to hide behind it.

'It's not reliable,' Mr Russell said crisply, 'and there seem to be several versions doing the rounds. You may need to consult your priest or whoever, but any further pregnancies would be extremely ill-advised. They would put your health in jeopardy as well as almost inevitably resulting in miscarriage.'

She nodded.

So that was it.

She explained it all to Peter when he got in from work. He said he would talk to Father Flanagan but they could hardly expect a special dispensation. A sin was a sin, after all, and the Pope was clear about interfering with mother nature. He did talk to the priest but never told Lilian about it beyond saying he'd got nowhere with him.

Two months later she first suggested adoption.

'No,' Peter shook his head.

'But why?' She had expected him to hesitate but not such immediate opposition.

'It's not the same. You don't know where they're from, what's in the blood. Could be anything in the background.'

She frowned, uncertain where his fears came from. 'They are babies Peter. If you bring them up the proper way . . .'

'No, Lilian.' He reached for her hand. 'This may be what God has chosen for us.'

Childlessness? Sterility? She pushed his hand away. 'No.'

He could be stubborn, well so could she. If adoption was the only way to have a baby then that's what they would do. Over the next year she bided her time. Worked on him. She put everything she could into their home. She cosseted him and made the very best of herself. She spent hours with her friends recreating the latest Paris fashions and Hollywood looks. She used make-up to emphasise her green eyes, add to the slight slant that gave her a feline look. She used the new foam rollers to create curly tendrils of hair that looked as if they'd escaped from her bun. She plucked her eyebrows and bought lipstick and nail varnish to match. She got new glasses, a frame that swept up at the corners.

She collected a range of Cordon Bleu cookery magazines and made new dishes. She tried out the latest foods on him, making spaghetti bolognese and risotto.

She tried to make him happy but the problem with sex soured everything. He would kiss her and she would feel his arousal but he would pull away, grab his coat and set off walking. What had been a vital part of their marriage was now a sin. Peter became increasingly irritable and withdrawn. She couldn't bear it. She missed his love and his touch.

She mastered the courage to go herself to the new priest who had recently joined the parish alongside Father Flanagan.

She explained the difficulty to him in a rush of words, staring at her hands to spare him embarrassment.

He said he would pray on the matter and advise her again. She went back a week later. The man said it was a very difficult problem. As a married couple, God's desire was to see a fruitful union. The institution of marriage was there as a home for the family, and sexual relations within matrimony were for the express purposes of procreation.

She knew all that. She nodded and waited to see if there was more. She needed a loophole. The priest talked about the rhythm method — that was acceptable in the Church's eyes. She pointed out that it had failed them and they dared not risk another failure.

'Another option—' he cleared his throat — 'would be coitus interruptus. Did she understand?'

'Yes, but wouldn't that be wrong, Father, because there'd be no chance of babies?' At least with the rhythm method it was like Russian Roulette — the unreliability meant babies got made.

'I'd be misleading you to say the Church would approve of such behaviour. I'm afraid it would be up to your own conscience. God has sent you a challenge, Mrs Gough. It may be that through meeting it you can enter a state of true grace.'

She clenched her teeth at the platitudes. She was flesh and blood. She wanted her marriage back and she wanted a family. How could that be so wrong?

One night when Peter had been out to the pub with his friends she ambushed him. Her period had just finished and she hoped it would be safe. She waited in bed and when he climbed in she reached for him. She kissed him. 'Love me, Peter, please, love me.'

'But what about . . .'

'Pull it out, before, you know . . .'

She was relying on the hope that the drinks he'd had would weaken his resistance. And they had.

It was wonderful.

Afterwards, while he slept, she thought of a solution. If she had her womb removed, then there would be no risk of pregnancy. Peter might still have to face the problem of wasting his seed but she was no longer prepared to feel guilty. She couldn't have his children but she would damn well have his love. If that made her a bad Catholic, so be it.

She went back to Mr Russell, who hemmed and hawed but eventually accepted that a hysterectomy would remove the risk of further complicated pregnancies.

And once she was over that her new campaign began in earnest. The plan to adopt.

* * *

Lilian had been physically sick the morning that the social worker called. A mouthful of cornflakes and her stomach, which had broiled in acid anxiety all night rebelled. Peter had managed to get the morning off work but his presence made her even more wound up. She rinsed her mouth with water and toured the rooms for the umpteenth time. All tidy. Could it be too tidy? The social worker might think they'd be too fussy to have a child messing up the house. Oh, God.

'She's here,' Peter called.

Lilian practically fell downstairs, pulled the door open hard and greeted Mrs Jenkins with a fixed smile. Her eye was twitching and she felt like something out of a Jerry Lewis slapstick film.

'Come in, please.' She couldn't work out how to wipe the stupid grin from her face without it looking peculiar, so she covered her mouth with her hand and tried to relax her lips.

They sat in the dining room, at the mahogany table that had been her mother's. Mrs Jenkins had two sets of forms to fill in and one to leave with them. Questions she asked related to all the facts and figures of their situation. Age, health, occupation, income, family in the area.

'Any existing children?'

'No.'

'Reasons for adopting.'

They explained.

'You'd want a baby, then?'

'Oh, yes. As young as possible.'

They had to supply references.

Then Mrs Jenkins wanted to see round the house.

'This would be the nursery,' Lilian heard herself saying, 'right next to our room. We haven't decorated yet, but we will do, of course.'

Before she left, Mrs Jenkins gave a speech. Adopting a child was a legal act, governed by the law. They should be fully committed before going any further. In rare cases if there was a problem with a placement then the social work department would try to assist, but that was exceptional and once they were approved and a child was placed with them they would have all the duties and responsibilities for the care of that child. Exactly as with natural parents. There would be no allowance or payment of any sort. Her report would be put forward and they were to fill in and return the form she had left them. The panel would meet to decide whether to approve their application.

Lilian kept nodding throughout it, hoping that wearing her glasses and the way she'd put her hair up would make her seem serious but not too frumpish.

If they were approved, the social worker concluded, their names would go forward to the Catholic Children's Rescue Society. Did they understand? Had they any questions?

When she had gone, Lilian sat heavily on the couch. 'She hated us.'

'She didn't, they have to be formal about it.' Peter stood by the door.

'I could tell, Peter. She thought I was too nervy, all that stuff about my health and my operation. And she turned up her nose when you said you were an engineer. They'll pick the richest people, the professionals, first.' She bit her knuckles, trying to bite back the tears that threatened.

'Lilian.' He moved to sit next to her. 'There are hundreds and hundreds of babies waiting for a home. You heard Father Flanagan last month, imploring people to come forward. We've a decent house, I've a steady job, you don't have to go out to work — that's all that matters. It'll be all right.' He put his hand round her shoulders and gave her a squeeze.

Lilian nodded, craving reassurance but terrified that this final chance to have a child might be snatched from her. And she didn't think she could bear that. She didn't know how she would go on living if she couldn't have a baby.

* * *

Lilian couldn't ring Peter at work with the news. Only something urgent, like a death in the close family, was permitted to interrupt him on the works floor. Instead she paced the house, smoked too many cigarettes and sorted all the junk from the spare room ready to shift into the attic.

When he arrived home she met him in the hall. She was covered in a layer of grime and wearing an old shirt of his over her messy slacks.

'What's going on?'

'They've approved us!' she yelled. 'For the adoption!' A sudden rush of tears disconcerted her but she laughed through them. 'Mrs Jenkins called this morning.'

'Good.' He nodded his head. 'Good.' And he smiled and drew her to him. 'Calls for a drink, I think. Martini?'

'Yes. And she said we may be contacted quite soon.'

They went through to the dining room and Peter made drinks. She chattered on, wanting to share every word of the phone call with Mrs Jenkins. She followed him through to get ice and back again still talking. She took a swig from her glass. 'And we'll need a washing machine.'

He raised his eyebrows.

'All the nappies. There won't be much else to buy. Our families will chip in — they'll spoil it rotten.'

He looked uncomfortable, glanced away. 'Yours might.'

She took another drink. She didn't want this to mar their happiness. 'Once we've a baby, Peter, they'll come round surely. They're just disappointed for us. I suppose they think if you'd married someone else . . .' She faltered. 'They blame me, I know that. Because I can't carry them.'

'Lilian, don't.' He moved closer.

'Yes, we'll celebrate. It's good news, the best. And those that don't like it can lump it. A toast.' She held out her glass. He raised his. 'Our baby.'

'Our baby.'

They drank. 'Let's get fish and chips,' Lilian said.

'And drink Martinis.'

'And get sozzled. And clear the spare-room stuff away.'

He looked at her. 'I've a better idea.'

'I love you.' She looked at his dark, wavy hair and the eyes that were almost black. He needed to shave, five o'clock shadows ringed his mouth and chin. He shaved twice a day.

He kissed her.

'Ow. Like sandpaper.'

'Refresh your glass, Madam?'

She winked at him and held it out. A moment's doubt swirled within her. What if she didn't love the child? What if the baby got sick and died? What if Peter found himself agreeing with his family? She lit a cigarette. Mother of God, give me strength, she prayed. It's going to be wonderful. We're going to have a baby.

* * *

A month later, Peter was arriving home late. He'd been delayed because Mr Ince had wanted to see him. He had felt a rush of hope at the summons and he'd been right. He was to be promoted to develop new production methods throughout the region. It would mean travelling, to visit their factories in Wakefield, Sheffield, Leeds and Hull. An extra five hundred a year and a company car. He was proud. He'd worked his guts out for this. He'd just stepped in the door when the telephone began to ring. He picked it up.

'Mr Gough? Sister Monica at St Ann's here. I have some good news.'

He was flustered. 'Oh, yes, Sister — right-o, erm . . . you better speak to Lilian.' Lilian was coming through from the kitchen having heard the phone. 'Sister Monica,' he said, holding out the receiver.

Her face blanched and she swallowed quickly. She blinked several times and took the phone from him.

'Hello, Sister.'

'Mrs Gough, I have some lovely news. We have a little girl here and I wondered if you and your husband would like to come and see her.'

'Oh!' a swirl of disappointment edged her excitement. 'We'd hoped for a boy first, Sister.' She glanced at Peter, who shrugged his shoulders.

'Would you like to have a think about it and call me back?'

'Yes.'

'And don't be worrying now. There's no hurry and I'm sure it won't be long until there's a boy for you, if that's what you've set your hearts on.'

'Thank you.'

She put the phone down, her forehead creased and her hand shaking. 'Now what do we do? It's a girl.'

'What did she say?' Peter hung up his sports coat.

Lilian told him.

'So it's up to us.'

'I know you'd like a boy,' she said, 'but . . .'

'Let's sit down.'

Once they were seated on the sofa in the lounge he said. 'I thought you did too?'

'I did. But now . . . I don't know how to explain,' she took off her glasses and rubbed the lenses on the corner of her blouse.

'You don't want to wait?'

'It's not that. She said it wouldn't be long before there'd be a boy available. It's more, well . . . this is random, isn't it, the luck of the draw. Like it would be if . . . if we were having one ourselves. We wouldn't get to choose. Do you see?'

'Fate? Down to chance?'

'I mean, we might not like her anyway. If I saw her and felt, I don't know . . . nothing, then I'd . . . well, I'd think about it very hard. Have you got a cigarette?'

Peter lit two cigarettes and handed one to her.

'Do you feel very strongly about a boy?' she asked him.

He thought for a moment. 'I would like a son, someone to carry on the name. But it doesn't have to be the first.'

She widened her eyes, the green glinting at him.

'Well, we may want to do it again,' he said. 'People do. Look at the Carters, they've got five.'

'I don't want five. Two would be nice. One of each. Oh—' she flung back her head — 'I just want a baby, Peter. I want to see her. I don't want to say no.'

'OK,' he said. 'We'll see her, see what she's like.'

She exhaled loudly. 'Oh, thank you!' She hugged him.

'Red-letter day.'

'Yes.'

'In more ways than one.'

'What?' She straightened up and turned to him.

'Mr Ince called me in. He's giving me the regional job.'

'Oh, Peter!' She clasped her hands together. 'That's marvellous. Why didn't you say?'

'I didn't get a chance, did I?'

'Oh, I knew he'd give you it! Congratulations.'

'And now I am going to get out of these clothes. Do you want to call Matron back?'

'Yes.'

'It'll have to be Saturday or Sunday.'

'I know.'

He took her hand and squeezed it. She looked alive with excitement again. After the tragedy of the first miscarriage it had been a horrific struggle to balance optimism and dread when Lilian got pregnant the second and then the third time. It was such a relief now to be talking about a baby without the shadow of miscarriage hovering over them. It all felt so simple in comparison.

'Go and ring then,' he said.

* * *

Lilian held the baby in her arms. She knew this would be her daughter. She touched a small foot encased in a lace bootee. The nun was murmuring about how beautiful she was, with the curls of dark hair and such a sweet face. Lilian knew this would be her daughter, her child, and in the same moment she faced the realisation that she would never *bear* a child. This baby would not share her blood, her looks, her nature, her background. She would never look at this child and see herself looking back, that particular shade of green in her eyes. She felt an immense sadness soaking through her, despair and bitter grief mingling with the love and hope that the child in her arms brought.

* * *

Joan

Carnaby Street was her favourite place. London was so different from Manchester. Things were happening here. Young people everywhere, parading the latest fashions, having fun. Jobs were there for the asking, if your boss got up your nose you could just walk away, there was always something else available. Joan had already had two. The first in a record shop, a place she loved because she could hear all the latest records, but the manager had wandering hands and bad breath and she got sick of his attentions.

There were plenty of dishy young men in London looking for a good time, money in their pockets. She got countless invitations but she turned them all down. She still felt uncomfortable about what had happened. She didn't want anyone to know she had stretch marks, silvery threads that meandered across her belly, and although she sometimes felt aroused she had no desire to sleep with anyone. The woman who had cavorted on desks with Duncan and then gone home and pleasured herself was a stranger. Like a flickering home movie from someone else's life; she had withered and died as Joan's baby had grown and been born. Occasionally Joan wondered whether she would ever want to do the normal things again. Settle down, get married, have a family. It all seemed so stuffy, really.

Her friend Frances had got married and moved to the outer suburbs with her new husband. Frances had given up work and become a full-time housewife. Joan couldn't imagine it. Be like being buried alive.

Her second job was with a record company. They needed someone to run the office. The place was crazy, an endless stream of hopeful youngsters ringing up or turning up, climbing the rickety staircase to the two-room let in a Soho backstreet, clutching song sheets or guitars or letters from the school music teacher. The place was owned by Roger, who had minor connections to royalty and no need to make any money from his hobby. He talked endlessly about the new sound, about rivalling the Shadows, about platinum discs and breaking America. As it was, the only success the outfit had was with compilations of ballads, Russ Conway style.

Joan had her black hair cut short, a stylish cut with a straight fringe. She bought false eyelashes and practically glued her eyes shut on the first attempt. She got dark eye make-up and white lipstick at Biba and saved from her wages to get a second-hand Singer sewing machine. All the dresses in vogue were simple shapes. She ran up an A-line in geometric material from the market and a dress with the empire bust line in gorgeous purple paisley for a fraction of the cost.

Roger liked her to look groovy, as he put it, never mind that half their clients were still wearing what their parents wore. She would give an impression of being really trendy and then the kids would go in and see Roger in his lair. After Joan had been there a month she had created some sort of filing system to show who they had seen and what, if anything, had been agreed. She often had to pester Roger to find out. And catch him straight after an act had left. He was irritatingly absent-minded.

Roger invited her to one of his parties. He had a huge house near Hampstead Heath and he boasted that the parties went on all weekend, day and night. He paid for caterers and cleaners and even people to serve drinks. With all that, Joan couldn't see why on earth he bothered with his little record label.

When she got there she didn't know what to do with herself. She smoked too much and drank too much and found herself outside by the terrace being sick behind a hydrangea bush. She fell asleep there. The cold woke her and she went exploring. The house was huge and, with music blaring from all corners and psychedelic lighting, she felt like she'd walked into someone's bad dream. People were petting on the stairs and dancing in one room to a live group who were hopelessly off key. Everyone seemed to be smoking reefers or popping pills. She opened one door and was shocked to see a bed covered with naked people. Not just one couple but several. A sea of breasts and pubic hair. A man's willy. She shut the door hurriedly, her cheeks aflame. She felt uncomfortable and walked home.

When Roger had his next party she wondered whether to go or not but he told her there were some business contacts there he wanted her to meet. He introduced her to Lena.

Lena was working in Soho, singing in a nightclub not far from the office. Although her English was very good she had a thick German accent and Joan had to concentrate hard to make out the sense. She was talking about Roger and how he had promised her some sort of record deal. They hoped to make a record soon.

'Have you written it?' Joan asked.

'No,' Lena threw back her head and laughed. She had bronze skin and her hair was streaked with gold and honey. She had very pale grey eyes. Joan thought she could have been a model or a film star if the singing didn't work out.

'Roger is the writer,' Lena said.

Joan pulled a face.

'You think it's a problem? No good?'

Joan shrugged. 'You'd be better off doing it yourself.'

'No. I can sing, but writing? Poufff!' she waved her hands in dismissal. 'What is wrong with Roger doing it?'

'First of all, it'll take him forever, and then it will be . . .' she leaned close and enunciated carefully, 'dull, square, boring.' She had heard his songs and tried to think of comments that wouldn't get her sacked.

'Joan, you write me a song.'

'But I've never . . .'

'If you don't, I'll have to do Roger's. Please?'

'He wouldn't like it.'

'We'll pick a name for you, he won't know.' Lena was animated, her face alight with the plan. 'What would you like to be called?'

'I can't . . .' She protested.

'Joan—' Lena grabbed her hands — 'my friend, please. Just try, promise you'll try.' She stared at Joan, an open look to her, eyes dancing, a smile stretching her lips. 'Please?'

'I'll try. But it might be rubbish.'

'You'll try?'

'Yes.'

Lena pulled her close and kissed her on both cheeks. Joan laughed with surprise.

'And what name?'

The question blew Joan straight back to St Ann's, to the registrar documenting the birth. And what name? Laboriously writing with a thick fountain pen. Her name and address, a careful line across the section for the father's details, and then, pen poised, he turned his shiny round face to her and peered over his glasses. *And what name*? Nearly two years ago now.

'Joan?' Lena nudged her elbow. 'You OK?'

'Day dreaming,' she said. 'I'll think of something.' And she tried to force her smile into her eyes too.

* * *

Lilian

'And this is Pamela,' Peter announced, lifting up the carry-cot. 'Pamela Mary Gough.'

'She's tiny,' his mother observed. She sounded pleasant enough but Lilian noticed that she made no move to touch her first grandchild. Frightened of waking her, or something else?

'Why don't you get settled and I'll tell Bernard you're here. Kettle's on.' She hurried away and Lilian took off her jacket and took it out to the pegs in the hall. She could hear Alicia calling Bernard in from the garden. He made models in his shed. Planes and boats, no — ships. He got upset if you called them boats. His fine attention to detail and his skills at his hobby went hand in hand with a complete lack of skills and gross insensitivity where people were concerned.

'Hrrumph!' had been his greeting when Peter first took her home. He was an electrician by trade, with his own business. Though Lilian often wondered how his customers coped with his offhand manner. The pair of them had never had a conversation. She dreaded these visits, Peter less so, though he readily acknowledged that his father was miserable company and that her family were more easy-going. 'You and Sally are chatterboxes,' he joked. 'You wouldn't notice if someone was mealy-mouthed, because you'd be talking nineteen to the dozen.'

Lilian wondered how much religion came into it. The Goughs were Protestants — Methodists, a creed that shunned pomp and circumstance, frowned on drink and, it seemed to Lilian, were uncomfortable with any emotional expression too. They could sing, though. Sang her lot out of church at the wedding. Peter had converted to become a Catholic. He'd studied and promised to follow the faith and now here she was encouraging him to go against the dogma. But the alternative was unbearable.

Peter had been an only child. His mother had never spoken about whether that was by choice. Lilian had a sister, Sally. They had quarrelled a lot as children but were close now they'd grown up and their parents were gone. Lilian had always thought three children would be a nice number. Three. Three miscarriages she'd had. And each time Peter's father had been too stiff and awkward to even refer to it. Had hardly come near her while she was there, as though what she had was contagious.

'It's just his way,' Peter defended him. 'He doesn't mean anything by it.'

And now there was Pamela?

Bernard appeared for lunch and the four of them settled to eat. Roast beef, Yorkshire puddings, roast potatoes, braised red cabbage, peas and carrots and thick gravy. It was seventy-eight degrees outside but the Sunday roast was made come hell or high water.

Peter talked about his promotion and the work he was doing in Sheffield. His mother chucked in the odd comment. An occasional nod or grunt from Bernard the only indication he was listening. No one mentioned Pamela. Lilian longed for her to wake up so she could tend to her and show her off. After apricot crumble and custard she helped Alicia wash up. Lilian talked about Pamela for a while — how she was a slow feeder and kept nodding off on the bottle. She had to tickle her feet to keep her awake sometimes. That she loved her bath and Peter sometimes bathed her at the weekends. But Alicia's response was so muted Lilian felt like she was talking to herself.

When Pamela's sudden, gutsy yell broke through the silence she put down the tea towel with relief.

Peter got his mother to warm the bottle while Lilian rocked Pamela. They had had her twelve days and every time Lilian looked at her she got a rush inside, her heart felt swollen as though it was bruised with emotion. There were moments when the child's vulnerability appalled her. Such tiny bones, the soft dips on her head where the fontanelles were yet to join, the translucent skin on her eyelids, soft pale fingernails. If she dropped her, hurt her . . . the pictures frightened her. Why did she think like that? She loved Pamela. She was her mother. She would do anything to keep her safe. So why did she have these flashes, awful images like nightmares. Blood and guilt. There was something wrong with her. You couldn't tell anyone about thoughts like that. They'd lock you up in Springfield or Prestwich, chuck away the key.

Peter handed her the bottle. The room was cool and once Pamela had started to feed it was peaceful. She looked out towards the small garden. It was full of roses. They had no lawn, only paving, between the rose beds. In the summer the roses looked showy, hot colours and big blooms. It was an adult's garden, all those thorns. No place for a child to play. What did it matter? Pamela would never come here to stay with Granny Gough. Her throat constricted, anger and sadness together. The baby spluttered and Lilian raised her upright and patted her back. The rich burp made Lilian giggle. 'Lovely manners,' she whispered, and kissed the baby's forehead. Pamela's fist curled round a strand of her hair. She pulled back, gently loosening the grip. When she offered her the bottle again, Pamela turned away from the teat.

Perhaps Alicia was just shy? No daughter herself, years since she's been around a baby. Not sure how to act with us?

'Let's go see.'

She found Peter and his mother in the dining room. He was engrossed in the paper and she was studying the crossword puzzle. Bernard would be back in his shed.

'Hello.' She stood beside him. He put the paper down, held his arms out to Pamela.

'I thought you might like a hold,' she turned to Alicia. 'She's happy now, had her feed.'

'Oh, er . . . yes.' Alicia looked dismayed, her mouth twitching and eyes blinking. Lilian handed her the child before she could demur, passing her the muslin square too, in case Pamela posseted.

Alicia held the child on her lap, a picture of uncomfortable tension. She didn't attempt to communicate with the baby but spoke to Peter. 'And you've got a new car?'

It took only thirty seconds for Pamela to twist and begin to whimper. Alicia looked helplessly at Lilian, who rescued her daughter.

She doesn't care. She swung her toffee-coloured hair out of the way and nestled the infant against her shoulder. She'd have more affection if we'd bought a bloody dog. She decided then that she would never come again. Blast tradition. She would not subject her wonderful, brilliant new daughter to these loveless afternoons of stifling boredom. If Peter wished to come, he could come alone. And if his parents ever woke up and realised just exactly what they were missing, then they could damn well come and see Pamela and Lilian in their own house.

* * *

Joan

'It's perfect,' Lena pronounced. 'I love you!' She leapt across the carpet and planted a kiss on Joan's head. 'Do it again, the chorus.'

'Walk my way,' Joan sang in a breathy voice and picked the chords out on the guitar. 'Make my day. You can take what you need but you're never going to take this away. Oh, baby, walk my way.'

When she had finished Lena sang the song all the way through, her voice rich and full.

'Wonderful. It needs strings, do you think? Or maybe a really moody sax? You're so clever, Joan. I knew you could do it. Tonight we celebrate.'

Joan laughed at her friend's exuberance. Lena wasn't all stuffy and bossy like you heard Germans were. She was like a child. Full of life and always excited about something.

'You're working tonight,' Joan pointed out.

'After.'

'Some of us sleep at night.'

'This is a special day. What do you call it — a letter day?'

'Red-letter day.'

'So?' She cocked her head, smiling as ever.

'OK.'

'Good. Ooh, wait till Roger hears this. Shall we tell him it's your song?'

'No. Only if it's a hit.'

'When it's a hit. It has to be. Forget Doris Day, Connie Francis, here comes Lena!'

Joan didn't enjoy waiting in the club for Lena. It was a seedy place, noisy and thick with smoke. Lena's act provided background but few of the patrons paid much attention, they were here for the exotic dancers who topped the bill. Joan worried that someone would think she was a working girl, a hostess who could be approached. She sat at a small table near to the toilets and avoided any eye contact. She drank her martini too quickly and sat twiddling her glass waiting for Lena to finish. When Lena swept up to her table Joan felt she'd been rescued.

'Come on.' Lena pulled her shoulder bag over her white mac. 'You hungry?'

'Now?'

'You English! In bed by ten, tea at five. You never grow up.'

They bought fish and chips from the corner and ate as they walked.

'Where are we going?'

'Club I know.'

Joan groaned. 'Another dive?'

'No, you'll like it. Come on, live dangerously.'

She followed Lena down a side street. A wooden sign proclaimed the Zebra Club. They went down steep basement steps to a plain door. Inside there was a large room crammed with dancers. About half of them were coloured. There had been places in Manchester where the West Indians went, but Joan would never have dreamed of going there. This seemed more mixed. On a small stage a trio were playing. At the tiny bar Lena bought drinks. Joan was aware of some of the men looking their way. Well, she thought, if Lena found a friend she should have just enough for a taxi home, if she was careful.

After the first drink Joan found herself relaxing. The music was good, quite varied too. They played some jazz and calypso-type songs with a strong beat. Lena insisted on dancing and got Joan up too. Some of the movements the black couples were doing were quite astonishing but no one seemed to mind and the atmosphere was fun. When Lena caught her yawning she dragged her to the ladies'.

'Here.' She took a couple of yellow capsules from her pocket.

Joan shook her head.

'Stop you being tired.' Lena put one in her mouth and bent to drink from the tap. 'They're great, really. Make you feel like you're full of champagne.'

Joan smiled.

'Try one.'

She might as well. Everyone else liked them. And it would be nice to have a bit more energy.

She took the pill and drank from the tap.

Hours later, almost four in the morning and in paroxysms of giggles the two wove their way, arm in arm, to Lena's flat.

It too was downstairs, a damp basement with a powerful smell of mildew and fungus on the ceilings. There was a main room with a tiny kitchen area in one corner behind a curtain. The toilet and washbasin were outside, in a small yard crammed with broken furniture. In the room Lena had a single bed, a small wooden table and two stools, an armchair that had seen better days and a wardrobe with a broken door. She had brightened the place up by putting multi-coloured crocheted blankets over the chair and bed. Posters adorned the walls: Adam Faith and Elvis.

Joan was still tittering and then she couldn't remember why they'd been laughing and that seemed even funnier. She collapsed on the bed, kicking off her shoes. Lena was singing as she switched on a lamp and the electric fire. She put a stack of records on the Dansette in the corner. The strains of 'Apache' by the Shadows filled the room.

Joan felt the bed bounce as Lena sat beside her. She felt a hand brush her fringe aside. Opened her eyes. Lena smiling, warm lips, her hair falling forward. Bending down. Lips against hers, touching her own, the faint stickiness of lipstick. Joan's giggles quietened. Her thoughts were scrambling, trying to run without legs. No, wrong, wicked. Mustn't. But she didn't move.

Lena sat up. Joan's lips were empty. A look passed between them. Lena's eyes like silver, swimming like mercury. Joan could smell smoke on her, and perfume. She should get up, move, break the spell, claim the armchair. Soon. She parted her lips, took a breath. Lena stopped smiling. She bent down, kissed Joan, the tip of her tongue tracing the inside edge of her lips. Joan closed her eyes, felt Lena's hand brush down her shoulder and over her breast, the lightest pressure that filled Joan's veins with warmth and sent small shocks of pleasure to her sex.

Joan moaned, moved her head a fraction, changing the pressure of the kiss. Wanting more. Everything. It was wicked but she didn't want to stop. The thought of the wickedness gave her an additional thrill and she felt her body stiffening and getting hotter.

But she mustn't . . . if . . . with a jolt of understanding she realised that however wicked it was Lena could never make her pregnant and a great feeling of recklessness and liberation made her moan and wriggle. She reached up with one arm, tangling her fingers in Lena's thick, smooth hair. Ran her other hand down her back, round the curve of her hip and along her thigh.

Lena made a gurgling noise and then parted from her. Her mouth was dark, the lipstick smeared and her lips swollen. Joan swallowed. Lena smiled, a small, intent smile, and began to unbutton her dress. Joan lay and watched her, her heart beating fast and anticipation tingling along the length of her spine.

MEGAN/MARJORIE/NINA

Marjorie

'Speaking. Hello, Sister.'

Robert Underwood noted the excitement in his wife's voice and she waved him over with one hand.

'Yes?' Her hazel eyes crinkled with a smile. She tucked her blonde hair behind her ear, fiddling with it, and then with the coiled phone wire. 'Oh, lovely. How old? Yes. When can we . . . Eleven. Thank you. Yes, he's fine. We'll bring him with us.'

She replaced the receiver. 'They've got a little girl. Four weeks old. We could have her in the next couple of weeks.' She grinned and flung her arms around his neck. 'Oh, Robert!'

He hugged her briefly. 'You're sure now?'

'Aren't you?'

'Yes.'

'Don't say things like that. I don't want Stephen to grow up an only child.'

'I know, but you're sure you don't want to hang on a bit — it'll mean more work.'

She frowned, examining his face. 'Robert, have you got cold feet?'

'No,' he reassured her.

The following morning they drove across town to St Ann's. Two-year-old Stephen clung between the bucket seats.

'Sit down, Stephen,' his mother told him and he obliged. 'Good boy.' People went on about the terrible twos and she'd seen friends' children hurl themselves to the floor in temper tantrums but Stephen was an angel.

Robert turned into the gateway for St Ann's and parked the car at the top of the drive to one side of the main entrance. Marjorie didn't really like the place — it was so imposing and she knew that beneath the bright chatter of the nuns there were terribly sad stories. When she came here she couldn't help but think of the girls who were sent here, the ones who would have to leave with empty arms. It had been the same last time when they had come for Stephen, but once she got him home she didn't think about that side of things. There was no point in dwelling on it all. This was the best solution for everyone.

She turned to look at Robert. He patted her knee a little clumsily, he wasn't one for fussing. She had liked his reserve when they first met at her brother's wedding. She had noticed the tall, sandy-haired man during the marriage ceremony. He had gone up to communion ahead of her and seemed to be on his own. It turned out he was a cousin of the bride, an optician with a new shop in Sale, and at the reception he had been seated opposite her. He had smiled quietly at the jokes and listened attentively to the speeches, while some of the other guests had made a show of loud laughter and called out quips to interrupt the speakers. Every so often she felt his eyes on her. Light-blue eyes quite different from her own hazel ones. She felt attracted to him and quietly confident of her own good looks. She was slender and she kept her golden hair long. It looked natural and fresh, and it suited her better than some of the more elaborate styles that meant spending hours under the hairdryer and left you reeking of setting lotion or permanent wave.

They had talked at the party, he had offered to get her a drink and explained apologetically that he didn't dance — two left feet. But he was good company, and dates led to a proposal and then a wedding of their own. And now here they were, about to meet their second child.

'Ready?' he asked her.

She nodded, her palms felt slippery and she'd butterflies in her stomach.

Sister Monica let them in and exclaimed with pleasure over Stephen and how grand he looked. He hid behind his mother's skirts. She lifted him up on to one hip so she could walk.

'They're all outside,' the nun said. 'It's great weather, isn't it. This way.' They followed her through French windows and on to the terrace at the back, where half-a-dozen prams were placed in a line.

'This first one,' Sister Monica said, 'she's asleep, but have a peek and we'll get some tea and if she's not awake by then we'll get her up and you can have a good look at her. Then you take a couple of days to think it over and telephone me to say what you've decided.'

'Go to Daddy.' She handed Stephen over and stepped closer and craned forward to see. The baby lay motionless, only her face visible between the white pram blankets and the white wool bonnet. The tiny cheeks were peppered with the minute white spots of milk rash, the nose was slightly upturned and the small, rosy mouth had a blister on the upper lip. 'Oh,' said Marjorie softly.

'She's a darling, isn't she? Just six pounds at birth but she's gaining well now.'

'Look, Stephen — little baby.'

Stephen looked, nodded solemnly.

'Let's have tea and you can tell me how you're all getting along.'

While the grown-ups chatted in Matron's room Stephen was occupied with a box of coloured building blocks. There were nine in the set and they worked like a jigsaw, the various facets formed a number of different farmyard scenes when put together. This was too sophisticated for Stephen, who instead built towers and lines with the cubes.

'He looks so strong and healthy,' Sister Monica told them. 'He keeps you busy, I'll bet.'

'He's very good,' Marjorie said. She didn't want the matron to think she wouldn't have all the energy to take on another child. She was being silly, she thought, they're crying out for places. It would have to be something terrible to not be considered and she wouldn't have rung if she didn't think we were right for it. 'He's marvellous,' she added.

Robert grunted in agreement. 'This little girl . . .' he asked.

'Yes. Now, her mother is very young, practically a child herself. She's a nice girl, lively and helpful.'

'Where's she from?' Marjorie said. Stephen's natural mother had been Irish and had come over to St Ann's to have the baby in secret.

'Lancashire,' the Matron said. 'Though the family are from Ireland originally. There are no family problems health-wise and the little girl, she's called her Claire, is great. She's had all her checks, of course.'

'When was she born?'

'May twenty-fourth, late in the evening.'

'My birthday!' Robert said, and Marjorie laughed.

'Well,' Sister Monica smiled, 'I think we can see the hand of God in that. Will I fetch her for you?'

'Yes, please.' Marjorie could feel a headache coming on with the sheer nerves of it all. She felt sick and excited all at once. 'We'll have to get new clothes,' she said to fill the silence. 'We can't put her in blue.'

Sister Monica returned with the baby in her arms. She sat beside Marjorie on the sofa and unwrapped the blanket. The baby wore a matinee jacket to match the bonnet, rompers and bootees. She was so tiny. Marjorie looked at the skinny legs, the petite feet. You forget how small they are. Stephen seemed huge by comparison. When Matron removed the hat the baby was practically bald.

'Oh, bless her.' Marjorie ran her hand over the fuzzy skull. The baby was awake now, blinking slowly and staring at the ceiling.

'Now, her mother is a redhead,' Matron said. 'And I think she'll turn out the same but you may want a baby with similar colouring to Stephen. He's very like you, Marjorie, with the blonde hair.'

'He is. But Robert's more gingery, it might be nice for her to look like him.'

'Yes, she'll have the blue eyes, too. Would you like to hold her?'

'Oh, yes.' Marjorie settled back so she could rest the baby across her lap and support the head in the crook of her arm. Sister Monica passed her the child and Marjorie settled her. The eyes, which had not yet acquired their colour, were very dark, almost black, and looked huge.

Stephen edged closer to the sofa.

'She's holding her head well. She's a strong little thing. Would you like a baby sister, Stephen?' Marjorie said.

He looked at her then back to the infant. 'No,' he said solemnly.

The adults laughed.

* * *

Megan

Most people at the factory knew where Megan had been. You didn't have to be a rocket scientist to work that one out. But apart from the snobby gits in wages and one or two holier-than-thous on the shop floor nobody made a meal of it. She knew for a fact she wasn't the only one, either. Annie Platt and Breda Carney had both been in the club with no wedding ring in sight.

Of course, it wasn't long before Brendan and she were courting again. In secret at first, both of them very, very careful not to let anyone catch on. They avoided their old haunts and met at places further from home. The waiting room at Victoria Station usually, and the reading room at Central Library one time. But you couldn't talk up there.

Gave Megan the heebie-jeebies. All these swots with their noses stuck in books and this loud silence and the great big ceiling like St Peter's in Rome or something and everyone creeping about. Made her want to make a loud noise and run away. But downstairs in the basement there was a cafe, that was all right, though none of the places were good for a necking session and she was just as keen as he was for a kiss and cuddle. They ended up fitting that in at bus stops and doorways and on the walk back up to Collyhurst. She told him plain though — no more than that, not till the bans were read and the church booked.

Brendan wanted to know all about the baby and it was great to be able to tell him. Her mammy didn't want to know. Put it behind you, darling, it's only more heartache, she said when Megan first tried. You did what was best, she said. That's all you can do.

After a few months Megan wrote to Sister Monica, asking if she could have a photograph of her daughter to remember her by. She got no reply. She wrote again when May came round and she imagined the child having a first birthday party, in a lovely white smocked frock with frilly knickers and a bow in her hair. She thought about her a lot, the weather and the blossom reminding her of St Ann's.

This time a small studio photo came back. Black and white. Looking at it was like a punch in the stomach. Claire, her baby — the name meant light and Megan hoped her life would be full of light and brightness — Claire was sitting up, a broderie anglaise dress on and bare feet. A sprig of close curls framed her face. Her hair would be red with both Megan and Brendan that colour but you couldn't tell in the photo and no one had coloured it in like the studios sometimes did. She must have studied that picture a thousand times that day, and when the children were all in bed she showed it to Mammy.

'Does she look like me?'

'Like spit. But Megan,' her mammy's voice sounded thin and pained, 'don't be upsetting yourself. You have to forget her.'

'I know. But it's hard.' She left the room not wanting to cry in front of her.

Brendan understood when she showed him. They had got the bus up Rochdale Road to Boggart Hole Clough, he'd sat upstairs and she down, just in case anyone got on, but they were OK. They wandered through the park and found a secluded spot to sit, surrounded by pretty trees, their leaves shivering in the slight breeze. He stared at the photograph, his face all blank and narrow like he'd seen a ghost. He shook his head. He didn't say much but she knew he felt like she did: that it wasn't fair.

They talked of marriage again and Brendan said he would go and see her dad.

'The apprenticeship.'

'I've two more years. The rules are clear. We can get engaged but they don't need to know. I just won't tell them.'

'There's other work,' she said. 'Vickers are crying out for people, and Universal Stores.'

'I know they are but this is a trade, Megan. I could work anywhere then, they'll always need printers. If I left now . . . I don't want to end up portering or on the markets.'

'Just seems so long.'

'I'll ask your dad. Least if we're engaged we can stop acting like spies.'

He began to kiss her. She could feel her breasts tingling. They were bigger since she'd had the baby even though the doctor had given her something to dry her milk up. As he unbuckled his belt, pulling at the zipper on his pants, he was still kissing her, French kisses. It made her wet and weak and hot for his fingers. She held him in her hand, made the movements copy the rhythm of his breathing.

'Megan,' he spoke softly in her ear. 'I've got a rubber johnny.'

She froze, shocked. He wanted to go all the way. Did she? Her mind raced about. It'd be all right, it would stop any consequences. Her body was hungry.

'Put it on then.' Her throat was dry.

While he sat up and fumbled she closed her eyes. Felt desire skip over her skin and quicken her pulse. Then he bent to kiss her again, moving over her. She wriggled her hips and opened her eyes to look into his. Cornflower blue, she thought. He nudged his way inside. 'Oh, yes,' she whispered. 'Yes.' She lifted her hips to meet him. She ran her own hands over her breasts, watching his face darken with lust. She began to unbutton her cardigan.

Three weeks later Brendan Conroy put on his Sunday best and walked round to the Driscoll's'. He had quizzed Megan about the best time to catch her father. She reckoned Saturday morning before the pub opened.

Megan watched from her bedroom window as Brendan came down Livesey Street. He'd got awfully long legs but he didn't stoop like some lanky lads did. He blew her a kiss and she pulled a face. Then she sat on Kitty's side of the bed, nearest to the door, and craned to hear.

She heard Daddy — '. . . of all the bloody cheek . . .' Then Mammy calming him down. Then nothing. But no door slamming, which meant they hadn't slung him out. Her stomach was twisted up and she felt lightheaded. If they said no, she'd die. If they carried on in secret they were bound to get caught and her daddy would make good his threat about seeing Mr Hudson, who Brendan was apprenticed to. They'd have to run away. Try and get to Australia or somewhere. They'd be pioneers, like the wagon trains you saw in the Westerns.

'Megan!' Her father's roar made her jump out of her skin.

She ran downstairs and into the parlour, where Brendan perched awkwardly on the edge of the armchair. Her father stood by the sideboard and her mother had the other chair. She noticed Brendan's socks didn't match and she could see the milk-white skin of his shins and the curly ginger hairs.

'You know what he's here for?' her father demanded.

'Yes.' She kept her chin up. She would not let him make her feel bad.

'And you want to marry the man who ruined you?'

'Anthony!'

'I'm not ruined,' she retorted.

'Huh!' He gave a bitter laugh. 'Says who?'

Megan was itching to argue with him but this was too important. He could think what he liked, damn her to hell. As long as he gave his permission he didn't have to like it.

'I want to marry him.'

'He's apprenticed.'

'We'll wait.'

'He's stuck by her,' Mammy said.

'Stuck too fecking close in the first place,' Daddy slung back.

Maggie Driscoll gasped and closed her eyes. She spoke with them shut, as though she was close to breaking and it was all too much. 'Anthony, the boy is here in good faith and he's asking you for your daughter's hand.' She opened her eyes and looked at Megan. 'I'm sure they've learnt from their mistake. It's over a year since the bairn was born and nearly two since she got caught. They are older now. We want them to make a good life. I've no desire to have them sneaking around because you've got stuck on your principles. The Lord tells us to forgive.'

No one spoke. Daddy craned his neck back as though he'd a crick in it and then rubbed at his face. He turned to Brendan. 'There won't be any monkey business,' he said. 'If I find out you've laid a hand on her before you walk down the aisle I'll cut your tackle off.'

Megan choked. It was a yes. The crude old git. All hot air. Did anyone honestly believe they'd get engaged but still wait another two years to touch each other? Mind you, every time Daddy looked at Mammy she must have fallen pregnant. Megan wouldn't be like that. They'd use johnnies and pity the Pope. No babies until they were ready. God would understand. Or the Blessed Virgin. She'd lost her child when they crucified him, she'd understand.

'Yes, Sir.' Brendan was bobbing his head up and down like a nodding dog on the back of a car, his face the colour of Campbell's tomato soup.

There was a pause. Driscoll looked at the clock and rocked on his heels. They were open in five minutes, Megan knew, and his thoughts were already with his first pint.

Mam broke the spell. 'Congratulations!' She shook Brendan's hand and hugged Megan and seemed genuinely pleased.

'I best be off,' Daddy said.

When he'd gone, Mrs Driscoll told Brendan, 'Be sure and let your mammy know. It'll be all round the Grey Mare as soon as the big fella gets there and everyone in Collyhurst'll know by tea-time.'

He nodded. 'Will you come?' He asked Megan.

She glanced at Mam, who smiled and dipped her head.

Megan stood on tiptoe and kissed Brendan on the cheek. Mrs Brendan Conroy, she thought. Thank God.

* * *

Marjorie

'You've made up your mind, already, haven't you?' Robert asked Marjorie Underwood when they were halfway home.

'She's lovely,' she said. 'What is there to consider? A different baby wouldn't be any better or worse. I don't want to wait any longer.'

He nodded. 'You'd better ring as soon as we get in, then.'

'Oh, Robert.' She laid her hand across the back of his shoulders and leaned over to kiss him on the cheek. Stephen had fallen asleep in the car by the time they got home and Robert transferred him to his cot. His face was flushed and damp around the temples and his hair was darker from the moisture. Downstairs Robert could hear Marjorie on the telephone, laughing and talking.

She was peeling potatoes when he found her in the kitchen.

'Probably a week on Thursday but Sister Monica will ring tomorrow and confirm if that's definite.'

'Happy?'

'Oh, yes.'

'As soon as I'm done with this I'm going to ring my mum. She'll be over the moon.'

'Stephen didn't seem too chuffed with the idea.'

She laughed. 'He's two. He doesn't really understand. We'll probably get a bit of jealousy. Your mother says you tried to smother John when he came along.'

'Still feel like it now and again.'

'Robert!'

'Something infuriating about the eldest, don't you think?'

'I wouldn't know. I'd have given anything for a playmate — older or younger. I hope they will get on, though,' she added. 'If she's anything like Stephen it'll be a doddle.'

* * *

Wind her more often.
Robinson's Gripe Water.
Give her a little boiled water on a spoon.
Try a different formula.
Rub her tummy.
Keep the milk cool.
They like swaddling.
Rocking helps.
Don't wrap them up tight.
Add half a spoon of sugar.
Make the feed warmer.
Let her cry.

They were all full of ideas but nothing made a blind bit of difference. She'd been back to the clinic, seen the health visitor and the doctor, but it all came down to this. Evening colic. Screaming for two to three hours at a time. Night after night after night. At first she had been terrified that Nina was in pain — the baby kept drawing her knees up, her face was red and creased and her cries were agonising. After two weeks of it, exhaustion and frustration had replaced terror. And now she just wanted it to stop. She fell into bed each night feeling as though she could not survive another day of it. She had tried changing the daily routine in a myriad of ways but still come six o'clock the pitiful screaming would start. Simple things like the chance to wash her own hair, have a bath, do her nails were completely impossible. She'd been taken over. And it wasn't fair.

She looked at Nina now, in her cot, a picture of fury and pain. Marjorie felt rage wash over her. She wanted to stop her, silence her, put a pillow over her to muffle the sounds. Her heart stammered and she walked from the room.

Robert was no use. He avoided the situation. His contribution to the living hell was to put Stephen to bed and then hide in the lounge with the radio or the television on.

She made a drink of Ovaltine and went back up. The screams seemed to drill into her bones, in the back of her skull and the roof of her mouth. How could the child scream so and not become hoarse? She put her drink down and lifted Nina from the cot. The yelling stopped momentarily and then resumed. She put her on her shoulder and turned the transistor on, raising the volume as high as it would go she sang along, her stomach clenched tight.

More racket for Deborah next door to get sniffy about. She'd been around and apologised after the first few evenings.

'Colic?' Deborah had said as though Marjorie had invented the explanation. 'You poor thing. We did wonder. She has got a powerful set of lungs on her, hasn't she? I never had anything like that with my three. They all went down at seven and not a peep from them till seven the next morning.' She gave a shrug and a smile as though apologising for this imperfection. Bully for you, thought Marjorie. She felt like hitting her. She was a failure.

Stephen had been good though. And no one could tell her why Nina had colic or even what it actually was. It would stop by the age of three months, the doctor had tried to reassure her. If we're both still here, she thought. That could mean another four weeks.

She lifted her cup in one hand and drank it while pacing about. Nina bawled frantically. Marjorie looked outside. It was dry, still light. She couldn't bear this.

She went downstairs and laid her in the large Silver Cross carriage pram by the front door. Put a blanket over her.

She went into the living room. Robert was watching Coronation Street. She would have liked the chance.

'I'm taking her out in the pram,' she said. I can't stand being cooped up with her any longer.'

He frowned with concern. 'Do you think that's . . .'

'What?' She snapped at him. Piercing screams reached them from the hall.

'If you think it'll help.'

'It'll help me.'

She walked fast around the block, pushing the pram. Trees lined the streets. It was a soft, pretty evening. The hazy evening light, the summer smells of night stocks and roses and honeysuckle, the dreamy quiet of the air seemed to amplify the wretched squalls Nina made. On her way she passed several people. She was sure that the looks they gave her were not sympathetic but were judgmental and suspicious. There she goes. Can't comfort the poor child. Not her own, of course. Some women just don't have the maternal instinct. Bad mother.

But she kept on and on, walking until her legs and arms ached and the night dew was falling and the child's cries stuttered into sobs and then quieted.

CAROLINE/KAY/THERESA

Caroline

Caroline sat at her grandmother's grave. She had brought a piece of heather from the tops, it had enough roots to take. There was no headstone up yet. They were still carving it, adding her name to that of her husband's. Both in the same plot. A purchase that had been made shortly after their wedding.

Caroline poked a hole in-between the turves of grass that were growing together over the mound and worked her fingers until it was wide enough and deep enough for the plant. She pushed the wiry, threadlike roots in and pushed the soil back packing it round them. Soft, rich, black soil. The colour of tar. The cemetery was exposed, out on the hillside beside St Martin's. You'll have a good view, Grandma. In this light with the haze burned off she could see right across to the other side of the valley. She could pick out the Colby's farm, the huddle of buildings and the foursquare farmhouse with its gravel drive. She saw a Land Rover bumping along one of the lanes and, further along, the silver streak of Dunner's Ditch, where water tumbled down towards Otter's Gap.

She loved these hills, felt comfortable here, unlike Mary, the friend she'd had at school, who yearned for the bustle of town or the headier excitement of Manchester with all the shops and coffee bars. Caroline found peace up here. No one to answer to, no one to bother her. But she felt lonely these days. Not a feeling she had been familiar with. An ache for warmth, for something to complete her.

Coming home had been a lesson in misery. Like a sleepwalker she had watched her mother set her endless practical tasks with some notion of keeping her busy.

Her mother had continued to act as though nothing had happened. No, that wasn't true. She had stopped touching her. Unclean. Caroline had felt her face burn when she realised. I've had the ceremony, they let me go up to communion now. If the Church can accept me, why can't you? Was her mother even aware of it? And her father, he was awash with embarrassment and hurt.

She hadn't a clue what she was going to do but she couldn't bear the thought of staying here. A life of nothing, a home scorched with shame. She cast her eyes around the graveyard and beyond. She was still alone. She stretched out the length of the plot to one side, where the grass was thick and green and dotted with white clover. She closed her eyes and let the sun heat her skin.

'Oh, Grandma,' she said, 'I had a baby, a little girl.' Words she could never speak, only to the dead. 'I gave her away.' She paused. 'No, they took her away. I didn't want . . . I wanted to keep her.' She remembered that moment, frozen, the babe in her arms, the nun coming towards her, turning to run and finding her way blocked. *No, no, don't take her*! She faltered, pressed her palm to her lips. No tears, empty even of tears. Just that ring of grief stuck in her throat like a bracelet.

She couldn't stay here to choke her life away. But how could she leave? There were three ways out. Marriage, hardly likely; college, but she'd have to go back to school and down a year and she had no great desire for learning; or work. Go into nursing or the forces, something where lodgings came with the position. She would ask at the library next time she went in.

* * *

Kay

The baby's face wrinkled and a tiny neat sneeze startled her awake.

'Oh, baby!' Kay Farrell chuckled at the bundle in her arms. She sat beneath the apple tree in the corner of their garden. The baby had been in the pram but Kay wanted to cuddle her. Dr Spock went on about routine in his book and Kay hoped that picking her up wouldn't end up unsettling her for her feed but she just had to keep holding the child.

It was a perfect June day, the leaves dappled in the sunshine, the scent of cut grass. Adam had done the lawn and was edging it now with the half-moon. She glanced across at him and then at the baby. Their baby.

'Hello!' She stared into the dark eyes. She looks so wise, Kay thought, as though she'd got it all worked out. She stroked the miniature hand with her little finger and was rewarded by the small fist clutching tightly. 'You *are* strong,' she said. 'Are you getting hungry? Mmm?'

Kay yawned. She had barely slept the last two nights. Excitement almost like a fever had bubbled around her body and she had risen countless times to check that the baby was safe. When she woke for a feed with small cries, Kay felt nothing but relief. She persuaded Adam to move the crib into their room after the first night. 'She can go in the nursery when she's bigger. I want to be able to hear her.' But even in the same room she couldn't hear the infant breathing and had to keep reassuring herself. So she was very tired and completely exhilarated. Once or twice she'd felt a moment of terrible panic, her stomach dropping and fearful thoughts assailing her like blows. They'd got the wrong baby, the mother might change her mind, they'll come and take her, we can't look after her properly. Unsettling moments that passed quickly but frightened her and cast a shadow on her happiness. Of course, it was possible the mother would change her mind, refuse to sign the papers when it came to court. You heard of that happening. She pushed the thought away.

'We'll be all right, won't we?' She spoke to the baby. 'Of course we will.' She closed her eyes, praying again. Prayers of thanks that now after all this time she had what she longed for.

Adam came over and knelt beside her, lit a cigarette and took a long pull on it. He was an attractive man — people said he reminded them of the singer Adam Faith with darker hair. He had that slightly rugged look and the dimple in his chin. Very occasionally she wondered if he'd like her to be slimmer. Lord knows, she had tried but nothing helped. She put on a few pounds every year and it never came off. She was big, not fat — she didn't like to think of it like that — but generously proportioned. Everybody couldn't be thin, after all. And she was big in all the right places. Like Marilyn Monroe. And Kay always made sure she looked her best: she had her hair permed and she never went out without doing her make-up. She wore scarlet lipstick. Adam never mentioned her size and he obviously enjoyed her in bed.

He sat back on the grass in the sun. 'She's awake?'

'Lunch time, nearly.'

'I could give her the bottle. While you get ours.'

'Yes?'

'Can't be that tricky.'

She laughed. 'You'd be surprised. Oh, Adam, she's so lovely. I can't imagine that some people wouldn't want her just because of that ear. It's nothing.'

She looked at the baby's left ear, which was little more than a whorl of flesh, the shell of the ear had obviously not grown properly prior to birth.

'She is lovely.' He leaned forward to look at the baby. 'Aren't you? Theresa, my pet.'

'Are you sure?' Kay glanced at him. 'About keeping the name?'

'We both like it.'

'And we could have Lisa for her middle name.'

'Theresa Lisa Farrell. Theresa Farrell. I prefer it without.'

'Yes, but if she has a middle name it gives her a choice. Some people don't like their first name, she could use Lisa then.'

'We don't need to decide yet.' He lay back and put his cigarette to his mouth again.

The baby's face furrowed and she turned a deep red. She twisted her head left and right and began to cry, a lusty sound as though some sudden calamity had befallen her.

'Oh, dear. Here—' she held the child out to Adam — 'mind your cigarette.' He ground it out between the roots of the tree. 'There. I'll make her bottle.'

He held the baby in the crook of one arm and walked over the grass singing 'The Grand Old Duke Of York', loudly and off key.

Kay went in close to tears, the swell of emotions overwhelming her. I am a mother, she thought. She is my daughter. She wanted to dance and pray and never, never forget the moment. She put a stack of records on to play, sang along to Jerry Keller's 'Here Comes Summer' as she got out the ingredients for salmon salad sandwiches. Jived round the kitchen to 'Three Steps to Heaven' by Eddie Cochran.

* * *

Caroline

Caroline was accepted into the nursing school at Manchester Royal Infirmary and began work in January 1962.

The regime was extremely strict. The new recruits lived in fear of the senior staff and Matron enjoyed a ferocious reputation and a godlike status.

The job was demanding. Caroline was responsible for bed-making, emptying bedpans, assisting other staff, lifting and assisting patients to use the toilet, serving drinks and changing dressings. She knew she hadn't much of a bedside manner and preferred the patients who were too ill to make small talk.

She missed the open air. The nearest park, Whitworth Park, was a flat space with trees and shrubs. She hungered for hills and huge outcrops of rocks, clean air and breathtaking views. Manchester was filthy. Her uniform was thick with grime before she'd finished her shift and the smog was awful. Caroline shared a room in the nurses' home with Victoria and Doreen. Doreen had come from Ireland, she was little and doll-like and made them laugh with her Irish sayings and her occasional bad language. Two months after they all started she disappeared.

'Her clothes have gone.' Victoria showed Caroline the empty drawers. 'Everything.'

'Maybe she was homesick?'

'She never said anything. Do you think we could ask someone?'

Caroline shrugged. She didn't fancy trying to talk to anyone about it. They'd bite your head off soon as look at you.

A new girl was allocated to take the room and still nothing was said.

In the end Victoria persuaded Caroline to join forces with her and approach Sister Mahr, one of the younger nurses who had a lot of contact with the new girls.

She led them into the nurses' station and shut the door.

'I'm afraid Doreen let herself and everybody down. She behaved improperly and found herself expecting.'

Caroline felt her face go cold, a prickle brushed across her neck and upper arms. She stared at the floor.

'Instead of throwing herself on the mercy of the societies that are there to help, she . . .'

Caroline swallowed, remembered the corner in the garden, the feel of the shawl, the weight of the baby cradled in one arm.

'. . . she tried to kill her baby.'

Victoria drew her breath in sharply, her hand flew to her mouth.

There had been no rumours, Caroline thought, not a whisper. If she'd collapsed in the hospital someone would have seen something, overheard enough to pass on.

'She went to an abortionist.' The word was shocking. Like a big, dark-red blood clot in the nurse's mouth. 'The police are involved.'

Caroline could feel heat blooming through her, replacing the shivers, pressure in her head. Oh, Doreen.

'What will happen to her?' Victoria asked.

'Nothing now. She didn't survive. They found her by the canal.' Her voice was bitter.

'Oh,' Victoria said softly.

Doreen. Little Doreen with her bright eyes and her delicate features. Why hadn't she gone to St Ann's? How on earth did she know where to find a person who did that? What did they use? She imagined a knife, a grappling hook, balked at the pictures.

A ewe had haemorrhaged once up on Colby's farm. So much blood and the ewe had struggled until its wool was crimson and then it had jerked, spasms racking it until it lay still.

Doreen. Did her family know? Would she get a proper burial? Caroline couldn't find the words to ask. Why had they come here? It would be better not to know, to imagine that Doreen had just gone home, fed up of the place.

'I want you girls to promise me that you will not speak about this to anyone else. It is a tragic thing and it would never have happened if Doreen had remembered the importance of staying pure. You give me your word?'

They both did. Victoria's voice shaky with emotion.

Caroline dreamt of Doreen that night. Doreen lay in her arms singing, a lovely ballad. She was wrapped in a shawl, sticky and dark with blood.

* * *

'Nurse!' The cry was like a bleat. The young man in the end bed. He'd been brought in that afternoon, his leg crushed by a forklift truck. He'd been in the army doing National Service for the last eighteen months. A year younger and this would never have happened to him. They'd abolished it now. He'd been in the last batch, called up in 1960. She took a look at him, his lips taut with pain, tongue gripped between his teeth. Pearls of sweat sprinkled on his forehead.

'I'll get Sister.' She hurried to the nurse's station and alerted Sister Colne, who administered more medicine.

'Sit with him a while,' she told Caroline. 'He's spiking a temp so keep him cool and he can drink if he's thirsty.'

Caroline took the cloth from his brow, dipped it in cold water, wrung it out and replaced it. He was hovering between sleep and waking, his eyelids fluttering up and down, his mouth working occasionally but no speech. The drugs would make him woozy. There was a rank smell from him, sour and unwashed. He wouldn't be bathed until the doctors examined him again in the morning.

It was warm on the ward and quiet now save for the snoring from someone at the far end and an occasional murmur from the depths of a dream.

Caroline closed her eyes for a moment, felt herself settle in the chair. Her head was heavy and she felt sleep steal over her like a cloak, creeping up her spine and over her skull, enveloping her shoulders. When she jerked awake some time later he was looking at her, his eyes made dreamy by the medicine.

'Hello,' he said.

She smiled.

'What's your name?'

'Caroline.'

'Paul.'

'The pain, has it helped?'

'Yeah. Where are you from, Caroline? That's not a Manchester accent.'

'Bolton,' she said.

'Ah, Bolton,' he mimicked her.

She smiled even though having the mickey taken was not particularly amusing.

'Get that a lot?' He surprised her.

She nodded. His hair was cut close, for the services of course. He had a strong face. She could imagine him as a man of action, no nonsense.

'This leg, what'll they do? Nobody's saying anything. Will they . . . ?' He faltered, looked away then back, his Adam's apple bobbed. 'Can they save it?'

'Oh, yes,' she said. 'It's only if there's gangrene or complications.'

Relief shone damp in his eyes. Light-blue eyes. She saw his chest fall as he exhaled.

'I don't understand,' he said. 'The operation?'

Oh, you poor man. 'They'll put a pin in, a metal rod, where the bones are shattered. You'll have a lump, scars.'

'And a stick? Charlie Chaplin. No more drill, then.' He spoke in a rush. Then gave a little hiccup. 'Sorry.'

Mortified, Caroline realised he was crying. She wanted to crawl under the bed and hide. 'Don't worry, please,' she said. 'I'd better go.'

He nodded.

She drew the curtains round so, although the light sleepers might hear the broken breathing coming from the cubicle, no one would have to witness him losing control.

* * *

His plaster cast was off and his leg looked sick beneath it, the skin like uncooked fish, greyish-white and damp. A smell too, cheesy. The skin had healed in puckered lumps along the outside muscle and across the knee. As if a child had started to model a leg from white plasticine and left it rough and unfinished. She betrayed no reaction as she wiped it gently with clean water and antiseptic and began to prepare the bandages.

She was fed up, another black mood, a miserable day. Most days were. A knot of resentment inside. She felt hot tears pressing behind her eyes. No reason for them. No reason for any of it. She stirred more plaster of Paris into the mix.

'Are you courting?' he said.

She looked sharply at him, two spots of red forming on her cheeks.

'Sorry,' he amended quickly. He watched her work, sneaking a look at her face now and then, large brown eyes, broad cheeks, her hair pulled back under the nurses hat. 'What would you do if you weren't a nurse?'

She shrugged. She didn't want to chat.

'What about when you were little then . . .'

Why wouldn't he just give up and shut up?

'. . . what did you want to be? I suppose it's different for girls — you don't have to be anything much once you get married — but boys it's always engine drivers and pilots and footballers. Or soldiers.'

No more drill parade.

'Farming,' she said.

'That's a hard life for a woman.'

Try this.

'What sort of farming?'

She thought of the ewe and of sick people, sick animals, mess. Grandma's allotment. 'Crops,' she said. 'Market gardening, a nursery.'

He raised his eyebrows.

And landscape gardening too. The chance to sculpt the earth, to plant it and make beautiful vistas, like they did in the grand old houses. Not the sort of thing a nurse from Bolton could aspire to.

She started to wind the bandages, feeling the plaster wet and cold and heavy on her hands. She wished he wouldn't stare at her so much.

* * *

He had several weeks of physiotherapy. He was moved out of the men's surgical ward. Caroline missed his company and felt a ripple of embarrassment when she realised she was manufacturing reasons to run errands to the convalescent ward. Then one day he came looking for her, using a stick now not crutches, with a rolling gait so he appeared to travel as far sideways as he did forward.

She turned from the cupboard she was stacking to greet him. They were the same height, she was pleased he wasn't taller. But why did it matter?

'You're doing well.'

He nodded. 'Discharge next week. Back home.' His family lived up in Yorkshire.

A crush of disappointment pressed on her heart. Silly, she thought.

'I wondered, your day off, perhaps we could have tea?'

'Yes,' she said quickly, then, 'Will they let you out?'

'Occupational therapy. Got to try getting on a bus tomorrow.' He tipped his head at the stick. There was a familiar trace of bitterness in his voice. She recognised it as a shield against self-pity.

* * *

Tea was a delight. He talked more than ever; about his army days, the boys in his regiment and his family. He asked after hers. She told him a little but threw questions back.

He reached out to touch her hand, his skin warm and dry against hers. She let his palm cover the back of her hand, a falling feeling inside her, like Alice in the rabbit hole.

'Caroline . . .' He licked his lips. She watched his mouth form different shapes as he chased words. 'Can I write?' He managed. 'Do you think, perhaps?'

Oh, Paul, yes. But if he knew. He thought she was young and innocent but she was spoilt. It just wouldn't be fair to him. He was a good man. She pulled her hand back. 'I don't think it's a good idea.'

His head reared slightly at the rejection and he ran his fingers along his jaw. 'I see.'

On the walk back to the hospital their conversation was strained and awkward. She felt the numb weight of depression settle on her. It would always be like this, it would never change.

And Paul had similar thoughts, cursing himself for being a fool. He should have known better than to expect her to take on a cripple. He should never have asked. What girl in her right mind would look at him twice? Yes, she'd been friendly and kind but that was her job. That was all. He must have been cracked to think there was anything more.

* * *

Kay

Kay Farrell was astonished at how much work one tiny infant generated. It wasn't just feeding and changing her, it was everything in-between too. Sterilising all the bottles and teats, sluicing and soaking and washing and drying the nappies, washing and drying and ironing the clothes. The daily walk, the bath. Life had been full before — keeping the house and garden in order, shopping and cooking and cleaning — but now it was hard to fit everything in. The windows were overdue for a clean, the pile of mending was becoming overwhelming. She tried to tell herself it didn't matter but it bothered her. Other women managed, why couldn't she? Was she doing something wrong?

She was tired too. Often numb by the end of the day when Adam came home expecting a decent two-course meal and home comforts. She had been going to bed earlier and earlier but Theresa needed a feed at eleven. Her friends with children raved about how easy Theresa was. Sleeping through the night, keeping her feeds down, easily placated when she cried. When they said that, Kay found it impossible to complain. After all she wasn't being dragged out of bed three times a night or struggling with three-month colic. But one day she did confide in her neighbour, Joanna, who was more outspoken than some of the others and had a devilish sense of humour.

'Bugger housework,' Joanna said.

'Joanna!' Kay snorted with laughter.

'Oh, come on. Does Adam notice?'

'Well, no, but . . .'

'But he notices you're tired? Headaches at bedtime?'

It took Kay a moment to grasp the reference. 'Joanna!' she scolded her.

'Look, Kay, you can have an ideal home and battle on exhausted with a neglected husband or you can give yourself a chance and make things a bit easier so you're fit company and you can enjoy Theresa.'

'I do enjoy Theresa,' she said defensively. Remembering the previous afternoon when Theresa had woken early from her nap and Kay had almost cried with frustration. 'You've no idea,' she carried on. 'It's wonderful. For heaven's sake, Joanna, I only said I was a bit tired.'

'Don't be so touchy.'

'Everyone else manages.'

'Like who? Here, have another biscuit.'

She took one, bit into it and considered. 'Violet.'

'She's got a cleaning woman.'

'OK, well, Muriel.'

'Her mother's practically living there, she does half the housework.'

'Ann-Marie.'

'Drinks.'

'What?'

'On the bottle.'

Kay's mouth fell open. 'Seriously?'

'Oh, Kay, you're so naive.'

'How do you know?'

'You can smell it. She's always sucking mints.'

'Maybe she likes mints.'

'And she fell over at our cheese and wine. Jerry had to take her home.'

'Oh, how awful. But in the day, she drinks?'

'Yes, Kay.' Joanna nodded her head slowly for emphasis. 'Soon as Jerry's left for work.'

'Crikey! Do you think we should do something?'

Joanna laughed. 'Such as? And Carol and Angela are both on pep pills. You could try those. Pep you up a bit. Doctor will sort you out.'

Kay pulled a face. 'I don't know. What about Bev? She looks great. Two children, house is always nice. She reminds me a bit of Sophia Loren, those sort of eyes. She's managing all right. She never looks like it's all too much.'

Kay finished her biscuit and waited for her friend to shoot her down. But Joanna had a funny expression on her face. One that Kay couldn't decipher. Joanna looked away.

'What?' Kay said. 'What's wrong with Bev?'

'She's having an affair with Ken,' Joanna said sharply and picked up her cigarettes.

'Oh, my God! Joanna . . . oh!' She didn't know what to say. 'Oh, Joanna. And here's me moaning on . . .' She drew out her own packet and lit a cigarette.

'Don't tell anyone.'

'No, of course not. When did . . . do they know you . . . ?'

Joanna screwed her eyes up against the smoke and shook her head.

'What will you do?'

'I don't know. I'd like to sue the bugger for divorce but I need some advice. And there's Damien to think about. It'd mean selling the house and I don't know how I'd manage. My typing's rusty and even if I went back to work who'd look after Damien? It's a bloody awful mess.'

'Wouldn't you get maintenance?'

'No idea. Oh, Kay, it's so horrible. I don't want to think about it.'

A rising cry from Theresa in her pram outside interrupted them. Kay went to fetch her in for a feed. Shortly after, the fish van arrived in the road — it was Friday — and both women went to buy fish for that evening's meal.

Joanna's revelation haunted Kay. It had been even worse because, having told her about it, Joanna hadn't wanted to say more and Kay found herself imagining the countless ways Joanna might have found out. How would she face Bev or Ken again? How did Joanna do it? If Adam ever . . . the thought chilled her to the bone. Was she neglecting him? If she was, surely he could understand, she'd such a lot on her plate. Had Joanna told her as some sort of warning?

That night when they were going to bed she broached the topic of a cleaner with him. 'A few hours a week.'

'Do we need one?' He sounded surprised.

'It would be a real help and I don't think it would set us back so very much. Violet has one. I could see what she pays, if she's reliable.'

He shifted in bed. Ran his hand up her thigh, pushing back the nylon nightie. Kay was tired. Her period was due and she felt grouchy but she didn't want to upset him. He murmured something.

'Is that a yes?' she said.

'Yes,' he replied. He slid his hand between her legs. 'Come here.'

* * *

Caroline

> *Dear Caroline,*
>
> *I hope you don't mind me writing but I am having to come back to the hospital for a check up on September seventh and I wonder if we might meet up? What shift will you be on?*
>
> *Life here is very quiet, though I sometimes go into Keighley to the pictures.*
>
> *Hope you are well.*
>
> *Yours sincerely,*
>
> *Paul*

She reread the letter, a bubble of excitement rising inside her. Two weeks away. She could swap her day off. She'd get her hair done. Don't, she admonished herself. He's a friend, that's all. I can't lead him on. But I wouldn't. Just company. It needn't mean anything else. She replied by return of post, arranging to meet him after his appointment.

She had her hair cut to shoulder length and bought some setting lotion and jumbo rollers so she could make it flick out at the ends. It made her feel grown up.

* * *

He looked well when he arrived, face and arms brown from the weather, prompting her to ask if he'd been working outside.

'Not working, studying. Balance isn't good enough to work — fall over all the time like some old duffer. Scares the sheep.' He gave a wry smile. He was more handsome than she remembered. Not film-star looks but nice. A lazy slant to his eyes like Dean Martin's, his eyes were even bluer against his tan. His hair was longer, floppy at the front, a dark-blond colour. The sun had brought out the light parts of it.

'I'll tell you about it. But we'd better get going, it starts in quarter of an hour.'

They watched the new Alfred Hitchcock film, *The Birds*. It was very scary and Caroline hid her face and gripped Paul's arm when it got really frightening. At least it wasn't a weepy. She had bought herself a block of mascara and some lipstick. Putting the mascara on had been a nightmare. Spitting on the little block then working up a paste then trying to get the stuff on her lashes with the little rectangular brush. So there was no way she wanted to see it all dribble down her face.

There was a coffee bar opposite the Odeon and they went there after. She got the drinks, realising it would be hard for Paul to manage with his stick.

'How's the hospital?'

'Same as ever.' She was sick of it, if the truth be told. The endless grind of dirty dressings and bedpans, the smell of sick bodies and pain and fear. Some days when it was time to get up she lay there and wished she could sleep forever. Once a month she made the trip home and there would be red salmon sandwiches and Victoria sponge and she'd get an hour or two up on the hills. She would go to Grandma's grave most times and say hello and wonder whether life would have felt any brighter with Grandma still in it. And she would climb up to a vantage point, to Little Craven or Goat's Head, and sit and let her eyes roam and let everything ebb away, all the feelings and the pictures and the words, let them empty from her, seeping into the earth like dew. Leaving her cleansed and grounded. Just bone and breath.

The city was choking her. Sometimes she felt like a mole, especially doing nightshifts — living underground, never coming up for air. Some of the other girls had got married and given up work. Married women weren't allowed to nurse. But Caroline could see no end to it. She couldn't go back and live at home again, the presence of her parents too much like a reproach. And what would she do all day?

She dropped two sugar cubes in her coffee and stirred.

'You look tired,' Paul said.

She concentrated on the spoon, the circles in the froth. She didn't want his pity. 'I'm fine.'

'I've missed you.'

'Don't.'

She saw his jaw tighten.

'So what's this studying?'

'Business. How to keep accounts, import and export, trading law, stock-taking. Correspondence course. I've picked quite a lot up.'

He missed me. She tried to concentrate on the conversation. 'You're thinking of setting up in business?'

'Yes. I've got some compensation through. Not heaps but enough to start me off.'

A crowd piled into the coffee bar, voices raucous, the boys teasing the girls and the girls giving lip back. Someone put the jukebox on, 'She Loves You' blared out. Caroline loved the song, it was a new group from Liverpool called The Beatles, but it was impossible to talk above the noise.

'Let's walk,' he said.

They headed for Whitworth Park. It was a dull evening, warm and humid, midges danced in clouds beneath the trees in the park, a gang of children kicked a ball about, their squeals punctuating the murmur of the city.

They stopped to sit on a bench. Paul propped his stick against the end. 'Caroline, there's something I want to say.' He spoke quickly, tripping over the words. 'I don't know what your feelings are for me but I meant what I said. I have really missed you.'

'Paul . . .' She felt her mouth get dry, her hands shook a little.

'Please, listen. The business idea. You talked about gardening. Well, I've been thinking, it could be a nursery. I've enough to buy some land and I could run the financial side, the paperwork. You'd be in charge of all the rest.'

'You want to go into business with me?' She was confused.

There was a pause.

'I want to marry you.'

'No!' she exclaimed.

'Caroline.'

'No, I can't.'

'Don't you care for me?'

'I can't marry you,' she repeated. You don't know about me. You don't know what happened. It wouldn't be fair.

He stood up, his face flushed. 'I thought you'd be sympathetic. See beyond the ruddy cane and the game leg.' He grabbed his stick and slammed it against the bench.

She stood too. 'Oh, Paul, it's not you. Don't think that. It's me. I can't. I don't deserve you.'

'Is there someone else?' He said tightly.

'No!' She exclaimed, then, 'There was before.' Did he understand what she meant?

'You still see him?'

'No.' She waited. 'I'm sorry.'

'It doesn't matter, really.' He felt for her hand, clasped it tight against his chest. 'If it's over, I don't mind, Caroline, really.'

'But Paul . . .'

'Marry me.'

She shook her head. 'You'll meet another girl, someone . . . better.'

'I don't want anyone else, better or worse. I want you.' He spoke urgently, his face creased with anguish. 'I've been going crazy. We could have a future together, a good one. Get married, buy some land. It was your dream . . . I thought you might feel the same.'

'I do . . .' she whispered. She blinked furiously. Tell him about the baby. Tell him now. No. She didn't want to think about it. It was too hard. She couldn't. She saw herself watering plants, potting on seedlings. Outside, rain and shine. No more antiseptic and bloodied dressings, enemas and vomit. Paul with her, sharing their lives together. She might never meet a man she liked so much. 'Yes,' she said.

'What?'

'Yes. I will marry you.' She was smiling and tears ran into the corners of her mouth. He gazed at her, his own eyes bright. 'Ow!' she said. 'You're hurting my hand.'

He kissed her then. Tentative at first as though he was holding back and then hungry. She thought how strange that she had promised to marry him before they had even shared a kiss.

PART THREE: GROWING UP

JOAN/LILIAN/PAMELA

Pamela

'Goal! What a goal!' Her dad leapt up and Pamela bounced off the sofa and back on again, her arms raised and cheering with him.

Geoff Hurst. Geoff Hurst had made it four-two and there was no way Germany could beat that in the remaining seconds.

'We won the cup, we won the cup, eee-aye-adio, we won the cup!'

Her mum stuck her head through the serving hatch. 'Have we won?'

'Four-two! And it was two-all at the end of full time. Two goals in extra time! Fantastic. Hurst was unbelievable.'

They watched the squad go up to receive their medals and the cup and hoist Bobby Moore on their shoulders. The Charlton brothers were playing, Pamela liked them best. Dad liked Alan Ball.

The beginning of the summer holidays and Pamela had plans. Mum and Dad had been saving all their cigarette coupons and they'd enough now to get a pogo stick. She'd helped count last night after tea. They said she could get one before Christmas, when, as she had pointed out, it would be too cold for it. Then they'd been to see *The Sound Of Music* the night before. It was absolutely brilliant. Pamela wanted her mum to get the LP so she could learn all the songs. The Nazis had been awful. She was glad she hadn't been a Jew then. Dad said there were still things like that going on, it wasn't always Jews. Like black children in America and South Africa who weren't allowed at school with white children. There were only two black children at Pamela's school but you had to be Catholic or pay lots of fees to go there. School was OK. The worst was when a gang came up, especially the big girls, and said, 'Are you a mod or a rocker?'

Pamela wasn't anything but you couldn't say that, they made you pick one. Sometimes if you got it wrong they pulled faces or pushed you. Sometimes they said, 'Who do you like best, The Beatles or the Rolling Stones?' She loved The Beatles, they were miles better, and her favourite was Paul because he was the most good-looking. Elizabeth, her friend at school, liked John because he was funny. But he wore glasses. Ringo was sweet but he had a big nose. She didn't know anyone who liked George best. George Best, hah!

In the middle of the holidays they'd go to Criccieth. They would set off really early in the morning and not even have breakfast and sing songs all the way. 'Summer Holiday' and pop songs like 'Pretty Flamingo' and 'Every Turn' by Candy and Dusty's new one, 'You Don't Have to Say Forever'. She knew all the words to that one and could sing it really loud and Dad would be the instruments, the trombone and the drums.

There was a caravan at Criccieth and it was *so* good. If she was an orphan and she had to live somewhere by herself she'd go there and live in a caravan. And get a dog. A golden Labrador that would walk to heel and fetch the paper. Auntie Sally had one called Queenie.

'Fancy a kick about?' Dad said and she leapt up.

'I'll get changed.'

She swapped her shift dress, the one with purple and green swirls on, for her shorts and PE top. And ran to get the ball. This was going to be the best summer ever.

* * *

Lilian

'Peter?' His breathing sounded strange. Lilian felt fear douse her veins with ice. 'Peter?'

She switched the bedside lamp on, put on her glasses and looked at him. He lay face down but even in the dim light she could see his skin was a horrible grey colour and when she put her hand out to touch him his pyjama top was soaked with sweat. She shook his shoulder. 'Peter.' There was no response, only the awful sound of his breath sucking in and out.

She ran downstairs, her heart thumping, stitch pains in her chest. She telephoned for an ambulance, watching the dial creep slowly back after each nine. Why nine-nine-nine, she thought, why not one-one-one? It would be so much quicker.

'It's my husband,' she said to the operator, 'I think it's a heart attack.' She hadn't named it till then, hadn't known she'd thought that till she said the words. She wondered what led her to that conclusion. 'Please hurry.' She gave her name and address and the woman reassured her that the ambulance would be there very soon. She ran back upstairs then, got on the bed beside him. 'There's an ambulance coming, it won't be long now. Peter?'

He was quiet. The rasping sounds had stopped. She tried to hear whether he was breathing but the blood was thundering in her ears. She put a hand on his back between his shoulder blades, looked for movements, but all she could see was her own hand trembling. He was dead.

Moaning to herself, she struggled to turn him over. He was heavy, always a solid man, not flabby but hard muscles, thick bones. His face was slack, dark blue eyes opened and vague. Don't think. She put her lips over his and blew into his mouth. There was a bubbling noise, that startled her. She moved away and a gush of liquid came from his mouth. She began to weep. No, Peter, no. I don't know what to do. She took another breath and bent and blew into his mouth again, and again. Nothing changed except his face became wet with her tears and the liquid that kept dribbling from his mouth.

The doorbell chimed and there was banging too. She left him, almost falling on the stairs as she clattered down them.

'He's upstairs,' she said to the ambulance men, 'he's not breathing.'

'We'll follow you,' the man said calmly, as though there was nothing to get het-up about.

'In here,' she said stupidly, then stood aside as they moved to examine him. One struggled out of his jacket, climbed astride Peter and began to pump his chest with his hands, stopping every so often to tilt his chin and breathe into him. After several minutes he sat back, exhaled and exchanged a look with his colleague. 'We're best taking him to the hospital,' he said to her. 'There's nothing more we can do for him here.'

She nodded, her mouth crammed with questions but too fearful to ask them.

The other man disappeared and returned with a stretcher.

They strapped Peter to it. She watched his eyes, praying for a blink, a wink, a glimpse of life. Praying endlessly, incoherent appeals running through her mind. They took him on the stretcher, negotiating the narrow stairs with difficulty, raising the stretcher to turn the landing, bumping it against the newel post. She winced as though he might be hurt. He can't feel anything, she told herself, and was dismayed at her lack of hope.

'We can take you with . . . ?'

'I've a little girl. Get a taxi. I don't drive. Peter . . .' She couldn't talk properly, missing connections.

They nodded.

She hurried back into the house to wake Pamela. Should she leave her with the neighbours? They had a seven-year-old too. She dressed herself then woke Pamela. She explained Daddy was ill, that she had to go to the hospital. Pamela begged to come too, promised to be good. Lilian was unsure. Children were usually shielded from such experiences. But she knew Pamela disliked Shona, the little girl next door. Lilian suspected her of being a bully.

'Please, Mummy, please? You've got to let me.'

'All right, put some clothes on quickly.' She rang a taxi that advertised an all-night service in the phone book. It was three thirty a.m.

At the hospital Lilian enquired at the Accident and Emergency Department and was told to take a seat. The place was quiet. The staff's voices echoed round when they spoke to each other. Lilian looked at posters about the smallpox outbreak and one about burns and scalds. Pamela sat beside her, knees together, toes meeting. She could tell her mother was upset and sensed it would not help to be asking lots of questions.

When the doctor came out to see them he asked Pamela to wait while he spoke to her mother.

Lilian walked silently alongside him into the small room. She was clenching her teeth tight, her hands called into fists, her tongue pressing hard against the roof of her mouth. Holding on.

'I'm sorry, Mrs Gough, there wasn't anything we could do for your husband. We weren't able to revive him.'

She nodded. Words, just words. Flying past like paper birds.

'It appears to be a heart attack but we'll be more sure of that once we've carried out a post-mortem. That's routine in a sudden death like this.'

Death. A feathery word, some owl lurching towards her.

The doctor looked at her. He must have said something. She'd no idea what it had been. She shook her head a fraction.

'Mrs Gough, had he been ill recently?'

'No.' Her voice sounded rusty.

'Any complaints?'

Only that he's dead.

'No,' she managed, horrified at the mess inside her head.

The doctor talked about forms and hours and releasing the body. He stood up then and she caught on that he had finished.

'Have you any family in Manchester?'

'Yes.' Her sister, Sally. She would ring her as soon as it got light.

* * *

Pamela

Pamela watched her mother walk towards her, eyes cast down and her steps a little unsteady. She paused by the bench and held out her hand. Pamela stood up and took it. Mummy's hand was cold and she held Pamela too tight.

She didn't say anything until they were back home. Mummy made her a cup of Ovaltine and sat opposite her at the kitchen table. She took her glasses off. It was just getting light. Like when they went on holiday and drove all night and watched the sun rise and the mist come off the fields.

'Daddy's not going to get better.' Mummy's voice sounded far away even though she was sitting right next to her. 'He's . . . he's gone to heaven, Pamela.'

It was a lie. He wouldn't go and leave her. She wanted to be brave but she began to cry. She couldn't help it. She loved Daddy, she was his best girl and he'd gone away and left her behind. It wasn't fair. It was stinking awful. She didn't want God to have him in heaven, she wanted him for herself. Mummy pulled her close and she breathed in the face-powder smell of her. Mummy stroked her hair, saying nothing.

'Why?' Pamela cried out. 'Why?' She felt her mother shake her head.

There was a horrid feeling in her tummy, a wrong feeling; everything dirty and mean and bad. Why couldn't it be

Grandpa who died? He was old and cranky. Or Granny. Or Mummy. No! She didn't mean that, really, God she didn't. But Mummy got tired and bossed her about and Daddy loved Pamela best and now . . . She'd been bad, the bad thoughts she had sometimes, the times when she was unkind or told a fib. She'd been bad and now Daddy was dead. She should have been good, all the time, like a saint, always good and kind and nice to everybody and then it would never have happened.

* * *

Lilian

Lilian rocked Pamela in her arms. Thank God she was here. Thank God.

'Why?' Her daughter's cry echoed her own thoughts, brought a twist of anguish to her guts. Why?

She'd been too greedy. After the miscarriages she should have let it be but she'd pushed. Maybe God didn't intend for her to be a mother. But she'd gone on and on about it, talked Peter round. Not just about the adoption, either. She'd been the one tempting him to disobey the Church's ruling on the sanctity of married life.

She looked at the clock. Nearly seven. He'd be getting up now . . . The room swam. She pressed her face into Pamela's tangled hair, her tears falling quietly. Would they take Pamela away? Fear coursed through her like acid. They couldn't. For the love of God after seven years. No. Don't be silly.

She looked up, her face wet and itchy, Pamela still cradled in her arms, one arm going numb. She stared out of the window. Saw the sky turning pearl-grey, heard the rattle of the milk float and the chatter of a magpie. She watched next door's cat parade across the garden fence and felt her cheeks grow cold.

She hugged Pamela and brushed her dark hair back from her face and told her to fetch a hanky. When the clock struck eight she rang her sister and had her first practise at saying the words. 'It's bad news. Peter's had a heart attack. He died last night.'

* * *

She had expected them to offer something, even though they hadn't seen much of them in the last few years. Peter had been their son, after all. Pamela was their granddaughter. So she'd expected a call or perhaps a note in the days after the funeral, discretely volunteering assistance. They knew she had nothing. The house would have to be sold and she'd have to find some sort of job, but these things took time.

The funeral had been miserable, how could it have been anything else? She had got through it like a robot. She'd taken the tranquilizers that the doctor proscribed and they'd made her feel sleepy and disconnected. She was determined to be dignified for Pamela, like Jackie Kennedy had at Jack's funeral. Composed. Sally had helped her with all the arrangements. Thank God Sally had been there. Practical and efficient, she was the one person Lilian could confide in. She could talk to her about how terrible losing Peter really was. She told her about hearing his voice and smelling his pillow and the strange things she felt compelled to do. The bizarre aspects of grieving.

Sally took Pamela too, on the worst days when Lilian simply needed to weep and thrash about, when she needed to let herself wallow in the pain, dragging up memories to lash herself with, reciting litanies of all they would never share, getting stupid with self-pity. All the things that Lilian hid from her daughter. Sally had Ian, a four-year-old, who Pamela loved to entertain, so it was a good arrangement all round.

Alicia and Bernard Gough had attended their son's funeral and gone back to the house afterwards. They had accepted commiserations from people and Alicia had been moved to tears several times. Pamela had been wary of them and they had made no special effort to talk to their granddaughter as far as Lilian could see. She herself hadn't had the strength to try and find common ground in their suffering, not that day, though she would try later when she was up to it.

The days rolled into weeks and there was no word from them. Then it was Peter's birthday. She sat in the lounge that afternoon while Pamela was at school and sorted through photographs, careful not to wet them with her tears. She chose three that she wanted to frame for herself and Pamela: a lovely shot of Peter with Pamela at the park, the pair of them sitting on the roundabout, caught laughing at something; and a solo shot of Peter in his tuxedo at a dinner dance, handsome, his black hair gleaming with Brylcreem slapped on to try and tame it. Sally had joked about him having girl's eyes, because of his long curling lashes. He was smiling and there was a cigarette in one hand. He was beautiful. She also selected a rare shot of the three of them. Pamela had been about five and a half, she'd lost her first teeth, two at the bottom, and her hair was tied up in bunches. They were at the front at Blackpool, Peter with a picnic basket in his hand and each of them with a cornet. She remembered the day, sunny with a stiff breeze. They'd gone back to the boarding house and Pamela had fallen asleep exhausted from a long day playing on the sands. She and Peter had made love in the cramped room, sand and suntan lotion on their skin and the taste of ice cream on their lips.

She sorted more pictures out for Alicia and Bernard. It would be nice for them to have some. She posted them first-class with a short note saying how she was missing him and how they must be too. She heard nothing.

* * *

She put the house on the market but interest was slow. A lot of people wanted something more modern — split level or at least with the living room and dining room knocked through. Then she got an offer. She began to look for places that they could afford. She hoped they could stay in the area and Pamela could continue at St John's, but it might not be possible. Then the buyer pulled out and it was back to square one. There was nothing in the bank and the Family Allowance went nowhere. Pamela needed new shoes. She began to feel panicky. She had to manage. She had to. There was no one else now.

* * *

She dressed as neatly as she could, aware of the aura of disapproval that always seemed to emanate from Peter's parents. She walked there. It was half an hour or so and it was a fine day, wind fluttering the first autumn leaves and the smell of wood smoke in the air. She was thirsty by the time she arrived and too warm from the walk.

She rang the front doorbell and after a moment saw the curtains in the bay window twitch. Then the door opened.

'Lilian.' Alicia had a tiny puzzled frown. 'What are you doing here?'

'I wanted to have a word with you, if . . .' She was tongue-tied. She had practised what she would say so often but it all ran away from her now.

'Oh.' Alicia stepped back and let her in. They went into the sitting room.

Alicia sat down, her feet together side by side. Lilian glanced down at her own feet, shoes dusty from the walk.

'Things have been difficult since Peter died. Financially . . .' It sounded too blunt, too direct. 'I'm trying to sell the house, of course, but there have been holdups. I've come to ask whether you and Bernard might be able to help us out.'

Alicia blinked, colour flushed her neck and she patted nervously at her lip with the knuckle of one forefinger. There was an appalling silence. Lilian could smell her own body odour. She cleared her throat.

'I'll have to speak to Bernard,' Alicia said.

'Yes, thank you. I'm sorry, if there'd been any other way . . . It's just these next few weeks till I sell the house and then . . .' she trailed off. 'Thank you.'

Alicia stood up and Lilian copied her. She had an urge to grab the woman, to get hold of her and shake her, shout at her. Did she mourn her son, did she cry for him in the night, did he walk through her dreams and call her name? Could she bear the thought of him in the cold ground, knowing she'd never hear his voice, watch him eat or smile?

'Did you get the photographs?'

'Yes,' Alicia said, betraying nothing. And turned to show her out.

* * *

She walked home feeling hot and humiliated. What, what had she done to deserve such . . . She struggled for words. She felt sick and parched. She stopped at a corner shop and bought a bottle of Coca-Cola. She drank it as she walked, trying to burp discretely when the bubbles repeated on her. It's for Pamela, she told herself, you had to do it.

Two days later a postal order for twenty pounds arrived and a note.

Dear Lilian,

We do hope this will assist you at this difficult time.

Yours sincerely,

Alicia Gough

It would buy groceries for a few weeks and new shoes for Pamela. It was the last time she ever heard from either of them.

* * *

Joan

Lena's version of 'Walk My Way' had been a monumental flop. Roger blamed everyone but himself. The discs were late being pressed, the distributors messed him about, it was the wrong time of year, the trend was for Americans or for male singers. Everyone wanted more Elvis Presley and Cliff. He ignored the fact that Helen Shapiro and Petula Clarke had each topped the charts. The fact that Roger had cut corners on studio time and session musicians and then had been late in liaising with all the other people involved and even had a design commissioned with the wrong title — 'Walk This Way' — might have had more than a little to do with it. Joan was bitterly disappointed but she didn't bother trying to tackle him about it.

Not long after that Roger shut down the company and Joan was out of work. He wanted to move into fashion, he said. More opportunities. Lena caught flu and was very ill. Joan nursed her. Joan worked for a temping agency, typing. Late in 1962 she sent 'Walk My Way' and everything else she had written since round to all the record companies. A week later, on her day off, she visited six of them. Two refused to let her past the receptionist. One told her they had a stable of writers and didn't take unsolicited work.

'You might want to add me to your stable,' she tried with a bravado she didn't feel inside.

'No room. Sorry.'

At the next place she met George Boyd — half-drunk and ill-tempered, wearing a ridiculous porkpie hat and a disreputable suit. He claimed not to have received her work.

'It's there,' she told him, 'that one.' She could see it on his desk.

'Let's hear it then,' he slung back at her.

'I don't . . .' She hated her voice but she couldn't miss the chance. Emulating Lena she launched into it.

At the end he shrugged. 'Not bad. Anyone ever tell you you could sing, they were lying.'

She felt her face flush at the jibe. 'Will you take it?'

'I could show it to Candy.'

Candy! This burke dealt with Candy? Yes, oh, yes! She swallowed. 'Yes. I'd want royalties, though, not just a flat fee.'

'Don't want much, do you?'

'Nothing wrong with a little ambition.'

He grimaced. Maybe it was meant to be a smile.

'Leave it with me.'

Not fully trusting him she had rung every week until he confirmed that Candy liked it and would record it for her next-but-one single. It would be released in July, the day after Lena flew home.

Joan saw her off at the airport.

'I wish you'd come,' Lena repeated, 'we'd be so happy.'

Joan shook her head, smiling. They'd been over this so many times. She loved Lena — her exuberance and her daring — and she owed her so much for showing Joan how women could love, but in her heart she knew she didn't love Lena enough to give up everything else. Things were just starting to happen for her and she adored life in London.

'You'll be happy,' Joan told her. 'You will.'

And she had been.

* * *

Lilian

'They say Friday at noon.' She handed the letter to Sally.

'But once you sell this place . . .'

'They won't wait. If the bill's not settled the bailiff's will take the furniture, anything of any value.'

'What's bailiffs?' Pamela came in from the hall.

'Never you mind,' Lilian said. 'Where's Ian?'

'Out here.'

'Well, watch him or he'll be after the china ornaments. Take him in the garden.'

'She's not daft,' Sally pointed out as Pamela left.

'I know, but she doesn't need chapter and verse.'

'I'll talk to Ed. I'm sure we can sort something.'

'Oh, would you?'

'Of course.'

'And we'd another couple looking round yesterday, agent thought they were very keen.'

'I'm not worried about being paid back,' Sally said. 'I know you're not going to pull a fast one.'

* * *

In the forty-eight hours that followed the phone was red hot with calls from Sally detailing the various conversations Ed had had with the bank manager and the accountant and everyone else. He would collect the money on Friday morning.

'Don't open the door. Don't let them in,' Sally told her. 'And make sure they don't try anything early. We'll be there by twelve.'

At half past eleven a white van drew up outside the house. Lilian watched from the upstairs window as two well-built men got out, both dressed in overalls. They made no attempt to approach the house but leaned against the van smoking.

'Where was Sally?' She'd tried ringing the house twice but there was no answer. If they took the furniture it would be that much harder to get settled somewhere new. And there were a few pieces that meant the world to her. Her mother's dresser, which had come from Wales when her mother married her father, the writing bureau that Peter had bought second-hand and restored. Somewhere for his engineer's drawings and books. Later when he worked away more it had become a place for all the family to use. The drawers held maps and stationery, photograph albums, certificates, a set of watercolours, dominoes and a chess game.

And the bed. The bed they'd shared, the bed where Peter had died. She'd heard rumours that the bailiffs couldn't take all the beds in a house, they had to leave you something to sleep on.

She went down and tried the phone again, praying for a reply. She listened to the ring, counting seven, ten, fifteen times before putting the receiver back.

She watched from the lounge as another car drew up. Ed? But he drove a Ford Popular. This was a Wolsey. A bald man in a suit and tie stepped out. He spoke to the men by the van. It must be the bailiff. She looked across the road to the houses opposite. They were all watching. Some behind the curtains other quite blatantly. Please, Sally. She went into the kitchen and lit a cigarette, sucked the sulphur of the match in her haste.

Knocking at the door startled her. It was only ten to twelve. More knocking. 'Mrs Gough.'

She went along the hall. She could see the man's head through the stained-glass panel at the top of the door.

'Someone's coming,' she said, feeling faintly ridiculous at shouting through the door. 'They're bringing the money.'

'They'll have to look sharp. We have a noon deadline.'

'They'll be here.'

'I have to advise you that we have legal powers to enter at midday and to remove items as we see fit.'

'I know.' Her voice trembled.

In-between smoking she bit at her nails, a habit she hated but found impossible to stop. She used to try every so often, when Peter was alive. She would put false nails on to fool herself and enjoy how sophisticated it made her look but she never managed to break the habit. It didn't matter much now, her nails would be broken anyway from all the extra jobs she was doing to keep the house shipshape.

I'm selling the house, she wanted to tell him, I can pay back the money then, more if it helps. But she had already had those conversations and they were like banging her head against a brick wall.

The phone rang and she raced to it.

'Mrs Gough, we've a Mr and Mrs Jarvis who'd like to view this tea-time if that's convenient.'

'Fine,' might be looking a bit empty by then, she thought.

Banging on the door. 'Mrs Gough, we need to come in now.'

She swallowed. Heard the clock in the dining room start to chime.

How could they let her down like this? Something must have happened. She ran upstairs and looked out, praying for a sign of Ed's Ford rolling down the street but there was nothing.

More hammering. She didn't want them to break the door down. She undid the latch, stepped back, her face set with dislike.

The three men ignored her. The bald man led the way and she listened from the hallway, her face stony, as he made comments about the items in the lounge, telling the others which to take. She heard them go out and into the dining room, more discussion, a burst of laughter at which she stiffened. They trailed past her and up the stairs. She went and hid in the kitchen. Lit another cigarette. The man in charge came and sought her out. He had a list. He offered it to her but she could not bear to take it. She looked away. He read it out. 'Matching armchairs and two-seater sofa, glass display cabinet, television . . .'

Even the television. And what would she tell Pamela when she came in and wanted to watch *The Monkees* or *Mr Ed*?

'. . . Welsh dresser, dining table and four chairs, writing bureau, vanity unit with mirror, Turkish rug, washing machine. We'll start moving it now. I need you to sign here.'

She sat there frozen but not unfeeling. Fury singing beneath her skin like sherbet. She heard them opening the drawers of the bureau. 'Where do you want us to put the contents?'

She sighed. The thought of the precious things, of Pamela's Holy Communion certificate, her baby bracelet, the photograph albums and letters from Peter when he had to stay the week in Sheffield or Leeds. She pulled herself up and went to fetch an old suitcase from under the bed. She began to empty the bureau drawers into it, trying to ignore the men, their patent impatience. When it was empty they lifted it up and carried it out. She would not cry, she bit her tongue, wiped her eyes, rubbed at the itching on her face.

'Lilian, Lilian.'

Sally and Ed, anxious, breathless.

She went to them. 'What—'

'It's all here!' Ed held out an envelope. Had a ruddy flat coming up Wilbraham Road! Sorry.'

She took it from him and went out to the man in the suit.

'It's all here,' she said, 'the money.'

He sighed and cocked his head on one side, looked at her as though she was a tiresome child. Please take it, she thought. Please.

'Cutting it a bit fine.'

She didn't trust herself to speak.

''Ang on!' he called to the lads. He pushed himself away from the side of the van and went to his car. He returned with a receipt, which she had to sign.

He spoke to the man and then drove off in his Wolsey.

'I'll put the kettle on,' Sally said. 'Look at that lot gawking, nothing better to do. Come on, Lilian.'

The men began to unload the van.

The tea was hot and strong and Sally put a splash of brandy in everyone's to steady their nerves.

There was no noise from the bailiff's men and Lilian thought they were probably taking the chance of a break themselves now the boss had gone.

When she finished the tea she went out to look.

The van had gone. They'd pulled out her stuff and left it there, higgledy-piggledy on the pavement. She didn't know whether to laugh or to cry.

* * *

Pamela

She'd done her maths. They were doing algebra and she liked it. Once you knew the rules you could work it out. English was trickier. They had to write an essay on My Ambition.

She had some ideas. One was to be a brilliant gymnast like Olga Korbut, who had just won three medals at the Olympic Games, or maybe a swimmer like Mark Spitz. Swimming was more realistic, because Pamela was in the swimming team but she couldn't do gym for toffee. Or maybe chess? She loved chess. She went to chess club after school and Mr Stenner said she had great promise. She got up to turn the LP over. Electric Warrior. T Rex. She moved the arm across, judging where the track started, and moved the little lever to lower it. Mum had bought her it for her birthday and she played it every day but there was only one scratch on it, because she was really careful. She didn't have many records. She wanted Rod Stewart next. As the opening chords began and Marc Bolan's voice sang out she returned to her work.

Her essay didn't have to be realistic, you could pick anything. One thing that would be good would be to bring peace. Stop wars like Vietnam and the trouble in Ireland and save all those lives. And Ban the Bomb and stop apartheid. All the things that were unjust. Like the Coca-Cola song said — teach the world to sing in perfect harmony. Her mum turned the telly off now when stuff about Vietnam came on. She got so upset. Pamela chewed the end of her biro and considered. She could be the first woman to walk on the moon. Hardly anyone got to do that. She liked the idea of floating, zero gravity. Mum had woken her to watch the moon landing. She said it was too fantastic to miss. So she'd got up at three in the morning and they'd watched Neil Armstrong climb down from the Eagle. You couldn't see his face in the big, bubble helmet but he sounded so happy and proud. Imagine going all that way seeing the earth and then when you came back looking at the moon and knowing you had stood on it. But it was only Americans and Russians went and you had to wee in tubes and eat pills or suck stuff from packets for food. It would be awful not to have real food. Outside, it was raining steadily. Mum was watching telly in the front room. *Monty Python* was on later. Her mum thought it was silly, which was the whole point. Usually she left Pamela to watch it by herself, which was less embarrassing all round, especially with some of the freaky cartoons.

She bent down to write. *My ambition is to be a world-famous chess player. A grand master, because no woman has done that yet.*

* * *

Joan

'Mind you, the Kinks have a huge following, and 'Hard Day's Night' is still selling well.'

'Bugger off, George,' said Joan.

He grinned, poured more pale ale into his glass and tilted back in his leather chair. The room was stifling, the windows painted shut years ago. A small, cream fan made a whining noise but barely shifted the smoky air.

'He will ring?' Joan slouched on the sofa. She was drinking Pernod and water, smoking Gauloises. Her Francophile phase. The taste of the drink reminded her of aniseed balls, of the weekly trip to the sweet shop with her threepenny bit. Choosing between flying saucers and sherbet fountains, Spanish and Kay-lie, gumdrops and sour apples.

There was a racket from outside. She went and peered down. Ban the Bombers. She couldn't open the window to shout her support but she raised her glass and blew a kiss to a guy dressed up like a clown. Most of them looked so ordinary she thought. She watched them pass. The atmosphere was good-natured. Strains of singing drifted up and the twanging sound of a skiffle band playing 'When The Saints Go Marching In'.

She slumped back on the sofa, adjusted her mini skirt. George had wandering eyes. He liked to look but he never tried anything else.

He peered across at her, narrowing his eyes against the smoke from his cigar.

'What?'

'You knew it was a winner . . .'

'We don't know yet.'

He used one hand to wave away her protest. 'Any other virgin, if you get my meaning, wouldn't have had all that stuff about royalties in their contract. But you knew.'

'Hoped, George. Not knew.'

He blew smoke rings. 'You'll need an agent.' He took a draught of beer, foam rimmed his upper lip. He wiped it with the back of his hand.

'You reckon?'

'You've copyright to watch, cover versions. Rights for this, that and the other. S'pose Sacha wants to release a French version, different tax laws and all that. What if the television wants it for a theme tune? You don't want to be bothering with all that. You need to keep churning them out.'

She balked at his description of her writing, pulled a face.

'You need someone to take care of the business side.'

'You?!' She beamed at him.

'Could do worse.' He cleared his throat.

'I'll think about it.'

The phone shrilled. Joan sat bolt upright, slopping some of the drink on her bare arm.

George winked. She'd never seen him move quickly for anything. He had all the ponderous calm of an old camel and a similar face.

He picked up the receiver and grunted his name. He listened intently, nodding, his mouth pursed in concentration. 'Tara, Bill.' He replaced the receiver.

'George?' It was bad news, she could see. Maybe they hadn't even broken into the top twenty never mind the top three. It had all looked so promising. Candy had sung it on *Thank Your Lucky Stars*. There'd been a rash of features about Candy too, all over the papers, linking her to a guitarist from Gerry and the Pacemakers. Every time she turned the radio on she heard it.

'Sorry, Joan.' He shook his head and sighed. 'I was going to take you out for a drink, bit of grub, but I don't know if I'm fit company . . .'

She felt sick.

'. . . not with you being the writer of this week's number one top of the pops.'

Number one! She screamed and leapt to her feet. 'You bugger, George! You rotten old pig! I thought we'd lost it. Number one. Oh, George!'

He raised his can. '"Walk My Way" by Candy, music and lyrics by Joan Hawes.'

She clinked her glass against his.

'Endless success,' he said.

'Endless success.'

'You, my dear, are going to make us both rich.'

She put her glass down. Hugged herself. Feeling childish but unable to contain herself.

'So what do you reckon? Bite to eat? Bottle of bubbly?'

'Definitely.'

He patted his pockets. 'You any money?'

'George!'

'Only joking. You can pay me back.'

'When hell freezes over.'

She wanted to run from excitement, turn cartwheels down the King's Road and shout her news from the rooftops. But she couldn't run in her heels and she'd never turned a cartwheel in her life. She contented herself with swinging her handbag and humming loudly as they went through the streets, her arms linked with George's. What a strange sight they must make. George with his rumpled, shiny suit, his porkpie hat and rolling gait and she with her thick, black hair cut short like Rita Tushingham in *A Taste Of Honey* and latest make-up, red beret and knee-high boots. Dolly bird and sugar Daddy? If only they knew, she laughed, and swung her bag higher.

* * *

Pamela

They got the ferry at Hull. The coach drove on and then Mrs Whetton told them all to bring their coats and any valuables with them. The crossing would take three hours. Thirteen, and

Pamela had never been abroad before. Everything fascinated her: the great metal structures in the boat, the excitement of setting off, watching the harbour side and all the men scurrying about with ropes. Then the launch. And the ship slowly turning, blasting its fog horn before they headed out to sea. She watched for a while. The buildings shrank and then disappeared from view and soon there was only the seagulls following in their wake and swooping down into the petrol-blue water.

'I feel sick already,' Eleanor told her. 'I'm always sick.'

Pamela grimaced. 'I hope I'm not.'

'Let's go in.' Eleanor led the way to the lounge. 'It's best to sit in the middle, where it doesn't tip so much.' She flopped into a spare seat. Pamela looked around. The place was almost full and there was a mugginess to the atmosphere which she didn't like. She didn't want to spend the whole journey sat in here, she'd feel better in the fresh air.

'Eleanor, I think I'd rather be outside.'

'It's cold though. I think I need to be near the toilet.'

Pamela felt the ship roll to the side and saw Eleanor's face slacken. She looked grey.

'Pam, can you get a me a pill from the Purser?'

'The what?'

'There's a place, through the doors there, near the bureau de change. The Purser's office, they have the tablets.'

'Fine. Hang on.'

She queued up, feeling responsible, and got a tablet for her friend. When the boat pitched more strongly she felt slightly queasy but it made her feel hungry rather than sick.

Eleanor had disappeared when she returned to the lounge but she came back soon after, looking deathly.

She didn't want anything else. She swallowed the pill then lay across two seats. 'I'm going to try and sleep,' she said. She curled up and closed her eyes.

'I'll be back later,' Pamela said.

She made her way to the cafe and queued up for a sandwich and a lemonade. She was horrified at the prices but she really had to eat something.

A family came in with two boys. The tallest glanced over at her a few times. She pretended not to notice but he was very good-looking. Thank God they hadn't been made to wear their uniforms for the journey. They were to save them for the performances. Just think, half of them would have been covered in sick. Not a nice picture for the Manchester Girls' Choir.

The family sat at a nearby table, the boy facing Pamela. She ate her sandwich slowly, aware of his eyes and enjoying the attention. She didn't move when she had finished but waited, fiddling with the packets of sugar on the table.

When the family got ready to move, Pamela got up and went to the top deck, where a few people lingered, some with binoculars, looking for seals or birds, she supposed.

She had almost given up hope when she saw him coming up the steps. The metal clanging as he climbed.

'Hello,' he said. 'A strong wind.'

'Yes.' She caught at her hair and held the unruly clump round her neck so she could see him.

'Are you German?'

He nodded. 'Erik.' He smiled. 'And you?'

What an awful name, she thought, for such a dishy boy. 'Pamela. I'm going to Berlin to sing at the choral festival.'

'You sing?' Amusement in his eyes. Did he think that was funny? Light eyes, almost yellow. It made her think of a cat, a lion or something. Yellow eyes, golden hair.

'What about you?'

'I never sing.' He crossed his eyes at her. Like Clarence, the cross-eyed lion on telly.

'No,' she laughed. 'Where've you been? Or going?'

'Ah! Family visit. My uncle lives in London. He was getting married.'

She nodded. Some hair escaped and slapped against her face.

'Shall we find some shelter?'

'Where?'

He winked. 'Follow me.'

* * *

There was a small recess on the deck below, a sunken rectangle big enough for the two of them, that offered some protection from the worst of the wind. Erik was easy to talk to. He was sixteen and told her he was going to be an engineer.

'My father was an engineer.'

'Yes? What sort of engineering?'

'I'm not sure. I don't remember much about his work. He died when I was seven.'

'That's bad.'

She shrugged.

'What will you be? A singer?'

'I don't know. I'd like to make lots of money and travel all over the world.'

'Where will you go first?'

'America – no, Australia. Somewhere really different.'

'America is good.'

'Have you been? Whereabouts?'

He talked and she listened. She was aware of her shoulder and hip touching his. She watched his hands as he talked. He wore an identity bracelet with his name on, a heavy gold chain. His skin was the colour of honey and there were fine hairs on the back of his hands. She could feel the vibration of the ship's engines in her tummy and excitement too at being here with him.

'Pamela, can I kiss you?' He said suddenly.

She turned to face him, looking at his eyes, which were serious now, the tawny colour ringed with black. His lips, fuller than hers, the shadow of darker hairs along his top lip.

'Yes.' She raised her face and he bent to meet her. His lips were cool and dry. She wondered for a moment whether she was doing it properly but then she let the sensation take over, eyes closed, feeling dizzy. She felt his hands on her. One at the nape of her neck, wreathed with her hair, the other stroking her back. It felt so good. She couldn't wait to tell Eleanor. This was going to be just the best week of her life.

* * *

Six years she'd been working. She started eight months after Peter's death and couldn't imagine her life without the job now. The first few weeks had been hell. She'd go to bed with her stomach clenched and nauseous at the prospect of the coming day. But she had stuck it out, she had to. It was the only job she could find that was near home and where she could do part-time and be able to pick Pamela up from school. Plus she didn't need any qualifications. And it had to get better, or maybe she had to get used to it. There were only two other women in the main sorting room and they seemed to be completely at home among the blue language and the practical jokes and the endless banter. She knew within a week that she had acquired a nickname: the moody widow. She tried not to be standoffish but some of the antics she found genuinely shocking and it was hard to pretend otherwise.

Finding a dead bird in one of her sorting cubicles had made her scream and another day the big joke had been letting off a stink bomb which made the back of her throat burn and her eyes water. There were dirty pictures from under-the-counter magazines sellotaped to the walls. She felt humiliated, hating the thought that the men might talk about her looks and speculate about what she was like under her clothes. Each day when she arrived she was greeted by a deafening barrage of wolf-whistles. She kept make-up to a minimum, her hair was cut short and practical and of course she had her glasses. She wore nothing that could be considered immodest but it made no difference. Even the older men acted like schoolboys and there was an astonishing amount of skiving went on.

She would end her shift with a headache from the noise and the tension, her teeth grinding together as she worked, ears alert for any mischief directed her way. Walking down to pick Pamela up she would try and free herself from all that. When she watched the news on television, barricades on the streets in France, students and workers, thousands of them ready for change, and people proclaiming a new beginning in the Czech republic, it seemed like the whole world was in turmoil. People talking about revolution and all she could do was fret about the pressure at work. By bedtime each day the dread began again.

After three weeks she was told to see the supervisor. She waited, biting her nails, until he called her into his office. There was a short-term vacancy in Lost and Missing, would she take it on until Norma came back?

She agreed readily. A tiny office down a corridor off the main sorting hall. Lost and Missing would be her refuge. She was taken in to Monica, who explained in heavily accented but precise English how they went about delivering the items with inadequate or absent addresses, or how they tried to trace items reported as lost.

Lilian was saved. Monica was a delight to work with after the others and soon confided in Lilian that she too was appalled by the general standards of behaviour. 'It is as if the teacher is out and they are seeing who can win the medal for the naughtiest boy. What I do is I smile, like this . . .' She beamed at Lilian, even white teeth framed by scarlet lips, 'and in here—' she pressed a finger to her forehead — 'I think, "You poor, pathetic creatures, you are a bunch of monkeys." Yeah? Apes, I think.'

Lilian smiled. They were like monkeys with their chattering and leaping about and their endless obsession with sex. She remembered being embarrassed at Southport Zoo when they'd seen a monkey fiddling with itself, the children squealing with laughter and pointing. She tried not to blush again as she had at the time.

'You're widowed?' Monica asked, once they'd got over the preliminaries about work.

Lilian was a bit taken aback at the direct approach but perhaps it was better to get it out in the open. 'Yes. What about you, are you married?' she looked at Monica's hand, no ring.

'Single. Waiting for Mr Right to come along.'

'Where are you from?'

'Spain. But my father was English. I came here after school and I seem to have got stuck.'

'Would you like to go back?'

'No.' She smiled again and pulled a face. 'Where I am from it is just farming, nothing to do. And Spain is a very poor country. There are better opportunities here, I think. I'd like to go to London maybe, that must be something. Have you ever been?'

'Once,' Lilian replied. 'For our honeymoon. It was lovely, so much to see.'

'Well, now we better get going. What you still need to see are the forms. There are a lot of forms in this office.' She rolled her eyes. 'Millions of forms.'

* * *

Norma never returned to work and Lilian became friends with Monica and two other women who worked in wages. The four of them sat together in the canteen. Lilian no longer felt like a belisha beacon shining to attract the attention of the pranksters. Monica invited the other three to celebrate her birthday with a meal out at an Italian restaurant in Albert Square. Lilian asked Sally to baby-sit and they agreed it would make sense for Pamela to sleep over at her auntie's.

Lilian hadn't been out since Peter's death and she had a rush of anxiety, worrying about what clothes to wear, how much money to take and what sort of gift to buy Monica.

* * *

Nevertheless she enjoyed the evening, caught herself laughing. Caught herself forgetting about Peter for a little while. It was peculiar coming back to the small terraced house that they'd moved into in Fallowfield and letting herself in and hearing the silence. Knowing she was alone, that Pamela wasn't there.

After that the foursome went out every month or so — to the pictures or for a meal. Lilian no longer dreaded work and she took some pride in being able to provide for herself and Pamela.

* * *

Pamela

She'd locked the bathroom door and taken everything off. She started at the top and worked down. Nice hair, black and wavy. Eyes a bit small but a nice deep-blue colour. Nose awful, much too long and it looked swollen at the end instead of smooth and neat. Ghastly complexion, blackheads and a million spots on her forehead and two on her chin. Eleanor had a facial steamer. She was going to borrow that. She'd tried Anne French and Clearasil and nothing worked. Nice ears, OK neck. Boobs too big and she was sure the left one was bigger. Big and lopsided. Flat stomach, good. Horrendous legs, big thighs and too thick at the ankles. Feet OK. She turned around and looked over her shoulder at the mirror. Bottom just awful.

She turned back. Maybe her boobs were even bigger because of her periods starting. Maybe they'd settle down and shrink a bit. Some people did swell up like that, didn't they? She pouted at herself and blew a kiss, touched the tip of one finger to her nipple. Watched the small, pink cone swell and darken.

'Pamela!'

She jumped. 'OK!' she yelled.

She dressed and flushed the toilet.

Downstairs she waited until they'd eaten before confiding in her mother.

'I've got my period.'

'Oh, Pamela.' Her mother smiled, a soppy look on her face. 'Everything all right?'

'Yes, it doesn't hurt, not yet anyway.'

'Some people get more cramps than others.'

'But I feel a bit bigger.' She tapped her chest, blushing. 'Did yours do that?'

Her mother hesitated. She was always a bit awkward talking about intimate things, secretive even. When Pamela had first seen tampons in plain sight in a friend's bathroom she'd been shocked. 'Not really. They were tender sometimes.'

'When did your periods start?'

'I was fourteen like you.'

'But they stopped really early?'

Her mother cleared her throat. Pamela began to feel embarrassed. She should never have asked.

'I had a problem with them.' Her mother shrugged. 'I had to have an operation and that was the end of all that.'

'So you wouldn't be able to have any more children,' Pamela said slowly.

'Yes,' her mother said quickly. She jumped to her feet and began clearing the table. Pamela didn't try asking any more. If the trouble was something that ran in families then her mother would have told her all about it, she was sure, if it was something important that would affect whether Pamela could have children.

* * *

Joan

'Scarborough?' George had said incredulously when she had told him about the house. 'You can't bleedin' well live in Scarborough!'

''Course I can. I can post you things, get the train now and again. I've had enough of London, George.'

'How can anyone have had enough of London, I ask you? This is where it's all happening, girl.'

'I've made my mind up.'

She had to get out. Seven years it had been, since she got that number one. Seven years of parties and clubs and the endless frenetic activity. Too many flings with too many strangers. It had been wonderful at first. And when 'Swing Me' followed 'Walk My Way' up to the top of the charts she had basked in the glory. Two number ones. There were nights at the Palais and others at all-night clubs. Times when Ray Davies from the Kinks or John Lennon and David Hockney, the artist, and Twiggy fresh from the cover of *Vogue*, and David Bailey, celebrity photographer, would be there. All the beautiful people. As the months went by it got harder to keep up. She was using uppers to stay awake and Mogadon to knock her out at bedtime. Speed and cocaine and god knows what for parties. Her hands shook now in the mornings, and she had begun to feel edgy. She'd lost weight and with it her energy. Some weeks ago she had woken up in bed with a strange woman and been unable to recall anything of the night before. Worst of all she hadn't written a decent song in months. Oh, she'd still been working, and George had sold most of them but they weren't a patch on her best, on what she knew she could do. When Jimi Hendrix died, Joan felt a stab of fear. A month later Janis Joplin died too. That could be me, she thought. If I don't get my head straight. Or she could just mess up, become more mediocre until she was a has-been. There were lots of them in the clubs and bars, talking about their heydays to anyone with half a mind to listen. She didn't want that. Leaving London was about survival.

'If you want me to, I can find a new agent.'

There was the merest whisper of alarm in George's face. Joan winked.

'Bugger off, Joan.' He pulled out a bottle of pale ale, removed the cap with his teeth. 'Where the bloody hell is Scarborough, anyway? Do they have running water and electricity up there?'

* * *

Pamela

Malcolm. He was very nice. But nice was the best she could come up with and it wasn't good enough. She'd met him at work, he was based at Stockport but the bank had brought him in when the flu epidemic affected staff at her branch in Northenden. It had been easy to say yes to a date. She'd even been excited about him for a while but now . . .

The hairdresser moved her over from the basin to the vacant chair. She'd fancied a pageboy cut but it was impossible with wavy hair like hers so she just kept it long and had the split ends trimmed every so often. Least it was a good colour, a glossy black. She didn't have to mess about colouring it with Harmony or Inecto to get an effect.

She had sensed Malcolm edging towards a proposal, imagining her ensconced in some nice, new semi in Heaton Mersey, just round the corner from his parents. Mrs Suburbia. Like Thelma from *The Likely Lads* on television. Ironing his shirts and having babies and making love twice a week laying flat on the bed with the lights out. He was so dull, so unimaginative. He thought prawn cocktails and a bunch of flowers were the height of romantic courtship. Or maybe that was the problem: he wanted romance — safe, dull, predictable — and she wanted passion. She wanted sex to be daring, challenging, naughty. It was so unsexy with Mal. Always the same routine, like brushing teeth or something. She fantasised constantly and she wanted to try out some of the milder ones but she couldn't see Malcolm taking her up against the wall or making her kneel on the floor and entering her from behind or chasing her and catching her.

She groaned. And she certainly couldn't imagine him letting her tie him up and tease him or shagging her in the shower. Crikey, even saying shag to Malcolm would be a challenge.

She glanced up at the mirror and wondered whether to try blue mascara to bring out the blue in her eyes.

The last time she had tried to vary the routine, waiting till he was as excited as he ever got then whispering that she wanted to get on top, she had felt his body stiffen and his penis soften. She'd tried to salvage things by staying where she was and saying *yes, more, yes, Malcolm* lots of times until he got back into his stride. Then Friday night they'd been back at The Steak House facing the same old evening and she'd had to stop it. She had watched him walk back from the gents, straightening his tie. She had waited until they were in the car before she told him.

'Malcolm, I'm sorry, I don't want to carry on seeing you.'

There was a clumsy silence and she heard him exhale loudly.

'Is there any particular reason?' He retreated into formal tones.

'Not really.' She could not be ruthlessly honest and hurt him. Why be so unkind?

'I just don't think we're right for each other.'

'Oh.' Pause. 'Is there someone else?'

'No.' Not yet.

'I'll drive you back.'

He didn't speak again. He drove her home and sat staring out at the road while she thanked him and got out. She felt lousy. She watched him drive off and stood on the pavement for a moment. She breathed in and smelt freedom. She had escaped.

And tonight she would celebrate. With good friends and probably too much to drink and some new outfit from the shop where she was headed as soon as her hair was done.

* * *

Two years later Pamela was on a training course at a conference centre near Rhyll. On the Friday night she spent much of the evening chatting to a trainee from Somerset, a man called Will. On the Saturday evening she slept with him and again on the Sunday morning. That afternoon they said goodbye. She went home exhausted and exhilarated. It seemed like the perfect arrangement — excitement, physical attraction, the mystery of strangers, the delicious opportunity to present herself however she wished. No boredom, no commitment, no complications.

* * *

'Mum, Mum?' Pamela Gough raced through the house, dropped her keys and bag on the table. 'Where are you?'

'Out here.' The voice came from the back of the house.

Pamela hurried through the kitchen and into the tiny stone-flagged back yard, ducking to avoid banging her head on the low door. Her mother was sitting on the old director's chair reading the *Manchester Evening News*. The headlines were all about the riots at Orgreave Colliery, there'd been a pitched battle between the police and the miners and their supporters. Lilian's father had been a miner and she was glad he wasn't alive to see what was going on now.

She turned to her daughter, reading glasses perched on the end of her nose.

'I got it, Mum, I got it!' She beamed with delight and thrust the piece of paper forward. 'I can't believe it!'

'Oh, wonderful! Oh, Pam, well done!' Lilian read the letter, speaking the final sentences aloud. 'And have great pleasure in confirming your appointment as manager at our Bradford Westgate Branch. I will be sending you details of our relocation package in the near future. Oh, Pam.' She smiled up at her daughter, narrowing her eyes against the brightness of the sky.

'Bank manager,' Pamela said, catching her lip between her teeth and widening her eyes in an exaggerated fashion.

'Not before time,' Lilian pointed out. It was Pamela's fourth shot at a branch of her own. Each time the disappointment of rejection had dealt a severe blow to her confidence. She couldn't do it. She was a woman and women never got the jobs. She wasn't good enough. She kept a bright functional front up at the bank but was unable to sustain it at home and Lilian was witness to the silences, the weary defeat in her posture, the lack of appetite and the inability to sleep.

Lilian suspected that losing Peter had hurt the child irreparably; she had adored Peter. She remembered the pair of them building castles from wooden bricks, sprawled on the floor, conferring, two heads of black hair. And racing along the sands at Criccieth, Lilian at the finishing line or judging the long jump. How on earth had he learnt to be a father like that when his own had been so remote?

Lilian also worried that her own deep unhappiness had been transmitted to Pamela. No matter how hard she had tried to continue to provide a warm, happy home for the two of them, in the quiet times of the night, in the privacy of her prayers and in the stock-taking of birthdays and New Years, she acknowledged that life had dealt her a cruel hand and that she was not happy. The best she could summon was contentment; that she was well, that Pamela and she were so close.

Endlessly she wondered how different it would have been if Peter had lived. A silly game. They would have stayed in the old house instead of moving to this little terraced house in Fallowfield, though it was a godsend for Lilian's work, only a stone's throw from the postal sorting office. There might have been more children, a brother or sister for Pamela . . . She shouldn't think like this, always wanting too much. That'd been her trouble all along. Not that she had wanted frivolous things; just a husband, a family, a nice home, close friends. But what was normal for others obviously wasn't in God's plan for Lilian. So she had lost one baby, then another, and a third. Then Peter. Pamela remained the light of her life, she could literally feel her heart grow warm each time she saw her, but even that love couldn't erase the sadness she carried within her.

'You aren't sure, are you, Mum? I could talk to them about commuting.'

'Don't be silly. You must go. It's what you've been waiting for, working for. There's a regular coach, or the train. You can come back for the weekend whenever you like. I'm so proud of you, Pamela.'

'I said I'd meet up with the girls later. Make a night of it.'

She nodded. 'Put the water heater on, you'll want to wash your hair, won't you? Do you want tea?'

'We'll be getting fish and chips later. But I'll get a butty now. Do you want one?'

'I'll do it.' She folded the paper up. She would save it for later, when she was alone. There'd be a lot more of that now Pamela was moving. Time she got used to it. She would not be maudlin, she admonished herself. Not like those parents who clung to their children and wouldn't let them go. Peter's mother had been a bit like that. Stiff with her when they were courting and downright cold about her granddaughter; anyone getting close to Peter was seen as a threat and earned her disapproval. Times past, she thought.

She busied herself with slicing bread and warming the teapot. Determined to deny the fearful flurry of questions about the future beating inside her, the panicky refrain, *Now what will become of me*?

* * *

Pamela

Learning to sail had been like coming home. The bank had sent management on a team-building weekend to the outward bound centre in Snowdonia. Pamela was the only woman and there had been plenty of innuendo among her friends about how much fun she might have with a dozen footloose men.

But it was sailing she fell in love with. There was something about the challenge of using the wind to travel the water and the undeniable kick she got from discovering she had real aptitude that reinforced the simple elation that she felt with the water flowing beneath her, the breeze in her hair and the smell of brine.

Towards the end of the course she'd asked Felix, the instructor, about any other opportunities. 'You've got the bug!' He grinned.

She nodded.

There are sessions here but you can't compare it to the open sea. That's real sailing.'

'And how do you do that?'

'Well, the wife, Marge, and I, we have a sloop, thirty-five footer, six berth, moored over in Holyhead. You could crew with us sometime.'

'Really?'

'Sure. We aim to be going out Whit week. There's always room for a friend or two. This'll be our tenth summer.'

'What will I need?'

He laughed and promised to help her with a list. She spent her next day off acquiring a sleeping bag and a good-quality waterproof jacket as well as woollen socks and leggings, hat and gloves and a small rucksack. She drove down to Holyhead straight from a strategy meeting in Manchester. It took an hour longer than she had anticipated, the route congested with lorries heading for the ferry to Dublin.

Marge was a small energetic woman with wrinkled, tanned skin, small black eyes like currants and a ripe Welsh accent. She cursed in Welsh and teased Felix mercilessly as a lazy bastard. A friend of theirs, Tom, a reserved man, made up the foursome. Pamela was never so happy. The daylight hours were full of work, handling the boat in the fine salt-spray, learning to tack and jib, to gauge the changes in the conditions and to navigate the seas. The constant song of the ocean in her ears and the ever-changing light filling her vision. The evenings, when they put into some small town or harbour, consisted of huge amounts of food, numerous bottles of wine and rowdy card games interspersed with rambling conversations and stories of other trips.

Well before midnight, Pamela would roll into her narrow bunk and fall asleep, lulled by the gentle rocking of the craft and the water lapping at her dreams.

The boat became her second home, apart from the winter months when the weather was too fierce. Marge and Felix became her firm friends. The following summer she crewed part-way for a tour of the Greek Islands. There were plenty of opportunities for casual encounters and though the boat was too small for secrets Marge and Felix were easy-going and, beyond the odd wink, didn't tease her about her conquests — at least not until the man in question had gone.

She loved the travelling too, and hungered for new sights, for foreign landscapes and food and climate. Those places that they couldn't reach by boat she visited in the winter — holidayed in Bali and Nepal, California and Zimbabwe. She worked hard and played harder. She and Lilian would take a short break every year, usually somewhere in Europe. Lilian joked that unlike her daughter she certainly hadn't got her sea legs as she spent all but the very calmest of crossings hanging over the toilet.

* * *

Joan

They met at the theatre. *Rosencrantz and Guildenstern Are Dead*. But you could say it was the house that brought them together. When Joan had first bought the place, investing her money from her run of songwriting success, she had acted sensibly. She had a vigorous and costly survey done which revealed a staggering list of essential repairs. On the basis of that she had beaten the sellers down and been able to pay for the work to be done. The house had been re-roofed, fully insulated and rewired. She had a new central heating system put in and an efficient boiler. The mortgage had been a huge responsibility but she had rented rooms out to actors appearing at the Stephen Joseph Theatre for the season. She soon acquired a reputation for offering upmarket digs, albeit at proportionally higher rates, and as soon as the season's entertainments were confirmed those actors with the leading parts and the higher incomes who didn't have allegiances to landladies elsewhere would ring and book their stay.

Joan regularly got comps from her lodgers. Penny had been at the theatre with two colleagues from school. In the course of interval chit-chat Penny had talked about looking for a house and the rising prices — she'd been married but was getting a divorce. Joan had a spare room. One of her actors had given back word after a more attractive offer from television. Joan had offered her the room to rent while she looked for a place. Penny came round the next day to look at the place and to explain a bit more about her situation. She had a child, a nine-year-old daughter. She was a teacher and was due to take up her first headship in Pickering after the summer. Previously her husband Henry had been able to take Rachel to school and bring her home. He was a self-employed accountant and could choose his hours. Now Henry had met someone else and they were going to get married as soon as the divorce became absolute. Rachel had been adamant that she wanted to stay with her father. Penny was still reeling from that. They had agreed that she would have Rachel to visit every weekend.

A child wasn't something Joan had bargained for but she didn't object, it was only going to be a temporary arrangement.

Joan hadn't imagined that anything else would develop. Penny and her dog moved in. Over the summer holidays Joan and Penny got to know each other. The theatre was dark, the actors gone for now. Penny would walk the dog each morning right along the bay. Early, before the holiday-makers hit the sands with their flasks and picnic rugs, rowdy children, knotted hankies and transistor radios. Joan asked if she might join her one day and the walk became a habit.

When Rachel came to stay Joan found that apart from her size she wasn't so very different from some of her more tempestuous guests.

Penny and Joan grew closer almost imperceptibly. They began to share meals and to accompany each other to social events.

Joan found herself watching Penny as she moved about the kitchen or while she prepared papers for school. She was drawn to her: she had a broad face, hair the colour of corn which she wore long, a generous body, more rounded than Joan's, and she had a bright mind; Joan relished hearing her talk, the intelligence and authority with which she considered ideas, encouraged her charges, commented on affairs was stimulating.

Joan began to feel awkward. She was falling in love. They had never discussed sexuality but a few choice, arch comments from one of the more camp lodgers had made it plain to all and sundry where Joan's inclinations lay.

But it was Penny who made the first move.

Joan had built a fire one night. The house was quiet. The next cast were coming the following Monday. Penny had finished work for the week. They sat watching the flames and drinking whisky, listening to classical guitar: John Williams.

She was laughing at Penny, who was lambasting Margaret Thatcher, describing how this woman had done her level best to shatter British society, wreck the Welfare State, close the pits, encourage individual greed, suck up to the Yanks, and then had the brass-necked cheek when re-elected to quote St Francis of Assisi: *Where there is discord, may we bring harmony . . . where there is despair, may we bring hope.* 'And what has she done since?' Penny demanded. 'Unemployment sky high, more privatisation . . .'

Joan was still giggling when she sensed a shift in the atmosphere. She glanced at Penny, who looked back at her steadily.

'Joan.'

Joan felt time slow, felt her blood thicken and warm at the tone. She opened her mouth a little. 'I . . .' Suddenly lost for words. She who crafted them, who selected and shaped words and rhythms and sounds to sway emotions to make hearts ache or soar or hips shake and feet tap. She had no words.

Penny moved from the big armchair still holding her gaze. Moved to sit beside her on the old, brocade couch. And kissed her.

A kiss, a stroke, her hands on Penny's neck and then slowly, cautiously running down her sides, hesitating. Another kiss and Penny's hands on her breasts, squeezing gently, Joan answering with a murmur, undoing the buttons on her cuffs. Silently they undressed. Joan was trembling with desire, shivering lightly. They lay side by side and she kissed Penny again. Her lips, her neck, her nipples. Moved down to kiss her belly, the inside of her thighs, her vagina. Feeling her own breath growing harsh, her sex clench and flush with heat. Penny calling softly. 'Yes, oh, yes!'

Afterwards they lay sprawled on the rug, drinking more whisky. Joan lit a cigarette and took a drag, narrowed her eyes and shook her head, a tiny smile on her lips.

'What?' Penny said, her fingers still tracing circles and figure eights on Joan's belly.

'Nothing. Just glad. I'd been falling for you. I didn't know what to do about it.'

'Me being an ex-married lady and all,' Penny teased.

'I didn't know if you . . . if it was just me. I wanted to be sure, I suppose. I never thought you'd get there first.'

'If we'd waited for you we'd have been old and grey. Bit scary though. You're sure?'

'Oh, yes.' She lifted Penny's hand and kissed her palm. 'Positive.'

* * *

Lilian

Pamela came home for a weekend every six weeks or so. In-between times Lilian ached with loneliness but was careful never to let on. She was determined not to cramp her daughter's style. Pamela was crazy about her sailing; she worked hard and played hard. No sign of settling down though she was twenty-eight already.

The evenings were the worst. She was still working days at the sorting office and dreaded the thought of retiring in two years' time when she reached sixty. She seemed to watch the television all the time, couldn't be bothered with her sewing any more. Even cooking for one was a joyless task. Often as not she'd open a tin and have a bit of toast with it. She still saw Monica and the others for an evening out and she'd friends through Church, where she helped out with jumble sales and fairs. She tried to keep busy.

The phone rang late one night. It was November, the weather was foul — cold, with gusts of wind and rain battering at the house. She had gone around and put newspaper down to soak up the rain leaking in through the kitchen window and checked the curtains in the other rooms to try and keep the heat in.

When she heard the ringing she assumed it would be Pamela or Sally or Monica. But none of them generally rang so late. Her heart kicked in her chest. Bad news?

'Hello?'

'Is that Marion?'

'Pardon?'

'Marion. Is Marion there?'

The woman's voice was slurred. The skin on Lilian's back tightened. Marion. Pamela had been Marion. This couldn't . . . A cold fear shot through her bones.

'I think you've got the wrong number.' She put the phone down quickly. And waited to see if it would ring again, chewing at her nails compulsively.

Her mind skittered round the prospect that she dreaded. But they couldn't do that, could they? They weren't allowed to. It was just a coincidence, that's all. She was holding her throat, her knees felt weak. She went and sat down. They wouldn't have this number, anyway, or this address. The phone was quiet. She finally went upstairs.

Lilian filled a hot-water bottle and put it at the foot of her bed. The sheets were clammy when she got in, there was a lot of damp in the bedroom in the winter. She warmed her feet then pulled the hot-water bottle up and curled round it. But even when the chill had gone she still couldn't sleep. Her back was tense and stiff, her stomach ached, stitched with fear.

She tried to imagine telling Pamela about the adoption but the prospect appalled her. It wasn't a good time. She'd such a lot on at work. And Lilian was sure the revelation would upset Pamela, it would be hurtful, and she was happy now, settled. She couldn't bear to spoil all that. If she did drag up the past what good would come of it? Pamela had had enough to cope with losing her father. Lilian was her mother, the only mother she needed. Plain and simple. That was that. But no matter how she argued to herself there was the grip of guilt dragging at her. She hadn't done anything wrong. She was just protecting her daughter. When she finally slept it was fitfully. She dreamt of Monica giving her a parcel for Pamela with the wrong name on it and when Lilian opened it there was a baby inside. And then she realised with horror that she'd left the baby in the parcel and she was going to be caught and punished. The doctor came in and told her the baby hadn't survived and she tried to run away but her legs wouldn't move.

* * *

Pamela

Bradford had made Pamela's career. Ten years later she had reached the highest echelons of senior management and been relocated to Head Office in Liverpool. Conditions were good. She earned enough to pay the mortgage and bills on the eighteenth-century stone cottage she had bought outside Chester and to finance her passion for travel. Money was not an issue. Lilian accompanied her on the nearer trips — a week in Venice, a cruise on the Norwegian fjords — but Pamela travelled further afield on her own.

She sat on the hotel balcony looking out over the fountains and the tropical gardens to the wild forest beyond. The Pavilion was an old colonial building dating from the times when Portuguese aristocrats holidayed here. The place was rich with marble, stupendous floor tiles, pillars and archways and gilt chandeliers. There was little wood, it rotted too quickly with the humidity.

It was her first trip to Brazil, though she had been to Mexico a few years before. It would be dark soon, and suddenly, no gradual dusk like at home, but that sudden dramatic plunge from blazing light to rich indigo night with a brazen sunset in-between. She sipped her lemonade and picked up the book she was reading. Once the sun had set she would shower and change. The anticipation of the evening to come made her smile. John, the Canadian guest, had wined and dined her for two nights. Third time lucky. Her experiences had taught her to take things at a moderate pace, at first anyway. She wanted a man who was prepared to get to know her a bit, to make intelligent conversation with a woman and enjoy her company as well as want to take her to bed. She didn't always meet someone on her holidays and she still enjoyed the pleasure of new sights and sounds and food and music. Being somewhere totally foreign. But a liaison made the trip something special. Back home the whole area of relationships was like a minefield. She had enjoyed a few brief flings but nothing that had ever gelled. Her status got in the way all too often. She was good at her job, good at the finances and good with people. Management skills had come easily to her and she was being selected more and more often for sensitive negotiations.

As the other women in the bank settled down and made full use of attractive maternity and parenthood packages or began to try dating agencies in their desire to find Mr Right, Pamela found herself reasonably content with a solo life. There were times when she felt lonely but many more when she was alone and at ease with it. She had good friends too, easily enough to fill a dinner table with when she chose to entertain. And she had her sailing.

She knew Lilian fretted about her. She didn't say much but Pamela knew she longed for grandchildren. Pamela couldn't think of a worse reason for having children than to please someone else.

She finished her drink and watched the purple and orange daubs of the sunset slide behind the tree canopy. For now this suited her. Freedom and the security of a good career. And the opportunity to be whoever the hell she liked with the men she met on her holidays.

It was time to get ready for John. She felt excitement ripple through her belly and into her breasts and her thighs. She had four nights left and she knew John was booked in for another week. If it all went as she hoped the remainder of her holiday would pass in a blur of sexual indulgence. Nights spent in the shuttered heat of the room and days spent in anticipation, with trips to the market, the mountains and the beach acting as interruptions to one long, shameless fuck.

The lights in the garden came on, coloured bulbs like Fiesta time. The noise of the crickets grew louder and shriller. She would wear the cream silk to set off her tan. All so much simpler than at home. No need to worry about the future, no questions about 'the relationship'. If all went well the future would be a handful of sexy memories and nothing else. She picked up her book and opened the screen door. Not long now.

* * *

Joan

Joan was working. Her desk was in front of the big bay window on the first floor. What most people would have called the master bedroom.

'But I have no master,' she had joked to Penny when she first showed her round. Only mistresses.

From her vantage point she could watch the tide come in and the boats inch their way across the bay. In the summer the tourists would come but this was her favourite season, with the winter sun like a ball of mercury, silvering the grey waves, and the clouds racing each other across the sky.

The room was spacious but warm. As well as her desk, it held a piano, a guitar, a bank of musical recording equipment and, either side of the open fireplace, shelves full of books. Many of these were collections of photographs. They were a source of ideas for her. 'Every Turn (Twists A Little Deeper)' had come to her one day while she was still down in London, flicking through a book. The photographs were black and white — street scenes, portraits and close-ups of natural elements, pebbles, the bark of a tree, reflections on water. She could never have explained the process by which these images became words, themes or tunes. It just happened. And 'Every Turn' had sprung almost fully formed, a morning's work.

That song had reached number three for three weeks and then been snapped up for a car commercial. Serious money. Today though she was making slower progress. She had the germ of an idea but she could see it as an image more clearly at this stage than she could hear it — footsteps in the snow, stillness, a parting. Not a dance number then, she thought wryly. She wanted a cigarette. If she had a smoke she would concentrate better. But Penny would never forgive her.

She saw the postman appear round the bend at the foot of the hill. Watched him wheel the bike up the steep slope, stop next door to deliver something and then disappear from view as he approached her front door. She heard the snap of the letterbox and the slap as the letters hit the floor.

A diversion. Time for coffee anyway. There were two letters — the contracts she was expecting from her agent and a gas bill. A postcard too. Berlin, Lena.

She read it while the kettle boiled, fussing over Kelly, the border collie that had moved in with Penny. A puppy then, but grey around the muzzle now. A grand old lady of ten. Seventy in dog years.

Darling Joan,

We're coming to London in February (must be crazy). M has an exhibition at the Tate. Will you come? We are still doing great with the gallery. How are you both? Any news about your Berlin trip?

Kiss kiss,

L

Joan laughed to herself. She'd been promising to visit her old friend ever since Lena returned to Germany the spring after they met.

She took her coffee back upstairs, settled at her desk. She could see a tanker out on the horizon and nearer a trawler with a cloud of gulls trailing it. The sky was darkening the waves a steely pewter now.

She looked at the mishmash of words on the paper. Nothing caught at her, nothing tugged further ideas. It was like fishing, she thought, trying to trap the words that swam inside her, haul them out into the light of day.

The phone interrupted her.

'Joan? It's Rachel. Can you ask Mum to ring me when she gets in?'

'Fine. How's things?'

'Oh—' Rachel sounded disconcerted to be asked — 'so-so.'

'Anything I can help with?'

'No. Nothing.'

'I'll tell her to ring.'

'Thanks.'

* * *

'She wants me to go over there,' Penny said.

'Why?'

'She wouldn't say why. Probably more problems with that pig of a landlord. I'll go now. Do you mind eating later?' She sounded relaxed about it but Joan knew that her demeanour concealed anxiety at the unusual summons from her daughter.

* * *

It was late, very late, when Penny returned. Joan had eaten an omelette and toast earlier, then returned to work. Preferring that to the dross on television. When she finally saw Penny's car creeping up the hill she went downstairs and switched the kettle on.

Penny looked exhausted, the grey pallor almost matching the grey that streaked her hair.

We're all getting so old, Joan thought. Me, Penny, the dog.

Penny sat at the table and rested her chin on her hands. 'She's pregnant.'

'Oh, no!'

'After all I taught her, drummed into her . . .' Her voice rose in frustration. 'A one-night stand. No protection. She could have HIV as well, for all we know.'

'What does she want to do?' She leaned against the counter, waiting for the kettle.

'She's all over the place, Joan. Talking about whether to keep it or have an abortion. She's nineteen. She can barely look after herself let alone a baby. What was she thinking of?'

I was nineteen, Joan thought.

'Oh, Joan, I'm sorry,' Penny exclaimed.

Joan wondered whether she had spoken aloud.

'But there's the pill nowadays and you can get Durex all over the place. How can I help her?'

Joan grimaced, turned for cups. Put them down. 'Stand by her, whatever she decides. That's all anyone can do.' She took a big breath, held it in. Christ, she thought, I'd kill for a cigarette.

* * *

Pamela

Summer 1990 Pamela spent crewing on the boat with Marge and Felix. They went from Wales to Southern Spain and into North Africa. After three exhilarating, exhausting weeks she was on the last leg of her journey home. She'd left her car at home to save bother parking and got the train to London from Portsmouth and then the London to Chester service. It was one of the old models. Shabby inside and out. There was little to see through the dusty windows. It was unreasonably hot and a peculiar stale, spicy smell filled the air as if someone had spilt curry on one of the heaters a long time ago.

She had the carriage to herself now. The couple who'd got on with her at Euston had left at Rugby. Not long to go. Taxi out to the cottage, a bath, some proper tea. Strange how it never tasted the same elsewhere, even with the same brand tea bags. It's the water, Lilian would say, but even that didn't seem plausible. How could all the water in every major city worldwide, and in all the other places she'd been to, be so different from home. Surely by the law of averages there'd be something similar in mineral composition or whatever in one of them.

Work tomorrow: back into drawing up plans for their strategy in Germany now that reunification was imminent, and there'd be all sorts of fallout linked to the Guinness scandal; they'd need to ensure their own house was in order so they weren't open to fraud on such a scale. Enough. She would not think about that now. Still on leave. She would think about Carlos instead. She could still feel where he had been, remember what a tease he had been, kissing her dizzy, till she was begging him to do more, to touch her.

Her mobile trilled. It was handy in her bag.

'Hello?' She shook her hair clear of the set to hear better.

'Is that Miss Gough? Pamela Gough?'

'Yes.' Her first thought was that someone from the office had got her days mixed up, ringing to fix an appointment for her boss. She'd switch off after this.

'You're related to Mrs Lilian Gough?'

Panic dried her mouth. 'I'm her daughter.' She felt the train sashay to the side, stared at the wooden window frame where someone had scratched T-e-r. She stared at the meaningless letters. Her heart went cold.

'This is Manchester Royal Infirmary. I'm ringing about your mother. She was admitted here a short while ago. She wasn't conscious. I'm very sorry to give you such bad news but your mother passed away a few minutes after she was admitted. I'm sorry.'

Pamela watched the letters spin and stretch and pool. She watched her own foot jerking with a will of its own. She felt a pull, increasing pressure as though she was being sucked underwater.

'Will you be coming to the hospital?'

'Yes.'

'Ask for Main Reception, they'll page me, June Kennedy.'

Pamela replied, the words saying themselves, as though there were two of her in the carriage. 'I'll be there as soon as I can. I'm on the train from London, the Chester train. It might take me a while.'

'No problem.'

'What was it?'

'Most likely a heart attack. It's still to be confirmed.'

'Thank you.'

'I'll see you later, and please accept my condolences. It must be a terrible shock.'

'Yes.'

She felt blank then, as though someone had slapped all feeling from her. T-e-r. Terrible. Terrified. Terminal. Mum's dead, my mother's dead. If she could only pull the communication cord. Stop the train, stop time. Back up a bit. To before she knew. Turn off her mobile and go home to her cottage and have that bath and a gourmet frozen dinner and then ring Mum. 'I'm back. It was wonderful.'

Whenever she had imagined this it had been so different. A long, slow decline, an illness, sitting at her bedside. The dilemma of care homes and sheltered housing. Visiting, nursing. In all her fantasies there had always been time to say goodbye.

* * *

It was horrible seeing her but she had to do it. She had never seen Peter and what he might have looked like had haunted her as a child. She had imagined his skeleton showing through or a scary look on his face. She had to view Lilian now to make it real and so she'd not plague herself with fancy notions of how she looked. They went into the room. Lilian was laid out on a trolley, a sheet up to her shoulders. She looked false. As though someone had made a poor copy of her. Her face was slumped, her mouth pulled down, she looked sulky or grumpy. Nothing like her usual expression. Her eyes were closed, no hint remained of their cat-like quality, the beautiful green colour. No glasses on now. Her hands looked more real — the familiar way her nails were bitten down. The wedding ring and engagement ring still there. Grief broke over her and with it came a whirl of bitterness, a flood of rage and fear.

How dare you, she thought, how dare you leave me. She wanted to shake her, wake her up, force her to put those arms about her, give her solace. Come back. A sequence of *nevers* flowed through her, surging like waves against the shore: never smile at me, never ring me up, never say my name, never share a menu, never.

How dare you go and die. She put her hand over the cold one and let tears burn and drip down her face. When she got tired she pulled the chair up and sat right next to the bed, lay her head against her mother's shoulder.

They had shared a bed after Dad had died. For months she had the comfort of her mother's soft warm body to save her from loneliness and fears. When had Lilian cried? Not in front of Pamela.

She could smell her mother's hairspray mixed in with the hospital smells and a trace of the floral perfume she liked, Lily of the Valley. Time passed. She let her mind float, bobbing from one memory to another. Time passed. She grew cold and nauseous. She felt filthy from the journey. There were things to do, an avalanche of things, but she didn't know how to leave.

It was dark outside when there was a knock on the door. Her aunt and uncle. The spell was broken. When it came to it, it was easier to walk out with them, off to be consumed by the practicalities of death. Leaving her mother lying there alone.

MEGAN/MARJORIE/NINA

Megan

He roared his head off when Father baptised him. Megan grinned. 'Sign of good luck,' she whispered to Brendan. Francine, in Brendan's arms, looked solemnly on, an anxious eighteen-month-old. He gave her a little tickle in the ribs and she wriggled and smiled.

'Aidan Stephen Conroy,' the priest said. They'd argued for hours over the middle name though they both liked Aidan. They'd had it in mind for Francine but then she turned out to be a girl. Brendan quite liked the idea of calling him Aidan Brendan but Megan pointed out that would be ABC in initials. Well, Brendan had retorted, it'll be ASC if you call him Stephen. That's OK, she'd replied with a logic that escaped him.

They went through to the church hall for the christening party. They'd done the buffet themselves with plenty of help from Maggie Driscoll and Kate Conroy. Proud grandparents. And the band were happy to play for a free slate at the bar. Michael, one of Megan's brothers, was doing the disco. She hoped he'd stay upright long enough to see them through to the end.

Megan told Brendan to get her a rum and Coke and settled down with Aidan and Francine at the centre table. From this vantage point she could see the whole of the room: the sweep of tables and chairs arranged around the wooden dance floor, the bar to her right, the stage at the left and ahead the entrance. Anyone coming in and she could see them. Aidan began to fuss again and she rooted in her bag for his bottle and the little jar of baby food.

She moved the highchair round and got him strapped in. His eager face was alight, burbling with anticipation.

* * *

Brendan set the drinks down and took Francine off. Two of Megan's sisters plus kids and both sets of grandparents sat down with her. She put Aidan in his seat, tied his bib on and started feeding him. The band struck up with a jig and like a flash the older crowd were up, twisting and whirling and giving it all they'd got. Showing the youngsters how it was done. Megan leaned over and took the ciggie her mammy had abandoned in her haste.

She looked over at her father, Anthony, whirling Mammy about. His face was the colour of beetroot these days but his hair was still black. He'd a belly like he was about to pop. Mammy looks old, Megan thought, the skin on her arms hung loose, her lips were thinner, eyes hooded as her face had succumbed to gravity. Maggie still sported ginger hair but it came from a bottle and in-between treatments it faded to the colour of pale rust.

Aidan had finished and was squirming in his chair. She lifted him up and sniffed at his bum, well-padded beneath the christening gown. 'Jesus, Aidan,' she complained, 'been saving that one up, haven't yer?'

When she returned from changing him she handed him over to Brendan, who was chatting with Billy from work. The disco was starting up and she took to the floor, which filled up to the strains of Herman's Hermits, 'Something tells Me I'm Into Something Good', a Manchester band and they'd got to number one. It had them all joining in, not that they needed much encouragement. She went up and got him to put on Candy's new one, 'Walk My Way' and 'Doo Wah Diddy Diddy' after that. She danced until she was out of breath. Francine toddled over and danced beside her when they all got into a line for 'The Locomotion'.

There was another drink waiting for her, she took a gulp and lit up. Billy stood up to leave them. ''S all we can do,' he said, 'wait and see.'

Brendan sighed.

'What's that then?' She sat in the seat Billy had left.

'There's talk of a takeover and there's more talk about modernisation.'

'Good or bad?'

'Bad, probably. Either could mean lay-offs.'

She saw his mouth tighten. Knew he was worried.

He recognised her concern. 'There's been rumours before,' he shrugged. 'Prospects might be better, now Labour's in. Harold Wilson, more in touch with the likes of us than the rest of 'em.' He bent forward, kissed her.

'What's that for?'

'The most beautiful woman in the world.'

'Oh, yeah. And you the biggest liar?'

Chubby Checker came on, 'Let's Dance'.

'Shall we?' Brendan cocked his elbow at her.

She ground out her cigarette, took another gulp of her drink. He was right. Could be owt or nowt. No point in fretting. Life was hard enough anyway with kids to feed and clothe and nothing getting any cheaper. But today was for Aidan and for them. This was a party and whatever troubles lay ahead they could still have a bloody good knees-up.

Brendan passed Aidan over to Granny Kate and the pair of them went over and into the circle that the dancers formed for them. Brendan winked at her, caught her hand and they launched into the jive that they'd first learnt as teenagers.

* * *

Marjorie

'Sit down!' Marjorie Underwood screeched at Nina.

'No!' The four-year-old glared back defiantly, then leaned forward and shoved her plate of food into the centre of the table. It knocked over a glass of Ribena, which bled across the cloth.

'Now look what you've done! You stupid child!' She lashed out with her hand. Nina ducked but her mother still managed to clip her across the head. 'Get upstairs.' Her voice was tight with anger. 'Now.'

Stephen stared dismally at his plate.

Marjorie pulled the edge of the tablecloth up to stem the flow of juice. Time and again the child pushed her to breaking point. Of course there was nothing wrong with a smack to instil discipline when the child was deliberately naughty like this but Nina's behaviour never seemed to improve. And when Marjorie smacked her she was often helpless with rage herself. The child made her see red, literally, a flood of orange in her eyes, a mist of bloody fury. Red hair. Red rag to a bull.

And at the end of these awful scenes she always had the sense that she had lost, that the girl had bested her in some obscure way. She would not cry and say sorry and have a cuddle. No matter how harsh the words that Marjorie used or how hard the slap, the girl would blink and swallow and look at her in defiance, vivid blue eyes bright and hard, her small mouth tightly pursed. Where did we go wrong? she thought for the umpteenth time. They had treated the two children exactly the same but Stephen had been so happy, so easy and biddable. Unlike Nina. Everything was a battle. Even as a tiny baby she had cried with a ferocity that had frightened Marjorie and had refused to be mollified. Her small face contorted with rage and her legs kicking as Marjorie paced the room almost demented with fatigue.

That evening when Robert came in she told him about the confrontation at tea-time. He loosened his tie and put his slippers on.

'She's definitely living up to the redheads' reputation. Vile temper.' He turned to find Marjorie in tears.

'I can't go on like this,' she gasped. 'I feel awful. There are times when I just want her gone.'

A shocked silence followed. She hid her face, appalled at what she had said.

'Marjorie . . .'

'I don't really mean it. It's just all too much sometimes. Like the day's one long battle with her. And I'm so tired. I can't sleep with worrying about it.' She ran her hands back through her silky blonde hair.

He came and put his arm around her shoulders. 'She'll be starting school in the autumn,' he pointed out. 'She'll have to buck her ideas up then. And it'll be a break for you. Do you want me to have a word with her?'

'She's asleep now. I do love her, Robert.'

'Of course you do.'

But I don't think I like her very much. The thought drenched her with guilt. She took a deep breath, wiped her face and went to dish up their tea.

* * *

Nina

It was sunny in the room even though most of the walls were covered in wood and all shiny. There were lines of sun coming in the windows and dust fairies floating in them, millions of them. They were practising for their first confession. You had to close your eyes and think very hard of all the things you'd done that were sins. And you even had to say bad things that you thought about, even if you hadn't done them and just thought of them. Nina had lots but she couldn't remember every single one. Then there was a list in the prayer book that you had to look at.

If God was so strong and powerful then why couldn't he make everyone be good all the time and then there wouldn't be any sins? No wars or robbers or lies or anything.

'Oh, my God,' Father Leary began, 'because thou art so good . . .'

They all joined in. You had to know it off by heart. And once you'd done confession then you could make your First Holy Communion. Nina had her dress already. There were tiny pearl buttons and lace round the sleeves. The lace was dead itchy. She wasn't allowed to try it on any more in case it got dirty. She had white gloves too and a headband, a tiara like something a Princess would wear but no diamonds, just white. And white shoes and socks.

Father Leary was nice. He smiled a lot. Not like Daddy, who only smiled at Stephen and mainly had a shut look on his face like you couldn't come in. When he got cross his mouth made a mean line. But he didn't smack her. Mummy did the smacking. She usually smacked her legs.

Father Leary had a nice laugh too. It made you want to laugh.

It was hard to be good all the time. The priest said the confession was to say you're sorry to God and that you had to try hard to be good after your confession. Yesterday she'd ambushed Stephen. She'd got the metal colander for her head and the sink plunger for her death ray and she'd waited behind the door on the landing and when she heard him coming upstairs she jumped out. 'Exterminate! Exterminate! I am a Dalek, I will exterminate you!' He'd jumped and screamed and she had laughed so much it hurt. He was bigger than her after all. He scowled at her and went off and she thought he might tell tales but Mummy didn't come. It couldn't be a sin that, being a Dalek, but maybe it was a bit mean. And teasing him about his books. He was always reading. Not fun stuff, like she got Bunty and there was good stories and pictures and always a free gift, like last week there was a hair slide on the front and it came through the door with the paper and it was great. But Stephen picked Look and Learn, which was more like school-y. And he read books without pictures in. She hated that sort. The pictures were always the best bit. But even when Nina was nice to Stephen and did kind things she would still think bad thoughts, they came into her head without her wanting them to, sneaked in so quick she didn't see how you could stop them.

She knew she would have to go to confession a lot. If she died in-between she'd be sent to purgatory and be tortured until they decided she could go to heaven. She didn't know what they used to torture you but it hurt a lot. In hell they had fire but maybe purgatory was different — bamboo shoots under your nails or that one where they put a rat on your tummy and then a cage over it and when the rat got hungry it ate a tunnel through you to escape.

'Nina.'

Startled, she looked up.

'Make your act of contrition.'

'Yes, Father. Oh, my God, because thou art so good . . .'

* * *

Megan

'All right, Megan?' Joe was on earlies, one in three weeks. She knew them all now, the regular drivers, but Joe was the most talkative.

'So-so,' she replied and put her fare on the metal dish. He rang her off a ticket and shoved the bus back into gear.

He waited till she was sat on the first seat before moving off.

'They've forecast snow,' he called over his shoulder. The bus was practically empty, sometimes she wondered if they ran it just for her. Now and then you'd get a student with a hulking great backpack off to India or Amsterdam on the Magic Bus from town but no one in their right mind would be on a bus at five in the morning if they could be tucked up warm in bed. Megan had no choice.

'My mammy'd say it was too cold to snow,' Megan called back. She lit up. They were bringing in rules about smoking, you had to go upstairs, but Joe didn't mind and there was no one else to bother. He'd a fag in his mouth like a permanent fixture, even got a little yellow-brown stain there above his lip.

'Never quite got it myself,' she continued. 'I mean, it snows at the North Pole, doesn't it, and up Everest an' all? Can't get much colder than that.'

'It's not the same in town, is it, the snow? All mucky by the end of the day.'

'That salt they chuck everywhere, the gritters and that, you should see what that does to the carpets. Burns 'em. It's corrosive, that's what it is. Ruins 'em if you let it build up.'

Joe swung the bus on to Rochdale Road leading down into town. 'Your Brendan had any luck?'

'No,' she sighed. 'Anything that comes up there's half of Harpurhey after it. And they take the youngsters. Pay 'em less.'

'Bloody crime,' Joe put in. 'When I started out you could always find something.'

'Like the buses?'

He laughed. 'Aye. Well they had conductors too in them days. Or the railways, markets, factories. Everywhere's hit now. Rolls Royce gone bust, did you see that? Dockers and engineers on strike, even the post office.'

She knew only too well. After she'd been off having Chris they'd cut back at her old place. When she went to see about going back to work they couldn't give her anything. Not even part-time. Orders were down and overheads were up. People blamed cheap imports and they were tightening their belts.

'Something might turn up,' he said. 'You live in hope.'

'Aye, you live in hope and you die in despair.'

'Keep doing the pools, lass.'

She watched the streets rattle past. Houses in darkness, streetlights still casting everything in an orange wash. It was perishing. They hadn't had the heating on all winter. Just using the gas fire in the lounge. They were living on beans and toast. She still tried to keep the kids looking nice but it was hard. Aidan only had to look at a pair of shoes and they started dropping to bits and Francine growing so fast they couldn't keep up. She'd even got them some stuff from the Oxfam shop in town. That was a real no-no. You were meant to give your kids the best, only the best, all new. Never cast-offs or if you absolutely had to then only in the family. She pretended they'd come from Woollies, they all had Ladybird labels in and you couldn't tell they'd been worn.

Brendan had taken her to task for it, thinking she'd been spending what they hadn't got, so she'd had to tell him the whole lot had only cost a couple of bob. She'd seen the fleeting look of shame cross his features and fought against the same feelings in herself.

'It doesn't matter, Brendan,' she said gently, 'it's just another way of keeping our heads above water.'

With no joy at the factory she now had four cleaning jobs and still they were spending more than they brought home. If she earned any more they'd dock his social. Two of the jobs were cash-in-hand as it was. Some fool somewhere had decided how much a family of five needed to live on. They must have forgotten to add a nought on the end because the amount barely fed them never mind all the rest — cleaning stuff, soap, plasters, tampons, school things, repairs, birthday cards.

Brendan had helped out on the Driscoll's stall for a couple of months but they all knew it didn't add up. People were holding on to their money and takings were rock bottom. Now and again he'd get a day or two labouring, on the motorway. Digging and lifting. He'd come back shattered, the sun or the wind peeled his nose and his shoulders and he'd have cuts on his hands and arms and sometimes was half-deaf from the drills but he'd have a note or two in his pocket. Enough for a bit of shopping or towards the gas or the electric. It didn't happen often. Too many after the same chance and besides it was wise not to push it, too many snoopers eager to catch them out and stop all their benefits.

Her stop next. She finished her cigarette and trod on the tab. Her day stretched ahead like an endurance test. Two and a half hours at the office block in town; five floors they covered, just the three of them. And that included everything from emptying paper bins and hoovering to cleaning toilets and polishing the big entrance hall with the industrial machines.

Then on to the nightclub, where it was clearing up tab ends and broken glass, wiping last night's beer from the bar and often as not someone's vomit from the floor. The carpet was past saving. Years of spills creating the dark, tacky residue that made your soles stick as you walked on it. Made her skin crawl, that carpet. Third job was a private house in Prestwich where she did a different floor each weekday and always the kitchen and bathroom. A consultant lived there, working at the hospital. She'd never met him, only his wife, who acted like minor royalty. She was often out, going off to coffee mornings and exhibitions and trips to Stratford or up to London, which was where they were from originally. How could you go up to London, Megan thought? The place was 300 miles south. It wasn't so much a direction thing, she'd said to Brendan, she reckoned it was more like a snob thing: London was better than everywhere else so London was up and everywhere else was down.

Once she'd done the big house she had to get two buses back home, squeeze in her own housework and fetch the kids. Sometimes Brendan went for them and she had half an hour with her feet up. Then it was three hours of bedlam while they were fed and did their homework and little Chris was got ready for bed. At seven she set out again to the comprehensive school. If she really pushed it she could do her section in an hour and a half but most nights she hadn't the energy to tear about. By the time she got back the kids would be asleep, Francine and her dad watching telly. She'd join them for a cup of tea and a final fag before turning in, the alarm set for four-thirty.

* * *

'Nina, Nina, there's no one meaner! Nina, Nina, there's no one meaner!'

The four girls surrounded her, their faces curled in snarls as they chanted their latest taunts, careful to have their backs to the staff supervising the playground. She could feel herself getting hot and the red bubbles growing inside. Wanting to smash their faces and pull the hair from their heads.

'Shut up, pigs!' she retorted.

'Takes one to know one!' Sophie Broom, the leader of the gang threw back.

'I know you are, I said you are, but what am I?' Veronica said. Veronica was the coward. Nina knew last time she had lashed out Veronica had run calling for teacher, leaving her three friends to cope with Nina's furious reaction, kicking feet and slashing arms. Veronica never came near Nina when she was on her own.

'If I had freckles like you, I'd get my name down for a skin-graft.' Rosie glanced at Sophie for her approval. 'There's millions of them.'

'Yeah. Looks like you're going rusty.' Sophie said.

Nina hated them. She felt her chest tighten, her hands go damp with sweat. She set her mouth, turned to walk away. One of them shoved her in the back between the shoulder blades. She couldn't stop herself then. She lunged and caught a fistful of shiny blonde hair, pulled it hard down, forcing Sophie's head towards the tarmac.

Someone grabbed her from behind. Other hands joined in.

'Get off!' The ringing tones of a teacher split the girls apart. Nina brushed the hair from her face, pulled her sweater round where it had twisted. She took some comfort from Sophie's flushed face and the way her hair was all messed up.

* * *

Mrs Day, the head, went bonkers. She would have to write to Nina's parents. If Nina couldn't control her temper then there would be no place for her in the school. It was unladylike and unacceptable. Mrs Day didn't bother trying to establish what had led up to the brawl and Nina didn't bother trying to tell her. Sophie was a clever pupil. Her father gave the school a lot of money. She didn't pick on anyone else, only Nina, so they all thought Nina was the troublemaker.

* * *

When she went back to her class she saw people's eyes flicking at her to see if she'd been crying. Well, she hadn't, so bully for them. She saw Veronica nudge Rosie.

'Sit down, Nina,' Mrs Sinclair said. 'And get out your Egyptian topic.'

Brilliant. She'd nearly finished her cover. She'd copied a mummy from a library book and she'd used bits of real gold paper from Dad's cigarette packets to do the stripes on the sarcophagus with. She'd filled in-between with a lovely blue ink from the Fred Aldous shop in town. She'd done a border of proper hieroglyphics down the sides, and across the top and bottom she was doing a row of pyramids with a Sphinx in each corner. All she needed to do now was to colour in the pyramids and it would be finished.

She knew Miss Sinclair would put it on display, she'd held it up to show everyone last time.

Nina sat down and opened her desk. The bottle of blue ink lay on its side, the top open and a thick pool of it all over her folder. Her work was ruined. She could smell the metallic fumes of the ink. She wanted to cry, her eyes burned like coals and her nose prickled but she wouldn't. She had left the ink at the other side, next to her pencil case. She knew she had. She looked across at her enemies. Saw the sly smile that Sophie shot Rosie and the prim curl on Veronica's lips, the way her shoulders jerked a bit with a mocking, silent laugh.

She plunged her hands into the pool of ink, spreading it over the whole of the cover, and then crumpled the paper up. Rotten stinking pigs.

'Miss!' She held up her hands and heard the communal gasp.

'Oh, Nina!' Miss Sinclair's voice was thick with frustration. 'After all that work. You'd done so well. See — a moment's clumsiness and it's all spoilt. How many times do I have to tell you girls to put the tops back on properly. Go wash your hands.'

'Yes, Miss.'

'And try not to get into any more trouble on the way. I think we've had enough drama for one day, don't you?'

* * *

Marjorie

She was in the middle of spring cleaning. A house like this was easier to keep up with than something larger but even so you'd be amazed at how much grime accumulated from one year to the next. They couldn't afford to be repainting and changing carpets whenever things got grubby but with plenty of elbow grease the place looked fresh and clean again.

She was methodical in her approach. A floor at a time, starting upstairs. First tidy and clear away the items that had a place to go. Put aside anything for jumble or good-as-new. Strip the beds. Remove and wash the curtains. That was a job and a half in itself. Filthy and tiring. Up the stepladder undoing all the curtain hooks, supporting the weight of the fabric on one arm. Curtains in to wash, or to the dry cleaners. Wipe down the pelmet and the curtain rails. Clean the windows. Shift all the furniture and vacuum underneath, more swathes of grey fluff and hair and lost things. Return furniture. Dust lamps and picture rails. Vacuum again. Wipe down the paintwork with a bucket of hot water and Stardrops. Polish the mirrors. When she was damp with exertion and groaning from the effort she would stop for coffee and a cigarette.

Doing the downstairs, she put on records to jolly her along: Tony Bennett or Burt Bacharach, Nat King Cole and Ella Fitzgerald. Downstairs was worse. The kitchen worst of all. Grease in every crevice. She had to dismantle and soak the Expel-Air, watch the water turn brown with the muck coming off it, till it was ivory-coloured again like it should be. All the crockery had to come out so she could clean the cupboards and put fresh lining paper in. The food in the larder and all the baking stuff had to be moved so she could clean the shelves. The drawers in the cabinets sorted out and tidied. The nets had to be soaked in Glo-White. The kitchen took at least a full day to do properly. Top to toe.

She had done their room and next was Nina's but she'd have a break first.

It was a system. She had learnt from her mother. It was different back then. A girl knew looking after a home and a family was the most important skill she could learn. It was expected that daughters helped out. Not now. When was the last time Nina had ever done anything with her? The pain of them rubbing along together hurt her still. It was a familiar pain. Like a tender tooth, deep and perplexing. She had dreamt of the joys a daughter would bring: shared interests, like going shopping together; up Market Street or down Deansgate to Kendal's for a new coat, arm in arm. You saw people like that. She felt a prickle of sadness in her nose. Daft. She could never work out whether it was her or Nina that had set the limits, or the pair of them together, but whatever it was they just weren't close.

In her darkest moments she would admit to herself that she despaired of the girl. Nina's bad temper and ill grace had left her disappointed and worn down. God knows she had tried to breach the gap, countless times, knowing as she did that Nina would lash out with clever words or pull back physically and wound her anew.

I've tried, I've done my best. That was her refrain. She had fed and clothed her daughter. She had bitten back the fresh remarks and sharp retorts that sprang to mind when Nina was behaving badly. Thoughts she never shared, not even with Robert.

Thank God for Stephen. Her lovely boy. Without him . . . well, she couldn't imagine. She'd have been a bad mother, wouldn't she? Unable to bear them, incapable of rearing them. Lacking the maternal instinct. But Stephen was her rock, her touchstone. And when she felt miserable about relations with her daughter she would think of him and her heart would lighten.

She stirred sugar into her coffee, lit a cigarette. She examined her hands. Red and chafed from the work, her nail polish chipped. She laid her cigarette in the ashtray and reached for the Nulon bottle. She poured a pool into her hands. Rubbed it in. The music changed. *Don't know why, there's no sun up in the sky, stormy weather* . . . Beautiful voice, Billie Holliday — sang like an angel and died penniless.

She picked up the cigarette, took a puff, felt the familiar melancholy ripple through her. Funny, she thought, all the torch songs that she adored, they never made her think of Robert or any old boyfriends or even film-stars. No, it was Nina. Nina who broke her heart. Nina who was her great unrequited love.

* * *

Megan

'We'd have to get a loan.'

'Who'd give us a loan?'

Brendan shrugged. 'They seem to be throwing it at people.'

'But we've no assets. This place is rented.' She saw uncertainty replace the eager expression that he'd had when he had told her about his uncle's carpet shop. She didn't want to spoil it for him but the prospect of further debts made her feel physically sick. 'You might be able to get one of those schemes,' she said, 'job creation or whatever they call it. Has Ronnie been making a profit?'

'Oh, aye. The trick is to get in while the stock's still there and the reputation. Any gap and we'll lose custom.'

'And he's sure he wants to sell up?'

'Definite. Belle would cuff him to the bed rather than let him work again. He knows his number's up. The doctor made it plain too. Nice and easy, no strain. They'll put him in for a by-pass.'

'You're sure about this, doing this?'

He nodded. 'It's not just selling the shop, there's fitting and all, they do the lot.'

'We'd need to talk to Ronnie. And the bank, we couldn't do it without a loan, could we?'

He shook his head. 'But Ronnie might accept half now and half over the next year. He knows how tight things are. I'd need to find someone to do the paperwork, the accounts, all that side of things.'

'Who did it before?'

'Ronnie.'

'Can't be that hard.'

'You know me and forms.'

'And figures!' She raised her eyebrows. 'I could have a go. If Ronnie showed me the ropes.'

He smiled quickly.

'Ring him now,' she said. 'See if it's all right for us to call round for a chat.'

'You don't want a bit longer to think about it?'

'No,' she said, 'we're not committing ourselves to owt, just going to see him.'

Besides, she thought to herself, if they didn't go straight away then she'd get panicky about the whole thing and come up with a million worries about it.

'Strike while the iron's hot,' she said. She looked in the mirror, pulled the elasticated band from her hair and shook out her curls. It needed a trim. Looked like a haystack, one on fire.

And what was the alternative to taking on the carpet business? Another twenty years getting poorer by the week, slogging her guts out and still having to watch the furniture fall apart and the cooker pack up and Brendan get more and more morose?

He slid his arms round her waist.

'You always were a fast worker.'

'I never heard you complaining.' She pushed his hands away. 'Go on, try him now.'

She watched him dial.

'Won't even have to change the sign, will we? Conroy's Carpets.'

* * *

Nina

Nina was sick of school, sick of her stupid, boring, useless parents and sick of being fifteen. She wanted to be nineteen. Able to do whatever she wanted. Get married or go round the world or have a brilliant job and loads of money but not be so old that she was just a boring old square with nothing worth living for. God, she thought, I hope I die before I'm thirty. Be dead famous, then die. Paint brilliant pictures or be a fashion designer and dress the stars.

She looked again at her revision plan, gazed back out of the window, where Dad was putting the new rotary washing line up for Mum. Event of the year. How exciting. Tears pricked her eyes at the bloody awful boredom of it all. She needed a ciggie. There were two in her secret bag in her wardrobe but she knew for a fact that Dad had a packet of ten Benson and Hedges in his coat. He only smoked five or six a day and now and then she would help herself to one if the packet was more than half full. He didn't keep count.

If she did another half hour then he'd be settled in the lounge and she could take the dog out.

The dog's the best person in this family, she thought, then giggled at the notion. Causes of the First World War. *As You Like It.* Alluvial Plains. She let her eyes wander over the headings and the blocks of time she'd allocated. What was the point? She didn't want to stay on at school a minute longer than was absolutely necessary. She wanted to get out, out of this house, away from this family, far away from this dump of a city.

She caught sight of her brother. Oh, brilliant. Now Stephen's helping too. Perfect Stephen. Expected to do so-o-o-o well in his A levels. University material. Not like his sister. She was a cuckoo. She didn't belong here with this lot, rotting in the suburbs. She felt permanently scratchy as though someone had supplied her with prickles instead of pores. There was this big myth that redheads had bad tempers and she did but it wasn't just a temper like losing it every so often it was like the steam was always building up and when she shouted or flew off the handle it was only a relief for a short while and then she was feeling cross all over again.

Stephen, O perfect one, brains and good looks, he wasn't ever mean to her no matter what she said. And she said some awful things. He never tried to get her into trouble. A blooming saint. That made it worse. Anatomy of The Earthworm. Respiration. Electromagnetism. Why couldn't she just have done GCEs?

Now the rotary dryer was fully erected and her mother was smiling like an idiot and Nina loathed how happy they were. They ought to get the priest to come and bless the damn thing. She ripped her plan in half. Began to draw pictures on the back, eyes and teardrops, shadowy people. Like an LP cover. She drew a sea of question marks and in the middle like it was floating she drew 'Nina' in bubble writing.

Maybe her real mother was scratchy too. Maybe that's where she got it from. If she found her at least she'd know whether it was in her blood. She scribbled out her name and turned the question marks into keyholes. *Nina has artistic flair, a good eye, strong technique, and applies herself diligently.* Best part of her report. For art. As low in the scheme of things as cookery, which she was rubbish at, and woodwork, which might have been good but most of the class were boys and they just messed about.

What could you do with art? Be an artist and starve? She liked it but she couldn't see it going anywhere. Be cool to do album covers or posters, like for films and stuff, but how did you do that? They never had those sort of vacancies in the paper. You'd probably have to go to art school, and for that you had to stay on and do A levels and there was no way she was staying on.

She was dying for a fag.

She listened and worked out that Mum and Dad were in the lounge. Stephen wherever.

She went down and poked her head round the lounge door. Dad reading, Mum watching *Upstairs Downstairs*.

'I'll take Joey out.'

They grunted.

She went to the small shelf by the front door, where Dad left his keys and loose change and cigarettes. Five left. Do-able. She took one and got her Zippo from her school-bag. She whistled for Joey and attached his lead.

Once they'd reached the banks of the river she let him off to mooch about a bit while she sat on a bench and smoked. The river was ugly, steep-sided banks shaped in stiff angular lines. Something to do with flood control. The river a grey-brown sludge between the towering banks, the banks covered in rough grass and clods of earth. Nothing like the rivers in stories. The rivers you imagined when you said the word river. A real river would have shallow banks, clear, burbling water; you could see the pebbles and the shadows of the fish. There would be stepping stones draped in moss and willow trees overhanging the edges, maybe a stretch of waterfalls making the water silver as it tumbled down.

She took a deep drag, held it and blew out.

This river went all the way to the sea. Somewhere near Liverpool. The Mersey. 'Ferry Cross The Mersey'. Good song, they'd re-released it. Bit sad but she liked that. Sad things were more . . . real . . . they meant more. Like Chloe, her best friend, cut-throat Chloe they nicknamed her because she was so down and talked about killing herself and how pointless everything was. Her loony way of looking at things meant she knew exactly what Nina was on about when she talked about being a cuckoo and her dumb, happy family and all that.

She whistled for Joey. The dog returned, delighted to be summoned, his tail beating, ears perked up. He licked her knee. She rubbed his head. She finished her cigarette and flicked the tab into the river. It could go all the way to the ocean.

She walked home quickly. The light was starting to fade and she was ready to go to bed. Not much revision accomplished but another day done. Another day closer to freedom. Another step nearer to the journey she was intent on making.

* * *

She had only asked once, that she could remember, when she was nine. She had learnt somehow that her adoption and Stephen's were not talked about. Close family knew, like Auntie Min and both the grannies and Dad's brother John. Other people must have known surely. Mum turning up to Church with a babe in arms, no former sign of pregnancy? Presumably people just took their cue from the Underwood's reticence. So she had learnt, not that it was shameful, but that it was private. Nobody else's business. Not quite a secret but as good as.

She'd been driven to ask after having a nightmare. So bad it had sent her to Marjorie's room. That was unusual, for she was a child who resented rather than sought out physical affection. She had always wriggled out of Marjorie's embrace, preferring to be unfettered. In the dream she had chopped Marjorie's head off. Robert had shouted at her and then she had pointed to her mother and said no harm was done. Her mother's head was back on but the face was that of a stranger.

She had reared up gasping and switched the light on. It was autumn and a moth batted against the shade, which gave her another shock, making her heart race and her breath hurt. With shadows biting at her heels she went to her parent's room. She let her mother hug her and delayed her return to bed by asking for a glass of milk. Her mother tucked her back in and kissed her on the forehead. She put the landing light on and left Nina's lamp off so the moth would leave her room.

The following day she waited until she could be sure no one would interrupt them and then asked her mother, 'When you adopted me did you meet my mother that had me?'

Marjorie froze, blinked fast, put the iron down and let her hands rest lightly on the edge of the board. Nina watched her.

'No.'

'What was she called?'

'I can't remember, erm . . . Driscoll, I think. Yes.'

'What was her first name?'

'I don't know, Nina. I don't think they ever told us.'

Her mum looked calm but Nina could tell she was really upset. She was squashing her hands together and her lips were tight. But Nina couldn't stop.

'What did she call me?'

'Claire.'

It was a shock. She hadn't expected an answer. Claire. Claire Driscoll.

'Did she have red hair?'

'Yes.'

'Why did she have me adopted?'

'Because she wasn't married. She wanted you to have a good home, a proper family. And that's all we know.' An edge in her voice. Putting an end to it. The lid on it.

Nina had gone out into the back garden, walked up the rockery to her perch by the birdbath. She felt hot and mean for asking all those questions. Horrible, but there was a bit inside burning bright because of the red hair. Red hair like Nina. She didn't even know her first name. But red hair, ginger. She knew that now. And Nina had been baptised Claire — Claire Driscoll not Nina Underwood.

She had never spoken to her parents about it since. She couldn't. They couldn't. So as she planned to find out more she knew it would have to be done in secret. She had learnt that from them. The way of secrets.

Maybe she would tell them, once she'd done it. But not before. Their hurt and disapproval would make her words come out all sullen and rebellious and this wasn't about that. About her life with them. It wasn't about them at all. This was about her — just her.

* * *

Marjorie

They were about to eat when the slam of the front door signalled that Nina was home.

'It's on the table,' Marjorie called out, and returned to cutting up the quiche.

Stephen noticed first. Made a little strangled sound and then glanced anxiously at Robert and Marjorie.

Oh, dear Lord. She'd shaved her head. Her lovely glossy red curls all gone, just stubble, like something from a concentration camp. 'Oh, Nina.'

Her daughter smiled and had the grace to colour a little.

Robert swivelled in his chair and dropped his cutlery. 'What in God's name . . . ? What on earth have you done?'

'It's the fashion. Suedehead, everybody's doing it.'

'Don't be so stupid. Have you any idea what a sight you look? What will people think?'

He was saying all the wrong things. Marjorie could see Nina recoiling then her chin rising, the defiance stealing into her piercing blue eyes.

'I don't care what people think.'

'That's ruddy well obvious. Well, you needn't think you're coming to Church looking like that. Like a ghoul.'

'Robert!' Marjorie tried to intervene. Yes, she looked a sight but teenagers were like that, well, some of them. It really wasn't the end of the world.

'I'm not going to Church any more anyway so you needn't bother. It's all a load of rubbish.'

A stunned silence greeted that little bombshell.

'It'll grow back,' Marjorie said.

'I'm not growing it, I like it.'

'Look in the mirror,' he said, 'you look ridiculous.'

Nina flinched. Marjorie felt her own pulse speed up as Robert's voice rose. 'Do you deliberately set out to hurt your mother and I? Do you get some perverted sense of satisfaction from causing upset? Eh? Are they going to let you go to school like that? You'll have to wear a scarf or something.'

'You can't tell me what to do,' her face was set, nostrils flaring.

'Oh, yes, I can, young lady. I'm your father and until you're . . .'

'You're not my real father.'

'Nina!' Marjorie felt as if a bomb had burst in her chest. 'Nina, stop.'

'He's not, and you're not my real mother and I wish you'd never adopted me.' She ran from the room banging the door shut behind her.

She could see Stephen's mouth working hard to contain his emotion. It was so hard on him. He was so settled, so grounded.

'It's all right, love.' She touched his hand. He shook his head.

'I've no appetite.' Robert pushed his plate away.

Please, she thought, looking at him. His eyes were lined now, the sandy hair sparse on top. Please don't go. She didn't say anything. Tears gathered in the corners of her eyes.

He pushed his chair back. 'I'll pop up to the club.'

The blessed golf club.

'See if anyone's up for a game. Stephen?'

Stephen shook his head.

What about me? she thought. She ran her hands through her blonde hair, pressing her fingers on her scalp. He walks away and leaves me with the mess. He's always shouting about how Nina has upset me but he never does a thing, not a damn thing, to make me feel better. Couldn't he just for once stay, give me a hug or just sit and hold my hand? Talk about it. Instead of running away.

'I'll be back in time for Mass.'

Marjorie could still feel the burning in her chest. *You're not my real mother.* She blinked to clear her eyes, hoping Stephen wouldn't notice. She wanted to ask Robert to stay but she couldn't, because then she would see that look in his eyes like a trapped animal and he'd pace about the house, his temper simmering, reproaching her, and she would feel she had made unreasonable demands. So she said nothing.

After he had gone she sat until Stephen had finished eating and then she cleared the table and began washing the pots.

She felt the misery settle on the house, soaking into the floors and the walls, seeping round the rooms like gas.

She listened for sounds from upstairs, for a movement that might mean Nina was coming down. Because this time Marjorie was not going to be the one bearing the olive branch. She wanted an apology. Nina's words had cut her to the bone. I'm the only mother she's got, real or not, she told herself. She had made allowances for her and given her the benefit of the doubt until she was fed up to the back teeth with it. She pressed her lips together and took a sharp breath. She rinsed the sink. Dried her hands on the tea towel. She looked with resentment at the pile of ironing: white shirts for Robert and Stephen, Nina's uniform, bed linen, tablecloths, her own skirts and blouses. With a sigh she went to fetch the iron.

* * *

Megan

She always did the monthly accounts sitting at the table in the front room. She could watch the street from there, see the world go by in-between filling in the columns and sorting the subtotals out. She had two months to do tonight and she wouldn't put it off any longer. But she was distracted. There had been a programme on the telly last night about adopted people tracing their parents. She wouldn't have had it on if anyone else had been in but Brendan had gone down the local, Francine was at her mates, Aidan God knows where and Chris tucked up in bed, so she was on her own. Brendan wouldn't have liked it.

'We have to put it behind us, Megan,' he'd said just before their wedding. 'It doesn't do any good this dragging it all out, look at the state of you.'

He was right. She upset them both when she started on about it all. It didn't help really.

'I know,' she said. 'OK.'

So they didn't talk about it anymore. When Francine came along they acted like she was the very first. They thought of Frances at first but Megan liked the French ending, made it a bit different. 'Besides, people might think Frances is a boy, you can only tell when its written down.' She was a real peach. A little doll with creamy skin and golden freckles and red curls like Shirley Temple. She won the May Queen when she was six and when she took her First Holy Communion she really was the best one there. Like an angel from an old oil painting. She turned out nice-natured too, no backbiting or whining. They got plenty of that from Aidan and Chris. Aidan was hell on legs, intent on a showdown with anything that drew breath, and Chris could whine for England, but she loved them all. Francine though, thank God she was the eldest. Lulled them into a false sense of parenthood, she did. Slept well, ate well, barely cried. She was out there now, hanging round the gate with her mates. Twelve years old and at high school.

She was already talking about doing nursery nursing. Loved the little ones. Megan didn't care what she did as long as she stayed happy and didn't get caught or end up on drugs. She didn't want her having a baby before she was grown herself. Not like Megan. Too young.

Course things were different nowadays, and a good thing too. At least you could choose what you did about it. Half of Manchester were single parents, no one batted an eyelid at teenagers pushing buggies. Some girls did it instead of getting a job, something to make them feel worthwhile. That was sad. But what else could they do. They watched telly and it was like the world was an Aladdin's cave of stuff you could have, places to go, but that wasn't the real world. Not if you lived round here.

She drew her thoughts back to the ledger and totted up the outstanding debtors column. Thank God for calculators.

While she had watched the telly programme she'd been on edge the whole time, holding the remote control in case someone came in. She watched these women talk about having babies adopted, things she had never told anyone except Brendan. Some of it rang bells, whole bloody sleigh–fulls, and she had to get the Kleenex before they got to the first ad break.

There was a helpline number at the end and she started to memorise it and then thought what the hell for? She'd never use it. And if she did she'd be on for hours talking her whole bloody life away and she'd promised it was behind them, hadn't she? Best left, like they agreed.

She'd three great kids, even Aidan had his moments and maybe he'd settle as he grew up. They'd a roof over their heads and now they'd enough money to manage, so why stir it all up?

Two of the women in the film had met the children they'd given up, grown-ups by then. She couldn't imagine that. When she thought of hers, she saw a baby or the little one in the picture she kept. What would she be like now? Three years older than Francine. Be nice to know if she'd turned out all right. To tell her that you'd done it for the best. That if they'd let you, you'd have kept her and got married soon as you could. One of the women had hired a detective to find her son. That wasn't right. It turned out OK in the film but you hadn't a right really, had you? You signed that away when you signed the papers. Imagine the upset if she tried that. Not just her and the girl but the younger children. What would they think? They hadn't got a clue. Laughter from outside made her look. Francine was pushing playfully at her friend Stacey. Then the pair of them doubled up with laughter again. Megan smiled. They were happy, weren't they? Only a fool would risk spoiling all that.

* * *

Nina

The music was very loud — 10cc blaring out and all the lights were off. Nina could see the tip of the joint glowing across the other side of the room and the glow lit up Chloe's face when she took a drag.

Nina had already had some, she felt giggly and sleepy and desperate for something to drink. She couldn't snog Gary until she'd had a drink. He was kissing her neck. She nudged him and told him.

'What?'

'A drink,' she said into his ear.

He stood up and was back in a few minutes with a bottle of cider. She drank from the bottle. It was very fizzy and cold and she had to stop every so often to let the bubbles go down. They shared the bottle for a while then Gary told her to come on.

He dragged her over the prone bodies and out into the hall. There was a red bulb so it looked like a film or something.

'Gary?'

'Come on.' He moved towards the stairs.

'What?'

'Nina.'

He was gorgeous-looking — soft, clear skin, wide cheekbones, a dimple in his chin. His hair was shiny and brown and fell to his shoulders. Hers was growing out and she looked like she had a red afro. They'd been going together for four weeks. It was her record. He lived near Chloe and was a friend of her brother.

'What if they . . . ?'

'*Nina*,' he said again. Not bossy but with a longing sound like he couldn't wait and it made her feel randy.

Upstairs there was a bedroom where all the coats had been put. Gary moved them on to the floor. She lay down on the bed and he turned out the light.

She let his hands roam up and over her breasts, squeezing them. She had a mini jumper on. She shifted position and pulled it over her head, let him fiddle and undo her bra strap. She could smell fresh smoke in his hair as it fell over her face, and the scent of the new Matsumi perfume she'd used. His breathing quickened. She moved her hand down and stroked the bulge of his crotch. He kissed her, his tongue warm and soft and tasting of cider. The last time they'd been together she'd made him come, rubbing his willy up and down. He had told her when to go slow or harder and he'd been really nice afterwards. He'd given her a finger-fuck till she was dizzy and gasping and wet, but she was too embarrassed to tell him what else she needed to make her come.

She undid his zip and touched him through his underpants. His erection stretched the cloth and she felt a ripple of excitement herself. She wanted him to touch her again. She slid her own tongue into his mouth, in and out, hoping he'd cotton on. He wasn't very bright, not school-wise. She wasn't exactly Einstein but she managed. His writing, she'd been shocked, it was like a little kids' and he couldn't spell for toffee. He wasn't clever with words, they didn't talk much, but he wasn't thick when it came to turning her on. He slipped his hand between her legs and pressed against the seam of her jeans. She moved against his hand, still fondling him with her own. He ended the kiss.

'Take your jeans off,' he said hoarsely.

She did, feeling the cool air of the room on her thighs. He removed his clothes and they lay side by side on the narrow bed. He rubbed her breasts again and when he rolled her nipple between his fingers she gave a mew of pleasure which made him swear softly. She touched his willy again, began to slide her hand up and down. He pushed a finger inside her, then another. She rocked her hips, straining. Wanting more. Flames danced along her arms and the back of her legs and she began to repeat his name to the rhythm he was using.

'Nina,' he said thickly, 'I want to do it with you.'

She felt a fresh flare of desire. 'Don't come . . . you know.'

'I'll pull out.' He kissed her and she opened her legs as he climbed over her. He withdrew his fingers and she felt him nudge against her. He pushed and slid in. She had expected more pain but it felt good. He braced himself on his arms and moved in and out. She wanted him to go faster, she gripped his buttocks. 'Yes, Gary, Yes!'

He pulled away, gasped.

'No!' she cried.

He flopped on the bed beside her. 'Oh, Nina, oh wow! That was great.'

She had a stitch in her side. She felt goosebumps break across her skin and the sour disappointment washed through her. So that was it. Big deal. She ached with frustration, tempted to move her hand and show Gary what would make her feel great.

The door flew open and the light snapped on. She pulled her knees up and wrapped her arms about herself.

'Bloody hell!' Chloe's voice. 'Sorry, but my dad's here and if you want a lift home you're going to have to come now.'

* * *

Megan

There were two couples browsing and a single woman. She always let them take their time, none of that rushing to make a sale. The longer they stayed the more likely they were to buy, and once they got around to asking her about a particular roll or for a quote she could do her sales pitch then.

Brendan was off on a big job. They'd swung a contract with the university, fitting heavy-duty carpets and wear-resistant cord in the new halls of residence. It was just the boost they needed. They'd be able to complete on the loan and give Ronnie the bit they still owed him. It was a bloody marvellous feeling, to be getting level and knowing that everything else they made they could spend on themselves, on the kids and the house. Another big contract and there'd be the chance of a holiday, a proper holiday, Costa del Sol or somewhere. Mind you, it was so hot this summer you didn't need to go abroad. An official drought, hose pipe bans and of course business in the shop had slowed down — most people couldn't imagine wanting snug wall-to-wall when it was blazing out there.

One of the couples asked for a quote. The woman reminded her of Mia Farrow, big eyes and that elfin look to her. Megan established the size of the house and whether they wanted underlay — which really was recommended if they wanted maximum life from the carpets and better insulation — and fitting. She gave them two estimates based on the roll they'd chosen and a similar but slightly more expensive version which she explained had a greater mix of wool and would wear better.

She let them hum and haw a bit but she knew they'd go for the better buy, you could tell money wasn't the main thing with them: they both had good leather coats on and his watch wasn't off Longsight market. She took the order and arranged a time for Brendan to measure up. They'd three lads doing the fitting but he tended to do the initial measuring. You only needed to be a few inches out and you could really cock it up. And that would eat into any profit you made.

She'd just finished with the customers when the phone rang. It was her sister Kitty. Megan was surprised. She never rang her at work.

'What is it?'

'Megan. It's Daddy. There's been an accident.'

'Oh, God!'

'He got knocked down. He's dead.' She broke down.

'Where's Mammy?'

'At home now, I'm with her here. We've just got back from the hospital.'

'I'll be over right away.'

* * *

Mammy had insisted on a traditional Irish wake with them up all hours eating and drinking and talking about Anthony. Open house for the whole parish.

He'd been a popular figure in the market and at the pub, though Megan wasn't quite sure why. He'd been addled with drink a lot of the time, he'd never been a particularly generous man, not even with his affections, though he got sentimental sometimes when he'd had a few. But he'd never been violent, he'd never belted them like so many she knew. Mammy had never had to cover bruises or lie about walking into doors. He'd been rough with his tongue, now and then and that was bad enough.

Megan passed around open rolls with thick slices of ham and beef on and a dish of pickles. Someone kicked off 'My Wild Irish Rose' and they all joined in, even her three sat by their Nana, though Chris's eyes were wide and fixed, the poor lamb was shattered. She'd never really forgiven her father for not letting her and Brendan get married back then. It had seemed such a cruel refusal. As the years had gone by she saw just as much of him but she felt distant from him. She'd lost the passion he'd inspired in her as a little girl when she had run to show him, tell him . . . Her kids had liked him well enough but he wasn't always there when they went round. Once the stall was shut Anthony preferred to relax with his mates rather than at home and his routine never varied. If it was within opening hours and not a meal time he'd be at the bar no matter who was coming to visit.

The kids were close to their Nana. Francine and Chris took after her in looks, redheads the pair of them. But Aidan was like Anthony, wild black hair and a rangy frame. Though where he'd got his contrariness from she didn't know. Brendan reckoned Aidan got his temper from the Conroy side. Like Brendan's father he was always ready to lash out before engaging his brain. Too handy with his fists by far. Only twelve and fetched home from school countless times for scrapping. He was sly too, which worried her more. He was trouble waiting to happen was Aidan and she hadn't got a clue what she could do about it.

CAROLINE/KAY/THERESA

Kay

'Happy Birthday to you!' The song reached its crescendo and Theresa blew out all the candles in one long blow.

Kay smiled and called the cluster of children to go into the lounge for pass the parcel. The party had taken days to organise and meanwhile Dominic's croup had kept her up in the night just as the twins had started sleeping through. Four babies in five years. People in the parish thought it was a fairy story. If they hadn't all been adopted there might have been less interest, though families did seem to be getting smaller these days.

She watched Theresa pass the parcel round and got ready to lift the arm off the record player. Theresa was a lovely looking child, thick shiny dark-brown hair, creamy skin that turned caramel in the summer sun and brown eyes like dark chocolate. Kay wondered sometimes whether there was any Spanish or Italian ancestry. She looked darker than her brothers, who all had blue eyes, but of them all it was only the twins who had a clear likeness to each other. They weren't identical but very similar.

But people saw what they wanted to see. Strangers often remarked on the resemblance between Kay and Theresa

— 'She's just like you isn't she?' Kay found it bizarre — they both had shoulder-length brown hair, cut with a fringe, but that was it really. There was little alike in their faces — Kay had chubby cheeks and a generous mouth, grey eyes, a motherly look to her, while Theresa was more delicate, like a little fawn with those big, brown eyes and long eyelashes and a small nose. Even more amusing were the comments the whole family would get on holiday, which veered from 'like peas in a pod' to 'they're all quite different, aren't they?' The Farrells' standard response was to smile and agree with either observation.

Kay stopped the music and waited while Jimmy's mother helped him take away a wrapper. She lowered the needle and 'Nellie The Elephant' rang out again. Four children meant a busy life but she had a cleaner every day now. She couldn't have managed otherwise. Adam's estate agency business had expanded and he'd opened a second shop in Chorlton-cum-Hardy. More people than ever were wanting to buy their own home and new Barratt's and Wimpy estates were being built everywhere. Modern homes with all the mod-cons and easy to look after. Adam would enthuse about the more stylish developments but Kay loved the character of their old Edwardian semi in Sale even though it was a magnet for dust and hard to keep warm. But he was talking about central heating before next winter. That would make so much difference.

She stopped the music and Andrew undid the parcel. Theresa looked across at Kay, eyes shining, a jelly stain on the neck of her party dress and crumbs round her mouth. She raised her shoulders and grinned, a little gesture of happiness that made Kay wink back. Nearly done, she was dying for a cup of tea and to sit down for a few minutes. Before then there was cake to parcel up and balloons to give out. Some of the other mothers would help. Not a man in sight though. Funny they never came to the parties, it just wasn't done. Never did much of anything in the house either. She wasn't complaining but just now or then it would be lovely to have a meal cooked for her or find a room tidied or the ironing done. The image of Adam hunched over an ironing board made her giggle.

She was happy. Of course, there were days when she snapped at the children or the hours before bedtime seemed to yawn ahead with nothing but demands on her. On the rare occasion that she left the house without a pram, a toddler on reins or a small hand in hers, she felt anxious, as though she had lost something precious and would get into trouble. The unease persisted, albeit at a low level, until she was back home, so she never really enjoyed the rare trips to the sales or a get-together with an old friend. Her social life revolved around the children and the network of women nearby who were at home with theirs. She was closest to Joanna. She didn't agree with everything Joanna said but she was honest and she was funny and you knew she wouldn't sit in judgment on you like some of the others.

Damien, Joanna's five-year-old, opened the next layer and grabbed the twist of floral gums that fell out. Two more layers, if she remembered correctly. She'd try and get Karen next, a whining child that she found hard to like, who looked close to tears at not having had a go. How different would life have been if she and Adam had been able to have their own family. She might have ended up with one like Karen. She'd no regrets. Not now. Though she did wonder what pregnancy would have been like, all that side of things. And breast feeding. Not many people did it, with bottles being so convenient, but she thought that would have been something special. She'd talked to Joanna about it once.

'Ghastly business. Tried it for a week. I'd bosoms like a cow, it hurt like crazy and the poor mite nearly starved to death. Ken hated it too.'

The odd thing about their birthdays was that she'd not been there when they were born. There were no anecdotes about the day like other people had. They didn't even know what time Theresa had been born or how the labour had gone. That was another woman's story. She always thought of her and said a prayer for her, hoping that everything had turned out all right, as well as a prayer of thanks for what they had been given.

Karen got her turn and then the final parcel made the rounds. The bat and ball in the middle went to Janey from next door.

'Home time!' Kay called out. 'Get your coats.' She handed each child or their mother a balloon and a piece of birthday cake. She saw people out and when they were all gone except for Faith she heard the woman's voice, etched with tension, 'For Christ's sake just put the bloody car down. Now!'

A caterwaul rose and Kay hurried in. Faith was gripping Andrew's arm and the child was obviously in pain. Theresa watched, her lower lip trembling. Faith's older son Oliver stood unblinking to one side.

'Faith?'

Her friend wasn't usually harsh. But with two youngsters and another on the way there were bound to be difficult days.

Faith let go immediately. 'I'm sorry.' She bent to put an arm round her son. 'I'm sorry, Andy. Mummy's very tired.' She rubbed his hair and straightened up, turning so Kay caught sight of her face crumpling. 'It's just . . .'

'Come in the kitchen,' Kay said. 'Theresa, you take Andrew and Oliver and Dominic out to the sandpit. Go on and I'll bring you all an ice-lolly in a minute.'

Kay sat Faith down, put the kettle on and offered her a cigarette. Faith took it, mouth working, wiping at her tears with the heel of her hand. 'It's Mick,' she said. 'He's gone.'

'Gone?'

'Left us. Walked out.'

'Oh, Faith. Why . . . what?'

'We've been rowing—' she gave a short laugh — 'endlessly. He didn't want another baby. He says I can't control the children. He expects them to be little angels, all the time.' She picked up Kay's lighter and lit her cigarette, her hand shaking. 'He was coming home later and later.'

'Do you think he was . . . involved with someone?'

'No. I just think he was avoiding the children. It can be frantic at tea-time, you know what it's like. Oliver is always teasing Andrew. Anyway, Mick's been drinking, more than he should . . .' She frowned deeply, pressed the back of her hand to her nose.

Kay got up and made the coffee. Put the mugs down, lit her own cigarette. Ate a slice of cake. Waited.

'Kay, please promise you won't tell anyone but . . . he . . . Sometimes he hits me.'

'Oh, God!'

'He always says sorry and things seem better for a while but . . . it's worse when I'm pregnant.'

'He hits you when you're pregnant?'

'Please don't tell anyone?'

'I won't. I promise.'

She could be trusted. She thought of Joanna — Kay had never betrayed her confidences about Ken's affair and one day Joanna had made some dry remark about Bev that revealed the whole thing was over.

'He hates me like this.' Faith lowered her eyes. 'I was so worried about the baby. I'm almost glad he's gone but I don't know how I'm going to manage.'

Kay was appalled. She'd no idea. But she wanted to know more: where did he hit her, how, when; did he shout, did they make love afterwards? A prurient curiosity that made her feel ashamed.

'You can sue him for maintenance, at least for the children. It's cruelty — you could divorce him.'

'I don't want to. I still love him. You probably think I'm mad. Maybe things will change, once the children are older, easier . . .' She faltered.

Kay bit her tongue. 'If I can help, if there's anything, take Andy and Oliver for an afternoon. Just ask.'

Faith nodded. 'Thanks.'

'And when the baby comes.'

'He'll probably be back before then. Wanting his marital rights. Did you and Adam, this late on . . .' She realised her mistake. 'Oh, God, Kay, I forget. I'm sorry.'

'Don't worry.'

'Well, it's blooming uncomfortable, I can tell you, and you'd think he wouldn't want me, looking like a barrage balloon.'

Kay smoked her cigarette and took a drink. 'Do you know where he's gone?'

'His mother's. She thinks the sun shines out of his you-know-what. She likes having him home again. She's on her own now,' she amended.

'When did he go?'

'Tuesday.'

'Have you spoken since?'

'Nope.' She crushed her cigarette in the ashtray. 'They never tell you about this part, do they? All the films and the books, they always stop at the altar. I keep thinking, How did we end up like this?' She sighed heavily. 'Sorry to put a damper on the party.'

'Don't be daft. And if I can do anything . . .'

'I know. Why can't they be more like us, Kay? They say women are the weaker sex but I don't see much sign of it. They waltz off but we have to keep going no matter what, we get stuck with the children. We just have to get on with it, don't we?'

* * *

Theresa

Theresa had made a whole row of sandcastles. She loved the little paper flags that Mummy had bought her to stick on top. There was a white cross on blue paper, a lovely red dragon, a Union Jack and a stripey one.

She needed seaweed now to make a pattern round them all, and some shells. At the water's edge she squatted down, selecting slippery strands of bladderwrack, with its leathery skin and bulbous pods, and fronds of the other slimy, bright-green weed.

Another girl came up close. She had a fishing net. Theresa watched the girl's toes disappear into the soft sand.

'There's a crab over there,' the girl said. 'In the big rock pool.'

'Can you see it?'

'I'll show you. What's your name?'

'Theresa.' She got up, leaving the seaweed.

'How old are you?'

'Six.'

'What's wrong with your ear?'

Theresa blinked. The question stung her, she felt a bit sick.

'Nothing.' She pulled her hair over it, hiding it. 'It didn't grow right.'

'Does it hurt?' The girl had a mean mouth. Theresa wanted her to shut up and go away.

'It looks horrible. Are you a bit deaf?'

Theresa grabbed her bucket and ran up the beach. When she reached the shingle she slipped, skinning her toes against the pebbles. She began to cry. She couldn't see the place where Mummy and Daddy and Dominic and the babies were.

She walked on. Stupid, horrid girl. She hated her ear. Mummy said it was nothing to worry about but she didn't know, she didn't have a lump like a slug on her head, did she?

She sobbed some more, her tummy hurt. She was lost. Then she saw her castles, the flags tiny specks in the distance and nearby Daddy rolling the big beach ball to Dominic. She squeezed her face to make more tears come and then ran to them. Mummy was reading, lying on her front on the blanket. The twins were asleep on the picnic rug. Theresa wailed so Mummy would hear her.

'Theresa, what's happened?'

She cried some more first, really loud to show how bad it was and then she told her about the horrid girl and hurting her toes. She saw Daddy look at Mummy and felt Mummy squeeze her tighter. 'It's not horrible, Theresa. Little girls like that say silly things.'

'I wish I was dead,' she said.

'Sshhh! Don't say that. We love you. What would we have done without you? When we fetched you home it was the happiest day of my life.'

Theresa swallowed, sniffed up her tears. 'Tell me,' she said.

'It was a lovely June day. We'd already been to see you once . . .' Her mother began the familiar story and Theresa relaxed back into her embrace. Mummy was big and soft. Theresa's skin was damp and sticky with salt and sand but warm where she touched her mother. She listened, waiting for the comforting words to work their magic and make her feel better.

* * *

Caroline

Things had unravelled after Davey's birth. As she nursed him and changed him her eyes kept blurring. Stupid unbidden tears. She kept telling herself that it would be all right, that no one would take this child from her, but the fear grew in her like a tumour until every situation became a tangle of threats.

The midwives told Paul she was overwrought, that she needed help, but when he offered to hold Davey while she bathed or rested she shrank away from him. He found her tearing the newspapers into tiny pieces. Talking of demons. The news was horrific, they'd charged Ian Brady and Myra Hindley with the Moors murders. He cursed himself for leaving the thing around.

After another week of sleepless nights and frantic panics Paul was at the end of his tether. He spoke to his mother on the telephone. She arranged to travel down from Yorkshire in two days' time. Reassured that help was on the way Paul went to find Caroline upstairs.

She had closed the curtains and lay on the bed. The air smelt stale. When he put the light on he noticed afresh how messy the room was. Nappies and baby clothes strewn about, a pile of ironing on the chair. Dirty glasses and cups on the bedside table.

Caroline winced at the light, looked at him with suspicion.

'I'm going to clear up a bit,' he said. 'All this mess isn't helping. Why don't you sit downstairs? I'll call you if Davey wakes up.'

She sighed and got up sluggishly. Her chestnut hair had lost its gloss and hung in lank strands, her complexion was sallow.

'Or would you like a bath?'

'Have you put the water heater on?' She spoke sullenly.

He sighed. No, he ruddy well hadn't. He didn't know how to do all this. The house was her province. 'No, but I can.'

'Don't bother,' she said coldly.

'My mother's coming to help us out.' He tried to sound matter of fact. He propped his stick against the wall, started picking up the baby clothes from the dressing tables and putting them on the bed.

'No!' she cried as though he had hurt her.

'Just for a few days, till we're on top of things.'

She stood there, her face crumbling, shoulders shaking.

'Oh, Caro,' he said gently. He moved towards her.

'No!' she yelled and swung away from him, stumbling and knocking into the bedside table, knocking the lamp over and a glass. There was a crash followed by a beat of silence then the stringy wail from Davey in his cot in the next room.

Paul moved but she was quicker, sobbing loudly. He followed her, feeling frightened but not sure why.

He watched her lift Davey up, hold him close, humming a tune broken by her irregular sobs. He wanted to join them, to comfort both wife and child but he knew there would be another rebuttal if he tried.

'I'll get on then,' he said. 'Call me if you need anything.'

He returned to their bedroom, his chest tight and a pulse hammering in his head. Glass on the floor. He went downstairs to get the dustpan and brush.

* * *

His mother's arrival seemed to make Caroline worse. From being moody and prone to tears she had started raving. A stream of accusations directed at him and his mother, dark mutterings about them plotting behind her back. His mother had cleared up the kitchen, prepared the baby's bottle and made a simple meal. Caroline refused to come down. She refused to eat. When he went up to see her she spoke more gibberish and acted as though she was scared of him, as though he intended some harm.

'Call the doctor,' his mother said.

He hesitated. 'Do you think so?'

'She needs help, Paul. He can give her something to calm her down.' She smiled at him. 'It's probably depression, getting a bit out of control. Call the doctor.'

By the time the doctor arrived Caroline had barricaded herself and Davey in her room. Davey was hungry — Caroline had not given him the bottle her mother-in-law had made up — and crying incessantly. Paul had begged her to open the door, reminded her that Davey needed his bottle, but she refused.

'Caroline, let us in now, the doctor's here, he wants to have a look at you,' he said. There was no response. He felt his temper rising at the stupidity of it all. 'Caroline,' he threatened, 'if you don't open the door I'll break the bloody thing down.' And how would he do that? With his poor balance it would be hard to put much force against it. 'I'll get the fire brigade,' he added.

He wasn't sure if she could hear him over the screaming baby but after a minute there was the bumping of furniture being moved. When he tried the door it opened.

Once inside, Paul took Davey from the bed and passed him to his mother. Caroline, perched on the bed, panting from her exertions but outwardly calm, watched them like a hawk.

'You remember me, Mrs Wainwright?'

'Oh, yes,' she nodded. 'You're the Devil. You eat the babies.'

An hour later Caroline was admitted to the psychiatric hospital. The doctors assured Paul that a short stay, the use of tranquilizers and possibly a session or two of electro-convulsive therapy would relieve her of her distress.

'Some women react like this after childbirth,' the psychiatrist told him. 'This is your first child?'

'Yes.'

He nodded. 'Most women get a bit weepy a few days after they've had the baby but this is something more serious, a form of depression. We still don't understand exactly why it happens and/or why some women are more susceptible than others, but it is treatable and I'm sure your wife will be back home, enjoying family life very soon.'

* * *

Kay

The lemon was rotten. It looked fine on the outside but when she halved it the centre was brown and slimy. She couldn't make a lemon cake without a lemon. Joanna might have one. Knowing Joanna, she probably had a plastic squeezy one to squirt into her gin. She certainly made a virtue of being a lazy cook and a fan of all the latest gimmicks.

Kay Farrell took her apron off and washed her hands. She checked on the twins, who had gone down for their nap half an hour ago. They were sound asleep, head to tail in the cot. They liked to share it for their daytime sleep. She went round the back at Joanna's, the kitchen door was always open. The climbing rose around the back door was in full bloom. She inhaled the scent. They must do more with their garden, get some nice shrubs. All they had was the lawn and the apple tree. Bit dull.

She let herself in and called out. 'Hello, it's only me!' She went through the hall into the dining-cum-living room. A blur of bodies on the sofa. Naked. Skin, limbs, hair. She froze. Joanna and Adam. Her Adam. The pair parting, scrabbling away from each other as she gawped. Her heart shattering, mind numb.

'Hell!' Adam stood, scooping up clothing to cover himself. Joanna remained seated, curling up, face averted, her pendulous breasts still moving slightly. Kay turned and ran. Her world crashing about her. Panic clutching at her throat. Betrayal flooding her stomach with acid, adrenalin furiously pumping her blood faster than she could breathe. The bastard, the bitch.

At home she steadied herself on the sink, tried to slow her breathing, drank water from the tap to wash down the bile in her gullet. Then she got out the brandy from the drinks cabinet, poured a tumblerful. She took a large mouthful, relishing the way it burned her mouth and made her lips tingle. She stuck a cigarette in her mouth, flicked the lighter. Her hand shook. Everything shook.

'Kay.' He stood in the doorway.

She wouldn't look at him.

'Kay, I'm sorry.' His voice was dry, like grass rustling.

'That's all right then, is it? That supposed to make me feel better?' she said coldly.

'Kay, I love you. This . . . it . . .' He moved into the room, sat down. 'It doesn't mean anything.'

'It means something to me,' she shot back. 'My husband committing adultery with my best friend. Means quite a lot, actually.'

'Kay—'

'Shut up!' She drank again, a fiery mouthful, sucked angrily on her cigarette. There was so much anger. It was like a great cannonball inside, hot and heavy and rolling, rolling.

How could you? she wanted to scream at him, How could you hurt me so, how could you risk all this, our marriage, our children? Why? Questions that had no answers.

'Get out!' she managed.

'Kay.'

She flung her glass at him, the drink splashing on his shirt and his neck, the tumbler crashing to the floor.

He hesitated.

'Fuck off!' she screamed. Words she had never spoken before.

He went.

She found another glass, poured another drink, smoked more cigarettes. Looked out at a brisk, bright afternoon and felt her eyes swim. How could it all be there, looking just as it had before?

When the twins woke she got them up, went through the motions of feeding and changing, the drink making her move a little more slowly, more carefully. She put Martin and Michael out to play in the garden. All the while nursing her anger, chewing over the shock of her discovery, seeing again Adam's darker leg against Joanna's, his buttocks, her breasts swaying as she sat and turned away. She wallowed in it, soaking up the misery, feeling the bite of jealousy and the ache of grief settle in, the streams of emotion seep through her till it was all she was. Every hair, every cell sharing in the pain.

She let her imagination run riot, fantasising about the two of them, her friend and her husband, digging out a conspiracy that dated back months — assignations, plans and schemes, efforts to cheat on her. She was a fool, such an idiot. How she had sympathised with Joanna when she'd told her about Bev and Ken that time. She had felt so sorry for Joanna, so glad that she and Adam were different. Hah! They had played her for a fool and that knowledge scalded her with shame.

When Theresa and Dominic got back from school she made peanut butter sandwiches for them and mandarin oranges from a tin. She let them watch Crackerjack and then she got them all bathed and into bed earlier than usual. She couldn't eat. She had a headache from the brandy but she didn't care. A headache was nothing. She smoked more cigarettes, drank strong coffee. Poured herself the last of the brandy.

He came back when it was dark. She heard the door, then his walk along the hall. She was sitting in the lounge. She hadn't put the light on.

'Kay.' He'd been drinking too. She could smell it on him as he came closer, a yeasty smell, beer, not the spirit she'd doused him with. He put his hand on her shoulder.

'Don't touch me!' she spat at him.

'I don't know what you want me to do,' he said in anguish.

'It's a bit late for that now, isn't it? I wanted you to honour our marriage vows. I wanted you to love and honour me, to forsake all others. To be true to me.'

'Kay, I promise—'

'You promise? You promise what?' she began to shout. 'You don't know how to keep a promise, you bastard! You rotten, cheating, bloody bastard! I hate you, Adam, I hate you for this.'

There was a silence. She heard the blackbird outside trilling in the dark, the hoot of the train in the distance. Adam's breath, harsh as though he'd been running. Then she heard him sit. The creak of the chair and a sigh.

'What will you do?'

'Well, I can't divorce you.'

He made a sound. Had she shocked him? Good. She wanted to frighten him, though, make him feel an ounce of what she was feeling. 'I don't know about the rest. Separation, maybe.' Had he any inkling how unlikely that was for her? 'I'd need to get a solicitor, maintenance for the children. And we'd need to stay in the house.' She wouldn't do any of it, though, would she?

'Kay, please. It was one mistake, a stupid, bloody mistake. I love you, and the children. You mean everything to me. There's no need to—'

'What? Take it to heart? Don't tell me what I need or don't need, Adam.'

'I just meant—'

'How long?'

'What?'

'How long have you been fucking Joanna?' She swore to shock him.

'Kay, really.'

'The truth, Adam. How long?'

A pause.

'A couple of months.' He cleared his throat.

'When did it start?'

'Kay . . . I don't . . .' He fell quiet.

'Don't remember? Why not? Do you sleep with the neighbours often? When?'

'Why?' He said softly.

'When?'

'Easter.' he cleared his throat again. Four months, not two. 'The dinner dance.'

At the Tennis Club. Kay had left early so their babysitter could get home. 'But Ken was there?' The four of them had sat together.

Silence.

'You didn't take her home. Where then?'

'In the gardens.'

She lit a cigarette, the flare from the lighter illuminating her face, the flame just catching a wisp of hair. She smelt the acrid stench as it shrivelled up, a tiny crackling sound.

'Where else?'

He didn't answer.

'Did you do it here?'

'No,' he said quickly.

Liar. 'Adam?'

'No,' he insisted.

'Where else?'

'Joanna's.'

'That weekend at Southport,' she said flatly. 'After the picnic? When we went horse riding?'

'Kay, please, don't.'

'Tell me, Adam.'

'Yes,' he said and sighed.

She felt her past unravelling. The memories distorted now by the image of them having sex. Bitterness flooded her anew. Joanna had lent her a stole that weekend. They'd all got drunk in the chalet bar. She'd been wearing Joanna's stole and Joanna had been borrowing her husband. How ironic.

'Since then, how often?'

'I don't know.'

'Lost count.'

'What's the point,' he yelled, 'dragging it all out. It's not doing you any good. I'm sorry. What more can I say?'

'The point,' her voice trembled with fury, 'the point is that I have a right to know. To know the truth. To know exactly what you have been doing. In her arms and between her legs. Twice a week, more?'

'No.'

'Once a week?'

He said nothing.

'And what do you like? When you get together? Fast or slow? Do you usually do it in the lounge or was today an exception? Do you satisfy each other?'

'Kay, that's enough!' he shouted.

She knew it would never be enough. No matter how many details she had she would never believe that he'd told her the whole truth. But she kept on.

'Who started it?'

'It's not that easy . . .'

'Someone must have made the first move, that night at the Tennis Club. You went outside together. Who suggested that?'

'I don't remember.'

'Oh, come on, Adam!'

'I was drunk.'

'That's handy. Drunk but not incapable.'

'She tripped, I helped her.'

'How gallant!'

'We didn't plan it, Kay. It just happened.'

'And today? Does Ken know?'

'No.'

'Because he's been unfaithful too, you know. Did Joanna say? With Bev, last time I heard. Regular Peyton's Place round here, isn't it? Must be catching. Have to hope none of you has picked up anything nasty, won't we? Spread like wildfire.'

Silence again. She drew on her cigarette, listened to the sizzle of tobacco. 'Do you love her?'

'No. It's just a silly fling. It got out of hand. I never meant to hurt you. Neither of us did. I'll make it up to you.'

What a stupid expression. How could he ever do that? He'd ruined it. Ruined everything. No matter how good things were in the future he had taken the one thing that you couldn't repair and damaged it. Time might reduce the sting and erase the clarity of the details but she would never trust him again. He had broken her trust and broken her heart.

And as for Joanna, she couldn't bear to think of that too. All those confidences, Joanna's sardonic tone, sharing secrets. All a front, a con.

'I'm going to bed,' she said. 'There's blankets in the spare room.'

'What are we going to do, Kay?'

'I don't know,' she said honestly. 'I really don't know.'

* * *

Joanna had the barefaced cheek to turn up at Faith's coffee morning two days later. When she arrived, Kay had two urges — she wanted her to slap her, she wanted to run and hide. Of course, she did neither, she ignored her completely and gave a tight smile when Joanna made one of her acerbic remarks that made the others laugh. It's as though nothing has happened. Kay was incredulous. So blasé about it. She hated her, with her flip comments and her boutique clothes and her rotten deceit.

Kay left early, exhausted at the strain of maintaining a facade. She was halfway home when Joanna caught up with her.

'Kay.'

'Go away.'

'Let me explain.'

'Go away. I don't know how you dare.'

'Don't be like this.'

'How do you bloody well expect . . . !' She broke off determined not to be drawn into talking about it.

'Some of us make mistakes.' Joanna put out her hand to touch Kay's forearm, Kay wrenched her arm away.

'We can't all be saints,' Joanna flared up.

Kay flinched. Was that how she saw her, how they saw her? Goody two shoes? 'Leave me alone. I don't want to see you again. Don't come to my house and don't even look at my husband or I'll make sure everyone knows what a slut you are, including Ken.'

Joanna gave up — contempt and then resignation crossed her face. She turned away.

Kay continued home, trembling with outrage.

* * *

She buried their friendship: when she chanced upon Joanna at the shops or the park or in Church she treated her like a stranger: more than that, cut her dead. Inside, she seethed with bitterness. Over the weeks that followed, Kay gradually engineered it so that Faith and she spent time together and drifted apart from the larger group of women. She mentioned that Joanna was too flip and implied that she had been bitching about people behind their backs. She told Faith that there was never a chance to have a proper chat in a big crowd.

She found managing the children and running the house increasingly hard, she felt tired and irritable but had trouble sleeping too. She made an appointment at the doctor's. He prescribed tablets, they would take the edge off things, he said, calm her nerves.

Slowly, begrudgingly, she resumed her relationship with Adam. As time went on there were moments when she forgot the damage that had been done, but she was aware that her love for him was tainted. And any affection and forgiveness was tempered by an abiding lack of trust and a current of suspicion that played through her all the time.

* * *

Caroline

He hated the visits. The first time he went, Caroline refused to speak to him, face blank, eyes heavy. He made an effort to talk but his words soon petered out. He sat and held her hand and tried to cut out the sights and sounds and smells around them.

After a week he asked the nurse if he could see the doctor but was told he'd need a separate appointment for that. He made one. Aware it would mean even more time away from the business.

The doctor said much the same as the first psychiatrist had. It was a question of time, she was responding well. He thought of Caroline's comatose state and wondered. Quieter than the creature who had shrunk from him, but better? The doctor couldn't tell how long she'd need. It can be weeks or months. You may need to make arrangements at home. Paul nodded.

When he got back, his mother had tea ready — fish in parsley sauce, mash and peas. He explained the situation to her, he knew she couldn't stay indefinitely. She offered to take Davey back with her until Caroline was well.

He hated the idea of being parted from the baby as well as his wife. He shook his head, in despair rather than defiance.

'Paul, it's either that or get someone to live in.'

'Which we can't afford,' he replied. 'We're already behind on orders. If I hire anyone it'll have to be for the nursery. Caroline worked so hard. Maybe we were too ambitious, got too big too fast. If we sold now—'

'You'll do no such thing!' His mother put her knife and fork down to talk. 'You were only saying at Christmas how promising things looked. You might not be able to do anything for Caroline at the moment, that's down to the doctors, but what you can do is make damn sure that when she does come home she's coming back to a thriving concern. Sell up!' she snorted.

'Point taken,' he replied.

'Self-pity never built prosperity.' She returned to her meal.

'I said, point taken,' he repeated.

* * *

Via one of the greenhouse suppliers Paul found a nurseryman who'd recently retired. Arthur was delighted to come and work on a temporary basis. Retirement had been the biggest shock of his life. And his wife's. Eileen Wainwright took Davey back to the Dales and Paul worked long hours catching up with the business and doing what he could in the sheds.

Caroline's manner during his visits began to vary. Often she was dull and withdrawn, looking at him with the same indifference that she had to her appearance. Her eyes were frequently narrowed — apparently the drugs affected them, making them less light-tolerant — and her hair unkempt. Her clothes appeared to be thrown on and were sometimes stained. Her only interest seemed to be in the cigarettes he brought her. Her fingers were stained yellow and even though he smoked himself he could smell the stale nicotine on her. He took her flowers and sweets too but the cigarettes were what she had most need of. Sometimes she would be excitable, her face flushed, her pupils shrunken, eyes glittering. She would talk breathlessly about inconsequential things, giggling inappropriately. He realised the medicines were responsible. She rarely mentioned Davey or asked about the business.

After a second month he asked to see the psychiatrist again. It was a different man. He was filling in for Mr Jeffreys, who had been taken ill himself.

'Mrs Wainwright.' He looked at the bundle of notes then at Paul. 'How have you found her?'

Paul told him. 'And I still don't understand why she . . . got like this.'

'Ah, if we knew that . . .' The doctor smiled ruefully. 'We don't really understand what is at the root of this sort of disturbance. Even in the medical profession you've different theories doing the rounds. Some argue there's a physical imbalance, a chemical reaction in the brain, and that might be passed on from one generation to another.' With a chill, Paul thought of Davey. 'But other people argue that social circumstances are more important, that events happen to an individual and pressure builds up and this is the explosion, if you like. Anything might tip the balance. Of course, relinquishing a child can't be easily borne, that must take its toll.'

'Pardon?' Paul frowned.

'Giving the baby up for adoption.'

'We haven't given him up. He's at my mother's.'

'Not this—' He stopped short, closed his eyes and balanced his head momentarily on his fingertips.

Paul stared at him. 'Caroline had a baby adopted.'

'I'm terribly sorry Mr Wainwright, I assumed you knew — the notes . . .'

'Oh, my God!' He rubbed at his chin with his hand, got halfway out of his chair, knocking his stick down in his haste. He sat back down.

'When?'

'I can't say any more. I've said more than I should have. I've spoken out of turn. Please accept my apologies. I'm sure your wife only wanted to spare you. She was probably ashamed of . . .'

Dear God. Caroline. Why had she never . . . Making out that Davey was the first. That he was her first. Dear God. Why couldn't she have just told him?

'Dear God.' He said softly and stood up again.

'Mr Wainwright.'

'Please, doctor, can you pass me my stick?'

He hurried to help.

'Mr Wainwright, I do hope . . .'

But Paul couldn't wait, not even to observe the social niceties. He left the room and made his way out of the hospital to the bus stop, his brain full of clamouring voices, his heart hammering in his chest and a great weight across his back as though his coat was laden with stones.

* * *

Theresa

She'd made a tent out of the big clothes horse and an old sheet. Martin and Michael were using it for their den. They were the Indians. Dominic had been playing too but he'd gone round to Jim's. Theresa was bored. She went inside and got her little transistor radio. Mungo Jerry were singing 'In The Summertime', which was just right because it was really hot. 'Spirit In the Sky' was her favourite, though. Mungo Jerry had been the poster in *Jackie* this week and she had put it up with the others on her bedroom wall.

She went out to the front and sat on the wall, the tranny beside her. The hopscotch she'd drawn had faded, so she got some chalk and did it again. The flagstones by her gate had the lines in all the right places for hopscotch. She searched by the drive for a stone, a flat one that wouldn't roll.

Belinda from down the road came out and Susie and they played for a bit but it was hot so they changed to Jacks. Belinda always beat her at Jacks. Her fingers must have been longer, because she could scoop up 'tennies' even when they were scattered far apart and still catch the ball.

Dominic came back but he wouldn't play Jacks. He said he'd play picture cards. Everyone got theirs. Theresa had forty-five. Nearly all from Typhoo. Some she'd won at school.

They propped a card up against the garage door and took turns trying to knock it down with theirs. Dominic won twice and gathered all the cards from the floor.

'Ask your mum if we can have the paddling pool,' Belinda said.

'Yeah!' Susie hated cards.

Theresa went in. Mummy looked tired just at the thought of it but Theresa promised to do all the blowing-up and the filling it and she said all right but get changed. Theresa had her loon pants on, bright-red, and a calico smock. Belinda had hot pants but she said she was allowed to get them wet.

The twins went bonkers once it was all ready, until Mum came out and shouted at them. They gave each other showers later, using the watering can, and Theresa sang 'Raindrops Are Falling On My Head', and then they played Butch Cassidy and the Sundance Kid, coming out of the tent like it was the building and all the Mexicans firing at them.

'Let's play Dying,' said Theresa.

'I'm not,' said Dominic.

'You can be first on.'

'It's best at the bank,' Susie said.

'Get dressed, be there in five minutes,' said Theresa.

The bank was at the top of the avenue, a big slope of green, quite steep. Dominic stood at the bottom and the others lined up at the top.

'Martin!' Dominic called out.

'Deadly snake,' Martin chose.

Dominic pretended to throw a deadly snake at his brother who squawked and fell down and rolled to the bottom of the hill.

'Michael.'

'Deadly snake.'

'Pick something else,' Theresa yelled. They were so dumb sometimes.

'I don't know.'

'Have a gun.'

'A gun.'

Dominic levelled his arm, forefinger pointing, and shot Michael. Michael clutched at his stomach and rolled down the hill.

'Belinda.'

'Machine gun.'

Dominic rat-tat-tatted and Belinda jerked loads and tumbled her way down.

'Susie.'

'Electric shock.'

Dominic pointed and she twitched and jumped and rolled down the hill.

'Theresa.'

'Drinking acid.'

She mimed the drink, then gasped and staggered, began to claw at her chest and stomach, pulled herself down the slope and died at the bottom.

'Martin 4 points, Michael 7, Belinda 6, Susie 6, Theresa 6. Michael wins.'

'You can't pick him, he was rubbish!' Theresa rounded on him.

'I can.'

'I wasn't.'

'I'm not playing,' Dominic said.

'Don't then, see if I care.'

He stalked off.

'You're on,' she said to Martin.

'Yippee!' he said.

'You've got to pick the best. The best acting.'

'Yeah,' he nodded.

They climbed the hill.

'Michael!' Martin pointed to his twin and grinned.

'Dunno.'

Theresa sighed and looked across at Susie and Belinda. 'Shall we go down the Tarzan swing instead?'

* * *

Paul never found the right time to ask her about it. When she first came home he knew that the most important thing was making her feel safe and happy, helping her to feel confident about looking after Davey while he held the business together.

The months passed. Caroline gave up smoking and put on weight. She was happier, though he always had the sense that he didn't really know her, not all of her, because of the secret she had kept from him and her natural reserve. He loved her quiet intensity. He watched her now as she examined the new mother plants with the nurseryman. She didn't say much but everything counted: a gentle joke and a fleeting smile that made her eyes shine nut-brown, a shrewd word about delivery dates. When Davey toddled up she simply put her hand down and he took hers and accompanied her while she worked. If he fussed she'd pass him stones or leaves to examine, a trowel to play among the furrows with, or she'd point out a butterfly or show him how to make a Snapdragon snap.

Deep, she was. She kept things to herself. He knew she needed her time away, she'd go off on one of her walks and come back more settled. He was fearful that if he dared to mention about the baby she'd had, he'd precipitate another depression; see her withdraw again back into the land of the demons. So he said nothing.

He surveyed the nursery grounds. They'd rented extra land for an arboretum and taken on another worker. It was touch and go, but you couldn't run a business without taking risks. He'd plans for an indoor-plants section. It was becoming fashionable for offices and banks to brighten their foyers with a splash of greenery. Bit like Victorian times, when an aspidistra or some parlour ferns were common in the shopping arcades and hotels and clubs. And if things went the American way, with purpose built shopping malls, then with his ideas and her green fingers . . .

'Paul!' She waved to him from the stock beds. 'Tell Joe we need more pallets.'

He gave her the thumbs-up and moved slowly off back to the yard. The weather was fair. Their first winter had been bitter, '63, when the country froze to a halt. The ground had been unworkable for weeks. There'd been heavy blizzards. Here in Somerset they'd escaped the smogs that choked the cities. Hundreds of people were ill, some died unable to breathe the poisonous air.

There had been days that winter when he'd felt like giving up. Chucking in the towel before they got enmeshed any deeper. But Caroline was tenacious. And convinced it was the right move. She never doubted and she never ceased working. She was strong, she'd big bones and a broad back and lifting and carrying and shifting were no problem for her. If the ground was too hard to dig she'd make cold frames or saw stakes, mend fences or prune the hedges. She'd never once complained. Shovelling snow for days on end. Coming in only when it got dark, her cheeks and nose red with cold, fingers numb. When he praised her she looked amused. Shrugged and told him that hard work was good for the soul.

He wondered sometimes who had fathered her child? If she had been willing? And would there ever come a point when she would confide in him?

* * *

Kay

The shaking started when she was on the bus home. She'd been fine in town: she'd not become confused or lost her purse or suddenly heard voices in her head mocking her.

But on the bus, out of nowhere, it all started. She began to sweat, she could feel her thighs and her arms burning, her armpits damp and her mouth dry. She looked out of the window, tried to distract herself with the view as they crossed the river into Northenden and the parade of shops, but she couldn't focus properly and that made her more panicky. She'd tried so hard. Four days now. Doctor Planer had told her it would be easier every day and also said if she felt really unwell she should start taking the pills again. No point in rushing these things.

She was scared to stop and scared to carry on. The tablets slowed her down. She put on even more weight, she felt dim and slow-witted. The children seemed to be an endless series of chores with little pleasure. She barely had the energy to play with them these days.

She was going to be sick. She stood abruptly, stumbled to the front of the bus. 'Let me off, please, I missed my stop.'

The driver slowed to stop at the roadside and opened the automatic doors. She walked back a little and leaned over the gutter, dry retching. Her mouth filled with saliva, she spat it out, deeply embarrassed at being a public spectacle.

She walked home in the rain, her only thought the salvation contained in the small brown bottle in the medicine cabinet.

It had been a silly time to try, she told herself. Too much going on. Theresa and Dominic were both settled in school but she still had the twins at home and Adam had had his best year yet, which meant more business dinners where Kay was expected to entertain and look lovely and relaxed. She simply couldn't manage it all without the pills. Not yet.

When she got in she reached for the bottle before anything else, shook the bright pink-and-yellow capsules into her hand and swallowed them. She'd try again when the time was right. Doctor Planer was right, some people needed something to calm their nerves and it was silly to get worried about taking them. After all, the doctor wouldn't prescribe them if they weren't safe.

* * *

Theresa

'I've always known,' Theresa replied to her friend Letty. 'As long as I can remember. Like a bedtime story.'

The four girls were huddled in the school toilet, it wasn't too poky. Theresa had claimed the radiator, Ruth sat on the toilet and Letty and Rita sat on the floor, backs against the wall, legs in woollen tights and thick crêpe-soled shoes stretched out before them. Each girl had a freshly lit Embassy Regal cigarette from the packet of ten they had clubbed together to buy.

'Do you know anything about your real mother?' Rita asked.

'Not much. She wasn't married, she couldn't keep me. I think she was quite young.'

'Would you like to meet her?'

'No. It wouldn't mean anything. It's never bothered me.'

'I'd be dying to know,' said Ruth.

'What if it was someone famous?' Rita asked.

Theresa smiled and shook her head.

'What about your real father?' Letty took a drag on her cigarette and held it in while she spoke. 'He might be looking for you now to inherit his stately home.'

Theresa laughed and shook her head again. 'They're not allowed. They have to promise when they give you up.'

'Well, how come you hear about these people finding their real parents then?' Letty said.

'I'd be allowed to but not them. Some people don't even know they're adopted. Imagine the shock if someone turned up on your doorstep and said you were theirs.'

'What about your brothers? Are they all from different families?' Rita asked.

'There's twins, thicko!' Letty shoved her.

'Apart from them.'

'They're the only ones that are related.'

'Why were they adopted?'

'Same thing. Their mothers weren't married. Well, Dominic's was but they weren't allowed to keep him. They'd had other children that had been neglected. The rescue society took him at the hospital.'

'Bloody hell!' said Ruth.

'It must be awful,' Letty said, 'having a baby and giving it up.'

'What else can you do?' said Rita.

Theresa winced. It was only a week since SPUC had brought their gruesome slide show into school and the Third Form had been forced to look at pictures of embryos and foetuses and babies and basins of blood accompanied by a savage commentary. Afterwards Father McEvoy had made an impassioned plea to the girls to stand up for Jesus and fight the wholesale slaughter of the innocents. There would be a LIFE rally in London, they were all enjoined to come and save the babies.

'If I got pregnant I'd keep it,' Ruth said.

'It's easier nowadays,' Rita said.

'I don't think abortion's always wrong,' said Letty.

'God!' Ruth shuddered. 'How can you say that?'

'It's got to be up to the person who's having it.'

'That's like saying murder's up to the person doing it,' Theresa said.

'It isn't.'

There was an awkward silence.

'Keep your legs crossed,' said Rita. 'Just don't let them go all the way.'

'You can get the pill from the doctor,' Theresa said.

'Clinic's better, that Brook place. Our Lucy goes there. They don't know your Mum and Dad like the doctor does,' said Letty.

Theresa finished her fag. Ground it out on the side of the wastepaper bin.

'If you had a baby though, it's your whole life gone, isn't it?' Letty said.

The bell for the end of break rang and the girls got to their feet.

'I'd never have an abortion,' Ruth repeated, bending over to stub her cigarette out. 'No way.'

'I'd never have a baby adopted,' Theresa said vehemently, her chocolate eyes flashing. And the declaration astonished her even more than her friends. Adoption had been fine for her, and her brothers. Why had she said that? She felt unsettled for the rest of the day.

* * *

Kay

The glaze is beautiful,' Faith said.

'You were right to use the deeper blue,' the pottery teacher told Kay. 'It's perfect for the red clay.'

Kay placed the large bowl on the work bench at the side of the kiln. It would look lovely filled with fruit and would give her something to talk about the next time she had to make conversation with more of Adam's business wives. The agency were involved in a takeover bid; if it was successful they'd be selling property throughout most of Lancashire. The expansion would mean more functions, more dinners. Thinking of Adam brought the familiar twist of anxiety to her stomach. Was she imagining it all again? It wasn't as if she'd caught him out. She shuddered at the memory. The sight of Joanna and Adam naked together was frozen in her mind, etched indelibly even after seven years.

But this time there was no evidence. No lipstick on his collar or perfume on his skin. No unexplained bills. Nothing except an air of distraction and the fact that he had been attentive. He brought her flowers, told her he loved her after they made love. He never did that, not usually.

She wrapped the bowl in newspaper to protect it on the way home. It was the final class of the year. She'd come back again in the autumn. She had the knack. Faith wasn't so sure. 'I might try French. I could still give you a lift, it's on Wednesdays as well.' Kay didn't drive, had never learnt, but Faith did. Faith was working now, teaching, and her mother looked after the children on a Wednesday night. Mick never saw them. The divorce had been acrimonious and costly.

Kay held the bowl on her lap in the car. When Faith drew up outside the house, Kay turned to thank her.

'I think Adam's having an affair.' The words came out in a rush.

Faith looked shocked. She turned the engine off. 'Oh, Kay!'

'It's just a feeling, I've no proof. I don't know whether to say anything to him or not.'

'Who is it?'

'I don't know.'

Faith looked at her, considering. 'If you're not sure . . . I mean, Adam's never done anything like this before, has he?

'Once,' Kay said. 'A few years ago.' She didn't elaborate.

'You never said anything.'

There was an awkward pause. Kay imagined Faith feeling hurt that Kay hadn't told her about it.

'I didn't tell anyone. It was a long time ago.' Implying it was before they met.

'What if you're wrong?'

'You think I should wait and see?'

'There are places aren't there, private investigators.'

'Oh, God! I couldn't do that.' She saw some seedy type in an old coat trailing after Adam, spying on him, taking horrid photos. 'You're probably right, I'd look a real idiot if I was wrong. It would be awful.'

* * *

But the feeling of unease wouldn't leave her, and suspicion made everything between herself and Adam seem shallow and false. She kept up the act for a further two weeks but the gnawing in her stomach grew stronger and she had vivid dreams where she came upon Adam with someone in their own bed and he laughed and pointed at the door and then he resumed having sex, his buttocks moving furiously, the woman beneath him obscured from view.

On the Saturday night they went to dinner with Adam's partner and his wife and another couple from the chamber of commerce. It was a pleasant enough evening but she couldn't relax. She thought about the tablets. She hadn't had them for eighteen months but at times like these she missed their numbing effects and began to feel edgy and anxious. It had been hell coming off them and staying off them and she'd no wish to go through it again. There were cases in the papers all the time, women who were addicted. Kay ate little of the meal and drank too much. She was able to disguise her inebriation because she was aware of it. She thought before speaking and was careful not to slur her words or knock her glass over.

When they got home Adam asked her if she wanted a nightcap. She accepted and watched him pour a Drambuie for her, a brandy for himself. He seemed at ease and when she spoke she watched him avidly for any sign of guilt or embarrassment.

'Are you having an affair, Adam?'

What she saw was shock; his face jerked as through he'd been slapped, his pale-blue eyes widened and then he looked wounded. 'No! Christ, Kay, why do you think that?'

'You've been preoccupied. And the flowers. You never buy flowers.'

He looked at her open-mouthed. 'I buy you flowers and you accuse me of having an affair?' he said incredulously.

'I didn't accuse you. I asked you. Maybe I need reassurance. After all, it's not beyond the bounds of possibility, is it? Look at last time.'

She saw his cheek twitch. They never referred to his fling with Joanna. He hated the reminder. He walked over to her and took her hand. 'I'm not having an affair.' He held her eyes with his, his pupils large, swamping the blue. 'Everything I want, everything I need, is here under this roof. I learnt my lesson, Kay.'

'I had to ask.' She squeezed his hand. 'I've been going up the wall. I'm sorry.'

He shook his head and pulled her to him. Held her by the nape of the neck. Kissed her. She let him. Catching hold of the relief that his denial brought and trying to quieten the whispering doubts that still clung to her.

* * *

Caroline

She marked each birthday. A little ritual that no one knew about. That in itself hadn't been easy with a business to run and a young family, but she had no qualms about inventing a trip to town, a meeting with a potential supplier or even, one year, a hospital appointment to account for her absence. She would find a quiet place, somewhere tranquil, usually where there was water and stones and trees. The first years after her marriage it had been the gorge where the Avon flowed and when they moved again she had found this place on one of her walks. Farsands Cove. Tiny, virtually inaccessible apart from a steep scramble down red-mud cliffs and through a stand of conifers. But once reached it had been her sanctuary.

She found herself a spot among the rocks. The tide was well out and the fresh wind had dried the beach. She sat down, rubbed her palms in the sand, picked up handfuls and let it trickle from her knuckles.

The ritual was simple. She would recall her time at St Ann's. She would try to remember as much as she could: the imposing building with its towers and gargoyles, doing the laundry, the perishing-cold bedroom she shared, the garden and the hours she spent bundled up on a bench. The other girls: Megan, who had been so lively and generous; Joan, who had been older but still in the same terrible situation. Did they ever think back? Remember her? She recalled the corner of the garden where she sat. The shawl she had brought. What else? Grandma dying and not being there for the funeral. Megan knitting. Porridge for breakfast. Her labour. The details still more clear to her than those of the boys'. And then it had changed.

The baby had become the centre of her life. Changing and feeding her. Holding her. Falling in love with her.

'A very good family,' Sister Monica had said. Caroline had nodded. Thinking, And I am not. Not good. Not family. What am I then? Nothing.

The worst part to remember was the night she had tried to rescue Theresa. She couldn't just give her up like all the others: it was wrong to let her go. She loved her so. Caroline would talk to her and she would listen, really listen, her tiny face running through all these different expressions. She was so beautiful. A shock of dark hair, eyes like pools in the night. She loved the smell of her, she would sit breathing in the scent from her skin, feeling the weight of her in her arms. My lovely, lovely girl.

They hadn't told Caroline what day the baby would be taken but her cot was next to the door in the nursery now. She would be next. Caroline had lain awake that night, her eyes hard and dry, her heart heavy and an awful pain in her stomach. It was wrong. She wouldn't let them do it. She had slipped out of bed and opened the wardrobe. Wincing when it creaked. But no one woke. She pulled on a dress and coat, found her shoes and the bag she had ready with her few possessions.

She tiptoed across the hall to the nursery, where Sister Vincent and one of the girls were meant to be watching over the babies. She couldn't see Sister Vincent but Deirdre was curled up on the truckle bed, out for the count. It was cool and Caroline was shivering but she could feel sweat sliding down the sides of her chest. Her heart was thumping in her throat. She went into the nursery and bent over the cot. She felt the familiar rush of affection, a dizzy sort of joy at seeing her little girl again. Quietly she pulled aside the blankets and lifted up the child, holding her against her left shoulder. She pulled the shawl from the bed and wrapped it around the baby's back. She walked out and down the passage to the front door, thinking at the same time that it would be a long time till the first bus. The first bus to anywhere.

The door was locked and she couldn't see the key. Her hands were shaking, she looked on the little table in the hall but there was nothing there. She could go out the back, then.

She turned and the snap of lights flooded the hallway, making her jump. Sister Vincent came towards her, her face hard. 'Caroline.'

She felt her eyes flood with tears, her cheeks slither, the shaking spread to her ribs and her thighs. 'Sister, I can't! I can't, I won't!' She buried her face in the baby's neck. Soft skin, silky hair. The smell of milk and powder. She cupped her hand over the small skull, felt the pulse beating through the fontanels, used her thumb to stroke the small nub of Theresa's left ear. 'Please?' she begged. 'She's my baby.' She turned but her way was blocked again.

Then there were more footsteps and lights and orders whispered and they took her into Sister Monica's office and she was shaking her head and begging them and they pulled the child from her arms.

She didn't see her again.

There was little to remember after that. A blur of pain and misery so she could barely swallow or talk. A stone inside her.

She thought about her baby every day. And once a year she came here to remember and to weep and to pray that one day the child would seek her out and she could begin to make amends. She would be fifteen years old today, practically grown up. Did she ever think of Caroline? Did she know she even existed?

She watched the sea suck and sigh through her salty eyes, blew her nose on one of the handkerchiefs she had brought. She prayed to the earth and the high, pewter sky and the wind to bring her daughter back. Then she walked the cove, searching for a small stone, a pebble or a shell. She would know the right one when she held it. This time she found a small, smooth, oval-shaped pebble, dark grey with lines of white terraced through it. She held it and it fitted her palm. She would take it home and put it in her special box along with the fourteen others she had. Her only mementos.

* * *

Kay

'Kay, Kay Farrell?'

A young woman stood on the doorstep: she was very slim, pretty, with long blonde hair and a lime-green crocheted dress. 'I'm Julie.'

Kay frowned. She didn't know the girl, was sure they'd never met. 'I don't think . . .' she began.

'I work with Adam.'

'Adam's not here,' Kay said stupidly. Monday to Friday, eight thirty to six, even later if business was booming.

'I know,' the girl said. 'Could I come in a minute?' She seemed tense, her eyes looked a little startled and she blinked a lot.

Kay hesitated but it would have been impolite to refuse. Why was she here? Was Adam hurt?

The washing machine was making a din in the kitchen so Kay took her into the dining room. The girl sat down. Kay offered her a drink.

'No, thanks. Adam hasn't said anything about me?' Half question, half statement.

Kay shook her head.

Julie sighed and closed her eyes momentarily.

'I'm pregnant,' she said, looking down at her hands in her lap. 'I'm having Adam's baby.'

For an awful moment Kay wanted to laugh, felt a cackle sitting in her chest. Pregnant? Preposterous. You can't be. He can't . . . He swore to me. She didn't speak but swung her eyes away from the girl out to the garden, to where the climbing frame stood.

Julie continued. 'He said he'd tell you but I think it was just another lie. I know he can't divorce you, the religion and that, but that doesn't mean he has to keep living with you.'

'Why are you here?' Kay spoke softly.

'I thought you should know.'

His baby. She was carrying his baby inside, beneath the trendy dress. A little Adam or perhaps a girl.

Fresh, fertile, skinny, ten years younger.

What was she? Barren, fat, dried-up and bitter. Up to her ears in packed lunches and clean football kits and table decorations. 'I'd like you to go.'

'He has to choose,' the girl said. She stood up.

Adam. Adam could have children. They had always said it was feasible. But not likely: his sperms had low motility.

'He's got to face up to his responsibilities.'

'Please, go.'

Julie moved into the hall. Kay walked after her, her throat constricted, her heart beating in her neck, her ears. She shut the door after her and sat on the bottom stair, her head in her hands. Talking quietly, cursing him, over and over, letting the tears slide down her cheeks, banging her fists on her chest and pressing them against her cheeks.

She thought of slitting her wrists or pouring the contents of the medicine cabinet down her neck. Something to surprise him on his return. See, she would say in her death, see how you have hurt me. See. You have killed me. But she couldn't. She couldn't leave the children. While she could breathe she would carry on. For them. Whatever he had done. Fuck him. Fuck him to hell and back.

* * *

Caroline

It was twelve years after Davey's birth when the depression returned in full spate, dragging her down into a tomb of defeat and dislike and black grief. She had been certain she would succumb earlier, with her second pregnancy when Davey was three and as her due date drew nearer she had become more worried about that than about the labour itself.

She had begged Paul to stay with her for the delivery and he agreed. The midwives wouldn't promise anything, they said they'd have to wait and see how she got on. The birth was difficult. They kept examining her and every time

Paul had to wait outside. One of the midwives tried to examine her during a contraction and only by screaming could Caroline get over how much it hurt.

After several hours she was still only five centimetres dilated and they gave her an injection to speed up the labour. The contractions that followed became unbearably strong, panicking her with their ferocity. They had a belt strapped round her to monitor the foetal heartbeat, that made it hard for Caroline to move. She wanted to kneel up but they wouldn't let her. She knew she had done that before, not with Davey but before. It was hard to remember Davey's birth, one of the things that had become cloudy and indistinct after the ECT. The midwives came in and looked at the screen and went away.

She began to howl and pleaded with them to give her something for the pain.

The doctor told the midwife to break her waters. They sent Paul out.

She had to lie still, tears leaked from her eyes and she thought she would pass out when they ruptured the sac.

'Please—' her voice was hoarse with pain — 'please stop it.'

They began to talk about an episiotomy. Then the baby went into distress, according to the screen, and she was wheeled through for an emergency Caesarean section. Paul wasn't allowed near her.

The baby had been fine, the spitting image of his brother. Caroline felt damaged. She wanted to go away from this place that had caused her such agony but she had to stay in ten days. She vowed not to have any more children.

The first weeks home she walked on eggshells. Any slump in her mood, any distressing thought, she seized on as proof that she was losing her mind again. But the weeks turned to months, she recovered from the operation, and Sean, bless him, was soon sleeping through the nights. In the intervening years she became accustomed to low-level unhappiness, the leaden feel of her life, and betrayed little of it to others. Everyone thought she was quiet, that she liked her own company. She could bear it. Anything was tolerable compared to madness.

But now Davey was twelve and Sean nine and out of the blue the terror began to suffocate her again. She fought it for a few weeks, immersing herself in work, but the lack of sleep and the endless tension built up, corroding away her control. She had violent, destructive dreams when she did sleep and when she was awake she would frighten herself with thoughts of suicide.

It was a relief to give up. She sat in the office, looking out at the yard and surveyed her desk. Suppliers to visit, a trip to Holland for the new range of bulbs, a meeting with the man who was importing the New Zealand plants. She barely had the energy to blink. Two of the lads were unloading compost, laughing. Probably laughing at her. She closed her eyes but the shadows came then, frightening her awake.

She had to go. They were watching her in this place. Hidden cameras. She took her boots off and her socks. It was better not to leave footprints. Harder for them to track you down. She walked out and along the road.

The cars roared past her, some bleating their horns and startling her. She fell in the ditch once, nettles bit at her arm and her bare feet. When she reached the roundabout she sat in the middle. The road was like a moat protecting her. She lay by the shrubs and watched the clouds. Even the grey hurt her eyes. Jesus was the Lamb of God but lambs were slaughtered. Doreen had been slaughtered. And her unborn child. Pulled inside out. *Let me keep her, please . . . Sister, I can't . . .* Some of the cars were spying on her too. The indicators recording her. She rocked to and fro.

Paul came later, with one of the lads who had been laughing. They put her in the back seat. He asked her things but she didn't know what his words meant. They were traps or jokes. Not to be trusted. She tried laughing but her mouth didn't want to. There was something she had to tell him. She squeezed her eyes shut tight till there were stars bursting and a band of pain. She looked at him. 'I'm going to the hospital,' she said. She saw his neck tighten and his Adam's apple bounce. He turned to the lad. Nodded. 'Collin's Hill,' he told him.

* * *

One day she told the doctor about her baby. When the words came back. But the memories were still full of holes, like moths had been at the shawl. She told her about trying to keep her and how they'd caught her and pulled the baby away. There was a hole inside where her heart had been. She never knew what had happened. If she was still alive, even.

The doctor told her she could always write a letter for her.

Caroline was shocked. 'No! I promised, at the court, they made me swear I'd never . . .'

The doctor nodded. Her big copper earrings wobbled. 'Yes, but you could leave the letter with the adoption agency, and then if your daughter . . .'

My daughter. Caroline felt the room sway.

'. . . ever wanted to find you she would have something from you.'

'Not my address. Paul doesn't, the children . . .'

'Fine.' The doctor held her hands out, trying to calm her. 'Just a note perhaps? If you'd like to, telling her that you think about her.'

Caroline tried to smile but she felt her face dissolve again and the tears made her thoughts all blurry.

They didn't give her ECT again and she was grateful. She had lost too many memories. She imagined her mind pockmarked with cigarette burns, precious moments from childhood and later scorched away.

It took her six months to write the letter to her daughter. Endless drafts in her head, then on paper, times snatched in private. In 1978, eighteen years after she had given birth, she posted the letter to the Catholic Children's Rescue Society.

They had just passed the new law which entitled adopted children to apply for their adoption records and made it much easier to get hold of them. If her daughter approached the agency Caroline's letter would be waiting for her. In it she explained the circumstances back in 1960 and a little of her memories of the few weeks they had spent together.

> *I have thought about you every day and prayed that you have been happy and that you have a close and loving family. I am married now and have two sons but I haven't told them about you, I hope you understand. I do hope one day you will write and tell me all about yourself.*

She did not put her address on the letter itself, panicked at the thought of Theresa turning up on the doorstep unannounced, but she attached a note of it for the society to keep on file so they could forward any communications to her. When her letter reached Manchester the clerk opening the mail was interrupted by a phone call. When she returned to sorting the mail she failed to notice the slip of paper that had got separated from Caroline's sealed envelope and was among the pile of discarded envelopes. She placed the letter in Caroline's file in the big filing cabinets, threw away the envelopes and began to sort through her correspondence for the day.

For weeks afterwards Caroline scanned the mail for unexpected postmarks or anything from the society in Manchester, aware that she was desperate to hear and terribly fearful in equal measure. Summer turned to winter then spring and her anticipation faded.

When she went to mark the May birthday, at the beach, she wondered if she would ever hear. Will I die not knowing? Will she write in ten years, thirty, forty? The uncertainty was cruel, like a slow water torture, dripping away, hope calcifying into resignation. She watched the waves break against the rocks, the pattern of foam eddying in the gullies. Heard the shriek of a cormorant. I've been suspended in time, she thought. My whole life since I had her, it's one long wait and the rest of it: Paul, the boys, everything, is like a dream and it'll never be real, never be enough until I can wake up and find out the truth. Like Sleeping Beauty waiting for a prince, for a kiss, for release.

* * *

Kay

They had half-a-dozen visits to the marriage-guidance clinic. It was deadly. Bitterness and confusion dragged out of each of them until the state of their relationship was displayed in tatters in front of them. The counsellor hadn't been at all judgmental but they had both made up for that. She came away from each session heavy with dismay, sickened by the depth of her anger. Worst of all was having to talk about the baby, Julie's baby, his baby. How she hated him for that. More than anything. And she grieved for the baby she had never had and felt an awful disloyalty to Theresa and Dominic and the twins.

She could never bring herself to voice the awful thoughts that haunted her, how she had wished Adam's love child dead, hoped that Julie would miscarry. Evil, unchristian. Adam wept his crocodile tears and said a million sorrys and talked of mistakes and being weak and a fool. He said she had withdrawn from him, been critical, grouchy, he talked about the tranquilizers and how sleepy they had made her. A hundred excuses.

The counsellor made them consider the future, what they wanted for themselves, from each other, what they could give. She asked them to consider separation as well as staying together. Kay panicked. She would not condemn the children to a broken marriage whatever the cost to her. She could not. But she could not forgive Adam either. It was a stalemate.

'Picture yourselves in five years' time.' The counsellor had smiled lightly. 'Think of three words to describe your marriage as it might be then.'

Adam huffed and puffed and eventually came up with stable, loving and safe. 'Faithful,' Kay said crisply, 'settled, friendly.' It was the best she could do and even those modest aims seemed completely unattainable to her.

Adam had promised her he would never stray again and begged her to believe him.

'I can't,' she said simply. 'I tried before and look where it got me. You want my trust. You can't have it. There isn't any.'

He sighed as though she was being obtuse or unreasonable.

The marriage became a convenient arrangement for raising the children. Julie had the baby, a girl, and Adam arranged to pay maintenance. He never saw his daughter. Theresa and the others knew nothing about their half-sister.

Once the twins started college Kay planned to take up training in information technology. Her independence was just around the corner. She was determined to build a new life for herself. And when she was sure of her footing she would leave Adam.

* * *

Theresa

'You may turn over your papers now.'

The last exam. Her eyes skimmed the paper, snatching at the key words of the four questions to see if her revision had covered all the items. Yes, more or less. The world-trade one would be the hardest, she'd have to waffle a bit, but the rest were items she'd gone over and over till she was sick to death of them. Three hours and it would be done. Freedom.

She began to write, her mind working more quickly than her fingers could. She finished fifteen minutes ahead of time and tried to read over her work, but by then she was exhausted, concentration spent, unable to think straight anymore.

She capped her pen, closed her eyes and sat back in her chair. Summer beckoned. Two weeks family holiday on the Costa Brava and then university. If she got her grades. Surely she would. She had worked so hard. The teachers thought she'd sail through. She needed a B and two Cs for Exeter, the course in geology.

'Couldn't you have found somewhere further away?' Her father had joked and her mother had gone all soppy and said, 'I can't imagine you not being here. Oh, I know it'll be wonderful for you and everything, but I keep thinking how did you grow up so quickly?'

'It's only three years, Mum. I'll probably be dying to get back to Manchester by the end of it.'

'I doubt it,' her mother snorted.

Theresa tried not to think too much about the actual move. It was exciting but a bit scary too. She was going into student halls of residence for her first year. After that she could move out to a place of her own, or get somewhere with friends. It would be brilliant. Her own place, own key. She'd had a silver key on her eighteenth-birthday cake. Key of the door. It used to be twenty-one but now you were grown up at eighteen. They still kept to twenty-one at the bingo place. She'd been with her mum once. To the Mecca. A fundraiser for the Catholic Rescue Society. Most of the people knew all the lines and they'd shout them out with the caller, and when there was a saucy reference the whole place would make a big 'w-h-o-o-o' sound. Theresa and her mum nearly wet themselves at some of the quips, and the characters.

The night before her eighteenth birthday she'd been helping her mum make vol-au-vents and her mum had spoken in that halting tone that Theresa knew as her important voice.

'Now, you're eighteen, if you ever want to trace your family, we wouldn't mind, Daddy and I. We'd understand.'

'I don't,' Theresa said, faintly embarrassed. 'I don't see any point.'

'It's just that we wouldn't want any of you to feel . . . well, that you couldn't find your natural parents, that we'd be upset. If it mattered to you, if it does in the future, then we'd be behind you.'

'Yeah, OK,' she said gracelessly and changed the subject. She hadn't wanted to before, why should she feel any different now?

'Stop writing now,' Mrs Evans called out. 'Pens down. Please remain at your desks while papers are collected.'

Outside in the glaring sunshine, Theresa joined her friends, swapping anecdotes from the exam. They wandered to the sixth-form common room and made coffee to go with their cigarettes.

'*Voila*!' Letty produced a bottle of martini and plastic cups. 'A little light refreshment.'

Oh, yes please! It was the last exam. It was all over. Theresa took a big swig. Someone put Stevie Wonder on full blast. 'Don't You Worry Bout A Thing.' Theresa finished her cigarette, drained her martini and felt a bubble of elation rise inside her.

'C'mon.' She pulled Letty to her feet and began to dance. Life starts here.

* * *

Kay

She had known she'd cry. She had worn waterproof mascara and had two neatly pressed handkerchiefs in her handbag. She held it in as much as she could, clenching her stomach and pressing her lips tight. But when they had made their vows she had felt her eyes fill and had to dab and sniff and hold on tight.

She and Adam had been so happy those first few years and then bang! Like hitting a brick wall at sixty miles an hour. The years since had been little more than a sham, a foundation for the children. Please, God, let it be better for them.

She glanced across at Craig's family. His parents seemed nice. They'd only met two days before. The Murrays had travelled down from Aberdeen and were staying at the Midland in town. Craig she knew better, he'd visited several times in the three years that he and Theresa had been going out. He had a dry sense of humour which caught her unawares many times. He wasn't good-looking, not in the conventional sense, his chin too narrow, nose too big, hair a mass of wiry brown curls, but he had a lovely manner and he plainly adored Theresa. Anyone could see that.

The two had met as postgraduate students at St Andrew's. He was in archaeology — tombs and bones, he declared in sonorous tones — and Theresa was a geology student. Craig had made various puns about rocks and hard places when he asked her out.

Kay watched as Theresa raised her veil and Craig leaned forward to kiss his new bride, and she felt the swell of emotion playing havoc with her insides. Who had decided that joy should make us weep? Adam squeezed her hand and she turned to smile at him, blinking hard.

The organ struck up and people prepared to follow the couple out of the church. She gestured to Dominic and the twins to get ready. She felt drained. There would be photographs now, then the reception, then a dance going on late into the evening. Hours before she could slip her shoes off and her girdle and lie down, and already she could feel a headache starting. Just tension. It was supposed to be a happy day but she felt silly and emotional and off-kilter. To do with her little girl being all grown up and married she supposed. Mrs Craig Murray. Theresa Murray. Tess, Craig called her, a nickname of his own which Theresa accepted without any qualms. Even though Theresa had left home six years ago for university, marriage put the seal on it. And they'd be so far away. Exeter had been bad enough but Craig had taken a post in Boston. Only for three years, Theresa had reassured her, we'll be back then. But Kay wondered. They were always saying it was hard to find posts in the UK. You read about the *brain drain* in the papers. She would miss her. And if they had children . . .

'C'mon, Mum!' Theresa yelled. She'd had her hair dressed long, always conscious of her ear, and found a broad lace hairband to frame her face and cover her ears. They had set her hair in ringlets and woven silk flowers through them to match her dress of ivory silk. Kay thought she looked like someone from a medieval painting.

The mother of the bride hurried to her place in the group. She had been going to WeightWatchers for six months in anticipation of this day, she'd lost eight pounds, that was all, eight rotten pounds after weeks of Ryvita and cottage cheese. The outfit she had bought — a light, grey jersey sleeveless dress and jacket — was her usual size, but it was the best quality, cut well so it looked simple and elegant. She had dyed her hair a rich brown and covered up the sprinkling of grey hairs she had. You couldn't see much of it beneath her large, grey hat, but she'd take that off once they had done the photographs.

'Now, everyone, say Manchester!' the photographer said. They all obliged.

'What about Aberdeen?' Craig called out.

'Go on then,' the photographer said, 'after three.'

She would miss her. It was so hard letting them go.

* * *

Theresa

The university in Boston ensured that all staff had adequate healthcare plans and when Theresa became pregnant there was no problem in covering the costs of antenatal care.

Her mother had been practically delirious when she'd received the news. Had rung them and then written, burbling with excitement. A few days ago a parcel had arrived: new baby clothes. She'd sent Babygros, vests, mittens and bootees — yellow and white. There was a second parcel with a note attached:

> *Theresa — these were what you had when you came to us, I've been keeping them for you, love Mum.*

She unwrapped it and found a shawl, silk-and-wool, with a delicate scalloped design, and a little hand-knitted coat in lemon. *When you came to us*. Someone had dressed her in these, got her ready for her new family. She wondered who. And who had provided the clothes? Had her real mother knitted the coat? She felt a little uneasy thinking about it. It didn't matter really. The shawl was lovely and she would use it for her own baby.

'She never had this,' Theresa remarked to Craig one night as they lay in bed, his hand on her belly feeling the baby wriggling inside. The sheets pulled back so they could see the movements too.

'She had you though. And Dominic and Martin and Michael.'

'But it's different.'

'Yes?' He waited.

'It's not a straight swap, is it? Having a child of your own or adopting one. They were probably encouraged to think of it like that when there were loads of us up for grabs.'

He looked at her, narrowed his eyes at the unexpected sting in her words.

'But you don't get *your* baby,' she continued, 'you don't go through all this feeling it grow and then having it and knowing it already, knowing it came from you. Ow!' She gasped as the lump stretched the skin on the left of her belly. 'It must still hurt. Being infertile. Even if you get a family through adoption. Mum's never given birth, I can't share all that with her.'

He drummed his fingers on the rounded lump still visible and it twisted away in response. She gave a little laugh. 'What about your mum, did she ever tell you what her labours were like?'

'Good God, woman—' he flared his nostrils and raised his eyebrows — 'are ye mad? Dates and times and birth weight and that was quite enough biological detail as far as my parents were concerned.'

'They're not that bad.'

'They are. Not quite under the gooseberry bush maybe, but pretty damn near. D'you think the wee one can hear us?'

'Yeah.'

'I can sing it a wee lullaby, teach it a little of its sacred Scottish ancestry.' He rubbed his hand over the dome, put his mouth just below her navel and sang: '*Ally-bally, ally-bally bee, sitting on his mammy's knee, waiting for his wee bobbie, to buy some Coulter's candy . . .*'

She giggled. 'It tickles.' She pushed his head. He grunted and kissed her belly. He continued to stroke at it in circles, making the sweeps a little wider each time.

She made a small sound in her throat. He knew exactly what it meant. He slid his hand down the slope of her belly, over the bush of pubic hair and slowly, slowly in amongst it. She arched her back slightly and twisted, offering him a nipple. He licked it and felt the reaction where his fingers lay.

As they made love she thought of the baby, conceived this way and soon to be born as a result. The whole thing seemed prosaic and precious and preposterous at the same time.

* * *

She felt sweaty and couldn't stop trembling. She was relieved though. They hadn't done a C-section on her. The rates in some of the hospitals were frightening. A testimony to the medicalisation of childbirth and to the triumph of technology over necessity. Plus there was the risk of people suing each other all the time. She'd heard things were more relaxed in parts of the UK. You could have home births and domino schemes where you just went in for the actual delivery and home as soon as you liked.

She had tentatively enquired about a home birth in Boston and the obstetrician had looked at her as though she had suggested stuffing and roasting her child at birth. So she had concentrated on stressing her desire for a normal delivery, even if that meant a long labour. Thank God the baby had been presenting in the right position and she had deliberately delayed going into the hospital until the contractions were well established. By the time she allowed Craig to get her into the car the pains were so intense that she was unable to sit down and had to travel in the back with her bum in the air.

Her waters broke in the corridor. A shocking sensation but one that amused her too. Nature triumphs again. She caught Craig's eye, the glint in her own helping him relax.

'They'll add it to the bill,' he hissed at her. 'Cleaning charges.'

They wanted to wheel her to the maternity suite but she couldn't sit in the chair and in the end they allowed her to walk, stopping every few yards to weather a contraction. Once there, she changed into a loose-fitting nightdress she had brought with her. Craig tried to help but his nervousness made him incapable of fixing the buttons.

A midwife checked her pulse, blood pressure, felt her stomach and said she needed to do an internal examination. She asked Craig to step outside.

'I want him to stay,' Theresa said. 'He's seen it all before.'

Craig raised his eyebrows. She wasn't usually so blunt, but needs must.

The midwife didn't press the matter.

'Eight centimetres dilated,' she announced. 'That's very good. If you just get comfy we'll pop this round you so we can see how Baby's doing.'

Theresa shook her head. She had read countless books on childbirth, attended classes, taken up yoga, and knew that if she put the monitor on her ability to move about would disappear. 'I don't want to lie down, not yet.'

'This is just so we can make sure all is well with Baby, we can see on the screen at a glance if there's any problem.'

Before she could argue, a contraction swept through her, robbing her of words. She pitched forward, leaning over the bed, and Craig hurried to hold her from behind.

'We'd rather leave it for now,' Craig said. 'You have those listening devices, don't you?'

The midwife nodded and went to get the sonic aid.

Theresa straightened up. 'Oh, God, she doesn't like it, does she?'

'Dinna fash yerself. You thirsty?'

'No.'

'Hungry?'

'No. Put that chair the other way round, I'll try sitting on that.'

He moved it and Theresa straddled the chair. She tried to relax, to let her body rest before the next flood of pain.

Four hours later she began to push, on the bed now but not strapped up. Kneeling on one knee and holding tight to Craig and to one of the midwives. She was thinking maybe a Caesarean wasn't such a bad idea.

'I can see the head!' Craig yelled. 'Oh, Tess . . .'

The child slid out and Theresa was aware of the bustle of activity, and the shaking of her legs. She closed her eyes, momentarily drunk with relief. When she opened them again she looked down at the infant, red limbs performing a jerky dance, the small face mobile and alert, huge eyes. They helped her to sit back on to the bed and handed her the baby.

'A wee girl,' Craig said.

'Is she all right?' She was desperate now to know, her eyes checking ears and fingers for anything missing, anything not properly formed.

'She's perfect.'

'Hello.' She stared at the baby. 'Craig.' She turned to him, her face wet with tears, screwed tight with emotion. 'Look at her.'

'She's beautiful.' Craig cleared his throat.

'No,' she squeaked. She shook her head and tears coursed down her face.

'What is it?'

She wept, trying to swallow enough to allow her to speak. 'She looks like me.' She took a shuddering breath.

'Of course she does.'

'No,' she said again, her voice high and out of control. 'You don't understand. She looks like me. That's never happened before. It's the first time I've ever known anybody who looks like me.' And she began to cry helplessly again.

PART FOUR: SEARCHING

MEGAN/MARJORIE/NINA

Nina

'We've been up half the bloody night. Your mother's been lying up there worrying herself sick and you waltz in, half-cut and stinking like a brewery.' As he yelled the chords in his neck stood out like ropes, his face was purple and some spit flew out.

Maybe he'd have a stroke. She was ashamed of the thought but what the hell. She was sick of him.

'Said I'd be late.' She tried not to mix her words up. She was going to throw up. Vodka and barley wine. Rotten mix. 'I need the loo.'

'I haven't finished!' he thundered. 'You're fifteen—'

'Dad, please.' Her mouth filled with saliva.

'Midnight. We said midnight.'

'Sorry,' she managed. She lurched towards the stairs but it was too late, she retched and a stream of vomit hit the carpet.

'Sweet Jesus!' he cursed.

'Toilet. Now!' Marjorie appeared at the top of the stairs.

Pressing her hands over her mouth, Nina ran up to the bathroom, her oesophagus contracting in preparation for the next eruption.

Her mother followed her and filled the basin while Nina hung over the toilet. When she'd emptied herself she wiped the strings of saliva from her chin and flushed it all away. She washed her hands and face. Marjorie said nothing.

'I'm sorry,' she said. 'I'll clear it up.'

'I know your idea of clearing up. It'll need bicarb to get the smell out and Dettol I shouldn't wonder. Go get yourself to bed. We'll talk about this in the morning.'

She couldn't resist the dig, thought Nina as she brushed her teeth. Her mother was always on about clearing up and being clean and tidy. As if being good at dusting or bloody ironing was in any way important. It was pathetic. And Stephen never had to do any of it, did he?

She drank some water. Her throat was raw and the sharp smell of sick clung to her. Shame. It'd been a good night until she'd had to come back here. They'd got into the Ritz, she and Chloe. They'd plastered loads of make-up on, it wasn't hard to pass for eighteen, they'd even memorised false birth dates in case they got asked.

They'd got off with two blokes from Warrington way. When they left the club the blokes were planning to drive back but it was obvious that all four of them wanted something else before they left. 'Bit of kissing and cuddling,' Grant had said to her. They'd all sat in the car and shared a joint. It was grass and smelt like hay, which struck Nina as hilarious after a few tokes. Then Grant had taken her round the back, where there was a little alleyway. Chloe and John got to stay in the car, which was his dad's.

They'd done it standing up against the wall. Knee trembler. He went on longer than Gary had ever managed and it was all right, but when he kissed her it was like he was hoovering.

After, on the all-night bus back, Chloe had told her that John had wanted to lick her down there. She'd said no. Nina wondered what it would feel like. She couldn't remember much else about getting home.

In her room she threw her clothes on the chair and got her nightie on. She kept stumbling and the room kept tipping.

She pulled the sheets and blankets up and turned off the light. The room swayed and her head began to thump. She put the light back on and pushed her pillow up against the headboard so she could sit up a bit. She hadn't really liked Grant. He'd made lots of jokes that weren't very funny and when she said anything he'd only half-listened, his eyes roaming round the rest of the talent. She knew he was only after one thing but he didn't pretend otherwise. Didn't matter to her. Could have been anybody. Wham bam, thank you ma'am. It made her feel good, not the sex so much but the fact that someone had picked her. Someone wanted her. The worst thing of all was to come home and you'd not copped off. That was the pits.

* * *

Megan

'I'm afraid he's simply not responding to any of the measures we've tried.' The head teacher frowned. 'And, as we said at the outset, there'll have to be some clear signs of improvement, otherwise Aidan would have to leave.'

'And then what?' Megan said. 'What is there for him then?'

Mr Brookes sighed. He reminded her of a baddie in a James Bond film, one of those public-school type actors whose sophistication hid real evil. Mr Brookes used fancy language and lots of slow sighs but he could snarl with the rest of them.

'If there were more resources open to us then perhaps things could be different.'

'His attendance is better,' Brendan tried. 'Up five per cent you said.'

Mr Brookes nodded once. 'But that's still only giving us fifty-five per cent, and his behaviour when he *is* in school remains unsatisfactory.'

'So that's it,' Megan said. 'Exclusion and he's back on the streets day in, day out.'

'For the school this is the only appropriate course of action.'

'Right.' Megan got quickly to her feet, a rush of anger flared through her chest.

'Megan?' Brendan stood too, confused by her sudden move.

'Mrs Conroy,' said Brookes.

'Don't bother,' she said, 'we get the message. And so will he. Thirteen and on the scrap heap. I know he's a handful, we know he's got problems. Do you think we haven't worried ourselves sick about it all? Not knowing if the next knock on the door's going to be the police saying he's been thieving again or he's been found behind the wheel of a wrecked . . .' She faltered, sniffed hard and set her jaw. 'We've done our best. Maybe it's not been enough but we haven't given up on him. Not like you lot. This school, you labelled him a troublemaker as soon as he walked in those doors and you couldn't wait to be rid . . .'

'Megan!' Brendan protested.

'It's true,' she retorted then turned back to Brookes. 'This solves your problem but it does nothing for Aidan. Did anyone here ever praise that boy when he *did* try? Eh? Not once did any of you really give him a chance, really put some time and effort into him . . .'

'We have six hundred . . .'

'You failed him!' Her voice rose and she pointed at the man. 'And it's a bloody disgrace.'

She walked to the door, trembling all over. She could feel a sheen of sweat on her forehead.

Mr Brookes cleared his throat. 'I'm sorry you feel . . .' His tone was languid, cool, he chose his words with care.

'Oh, don't bother! Save your breath.'

She walked out.

Brendan followed her, his eyes flicking to her and away several times as if he was worried she might start in on him next.

In the car she put her head in her hands. 'It's like waiting for an accident to happen. Like those dreams you have where the brakes don't work or the steering wheel comes off in your hands. It's driving me up the wall, Brendan. If I only knew why he was like that, what makes him so unhappy he's got to get into all this bother. The next time he's caught it's a detention centre and that'll just make it worse — schools for crime, they are.'

'Megan, you said in there, we've done our best. And we have. We haven't slung him out or let him down, have we?'

She shook her head, pressed her lips together as her eyes smarted.

'But it's not enough,' she whispered. 'Why couldn't we make him happy?'

'Come here.' He put his arm round her, pulled her closer. 'It'll be all right.'

Oh, Brendan, she thought, no, it won't.

* * *

Nina

She had no idea how to go about tracing her mother. She went to Didsbury library and looked for books. There were two on adoption; she flicked through them quickly; there were lots of different people's stories about what had happened to them. She didn't want to read all that, just find out how to get started. At the back of one she found a list of places and she copied them down but she didn't understand how it all fitted together.

Maybe she could try Central Library, they should have more books and maybe something directly about how to trace someone. She hadn't been to Central Library for yonks. She'd joined once when her art teacher had got on to them all to use it for a project on the cubists and the impressionists. She still had her tickets.

She told Marjorie she was going to town.

'Take this—' Marjorie opened her purse — 'in case you see something you like.'

'Thanks.' She felt awkward. If Marjorie had any inkling of where she was really going . . . The thought made her stomach clutch, a cold, rolling feeling as though the tide had come in. But if she refused the money how could she explain? She nodded and pushed the money into the back pocket of her jeans.

The library sat on the corner of Oxford Road and Mosely Street. A circular building, white stone with a domed roof and columns that made her think of postcards from foreign holidays. She went up in the cramped lift to the social sciences section. There were several books on adoption. She skimmed through and selected a handful and took them to a table to look at. She had brought pen and paper with her. Some of them used charts and tables to show the paths you could try to find someone — there were lots of different possibilities, but finding out if your birth mother was married was important because the name would change. Was she married? Had she had any more children? She felt dizzy when she tried to imagine that. She shut the book and opened another. It talked mainly about the need for counselling at every stage and said that counselling was mandatory for getting records. There were other places you could try too, like electoral rolls if you knew where they lived. One paragraph said the mother sometimes sent a note to the agency so if the child came looking they could find her. Imagine that.

She made notes but it all seemed to be a tangle and there were places that sounded the same but had different addresses so she wrote both down. By the time she had finished she felt overwhelmed. She put the books back and got the lift down to the cafe for a drink and a smoke.

The cafe was so gloomy, a real dive. She wondered whether they made it look like that on purpose so people wouldn't use it much. There weren't that many seats and the staff acted like they'd rather slit your throats than serve you drinks.

She smoked hungrily and washed away the parched feeling with swigs of coffee. She was just finishing when Tracy Metcalfe, who'd been in her class at school, swam into view.

'Hiya, Nina. Fancy seeing you here. What you doing?'

Nina held herself still. Tracy had a gob like the Mersey Tunnel and was reputed to have done it when she was just thirteen. Tracy was a greaser with an eye for weaklings. Nina was no pushover but you didn't want to get on the wrong side of Tracy Metcalfe. And what the hell was she doing at Central Library?

'Having a ciggie. What about you?' Nina tried to erase any sign of panic from her eyes.

'That'd be telling!' Tracy winked, swung her leather shopper off her arm.

Nina grinned.

Tracy sat down.

'I've got to get my bus,' Nina said.

Tracy nodded. She rooted in her bag for Number Six and Zippo lighter. 'Tara!' She clicked the lighter and sucked hard, flung her throat back in a gesture of pleasure.

Nina fled.

Back home she went slowly upstairs and put her notes in among her art folder. She was confident no one would rummage through that. Her mother was hoovering the dining room. Nina put the kettle on. Stephen came in the back door, saw the gas was on.

'Make me one.'

'Make your own,' she said.

'*Nina*.'

'Well, when did you last make some?'

'Yesterday.'

'Not for me you didn't.'

'You are so childish.'

'Fuck off!' she said. And saw his shock. He never swore. He looked at her but he didn't even look mad just sorry for her or something. He shook his head and walked out. Making allowances.

She hated that. Hated him. She didn't need his fucking pity. She stood there, her arms locked across her body, her back rigid with tension. She'd show him, she'd show them all. Her real family, they'd be different. They wouldn't pity her or feel disappointed in her. They'd understand. Well, it would probably just be her real mother but they'd be able to talk to each other. She'd be accepted for what she was, not what she was expected to be in someone's boring little mind.

The kettle began to whistle and she turned off the gas. Her mother came in rolling the hoover. 'I'd love a cuppa, Nina.' She pushed the pantry door open and put the hoover away.

Nina poured water into the pot and swilled it round, went to open the caddy.

'How was town? Did you get anything?'

'No.' her skin prickled and her breath caught in her throat. 'No, I didn't see anything.'

* * *

The following day she tried to make sense of the notes but she wasn't sure which place to start with.

'Ring Social Services,' Chloe said when she told her. 'They'll know.'

She found the number in the phone book but it was another two days before she got the house to herself and a chance to use the phone. It was engaged at first, then she got passed on to a different department.

At last she spoke to someone who could deal with her. The woman asked her if she had her original birth certificate.

'No.' Mum and Dad might have it but she couldn't ask them.

'Do you know what your name at birth was?'

'Yes.' Claire Driscoll.

'Good. If you know your name you can buy a copy of your original birth certificate. I'll tell you where to write. When you've done that it will give you information about your birth mother and where she was living when you were born. Then, if you wish to, you can apply to see your adoption records — they are usually kept by the agency who arranged the adoption. But those aren't automatically handed over, you have to see a social worker before you get them. We make sure everyone has that basic counselling before they have access to their records. A lot of people find it very helpful.'

Nina was scribbling down as much as she could.

'So, first I need my birth certificate?'

'Yes, you write to the General Records Office and they will send you a form. I'll give you their address in a minute. They make a small charge, a few pounds or so, for a copy.'

'Right.'

Nina wrote the address down.

'When you've got your birth certificate you can ring here again and we can make an appointment with a social worker.'

'Thanks.'

She dropped the receiver as she replaced it, her hands were trembling. God. Maybe she should just leave it? She looked at what she had scrawled on the paper. If she just got the birth certificate, it didn't mean she had to do anything else. Before she could get any more confused about it all she went up to her room, got out notepaper and an envelope, wrote asking for her birth certificate, sealed the letter and addressed the envelope. She sent it that afternoon, a sense of occasion. She would have to watch the post. A thrill made her want to run, or jump up and down. It was exciting, there was an undercurrent too, a pull of guilt as though she had done something naughty and might get caught. But it was done now. No turning back.

* * *

They told her to apply again when she was eighteen. Nina was furious. 'I can get married,' she ranted to Chloe, 'leave home, work in a poxy little job for forty hours a week, but I can't find out who I am!'

'Could you find her without those papers?'

'Chloe, I don't know her full name. I can't do anything till I have that. I'll have to wait. They said it might be different if I had my parents' permission but there's no way I'm asking them. They'd go mad.'

'You don't know that.'

'I do know that. But the day I'm eighteen I'll do it.'

Chloe leaned forward into the mirror and applied thick black mascara to her lashes. 'What if you don't like her?'

Nina shrugged. 'It's all right for you, least you know where you come from, who you look like.'

'Yeah, the bloody Adams family!'

'Give over.'

'Pink or yellow?' Chloe held up eye shadows.

'Pink — and you should do your mascara last.'

'Says who?'

'Well, you'll get pink all over it now, and then you'll have to do it again.'

'Are you coming like that?' Chloe raked her eyes over Nina's unadorned complexion.

'No.'

'Well, get a move on. It's a pound more after nine o'clock.'

* * *

Marjorie

She loved this place. And it was always such a contrast with home. Each summer she'd be surprised afresh at the rough plaster walls, the stone-flagged floors, the simmering views over gauzy hillside terraces and fields. The hillsides were mauve and olive from the wild thyme and lavender. She relished the sound of cowbells in the air and the incessant chattering of the small birds that swooped in and out of their nests under the eaves, the smell of sun-baked pine.

They had all their holidays in southern France.

It had been an idyll, but now . . .

She waited in the sitting room, close to the drive for any sound that would interrupt the shrilling of the cicadas, swivelling the bracelet on her wrist. Moths batted against the windows, crazy for the light.

At last she heard the crunch of gravel and hurried to the door. It was Stephen on his butcher's bike. He slithered to a stop and propped the bike against the wall.

'She's in the square,' he said. 'She's been drinking. She was in the fountain.'

'Oh, God!' Marjorie closed her eyes at the thought.

'Dad's bringing her back.'

'Come in.'

'I hate her, Mummy,' he blurted out, his normally placid expression twisted with dislike. 'She ruins everything. She doesn't care about anyone but herself. Her top was all wet. Everyone could see.'

She shared his shame and anger. 'Oh, Stephen!'

'Why do you let her do things like that?'

What do you expect, she wanted to say, what can we do? If she's hell-bent on raising Cain how can we stop her. Lock her up?

'I'm sorry. You mustn't let it spoil the holiday.'

'Frederique came out of the restaurant and asked her to get out and she just made fun of him. You could see how upset he was.'

He began to cry and she pulled him close. He was taller than she was now, his chin on her head as he cried. Compassion choked her. And guilt. Could they have done more? What, though? Oh, my poor boy. It's so unfair. Thank God he was off to university in October. Away from all the awful arguments.

She heard the sound of a car drawing closer. Stephen pulled away. 'I'm going to bed.'

'There's milkshake in the fridge if you want to take some.'

She let him go and watched as the car headlights swept in at the end of the drive, picking out the Bougainvillea that scrambled along the wall. Her stomach fluttered with dread at the shouting match to come.

Robert cut the engine and snapped off the lights. Nina was still. Thank God she's not singing.

Robert opened his door. 'Get a towel,' he called.

She went in and fetched one of the beach towels from the drying rack in the kitchen. When she returned, Robert was by the house. He took it from her and opened the passenger door. Marjorie half-expected Nina to fall out like some comic drunk but she didn't move.

'Get out,' Robert said coldly, holding the towel up, the gesture at odds with his tone.

Nina got out slowly. As she stepped away from the car the light from the lantern by the front door fell on her.

Marjorie gasped.

Nina's face was cut, an angry gash bled below one eye, her eye half-shut. Her upper lip was split and swollen. Her wet blouse was torn and Marjorie could see another mark on her upper arm. Her hair was plastered to the side of her head. The cloud of moths batted against the light, casting shadows over Nina's wounds. A bat flew swiftly above.

'What on earth's happened?'

Nina looked blankly at Marjorie.

Robert draped the towel around her.

'Nina?'

'Leave her,' Robert instructed.

'Robert?' She didn't understand.

'Go to your room,' he told his daughter.

She began to move slowly, walking stiffly, her face still expressionless.

'But she's hurt.'

'Let her go.'

'What on earth has happened?'

'She's had a bloody good hiding, that's what. Knock some sense into her. And not before time.'

She stared at him incredulous, felt the hairs on her arms prickle.

He gave a short humourless laugh and shook his head. 'She's had it coming, Marjorie. There are limits. Should have done it years ago.' He went inside.

She moved, balanced against the little archway to the side of the door. Traditionally a shrine to the Virgin Mary.

She looked up at the sky but in place of the stars she saw only the brutal damage that Robert had done. It was wrong. No matter how far Nina had pushed him, to do that . . . break her face, beat her up. She covered her mouth with her hand. She felt sick. She closed her eyes and prayed: *Sweet mother of God, help me. Oh, God, help me.*

* * *

Nina

Life was a mix of work and waiting. She'd got taken on by British Home Stores at the Arndale Centre. She knew her parents were disappointed. They had wanted her to get more qualifications. 'I've five O levels,' she told them.

'Well, why stop now?' Robert Underwood demanded. 'You're a bright enough girl, if you'd only apply yourself . . .'

'I don't want to. I've had enough of all that.'

'You could even go to art school,' he said in desperation. He'd always regarded her success in art as an amusing but essentially irrelevant achievement.

'I'm not going back, I'm going to get a job.'

'You're cutting your nose off to spite your face!' he shouted.

'You don't even listen. You never try to see my side of things!' She had slammed out of the room. Silence clouded the days that followed. Cold disapproval. She comforted herself with the thought that she would save once she was working and she would get enough to put a little deposit down on something. And before long she'd have a place of her own and he'd have to eat his words.

But saving hadn't been easy, she didn't know where all the money went. She gave Marjorie some for her bed and board and she bought quite a lot of clothes from work, where they got staff discount. She got the chance to move into window dressing after her first three months. A chance to use her eye for colour and design.

On her eighteenth birthday she wrote again for her birth certificate. It took almost six weeks for it to come after she had returned the fee and the application form. Nina had stopped watching the post quite so avidly. It was Stephen who brought it into the kitchen, where Marjorie was clearing up the breakfast post and Nina about to leave for work. It was a training day.

'Official letter for Nina.' Stephen waved the brown envelope.

She snatched it from him. She saw the postmark and her stomach swooped.

'Who's it from?' Marjorie asked.

'Work, something to do with the tax office. I'll be late, better go.'

She didn't dare open the letter on the bus, she needed to do it in private. She was eager to know what it said but also frightened. It was like opening a Pandora's box.

She tried to pay attention as they went through the forthcoming season's plans, stock returns and health and safety but her mind darted back to the envelope all the time. She waited until after tea at home to go up to her room and open the letter. She used her nail file to slit it open. She drew out the certificate and unfolded it. Pink paper, the headings all in red ink. Her eyes flew across the columns. Megan Driscoll . . . Collyhurst . . . Claire. She forced herself to stop and read it slowly.

> *When and where born: Twenty-fourth May 1960, Withington Hospital, Nell Lane, Withington.*
> *Name, if any: Claire.*

She had looked up Claire and it meant clear or bright, a nice name.

> *Sex: girl.*
> *Name and surname of father:* just a dash across the page.

Name, surname and maiden surname of mother: Megan Agnes Driscoll (factory worker), 14 Livesey Street, Collyhurst.

An address, a proper address. Some places put down the mother and baby home, she'd read, but this was her real address. She couldn't sit still, she jumped up and walked slowly about, continuing to read.

Occupation of father: another line struck through the column.
Signature, description and residence of informant: Megan Driscoll, mother, 14 Livesey Street, Collyhurst.
When registered: Twentieth June 1960.
Signature of registrar: D.H. Coombes, Registrar.

And at the edge of the page, D.H. Coombes had written *Adopted* and signed it.

There was nothing about how old Megan had been. She scanned it again to make sure. *Megan Agnes Driscoll.* And the address. With that she had some place to start from. She read and reread the piece of paper. Megan, wasn't that a Welsh name? But Driscoll sounded Irish. There were loads of Irish in Manchester. Collyhurst was just out of town. She had passed through there on the way to Leeds on the coach. It was a run-down area, lots of slums. She thought they'd knocked quite a bit of it down.

She could look it up in the A-Z, see if it was still there. She wanted to go there now. Daft. She told herself to calm down, sit down. Her ears were buzzing with the excitement and her heart felt like it was too big. That'd be great, wouldn't it? Have a heart attack and die before she could trace her. Marjorie and Robert finding her, the certificate clutched in her hand. Wracked with remorse for never understanding her.

She pulled out her portfolio from under the bed, brushed off the fluff and dust and untied the ribbon. She got out her folder and looked again at the notes she'd made from the books and from the phone call with the social worker. She could use this now to write to the adoption agency, the Catholic children's place, and to ask them for her adoption records. But she'd be expected to have counselling from someone before she was given them. She might as well see what they had. There was nothing to stop her seeing if the house was still there in the meantime.

* * *

She went the following Saturday. Collyhurst was awful. Even worse on foot. She felt out of place and some boys had called out at her, made dirty suggestions which made her feel frightened. There was no 14 Livesey Street. The whole lot had been flattened. There was just a big patch of waste land and, beyond the railway bridge which crossed the street, there was a primary school and a scrap yard.

She had passed some shops a few minutes down the main road with a newsagents amongst them. She retraced her steps and went in. She had practised a story, which she trotted out to the woman behind the counter and the customer she was chatting to. Nina said she had moved away and lost touch with relatives who had lived on Livesey Street. When had they knocked the houses down?

'Be a good few years now,' the shopkeeper said. 'You could try asking at the Housing. Some people went out to Wythenshawe. What were they called, love?'

'Driscoll.'

Recognition lit the woman's face. 'Anthony Driscoll. They had a stall on Tib Street for years. Don't think they've got it now though.'

Would that be Megan's father? Nina's grandfather.

'And Grey Mare Lane,' the other woman piped up.

'I couldn't swear to it but I think they moved out to Wythenshawe when they did the clearance. Try the Housing, they should know.'

Nina nodded and left.

It was cold and she struggled against the wind as she walked back along Oldham Street to Piccadilly Gardens. People waited at the bus stops, many of them poorly dressed and carrying bulging shopping bags. Nina was aware of her neat, new clothes — one of the perks of working at the shop. A couple of tramps were begging and Nina gave them some change. The wind seemed to howl down the street, lifting litter and dust and blowing over a sandwich board outside one of the shops.

Wythenshawe was the other side of Manchester, near the airport. A stall on Tib Street and Grey Mare Lane, a market. Nina had never been there but it would be like the market in Longsight, she thought, cheap and cheerful. Was that what Megan did? Worked on the market with her family? Outdoors in all weathers. She might be really common, swearing and rollers in her hair, like Hilda Ogden off Coronation Street. And what would Megan make of Nina? A right snob? But then when she was adopted that's what people wanted, didn't they? A better life, a good home for their child.

* * *

In Piccadilly the pigeons flew in an arc around the gardens. The place was noisy and busy and her bus was full so she had to stand all the way back. If she got stuck tracing Megan she could always try finding her father first in Wythenshawe, look in the phone book. Nina was getting closer. The bus lurched to a halt suddenly as the driver swerved to avoid a car. People muttered and cursed. Nina straightened up, smiled at the woman who'd bumped into her. She must tell Chloe. What next? She could try and find a marriage at the records place so she'd know if Megan had changed her name, or she could just go up to the markets the woman had talked about and see if anyone knew where the family had moved. Or try the Housing Department, but she thought they might be a bit cagey about giving details out unless you could prove a connection. She could even put a little advert in the paper. But that felt scary. How would people contact her anyway without Marjorie and Robert finding out? It was probably best to wait and get her proper records. After all, Megan might have sent details of where she was so she could be easily found. Yes, she'd hang on and do that first.

* * *

'There are only the formal records, I'm afraid,' the counsellor said. She held the large manilla envelope in her hand. Nina wanted to snatch it from her.

'Sometimes there is a letter or photo but that's less likely because of the time when you were adopted. In the sixties your birth mother would have been told very clearly that she was giving up all right to you, she had to swear in court, to make everything legal.' She drew out the papers. 'I'll just explain what's here and then I'll give you a little time to yourself if that's what you'd like?'

Nina nodded. Get on with it. Her palms were damp and her throat felt as though she'd overeaten.

'This is the History Sheet.' She showed Nina a typed-up form. 'It would have been made by the social worker when your mother first applied to the society for help, and attached are some notes obviously made after you were born. Then there's this medical record — all the children had to be examined by the doctor, of course. I'll be next door if you need anything or want to ask any questions.'

Nina felt disappointment steal through her. There was so little. She read it through slowly. There was some new information. Her mother's age — sixteen, only sixteen — and a note that she had been a packer in a factory. She read the handwritten sheet.

24/5/60 Baby girl born at Withington. Both well.
27/5/60 Baby baptised Claire by Father Quinlan.
10/7/60 Baby placed for adoption with Mr and Mrs Underwood, 29 Darley Road, West Didsbury, Manchester.
12/7/60 Megan discharged home.

Two days after, oh God! She wiped at her eyes. Looked at the medical form — nothing there of interest except her birth weight, six pounds twelve ounces.

Nothing about who the father might be or how Megan came to be pregnant.

No letters.

No photo.

She had been expecting so much more.

Maybe Megan didn't care, hadn't cared. Maybe 'Claire' had been the result of some silly mistake, larking about with some loser from the market or the factory, him taking advantage and bingo, a bun in the oven. A problem to be got rid of. Forgotten about. These days she'd have an abortion, it was illegal back then and dangerous. Nina was furious. She hated her. How could she just leave her like that? Walk away and never, not once, think about her and leave some sign.

When the counsellor returned, Nina tried to hide her rage but it was too big for that, clambering all over her.

'I want to punch her,' she blurted out. 'That sounds stupid doesn't it?'

The counsellor talked about anger and emotions and how she might feel lots of different things and try to accept them. She gave her leaflets and a magazine. She told her to take things at her own pace and to come back any time if she wanted to. She talked about the importance of using a go-between if she tried to find her mother, an intermediary she called it. Less threatening all round. Nina nodded to show she was listening but already her thoughts were racing ahead. She'd find her, see what she had to say for herself.

'Some people wait a long time, years and years, before they are ready to start tracing, some don't go further than this, it's enough for them.'

Not for me, Nina thought. Can't stop now. It was the only thing she could think of. She had to do it, the sooner the better. Whatever it was like.

* * *

'We don't know where to turn, Father. It's affected the whole family. I'm only glad Stephen doesn't have to put up with it.'

'He's gone to Birmingham, is that right?'

'Yes, he's doing really well. But Nina, this constant depression. Moodiness. I can't remember the last time there was any joy in the house. It's like walking on eggshells.'

'Adolescence is a tricky time,' he agreed, 'hormones all over the place, identity crisis, the rest of the world all seem to be against you. But it will pass.'

'Will it? I don't know, I think it's more than just the usual teenage ups and downs.'

'You're not the first parent to sit here and say that. When you're in the middle of it, it seems never ending. Talk to your husband, try and share this, support each other.'

If only, she thought. Robert had completely withdrawn from any attempt to be a father to Nina. He endured her presence at mealtimes and that was it. Marjorie felt as if they were all actors pretending to be a family but with no conviction.

None of them ever referred to the night in France. Marjorie had tried to talk to Nina about it. Just the once. 'I'm sorry,' she had said the following morning as the two of them sat on the verandah eating bread and apricot preserve and drinking coffee. The sight of Nina's face sickened her. 'Nina, I'm sure he never really . . .'

'It wasn't you,' Nina said. 'You don't need to be sorry. I don't want to talk about it, anyway.'

It was like a boulder of shame rolling round the house, like a leg iron they each wore, silent and invisible but dragging the life from them. She could never tell the priest about it. That would be disloyal. And Nina had been difficult before then.

She knew Nina continued to drink too much, probably meddled with drugs as well but she no longer flaunted her abandonment for the family to see. She spent a lot of time at her friend Chloe's. She had become secretive, withdrawn and uncommunicative. The fight had gone from her and now she was sullen instead.

'I don't know how to help her, Father. There doesn't seem to be anything I can do.'

The priest nodded. 'Listen,' he said. 'That's all you can do. Be there for her and listen.'

What to, she thought, the sound of silence?

* * *

Nina

'Have you no regard for your mother's feelings?' Robert thundered, his face dark with rage.

'I never asked you to,' Nina retorted and then, sensing rather than seeing her mother flinch, she reined in her temper. 'I wasn't going to tell you, I knew you'd be upset. I've a right to find out about my own background. Lots of adopted people do it.'

'Stephen hasn't.'

'This isn't about Stephen, and it's not about you. I'm not doing it to hurt you, I'm doing it because I want to — for me. I'm sorry if you're upset.' She could hear her voice shaking and hated herself for it, 'but those are my papers and I want them back.'

'Why?' Marjorie asked. 'I don't understand why you have to drag it all up. Weren't we good enough? We love you like our own . . .' She couldn't continue and Nina looked away.

'I want to know, that's all.'

'She didn't want you,' Marjorie said. 'What is she going to feel like when you barge into her life?'

'I don't know.' She hugged her arms tight to her body.

'It's downright selfish. You go trampling all over people's feelings, not a thought for anyone else. Well, I suggest you think about this very seriously before you carry on.' He thrust the papers at her. 'And I, for one, don't want to hear another word about it. You are our daughter. We clothed you, fed you, taught you right from wrong, or tried to. This woman has never been a mother to you.' He sighed, his face folding into weariness. 'I don't know where we went wrong with you, Nina, but if you want to break your mother's heart you're going the right way about it.'

She closed her eyes. There didn't seem to be any way to make them understand. None of this should have happened. If her mother hadn't gone into her room, Nina on the bed and the papers ranged all around her. The distinctive colour of the birth certificate, the bold headings for the Catholic Rescue Society. Too late to try and scoop them up, her mother's eyes had drunk them in, looked at Nina, wounded. She tried to explain. Marjorie had made a small sound of distress and had run stumbling into Robert, who had taken her downstairs. Nina had waited for the summons. She had collected the papers together and, when he called, taken them down. Thinking with some small, uninformed part of her mind that they might care to know something of her story. Stupid. They couldn't see past their own injured feelings. They certainly weren't interested in anything she thought or felt.

'I'm sorry,' she repeated quietly and left them. In her room she stretched out fully clothed on the bed and stared at the ceiling. She wished she could cry. To let the hot churning inside go, but she couldn't. She had liked that about herself in the past: her resilience, the strength she had, but now it felt like she was choking, a chain around her heart.

I must get out of here, she thought. And soon. She lay there until the room grew dark and she climbed under the covers to get warm.

* * *

Megan

'Is that Megan?'

'Yes.'

'This is Claire.'

'Claire?'

'I'm your daughter.'

'What?'

'You had a baby in 1960, May twenty-fourth. You called me Claire.'

A rush of images flickered through Megan's mind — a matinee jacket, the prams in a row at the back of the house, the turrets on the building, her mother leaving her there, Joan and . . . the other girl, Caroline, the quiet one who tried to run away. Her own horrific labour, screaming for her mother, getting the photo . . .

'No,' she said, 'no, I can't. I'm sorry. There's been a mistake.' She put the phone down.

Her stomach clenched with spasms. She breathed in sharply. Dear God, what a mess! Oh, God! She half-expected the phone to ring again but it didn't. She heard the *Neighbours* theme tune start up. Time to get the tea on. Carry on as normal. Chicken and mushroom pies from the freezer, new potatoes, peas. Tea, wash up, telly, bed. Just keep going. Pretend it never happened.

* * *

When Brendan woke later that night she was sitting in the chair in the corner of the bedroom, a blanket round her.

'What's up?' He rolled over. He could only see her silhouetted against the window. The moon was up and it was lit up like a football pitch out there. 'Too hot? Am I snoring again, or what?'

'Brendan.'

Oh, God. He could hear the weight in her voice.

'I was thinking about Claire.'

'Ah,' he said, waited.

'If she ever tried to find us, what would we do?'

He breathed and released it slowly. What did she expect him to say? 'Well, I suppose she'd have a right, wouldn't she?'

'And Francine and the boys?'

He sighed again. 'It'd be awkward,' he said. 'I wouldn't fancy having to explain it to them.' He paused. 'Hell, Megan, we were only kids, we did what we did for the best.'

'That's what they all told us.'

'What's brought all this on?'

There was no reply.

'Megan?'

'She rang up.'

'What?' He sat up higher, turned the lamp on.

She turned her face, shielded her eyes with her hand. 'Today. She rang here. It was such a shock. I thought I was going to collapse.'

'What did she say? What happened? Are you sure it was her?'

'She just said is that Megan, I'm Claire. Your daughter. She gave her date of birth.'

'Good God!' He ran his fingers through his thinning hair several times, looked at her. 'Bloody hell!' he said.

'How did she find us?'

She shook her head, pulled her curls back and held them in her fist.

'How did she get the number?'

She shook her head again, let her hair loose. His questions were irrelevant in the light of what she had yet to tell him.

'Bloody hell,' he repeated. 'Why didn't you say 'owt?'

She sighed. 'It was such a shock, hearing like that, and I just kept saying no. I told her there was some mistake. I hung up.' She looked across at him. 'What if she never tries again? What if she does? I don't know which'd be worse. Oh, Brendan, what have I done?'

* * *

Nina

She didn't want to eat. Just looking at the food made her feel nauseous, brought a metallic wash into her mouth.

She'd skipped lunch at work too. She hadn't felt like it and then someone had come in and said there was a fire up at Woolworth's. People had been trapped inside, banging on the windows. On the bus home they said ten people had died. You heard stuff like that, saw the building and everything and people expected the world to carry on as normal.

'I'm not hungry.' She pushed herself away from the table.

'Nina . . .' Robert started.

'Leave her,' Marjorie intervened.

In her room Nina sat on the floor, back against the bed. She was wiped out. She had intended to look at flats at the weekend but she couldn't face it. Nothing mattered any more. Megan wouldn't give her houseroom, denied she was even her mother. How could she do that? She'd always been a disappointment to Marjorie, it was mutual, but she never expected to be cut off like that. The rotten cow. Self-pity made her throat ache.

'You should write,' Chloe had said. 'It must have been a shock for her, coming on the phone like that.'

'She'd probably chuck them away if I did.'

'You can't give up now. I bet if you give it a bit of time then write a note . . .'

'And what the fuck do you know about it?' She rounded on her friend.

'Pardon me for breathing!' Chloe was stung. 'I'll come back when you're fit company.'

That was rich coming from someone who spent ninety-nine per cent of her time moaning and being moody.

Chloe had hesitated at the bedroom door. 'Fancy the Ritz tomorrow night?'

Nina had shaken her head. She didn't fancy anything.

She sighed and let her head fall back against the edge of the bed. How could she hang up on her like that? Maybe someone had been listening, making it impossible for her to talk? A flicker of hope.

She stirred herself and found pen and paper. After an hour she'd got nowhere. Everything she thought of sounded like some sloppy love song. How did you write? What did you write? Sod it. She flung down the pen. What did she want? To see her and to find out why. She could hardly write that, could she? Bound to get slapped back.

She felt her anxiety rise, peeling up her back, knotting her stomach. She began to rock. It was getting worse. She'd had to leave work early on Thursday, claiming she felt sick. She'd been dressing the homewares window and had felt a powerful impulse to smash the glass, to watch it shatter and scream through it to the passing crowds. She was going mental. She must go to the doctor, see if he could give her something. But each time when the horrible feelings had gone she hoped that was the end of it.

She heard Marjorie coming upstairs and kept still and quiet. She heard the timid knock. 'Nina, are you all right?'

'I'm going to sleep.' She couldn't face her now.

'Would you like some toast or a drink or anything?'

'No, thanks.' Food turned to shit in her mouth, it was dirty. She couldn't bear the feel of it.

But she didn't sleep. She spent the night with the light on, hugging her knees, rocking and waiting for the dawn. Sick and tired and fearful of the demons inside her — nameless, faceless and getting larger by the day.

* * *

Marjorie

She hated ironing though it wasn't a chore she could get out of. She put the radio on and began on the shirts. Nina looked like death warmed up these days. She'd not eaten anything at breakfast, though she had pretended to and then slunk back to bed. The doctor had got her on sleeping pills but only for a limited period. There was a crash from upstairs and the sound of something breaking. Marjorie set the iron down and hurried upstairs.

'Nina?' She opened the door without knocking. The bedside lamp was on the floor, Nina was on the bed, eyes closed.

There was the sharp smell of vomit. 'Nina?' The bottle of pills was beside her, the lid on the floor. Oh my god. She rang an ambulance, her heart thudding in her chest, praying frantically.

Marjorie was at the hospital all night while they pumped her daughter's stomach and monitored her. Robert came too but when it was clear Nina was out of danger Marjorie sent him home. She could feel the irritation smouldering underneath his concern. His presence just added to the tension.

The following morning Nina was pale, withdrawn, submissive. For a moment Marjorie missed the turbulent, prickly young woman whose anger was so much healthier than this apathy.

After rounds they told Marjorie that Nina was being discharged; she was on antidepressants and had an outpatient appointment for the psychiatric unit.

'Gave us all a nasty scare but she should respond well to the drugs. Any worries, contact your GP.'

Robert couldn't cope with it, had no idea how to respond. Gave Nina a stiff little hug when they got back from the hospital.

Marjorie was more forthright. 'You scared the life out of me. I love you, Nina. I hate to see you like this. If you'd just talk to me.'

Nina was tired and unresponsive. The tablets coated her reactions like polystyrene. She was muffled, dopey.

Time passed, she returned to work. Slowly, steadily, she came back. But not the old Nina. It was as if the light had gone out inside her.

* * *

Megan

Her stomach lurched and she stepped into the nearest shop doorway. Panic made her want to run so the girl wouldn't see her but she told herself to 'get a bloody grip Megan' and she stepped out again. She could still see her, back view, fifty yards away, in a green coat. The hair was exactly the right shade, the same as Francine's, the same as hers. She was tall though, tall as Brendan. She followed the girl along Market Street and into Littlewood's. Megan pretended to examine leather coats by the door, bomber jackets, like Francine was angling for. She kept one eye on the red hair. Then the girl turned to leave and with a swoop of relief Megan saw she was much too old, late twenties at least.

The same sort of thing had happened half-a-dozen times in the months since Claire's phone call. It always caught her unawares and she felt so daft. She was being haunted: not by a ghost but by half the redheads in Manchester.

There'd been no more phone calls. The memory of the girl's voice, Claire's voice, and her own denial cut at her. She shouldn't have said no. If she'd only had more time, it had been such a shock. She thought of Claire ringing again with a mix of hope and fear. She longed to put things right but she didn't like to think of telling her other children about her. Perhaps it would never come to that.

A weight of disappointment settled on her and she felt like getting straight on the next bus home. But she'd only have to come in again next week to finish her Christmas shopping. She'd got sweets for her nephews and nieces, she'd exchanged most of her books of Green Shield stamps for a cassette player for Chris, who at thirteen had discovered punk rock. Bloody awful noise. He walked around looking a right sight with ripped black clothes, zips here and there, head practically shaved and a safety pin in his ear. It was all show with Chris, though. Little lamb, he was. Not like Aidan.

Maybe it was best Claire had not tried again, after all, Aidan wasn't exactly an advert for happy family life. He wouldn't be home for Christmas. He wouldn't be home for another eighteen months and how long he'd manage to stay out of trouble then was anybody's guess. When she visited him she could see the place was only making him worse. Not borstal but good as.

He'd been scared at first, she'd seen it in those first few visits: licking his lips, his knee twitching, signs a mother recognised. She was devastated. She'd still no idea why it had all gone wrong. She wanted to cuddle him better but he was a gawky fifteen-year-old and when she put her arms about him he wriggled free. As the weeks went by he started playing the hard man, growing a skin of disaffection.

The last time she'd been, his first words were, *How many fags did you bring us?* Not *Hi, Mam* or *Thanks for coming*. She wanted to shake him, to tell him that how he dealt with this place, and what he did after, would set the course for the rest of his life, that there weren't any more chances. She could give him love and help but you couldn't give a thing to someone who was turning away from you. She told him, without the shaking, and he sighed and shuffled on his chair and gave her a dead look with his eyes.

She checked her Christmas list. Francine wanted a watch. There were a couple of jewellers on Shude Hill she could try.

Francine had started her nursery nursing course. Megan had tried to talk Francine into staying on and going for A levels if she did all right in her exams but the girl didn't want to.

'Keep your options open,' Megan had said. 'If you got more qualifications you'd have a chance of more jobs, better money. There's two million people out of work, you know. A piece of paper will go a long way to getting something.'

'I want to do the nursing,' Francine insisted. 'I've had enough of school.'

Well, if it didn't work out for her with the nursing she could always work at the shop. Bit boring really but she was good with people.

Francine was courting. She and Shane seemed serious. He was a mechanic. They were saving for a deposit on a flat — rent, not buy. Megan had told her not to rush anything but Francine told her to stop fussing. 'Frightened I'll make you a grandma too soon? You needn't worry, I'm on the pill.'

Megan had looked at her. The Church still banned Catholics from any form of artificial contraception and sex before marriage was forbidden. The bishop sent letters round every so often reminding his parishioners of the edict. But the bishop hadn't got a sixteen-year-old daughter, had he?

'Good,' she said. 'Don't forget to take it.'

Francine beamed, pleased that her mam was understanding and hadn't gone all religious on her.

At least if she was protected, Megan thought, and things didn't work out for her and Shane, there wouldn't be a baby in the middle of it all to consider.

* * *

Marjorie

The doorbell rang. She wasn't expecting anyone but it could be a door-to-door salesman. There seemed to be more and more of them; wanting to demonstrate the latest vacuum cleaner or sell you household insurance or tarmac the drive. A sign of the times. Rising unemployment. The winter of discontent they called it and it had been awful, with countless strikes. People will always need glasses, Robert said, though they might patch the frames with Sellotape if times were hard. More and more people were trying contact lenses and he'd started stocking those too.

'Mrs Underwood?' Two police officers in uniform, a man and a woman.

'Yes?' She held her breath.

'Stephen Underwood's your son?'

'Yes,' she whispered, her throat suddenly dry and her chest tight.

'Can we come in a moment? It's about Stephen.'

'No.' She tried to shut the door, they moved into the way. She pushed harder. 'No,' she repeated, her voice cracking. 'No.'

'Mrs Underwood, we need to come inside and talk to you.' The man eased the door back. She moved away. The woman stepped inside, took her elbow. Marjorie twisted aside. 'No.' Her thoughts scrambling to get away.

'Come on, now.'

She let them lead her into the lounge. Her heart was galloping. She sat down, her belly heavy with dread.

She watched them mouth words, silly little words: car, roundabout, passenger, revive, failure. Silly, little words, each tearing a bit of her soul. The dread rose, flooding her throat, full of love and anger and breathtaking pain. She opened her mouth hoping that if the roar of it were loud enough it would drown out the man and the woman and bury the stupid, little words. Force them away, back down, anywhere. Stephen. Into the past, into another time, another place. Oh, Stephen. 'No-no-no-no!' she howled. 'No-no-no-God-no!'

The words floated free, too strong to be shouted down. Once spoken they soared above like balloons cut free. And burst like her heart. Stephen. Dead.

* * *

Nina

She couldn't believe it. Even now. It was like some gross practical joke. Like God had looked down and seen what a mess she was in and how bloody fed up she was. He knew how when she looked in the mirror this ugly, fat cow was there and when she looked inside herself there was just a black hole. Everyone hated her. And then God had looked at Stephen, last year of university, studying chemistry, lots of friends, popular and hardworking, even a steady girlfriend, attractive now he'd grown his blond hair longer. And God had decided to take Stephen. Not her. Or maybe he'd gone eenie-meenie-miney-mo. And Stephen was dead. When it should have been her. They all thought that. Even she did, for heaven's sake. 'Course, no one said a word, but you'd have to be mental not to think it. And she'd been such a bitch to him. Teasing him for being boring and goody-goody when he was just a boy, just a nice boy who'd learnt his manners and didn't have to put up with everyone hating him. He was dead and it was like they all were.

Her mother. The sound of her mother weeping was the loneliest sound in the universe. And Nina couldn't help her, she didn't know how. She felt responsible. It was her fault really. Her father cried too. She'd never seen him cry, but that first day he'd sat there, his red face all furrowed, eyes shut and these awful huffing sounds coming out of him. Her mother went and held him and Nina stole away. She shouldn't be there. She went upstairs and listened to them cry. She felt the pressure inside, a lump in her chest, but she couldn't cry. There was no release.

The weeks passed, Christmas and Easter came and went; their only significance was in marking Stephen's absence.

She knew she should leave. Get away so her mother wouldn't have to face her every day. See her and not Stephen, feed her and not Stephen.

Chloe invited her to move into a house she had found. It was a dump but they could sort it out a bit. Put some cotton throws over the furniture, get a couple of beanbags and some coloured light bulbs. She hadn't seen much of Chloe, who'd started a nursing course and was going out with a punk called Ali. She said yes. Spare her mother. And she'd be able to diet if she needed, without her mother watching her eat, forcing her to eat. Now she had to tell her parents.

She told them over tea.

'Oh,' her mother said softly and Nina glimpsed pain in her eyes.

Her father looked at her with incomprehension. Then he gave a short, humourless laugh and shook his head.

'Robert . . .' Marjorie said.

He held up his hands. 'I won't waste my breath.' He stood up.

'What?' Nina said.

'Never mind.'

'No, what's the matter?'

'Nina, it's all right.' Her mother tried again.

'You don't get it, do you? You really don't get it. You're so bound up in your own selfish little world . . .'

'No!' she protested. The loathing in his voice taking her back to the beating, to the ferocity of his blows. 'I thought it was the best thing to do.'

'For who? For Nina?'

'No.'

'Robert.'

'Your brother hasn't been dead a year and you think it best to . . . to just walk out? Very thoughtful.'

She was horrified at how he twisted it all.

'Mum,' she turned, seeking her response, wanting her to say it wasn't so, that she didn't agree with him.

Marjorie prevaricated. 'You have your own life to lead. It's all right.'

But it wasn't. She'd messed it all up again.

* * *

Marjorie

Stephen had gone. It was still too soon to know whether she could ever come to terms with it. How could you? It was something to be borne. She felt as though they had torn a piece from her. Each day was a struggle. She found some solace in prayer and she had begun to go to Church daily.

And she knew Nina would leave, they were losing her, one way or another. She'd either starve herself, or start taking drugs or simply move out and drift away. Robert had washed his hands of her. The two of them were strangers. He had no affection for her, no regard for her. He was unable to forgive, either Nina or himself. Most of the time the old aggression was replaced by a cold indifference. How Stephen would have hated it.

She knew Nina would pursue her natural family, with or without their approval. She suspected that had something to do with her problems now but she wouldn't talk about it. They didn't seem to know how to talk as a family any more.

Marjorie sighed. She hadn't had children to lose them like this. It was different for Robert, he had his work; men weren't involved in the same way. She loved Nina in spite of everything. She couldn't help it. It wasn't something you could choose. Nina might be exasperating and prickly and sullen but she loved her. She was so thin now, gaunt, very fashionable according to all the models in the magazines but not healthy. She had seen how easily she tired, how weak she was becoming. If she kept on . . .

Maybe they would never be as close as she had hoped for. Maybe Nina would always be hard work, veering from depressed to defiant, but Marjorie was sick of feeling that she was to blame somehow. Nina was Nina. If she just let her go she could imagine herself down the line somewhere regretting not having tried harder, resentful and lonely. She didn't want that. She would keep trying. She was a mother, for God's sake, infinitely giving. A doormat, some might say, or a martyr, but rather that than abandoning her daughter. She would not give up, ever. It was impossible to talk to her but she could write it down. Write to Nina, put it all on paper. How she loved her, how she had come into their lives, her hopes that Nina would find happiness, her complete acceptance that Nina might want to trace her birth family, wishing her well with it, her sorrow that she had been so unhappy. She would write it all down, in black and white. A love letter. Not for the daughter she had dreamt of but for the one she had. *My dear daughter, Nina . . .*

* * *

Nina

She walked past the house twice. Her bowels had turned to water and she was biting her teeth together, jaw rigid. She couldn't see in. There were net curtains at the windows. A small front garden, little picket fence, for show more than anything. She'd used one like that in her spring fashion window, set off with green catkins and the season's gauzy prints, a high-street version of the see-through styles that the more daring wore in London. She walked back more slowly. Number sixteen. Sweet sixteen. Megan had been sixteen when she had her. She came to a halt at their gate. She felt exposed, half the street could peer out and see her, spot a stranger prowling about. She bet people round here all knew each other, kept an eye out. The only privacy once your door was closed. It was quiet now, people out at work, but she could imagine it later, kids out on their bikes and roller blades, in and out of each other's houses. Roaming in a big gang.

Not like her and Stephen. They'd never played out much where they lived. He was too fond of his books and she found herself falling out with the few children there were. Either bored with them and losing her temper or finding herself made into the victim. Carrot-head, Ginger.

She was startled by the clunk of the door opening. Saw the woman — red hair, long, green dressing gown — open the door to let a dog out. Red hair. Nina felt her limbs go heavy. Rooted. The woman looked out, straightened up, her hand moving to her throat, clutching at the collar of her dressing gown even though it was fastened.

Nina took a step, then another. Placed her hand on the gate, unsmiling, her eyes fixed on the woman. 'Megan,' she said.

The woman nodded, a fierce little movement and her mouth trembled.

'I'm Claire.' Thudding in her head. Please. Oh, please.

'Yes.' She put one arm out towards her then lowered it. Her bright-blue eyes were brimming. She nodded again. 'Hello, Claire. I think you'd better come in.'

JOAN/LILIAN/PAMELA

Pamela

It was a year of reminders. A parade of events each highlighting her loss. The first birthday without her mum, first Christmas, first time planning her holidays without seeing if Lilian fancied a week somewhere.

She had left the little house in Fallowfield for months. There was no hurry. It wouldn't be hard to sell, there were always landlords after houses to let to students in that area. It would go up for sale when she was good and ready. Her Aunt Sally offered several times to help her clear it out, but each time she said she'd wait a little longer.

She dreamt about her mother frequently. She saw her too. Round the shops, in her garden, at the market, passing the leisure centre. The first couple of times she was petrified, thinking grief had made her mad, but two of her friends who had lost parents reassured her that it was commonplace. Someone lent her a book about bereavement. There were nights when she poured over it, eager for reassurance.

Work was fine. It helped. There she felt safe, valuable, capable.

In May she was ready to face the clear out. She booked a week's leave, the week before her birthday, and tackled it with a combination of practicality and ritual. Clearing the house was also a way of making her farewells. It was the last link to the years she had shared with her mother.

She had been back twice since her mother's death, twice in the blur of time before the funeral when she had cleared the fridge, taken meter readings, chosen clothes for her mother to be buried in, emptied the bins, removed jewellery, video and telly, her will and bank books, which she had kept in a biscuit tin in the kitchen. Pamela had left a spare key with neighbours in case of any trouble.

She drove over from Chester. There was no parking immediately outside but she found a space further down the road. Put her steering-wheel lock on.

Opening the door she allowed herself the fantasy of her mother being there to greet her — a generous smile, easy familiarity, her genuine delight whenever Pamela came home. Her stomach tightened as she stepped inside. She took a breath. The house smelt stale. It was resolutely empty. She put down her bag. A pile of junk mail lay on the floor. She checked through. There was nothing personal. She wandered round the rooms, she had to visit them all, some silly superstition. She was oppressed by the emptiness and silence.

Tour completed, she switched the mains back on in the kitchen and turned the stopcock on for water. She lit the gas fire in the living room to take the chill away. She opened the back door to let some fresh air in and saw the lilac was still in bloom. Its scent hurled her back through the years and tears filled her eyes. 'Oh, Mum,' she said aloud, 'I do miss you.'

She found scissors in the kitchen draw and cut branches of the lilac, got vases from the shelf and put the fragrant sprays round the house.

She had brought tea and milk with her and after she had finished her drink she got out her notebook and pen and went through the rooms making a list of things she needed

— bin-bags, labels, boxes, string, old newspapers, tissue paper, Sellotape — and a list of items she would like to keep.

In her old room she sat on the bed. The walls were still painted in the lemon colour she had chosen as a teenager. The curtains still a hessian weave which let all the light in. Once she'd moved out, her mother had bought a cornflower-blue duvet set to replace the old candlewick bedspread and sheets and blankets from before. She had been happy here on the whole.

She peered out into the back yard and the alley beyond. From here you could see rows of terraces like a brighter version of the Coronation Street title sequence. It had been a good place to grow up. Plenty of children, a park not far away. She'd been pally with Natalie from next door. One summer they had rigged a message system up between their bedroom windows, string and yoghurt pots. Last she'd heard, Natalie had moved away, somewhere down south.

She stepped away and turned to look in the mirror. It was a nice mirror, oval with a dark frame. She'd take it if Aunt Sally didn't want it.

She rang her aunt and explained what she was hoping to do. Asked if they would come and see if there was anything they'd like. 'I'm going to get one of those charities to take most of it, for the homeless or whatever.'

'Well, I can come tonight.'

'There's no rush.'

'You can stay with us, Pam, we've plenty of room.'

'Thanks, but it feels fine here. I'd like to be here.'

'Come and have tea with us, then.'

'Yes. Tomorrow or Wednesday?'

'Wednesday's good. Ed has his craft club tomorrow, so we generally have a fish supper.'

'Right.' She didn't quite catch the logic but it didn't matter. She had heard that Ed's health wasn't good, he was becoming very absent-minded, losing track. Sally took him to various clubs for the stimulation — and to give herself a break.

'So, we could come down in the morning, if you like?'

'Fine, see you then.'

She rang off. Considered her list. There was a mini market at the end of the road. They should have most of the stuff she needed and they might have some boxes. She could get something for her tea too.

By the time Aunt Sally and Uncle Ed arrived the following morning Pamela had assembled a pile of objects she wanted to keep in one corner of the lounge. After a little hesitation Sally soon gathered a pile of her own. They offered to help her fill bags and wrap china but she encouraged them to leave. She was more comfortable doing it on her own. She saw them out, promising to be at their house for five the following day.

She went up to her mother's room. All Lilian's clothes needed packing up. Pamela would never wear any of them — the patterned jumpers and blouses and skirts were a world away from the power suits she wore to work or the plain cotton leisurewear she wore when sailing or relaxing. She began to fill bin liners. The first armful of jumpers still smelling of her mother's perfume and cosmetics. She emptied the drawers and then began on the wardrobe. She slipped dresses and suits off hangers and folded them up. Some brought back memories: the silk skirt she had treated her mother to when they went to Paris, the stupid jacket that she had bought in Lisbon and hardly ever worn. Her old camel car-coat, worn round the cuffs but so comfy she had insisted on keeping it. Pamela had once tried to find a replacement but there was nothing exactly that length.

In one of the compartments at the bottom of the wardrobe she found a slim cardboard box, rectangular with a pattern of faded roses on it. She opened it expecting a chiffon scarf or kid-leather gloves. But inside were a batch of papers.

She sat on the edge of the bed, surrounded by half-full bin liners, to examine them. A letter from a Sister Monica wishing them every happiness. She shrugged, her mother had friends connected with the Church but she didn't know the name. A scrap of paper with *Sat — 10.30 — Girl* scrawled on it. Her mother's writing. And a birth certificate belonging to someone called Marion, mother's name Joan Hawes. The same birthday as hers. She felt a rush of confusion. Had she had a twin? Don't be stupid, different mothers. Why had Lilian got someone else's birth certificate? She looked again and as comprehension dawned she felt a wave of confusion and horror. Oh, my God, the truth slapped at her, it's me!

* * *

'Why didn't she tell me?' Pamela, still pale with shock and sick with the upset, demanded of her aunt. She had driven straight round there.

'I don't know. I don't think she ever set out to keep it from you. When you were very small I remember she and Peter talking about explaining to you when you were older. Then, with your father dying.'

Except he wasn't even my father, she thought bitterly.

'It must have got harder as time went on,' Sally said.

'You knew. Who else?'

'Just close family.'

'I can't believe it!' Her face stretched with indignation, her indigo eyes glinted. 'You should have told me, *she* should have. I'm almost thirty-one years old. Can you imagine what it's like to suddenly find it's all been a sham?'

Sally looked worried, her brow creased. She caught her lip between her teeth. 'She was a mother to you, that wasn't a sham.'

'But she let me go through my whole life thinking I was theirs, and I wasn't.'

'You were all she wanted. She'd been to hell and back before they got you.'

'What do you mean?'

Her aunt sighed. 'She lost three babies, miscarriages. The last was very late on.'

'Oh, God!' Pamela put her face in her hands.

'They said if she fell pregnant again it could kill her.'

'Tell me about it, everything you can remember, please, all of it.'

* * *

Joan

The clinic was crowded and far too hot. Joan craved some fresh air but was worried that if she left she might miss her name being called. There were women of every age, shape, size and colour. All here to see Mr Pickford. She no longer pretended to read the magazine on her lap but rested her head back against the wall and closed her eyes, imagining the bay, the way it looked, not yesterday with a summer blue sky and white caps on the waves, but on a calm November day, a sea fret curling from the water, the gulls arced like nail marks in the sky. Visualisation, they called it in the support group. It was supposed to help in the healing process; a calm place to take yourself. Along with raw food and aromatherapy and the more toxic treatments that Mr Pickford provided. But was she healing, or dying?

She steered her thoughts away, to work. Good news. There was a chance that 'Walk My Way' would be used for a new television drama series; the '60s were back in fashion. Her agent was cautiously optimistic but these things took forever, it seemed. Even if that didn't come off, Paramount — well a company who worked for Paramount — had commissioned an original slow ballad for a bittersweet romantic comedy. She'd read the treatment and put a few ideas down on tape. They'd liked two of them and asked her to develop them. Plus she'd sold several recent songs to the pop market.

'Joan Hawes.'

She put the magazine on the low table and followed the nurse along the corridor. She suspended her thoughts, focused on the carpet, the paintings hung on the wall.

Mr Pickford shook her hand warmly and gestured that she should sit. He took a moment to check her notes. He drew a small breath and looked across at her and she knew. A flutter of compassion in his eyes told her everything. She blinked hard and pressed her knuckles to her lips as he spoke. The words bumped past her — *secondary, extensive, chemotherapy, hard to say.*

She didn't need the words anyway, the message was clear. She was dying. They could poison her and chop at her and hook her up to pumps and tubes but they would only be prolonging her illness.

'I want to go home,' she said when he had finished. 'I don't want any more treatment. I want to be at home from now on.'

He nodded. 'You have support?'

'Yes. What about medication . . . if . . . when . . .'

'Your GP will be able to prescribe. I can write.'

'Yes.'

She was relieved he offered no opposition to her quick decision, that he had no desire to push desperate last treatments on her.

'I'm sorry,' he said.

She bit her tongue and nodded. Sniffed. 'Thank you.'

The nurse knew or else he'd sent some sort of signal to her. She asked Joan if she would like to make an appointment to see the counsellor. She shook her head, her eyes swimming over all the women in the waiting room: the young girl with the dreadlocks and her mother, the one with the wig, the woman in the sari whose little boy had fallen asleep on her lap, the very old woman with skin like crêpe, the business woman concentrating on her laptop. All the women. 'Can you call me a taxi? To the station.'

'You've come on your own?'

She nodded. Penny came when she could but today's appointment clashed with her school inspection. She had considered ringing in sick but Joan had persuaded her to go. 'If I need more treatment I'd rather you took the time then.' And if I'm dying.

'Yes, my friend couldn't come today.'

'I'll get you that taxi.'

It ran in families. They'd talked about that in the group, fearful for their daughters and granddaughters. They implied she was lucky, no children to worry about. She had thought about owning up but it didn't seem fair. Their children were real, they had names and faces, they came to the hospital and saw their mothers, they shared their lives, they heard them throwing up after radiation treatments, saw the clumps of hair in the bathroom bin, heard the talk of biopsies and percentages, prosthetics and remission. They loved them. Her daughter was barely fact, someone else's daughter now.

* * *

Pamela

The waiting room was decorated in pastel colours. The walls held a display about adoption — clippings from recent newspaper articles, child's drawings, poems. A leaflet rack had caught her attention on her first visit. *Tracing Your Family, Sibling Attraction* (oh God!), *How To Search.*

She had found out about the adoption charity in a leaflet from the library. She had spent most of the first session in tears and inarticulate, and when she had managed to talk it had been about the deaths of her father and mother rather than about discovering she was adopted. The second session had been just as harrowing, though she'd talked more about the adoption.

Today she would see her adoption records. They had been easy to get hold of. The counsellor, Donna, had been surprised that Lilian had Pamela's original birth certificate.

'It's most unusual. Someone must have given it to your parents. Anyway, it means we have the details we need if you decide to send for your records.'

Donna had talked about tracing too but Pamela would never do that. It would be like a betrayal.

'Pamela.' Donna invited her through to the room. There were couches and easy chairs, a box of tissues prominent on the low table. Her hands felt clammy as Donna talked about having the records and drew them from a folder.

Pamela read the details.

> *Joan Hawes, shorthand typist, aged nineteen. Father unknown. Baby expected April, possibly later. Family don't know she is pregnant. Plans to move away after baby is born. Baby girl born May twenty-fourth. Baptised Marion. Sixth July, baby placed for adoption with Mr and Mrs Gough, 8 Skinner Lane, Chorlton.*

'What's this—' Pamela pointed to a sum: two figures added up to make £4.10s.6d — 'her bill?'

'Yes. There would be a charge for the nights she stayed there and the smaller figure would be for the baby.'

Me. Sudden tears blinded her. She pulled out a tissue. Donna said nothing. Pamela wiped her eyes and read on.

Discharged, July tenth. Four days later.

'I can't imagine it.' She blew her nose. 'I know I've never had a baby but walking away . . .' She blew her nose.

'It's very difficult. We see birth mothers who tell us it's affected their whole lives.'

'There were so many lies,' she said. 'I asked her, my mum, Lilian — I asked her once what time of day I was born, for a chart, astrology thing, and she told me, made it up. She even told me what my birth was like.'

'What did she say?'

'"Straightforward." She'd had three miscarriages before they got me and she never told me about any of that. I thought we were close. I thought we had a really good relationship.' She stopped talking and put her hand to her mouth. It hurt too much. After a minute she began to talk again, haltingly trying to pick her way through muddled thoughts, around feelings that caught at her like brambles.

'I've never really had a serious relationship. I've never been close to settling down or getting married or having children. I used to think it was work, putting everything into that and . . . it didn't seem all that unusual, lots of single women, modern times, but now . . .' She paused. Donna listened. 'First Joan, then my father, now Mum. They've all left me.' She turned to the other woman, her face creasing, eyes hot with pain, lips stretching with grief. 'They've all left me,' she cried, 'and they all lied, it's no wonder I can't trust anyone.'

* * *

Joan

'It's all coming to you, there's no one else. Tommy's no need of anything. There's just George. I'd like him to have the platinum discs, for "Walk My Way" and "Swing Me".'

Penny nodded. Joan knew she was fighting not to cry. But what did it matter? What were a few more tears between friends. More than friends. Lovers, soul mates.

'I want to be cremated,' she said. Penny made a small choking noise. 'And my ashes scattered on the sea out there. I've written it all down. It's in the blue box with the will. Oh, Penny, come here!'

She gathered the weeping woman into her arms, stroking her coarse hair. The texture had changed over time as Penny's straw-coloured hair had gone grey.

Joan rested her chin lightly on Penny's head, felt Penny's hot, damp tears on her neck. She looked out through the window to the horizon. Almost noon and a strange brilliance, bright as neon, stretched the width of the skyline. Above it storm clouds hovered and solitary seagulls were tossed by mercurial winds.

'I don't want to leave you,' she said quietly when Penny had calmed down. 'You know that. I haven't given up. I still love you, I still want to share my life with you, stay here . . .'

And there were all the other things too. All the tunes in her head, the verses, the phrases and words waiting to be found and shaped and completed. All the songs she wanted to write. Would never write.

'Joan—'

'Sshhh. But if it is time, if I have to go, then I want it to be here, to be with you, to make the best of it. A good death.'

'I know. I'm sorry.'

'Don't. Don't be sorry. No regrets.'

'No.' The women clasped hands.

'God, I must look ghastly,' Penny said.

Joan surveyed the bloated red nose, the watery eyes and blotchy skin. 'Yep.'

Penny laughed and fought not to cry again.

Joan laid her head back against the headboard. 'Get me a drink?'

'Tea?'

'I was thinking Pernod.'

'Pernod? Do we have Pernod?'

'No, don't think so. It used to be my special drink, for celebrations, years back.'

Penny raised an eyebrow. 'We're celebrating?'

Every moment, Joan thought. She shook her head. 'A glass of red.' It might make her nauseous, sometimes it did but she loved to savour the taste. And she might manage another couple of hours before her next medication.

Penny went and returned with two glasses of wine. She climbed on to the bed beside Joan and they sat peaceably for a while. Penny spoke first; Joan caught the nervous edge in her voice before she made sense of the words.

'Joan, the baby you had, the one that was adopted. Do you want to do anything? Try and contact her?'

Joan stiffened. 'No.' Definitely not. 'It wouldn't be fair. I'm dying. I couldn't expect . . . I've never considered it before and it wouldn't be right now. And I think if she'd wanted to find me, well, she'd have done it by now.'

'Would you have liked that?'

'I don't know,' she said honestly. 'It's difficult to think about. It was a very unhappy time. Having a baby was the last thing on earth I wanted. I know I did the right thing and I've tried as much as I could to put it behind me. If she'd come looking, it would have brought it all back. I think that was part of why I moved to London, to create some distance.'

'You've never really talked about it.'

'I don't think I can.'

There was a pause but Joan sensed Penny needed to hear more. She took a breath, sipped her wine.

'What did you call her?'

'Marion. I liked the name at the time, that's all. No other reason.'

She had a giddy surge of memory. Little Megan, the one with red hair, talking about names and initials and Joan not wanting to pick a name, not wanting to choose clothes, not wanting any of it. 'It was awful, Penny. There was another girl there at the time, Caroline she was called, very young — only sixteen — and her grandma died and they wouldn't let her go to the funeral.'

'Oh, god.'

'Would have let the cat out of the bag you see.'

'Thank god times have changed.'

Joan drank some more and felt a wave of fatigue flood her limbs and up her spine.

'I think I'll rest a bit.' She put her glass down.

'Shall I leave the curtains?'

'Yes.'

'Penny?'

'Yes?'

'Love you.'

Penny nodded and kissed her softly on the lips.

Joan lay, facing the sea, eyes drifting open now and then. Noting the slow progress of the storm clouds, seeing how the sea changed from silver to lead. She could feel the electricity on the air, hear the snap of the wind in the eaves of the house. She shut her eyes and watched lightning sizzle and heard the low rumble of thunder leading to the crack at its heart. And she prayed that wherever Marion was, whoever she had become, that she was happy and healthy and loved.

* * *

After getting her records and a couple more sessions crying to the counsellor Pamela had put it all on one side and got on with her life. Work was frantic. There were mergers going on with the Netherlands and Portugal. She spent four months in Lisbon and considered emigrating but there never seemed to be time to look into the pros and cons. When she did return to her cottage it felt just like home and she knew that she would have to keep it, and had she the energy to keep two homes? There was no time for anything. She still missed her mother, still caught herself wanting to ring and tell her good news, ring and say she was home, and then found herself hurting afresh as she remembered that she was dead, still dead. Would always be dead.

Curiosity about her background emerged very gradually, in fits and starts. She would go for weeks without giving it a thought then a chance conversation or news item would catch her unawares. I'm adopted too, she would think. She began to wonder more about Joan. Who had been the father? It still hurt to think that Peter, her beloved father, was not her natural parent. They had been so close. She remembered how he would play with her, football and snakes and ladders. Almost like a child himself, except he also told her about the wider world, injustice and the need to fight it. He'd talked about apartheid and human rights — to a six year old. They'd released Nelson Mandela this year; there would be a new South Africa but only last week they'd seen pictures of the Serbian death camps. Was the world any more humane since he had died? It didn't seem so.

And her natural father, what would he be like? What if she was the result of rape or of incest? What had happened to Joan afterwards? If she tried to trace her what might she find? An alcoholic, a derelict; she might be in prison or on the streets. She could be happily married with grandchildren by now. Did she ever think of the baby she had given up?

Her curiosity grew but she resisted it. Then Sally died. Ed was already in a home, his mind had gone and Sally had not been able to care for him herself. 'I can cope with the feeding and changing and all, it's the fact that he's not there, that he doesn't love me anymore that's getting me down so,' she had told Pamela the last time they'd spoken.

As she stood in Southern Cemetery, one of a handful of mourners, she realised that her past was gone. There was no family any more, no one to tell her how it was, no one who remembered her father or could remind her of her childhood. Ian, Sally's son, was there, but he didn't remember Peter and he lived down in Cornwall. They'd probably never see each other again. There was no past and as she looked ahead there was no future either, no children, not even any nephews or nieces. The sense of being completely alone and unattached shook her to the core.

Two weeks later she wrote to the National Organisation for the Counselling of Adoptees and Parents and applied to go on their register. If Joan had ever done the same they would find a match.

NORCAP wrote to tell her there was no match. She was bitterly disappointed. In-between business trips she tried to trace the Hawes family from the electoral records. But although she was able to find the parents resident in Manchester until 1978 there was no mention of Joan. Where had she gone afterwards? It took hours to get nowhere and she gave up for several months but then resumed her search. This time she searched the records for a marriage. She found several Joan Hawes and spent time and money contacting the relevant registrar's departments only to find that each was a false lead.

Frustrated, she went back to NORCAP and contacted a researcher that they recommended. She met with the man and passed him all the details she had gathered. Later that night she flew out from Heathrow on her way to an international seminar in Harare. She wondered whether she would ever find Joan. And if she did would Joan agree to see her? Some people refused. How would she bear that rejection? She sat back in her seat and said a quick prayer to St Christopher, something she did whenever she travelled by air. The cabin lights dimmed. Joan seemed to have sunk without trace. She had read in the newsletters from NORCAP of people spending ten, twenty — more — years and not succeeding. The plane banked after take-off and Pamela looked down at the lights scattered below. What if Joan had emigrated? What if they were looking in the wrong country?

* * *

Joan

Morphine played strange tricks on her, mixing up the sounds and pictures so that the seagulls' shrieks became the cries of a child and the shush of waves on the beach a woman's breath.

Rachel, Penny's daughter, came in with the baby, already a toddler, and for a moment she saw Penny with a child in her arms. So alike. Mother and daughter. And now three generations in the same house. The child was a boy. Tiny, with caramel skin, crinkly black hair and shiny brown eyes. Complete contrast to Rachel and Penny with their straw-like hair, pale skin, apple cheeks. She wondered how it would be to raise a child so different from yourself. Not to see yourself reflected in the plane of a cheek or the shape of the mouth or the curve of the wrist. Would it be easier, would you allow the child to be more of themselves and less some minor version of you? Would you find yourself in them in other ways: their temperament or gestures, the way they laughed or their footsteps, their talents and dislikes?

When she had first seen her own baby, she had been shocked. A living child. Her very existence was incredible. Unreal. Joan had never been able to see beyond the pregnancy. That was where it all would end, she imagined. But this; this tangible, human creature . . . she had never really bargained for this. Or the appalling slew of emotions that assailed her.

She's me, she'd thought. And immediately dismissed the bizarre notion, but it lingered like a smell. She could not face the child. Literally. She had to handle her to feed and change her but she avoided looking at her. She did not trust herself to meet those eyes, to gaze at that face. To admit those feelings. The memory brought anxiety and she turned away from it.

It was good that Rachel would be here with Penny in the coming months and what a perfect place for the boy. Room to play, the beach on the doorstep.

Rachel had gone. Joan had slept maybe. She wasn't sure. There was a tune in her head. A lovely tune, haunting. A bit like Acker Bilk's 'Stranger On The Shore' — the yearning, that opening sequence that went straight to the solar plexus. She listened to it fade. They came like that sometimes, so intense. Unbidden. Usually the tune but sometimes the lyric. 'Spring Lament' had been like that. A gift. Maybe a burden. Too close for comfort. *It's May again, blossoms, swaying in the rain again, another year and still I dream. And the bluebells make me blue, wonder where are you?* She had written it down and the process had drained her. It became a favourite with the jazz singers; the syncopation and the key changes a challenge for interpretation.

She shifted her weight in the bed and felt pain stirring again. She closed her eyes, hoping to escape into sleep for just a few more minutes.

* * *

Pamela

Her stomach went into free fall when she got the message to ring the researcher. She made a coffee and got pen and paper ready before returning the phone.

'I'm afraid I've some sad news,' the man said. 'I managed to trace your mother, she was living in Scarborough but I'm afraid she died last year. I'm very sorry.'

They all leave, they all go. Last year. Only last year.

'I've written a summary of what I've been able to establish, I'll fax that to you?'

‘Thank you.’

‘There is something else, Pamela. Joan had a close friend, they shared the house for many years. I’ve had a word with her and she asked me to tell you that she would be very happy if you wanted to get in touch. She has some things, things of Joan’s that she’d like you to have.’

He continued to talk but she couldn’t concentrate. She felt as though someone had thumped her very hard, knocked the stuffing out of her. She managed to remain civil and conclude the call. Then she remained sitting, stunned. The coffee cooling and the room darkening. She sat and let the thoughts shuffle round, slow and painful, and a part of her observed how numb she felt and she wanted to stay like that, not to feel the full impact of the news.

* * *

A couple of months later, having spoken to Penny on the phone, she made the journey to Scarborough, the seaside town perched on the East Yorkshire coast.

‘Come in. I’ve made soup and sandwiches,’ Penny greeted her. ‘You must have been travelling for hours. The bathroom’s upstairs, first on the right, if you want to freshen up.’

‘I will, thank you. It’s a beautiful house.’ She took in the stripped wooden banisters, the large airy hallway with its abstract rugs and warm terracotta walls.

‘It is, it was in quite a state when Joan bought it, but she completely refurbished it. The kitchen’s through here when you want me.’

‘Thanks.’ She was relieved that Penny had already referred to Joan and so easily. Upstairs she practised a smile in the mirror. She had butterflies in her stomach. Would she be able to eat?

The kitchen was warm, the savoury smell of soup and the yeasty scent of warm bread made her mouth water.

Penny had set the table for two, a white linen cloth, a small vase with freesias in it. Simple. Beautiful.

'It's only vegetable, I didn't know if you were a vegetarian.'

'No, but that sounds great.'

She placed the pot on a mat at Pamela's side with a ladle. 'Please, help yourself. I'll get the bread.'

Pamela poured herself a modest serving, relieved at not getting drips on the cloth, and then accepted a warm roll. It was just possible for her to swallow but she remained nervous. She broke the silence. 'You lived here with Joan?'

'Yes. She'd always had lodgers, a lot of people from the theatre would come for the summer season. I moved in in '79. Over twenty years ago now. I had quite a journey to work. I was headmistress at a school in Pickering, that's about twenty miles from here. But Joan worked from home.'

'And she wrote songs?' One of the facts Penny had told her when they had spoken on the phone.

'Yes. Do you write?'

'No.' She smiled and shook her head. 'I'm not musical, not really. I sang in a choir when I was at school, nothing since.'

'You're in management?'

'Banking.'

'Is it very pressured?'

'Can be. But I must be doing something right, they keep promoting me.'

'Joan was good with money. Shrewd. She was investing and sorting out a pension years before most women even thought about it.'

'Were they well off — her family?'

'No, not particularly. She made her money writing, which is nothing short of miraculous, I'm told. But she had a hit very early on and she insisted on a particular clause in the contract, which made her a great deal of money. That's what I mean about shrewd. That more or less paid for this house. "Walk My Way", you've heard it?'

Pamela frowned.

'Bit before your time,' Penny laughed. 'Nineteen sixty-four. You'd only have been four. But everybody and their brother covered it after that. I've got a copy for you. And lots of photographs.'

They finished eating and Penny cleared the bowls away. 'You're very like her.' She shook her head. 'It's quite uncanny. Her hair was straight, but apart from that . . .'

They had always told her she took after Peter with her dark hair and blue eyes.

'Would you like tea or coffee?'

'Tea, please. Just milk.'

'Why don't you go up and I'll bring this. Have a look round. It's her study, I thought you'd like to see it. All her things are there. The top of the stairs at the front on the right.'

Pamela escaped gratefully. The soup had been light but she still felt her stomach churning. She could feel the tension in her neck and along her spine, the strain of the unfamiliar, highly charged visit.

The first thing that struck her was the view: a panorama of the bay, right round to the headland and the sea and sky stretching away on a palette of greys and blues. The desk was quite clear. But this was where she would have sat and written.

Pamela looked back out to the water. The sea was choppy, the outlook bleak, elemental. She had sailed not far from here a couple of years ago. They had fought bitter easterly winds and had to tack for several miles. She had never imagined . . .

She turned to the fireplace and examined the objects on it. Driftwood, postcards, a carving of dolphins, a small cowbell, a harmonica. There was nothing of herself in any of this. She felt unsettled.

On the piano there was a collection of snapshots in frames. Nothing formal; no weddings or graduation photos, no airbrushed babies on sheepskin rugs. Penny on the beach, Penny with a younger woman by a palm tree, Penny crouched beside a dog, with a baby. With a jolt she realised that Penny was more than a lodger or companion. Embarrassment made her cheeks burn. Not at the fact of it but at the possibility that she had already said something crass in her ignorance. But how was she to know? On top of everything else it was too much to take in.

Penny brought up the tea and they sat on the sofa by the fireplace. Penny gestured to a pile of albums. 'There are loads here. Anything you want copies of we can sort that out and most of these should come to you anyway. I've all her family's here. Joan's parents are both dead and she only had one brother, Tommy. He emigrated to Australia. He took what he wanted after their mother died. They didn't keep in touch, just Christmas cards. I found this one last night. She would have been your age in this.'

Pamela took the small, square, black-and-white photograph. She inhaled sharply — it was like looking at a version of herself, the same-shaped face, the long nose, same shape eyes, even the curve of eyebrows exactly alike. Like sisters. Like mother and daughter. She took a breath. Why couldn't you wait?

'And this must have been just after she had you, she moved to London . . .'

* * *

On the train home she stared dry-eyed out through her own reflection, replaying fragments of Penny's narration, her own clumsy questions.

'When did she tell you about me?'

'I'd known her for a while. I had just left a very difficult marriage and I'd been talking to her about the whole business of regret. She said there was only one thing she had regretted and that was having a baby and giving it up for adoption.'

'Which bit did she regret? Having me or giving me up?' The bitter question appalled her. Penny would think her so rude.

'I don't think she could separate the two things,' she said carefully.

'Did she say who my father was?'

'No.'

'Never?' Surely she would have said something, let something slip.

Penny shook her head. 'No. He was married, that's all she ever told me.'

She would never know, then, it wasn't fair.

Penny had talked about Joan's illness. 'The nurses were wonderful, they made her so comfortable. We put her bed by the window so she could see out. It's at the front like this room. She loved that view. It's not a pretty place, it can be wild some nights, but she said it inspired her. I suppose she didn't write pretty songs really . . .' Penny had got upset at that point and apologised and wiped her eyes. Pamela thought of Lilian losing Peter.

'These were hers. I'd like you to have them. And these were her mother's, heirlooms.' She had taken the pieces of jewellery.

'This is the song, "Walk My Way". I bet you'll recognise it when you hear it.'

'She said Marion was just a name she liked. There's a friend in Germany too, she knew Joan when she first went to London. If you ever want to meet her I can put you in touch . . . Your mother died very suddenly, you said?'

'Yes. My father too. I was seven when he died . . . It was only when I was clearing out Mum's house that I found out . . .'

'Oh, Pamela, it must have been awful.'

'If I'd known . . .'

Maybe I'd have got here sooner, maybe I'd have heard her sing, found out who my father was, taken her sailing.

'I may be talking after the event,' Penny had said, 'but I think she wrote this one about you, "Spring Lament".' A slow, haunting ballad.

It's May again, blossoms, swaying in the rain again, another year and still I dream. And the bluebells make me blue, wonder where are you? I'm not dancing, no romancing, only glancing over my shoulder, another year older and it's May again . . .

The train entered a tunnel, the clattering got louder and the lights flickered on and off.

Too late now. Never know you, nor him. You should have left a note, something. Whatever you thought of him — a one-night stand, a drunken party . . . still my father. I had a right to know where I come from. Who I am?

As the train emerged she found herself blinking at the light. She felt empty and overwhelmed at the same time. So much to take in. With time perhaps she would feel better. She could take some leave, see if Felix and Marge had any plans. Sail away — let the waves rock her and the space of the sea and the sky stretch around her. Make her peace. She pulled the photo from her bag and gazed at it again and watched it blur as her eyes filled with tears.

CAROLINE/KAY/THERESA

Theresa

'Does it make you curious?' Craig asked her, rubbing his thumb along the sole of the baby's foot. 'Make you wonder about your own background?'

'No,' she said shortly.

He looked at her, brows raised at the edge in her voice. 'Not at all?'

'Craig, she didn't care enough to keep me, why the hell should I want to know any more about her?'

'Whoa!' He held up a hand to her. 'Steady on. I just thought having Ella might make you inquisitive. Now we're back in the UK it wouldn't be so hard to get information. And she probably did care, you know, they were very different times.'

'And I wasn't exactly perfect.' She cupped her hand to her ear, a habitual gesture.

'That's ridiculous.'

'What?'

'She wasn't married,' he said. 'You know that much and she went into the mother and baby home to have you so she'd already decided to place you for adoption even before you were born. It wouldn't have anything to do with what you were like.'

'Nothing personal.'

He frowned. 'Why so defensive? You never used to be so prickly about it.'

'Craig, don't analyse me.'

'Just an observation. Your parents are more laid back about it than you are.'

'I'd never do anything about it even if I wanted to. I wouldn't treat them like that. I think it's awful the way people from really good families, happy families, go off . . . it must be so hurtful. I'd never do that to Mum and Dad.'

'What if she traced you?'

'I wouldn't see her. It's none of her business, my life. Nothing to do with her.'

He pursed his lips and exhaled noisily. 'Jeez, I better change the subject.'

'You think I'm being unfair?'

'It can't have been easy for her. It must have been heartbreaking, when you think of it.' He nodded at Ella on the bed between them.

'You don't know that, Craig. I just think . . .' Her mouth tightened and she stopped.

'Go on.'

'I think it was terrible, to leave me . . .' Sudden emotion distorted her face.

'Oh, Tess!' He moved closer. 'I'm sorry. I've put my foot right in it.'

'I *am* more bothered by it. Since having Ella. I get really cross. I look at her and hold her and I adore her and I think that was me, all those years ago, that was me and she abandoned me. I'm twenty-five years old and suddenly it matters. And I'm so angry inside, like it's only just sunk in what happened to me. And then I feel guilty about Mum and Dad. And feeling this way. I was only a few weeks old, it can't have mattered really, not so tiny, but I can't bear to think about it.' She cried, 'Bloody hormones.'

He held her and kissed her hair.

The baby woke then. Her mouth stretching, a cry gaining volume.

'Perfect timing.'

She laughed and pulled away, reached for a tissue to dry her face.

'I'll make you some tea?'

She nodded. 'And crumpets. I'm ravenous again.'

Like mother, like daughter, he thought, but bit his tongue just in time. The phrase might seem loaded given Theresa's state of mind.

She turned to plump the pillows up behind her. Lifted Ella from the bed and let her latch on. She wouldn't think about it again. It was all too upsetting and she had enough to deal with coping with all the demands that a new baby brought.

* * *

'Craig! Craig!' The terror in her voice brought him, taking the stairs two at a time, banging his elbow on the door jamb in his urgency.

'What?'

'Ella.'

Theresa stood beside the cot. Inside, Ella was jerking and bucking, her back arched, her limbs flailing, face contorted.

'It's a fit. She's having a fit.'

'Ambulance!' He wasted no time.

Theresa put her hand on the baby's stomach, willing the terrifying movements to stop. Epilepsy, brain fever, a seizure. Fear sang through her veins. She wanted to lift her up and cradle her but was frightened she would do more damage if she moved her. If she dies . . . the thought took the ground from under her, she clung to the cot side.

Craig reappeared. 'They're on their way.'

'What do we do?'

'Nothing. They'll be here soon. Oh, God.'

Ella's limbs tremored then stopped. Her features slackened, the red drained from her face, her abdomen sank back on to the mattress. She began to whimper. Theresa lifted her up, cradled her against her left shoulder, gently rubbing her back, making soothing sounds. 'Is she awake?'

Craig checked. 'Yes, she looks fine. Bit sleepy.'

'Where are they?'

'Here soon. You poor wee babby,' he said to his daughter.

* * *

At the hospital they needed to perform a battery of tests to try and establish the reason for the seizure. Family history was one of the questions that kept being raised.

Craig had already rung his mother and established that there was nothing on either side of his that he could have passed on.

'I'm adopted,' Theresa told the consultant. 'I've no idea.'

They took turns sitting by her bedside. They allowed Theresa to stay the night, sleeping on sponge block on the floor. She barely slept in the unfamiliar place. The sound of other children sleeping, the whir of heating and clanking of pipes competing with any sound from Ella, so she strained to hear, bracing herself to call the staff if her breathing altered or there was any sign of discomfort.

After two days and three nights there had been no repetition, they had made no positive diagnosis and Theresa was dead on her feet.

'Some of the blood tests are still being completed,' said the consultant, 'and that may tell us more, but I must say there doesn't seem to be any clear indication at this stage.'

'Would it help if you knew more about my family history?' Theresa said.

'It would help us to rule out or factor in genetic predisposition, but at the end of the day it might not give us an answer.' She nodded. She could feel Craig's eyes on her, questioning, would she? She continued to look at the doctor, not wanting to make a decision about it here, in front of a stranger.

They took Ella home. If she had any further seizures they should bring her back to the hospital immediately. They had a list of do's and don'ts. Don't use duvets, cot bumpers or too many blankets, don't overdress the baby, make a note of any symptoms that precede a seizure — aversion to light, vomiting, diarrhoea, high temperature. It was like living with a time bomb.

* * *

The following evening she sought out Craig in his study, where he was preparing lectures.

'You think I should find out my medical history, don't you?' She lowered herself into the easy chair.

He put down his pen, blew air out through his mouth. 'You heard what the doctor said: "It might help them get to the bottom of it".'

She rubbed at her forehead. 'That's all I'd want,' she said, 'just the medical stuff.'

He waited.

'I'd just be doing it for Ella.'

'I know.' He looked at her.

'It's scary. Even that.' She frowned, eyes suddenly wet. 'Don't know why.'

'The unknown.'

She agreed. 'And ignorance is bliss. But if there was something, in my genes, and I hadn't tried to find out . . .' she shook her head.

He moved around his desk and stood behind her, hands on her shoulders, bent to kiss her hair. 'I love you,' he murmured.

'Me, too.' She kissed his hand. But her thoughts were distracted, strewn about like dropped papers, and she felt only dread at the thought of the journey ahead. The unknown stretched before her like a chasm, black and bottomless.

* * *

She was walking the Pennine Way, the whole of it, from Edale to Kirk Yetholm, right along the backbone of England. On their visits to Paul's family in Settle she had walked a lot in the Yorkshire Dales, she had done the three peaks — Ingleborough, Pen-y-ghent and Great Whernside — and had promised herself one day she'd walk the whole length of the hills and here she was. Bliss.

She had left Malham that morning carrying her pack. It was a fair morning, bright and blustery, the sort of day when you could see right across the fells, pick out tiny sheep clinging to hillside tracks and watch the clouds chase across the sky, skimming shadows over the undulating green swards. Most of this section was treeless. The lower slopes would once have held forests but these had been cleared hundreds of years before for farming. The Romans had marched over here, building their long, straight roads, some of which were now part of the route.

Limestone country, and the white rock gave a bright, luminescent feel to the landscape, so that even in the foulest weather it never had the bleak, god-forbidden look of places like Dartmoor with its darker stone, where she had walked the previous summer.

She checked her map and followed the lower trail, which would take her down the hillside to meet a path rising from the hamlet below. She let her thoughts ramble as they did whenever she walked. Not concentrating on anything but aware nevertheless that there was an accounting going on. A weighing up of what she had made of her life, a consideration of what she would like to change, an assessment of her emotional health.

As she rounded the corner she found a stile set in the drystone wall. Just beyond it was a cairn of stones and, following tradition, she found a small pebble to add to the mound. Large rocks, fissured and worn, scattered the area and she decided to stop and have lunch among them. She had brought a piece of the creamy Wensleydale cheese, bread rolls, tangy orange tomatoes, locally grown, a flask of coffee and some flapjack. She ate and drank and then closed her eyes, savouring the quiet that was interrupted only by the peewit of the lapwing or the melancholy cry of the curlew and the barking call of grouse.

She felt safe on the hills. The nearest she got to peace. 'The one place I can't follow her,' Paul joked. And there was some truth in it. She relished the solitude and gently avoided linking up with other walkers, preferring a brisk 'good morning' as she passed them to any conversation.

She would be forty-three next birthday. Her hair was showing grey and every day brought more wrinkles but she felt reasonably fit, work kept her active.

Davey had joined them in the business. He was less interested in the plants but a natural at the landscaping and the structural side of design. People wanted more than a patch of lawn with borders these days and Davey was developing that side of things. He seemed happy with it. She didn't need to worry about him. Sean was settled too. Doing a computing course. She barely understood what he did but he was happy and had good prospects and he was engaged to an energetic young woman in PR whose confidence was breathtaking.

She had never heard from the Children's Rescue Society. She had never stopped hoping but sometimes it was hard.

She stirred herself and packed up her rubbish. She hefted the rucksack on to her back, groaning a little at the mild ache in her shoulders. She skirted the rocks and regained the path.

* * *

Theresa

'How was it?' Craig put his briefcase on the kitchen counter, pulled out a chair.

'Awful. Just like I expected. Why on earth they can't just send you the stuff in a sealed envelope and let you get over it in private . . .'

He raised his eyebrows. 'It's a safety net, I suppose. Someone to listen, could be quite traumatic . . .'

'Craig, there was a letter.'

'What?'

'A letter. From her.' Her face crumpled, her brown eyes glimmered. 'I never thought . . . It's all very nice but I didn't want . . . I just . . .'

'Tess.' He went to hug her. She pulled away after a minute and handed him the white envelope.

He drew out the paper and read it. He blinked several times, his Adam's apple bobbing up and down. 'Jeez. She was sixteen. Caroline.'

'You think I should write back?'

He shook his head in bewilderment. 'God knows. This was written in nineteen seventy-eight. She's not heard anything in all this time . . .'

'So I should feel sorry for her,' she said resentfully.

'No. I don't know.'

'I feel cornered,' she said. 'I didn't want this. I didn't ask to be born. I didn't ask to be adopted.'

'What did the counsellor say?'

'"Take some time".' We haven't got time though, have we? I still need to know about the medical stuff. There's nothing here—' she gestured to a large, manilla envelope — 'only a basic check they do at the home.' Her hand sought out her ear. He didn't miss the movement.

'I feel so cross, there's nothing to help with Ella, nothing. So that means if I want any more I need to trace Caroline and then write or get the agency to write and ask specifically. And what if it's on my father's side. There's no indication who he was. It's a nightmare.'

She looked at him. He looked haggard, his face creasing. She knew what he was thinking. 'Don't worry, I'll do it.'

'This counsellor could write for you?'

'First we'd have to track her down. There's no address on the letter. And they haven't any record of where she is. She could have left her address.'

‘Maybe she doesn’t want to be found, a new family and all. She just wanted to leave something for you, wanted you to know.’

‘Wanted forgiving?’

‘That’s a bit harsh. I know I can’t really imagine what it’s like for you but she was sixteen, Theresa, a schoolgirl. She obviously thinks about you . . .’

‘Don’t. You’re right, you don’t know.’

* * *

In the days that followed she found herself obsessed by thoughts of Caroline. She read and reread the letter, her feelings swinging from fury at being abandoned to compassion for the woman. She tried to imagine Caroline. She’d be forty-two. Married, two sons. Was she happy? Moments of spite pricked through her thoughts — hope she’s lonely, lost without me, hope she’s regretted it. She despised herself for such petty, cruel impulses. She was tearful too. When Craig was out she allowed herself to indulge in bouts of weeping, wondering where all the tears came from, whether this was a delayed case of postnatal depression. She was exhausted. She had to act.

‘I’m going back for more counselling with Helen next week. I’m all over the place with this. I’m going to start the tracing. Mum will have Ella for me.’

‘What does your mum say about it all?’

‘Haven’t told her yet, there wasn’t a chance really, just said I had a meeting. I don’t want to upset her. She’s on the waiting list now, for the hysterectomy. She’s a lot on her plate. I just need to find the right time.’ She felt awful keeping it from Kay, but she was frightened of what her reaction would be. She couldn’t bear it if Kay was distressed by it. It might be best to wait until she’d had her operation and recovered.

* * *

Ella thrived but their pleasure in her was shadowed by the fear that she was ill. That something lurked inside her waiting to rear up and create fresh delirium, fresh traumas.

At the age of eleven months she had a second fit. It was a mild Tuesday morning. Theresa went to the lounge, where Ella was asleep on her playmat, a loose cotton blanket covering her. Theresa heard a strange sound and when she went to investigate she found the child wracked by spasms, her eyes glassy and protruding like marbles, her legs quivering. She dialled 999 and went on to autopilot.

The stay at the hospital was like a rerun.

'If only we knew why,' Theresa told the doctor. 'It's not knowing what's wrong that makes it even worse.'

'I'm going to order a CAT scan — that's where we take a picture of the brain — and I want to refer you to a neurosurgeon.'

Theresa went dizzy with fear, she laced her fingers tight with the strap of her handbag. A brain tumour? Brain disease. She tried to listen while he talked on about being cautious and keeping things in proportion and all she could imagine was a tiny coffin. It was all she could do to stay in the room.

'Good grief, Tess!' Craig said as they walked back to the ward. 'How do people cope?'

* * *

'How can I go back to work with all this?' she said to him some days later.

'What are your options? You can stay here, at home with Ella, and leave your career on hold indefinitely, or go back to the department, get on with your life. The nursery's in the next block, we can make sure the staff are fully briefed. Your call.'

She frowned.

'Tess, giving up your work won't make her better. It's not about sacrifices. If you want to stay home because you'd rather do that than go back to the university that's a different issue.'

'I don't. I want to go back. There's a lot going on in the department. I want to be part of that, and they'll let me do part-time.'

'There's your answer. Try it at least, see how it works out.'

'Yes.' she nodded, raked her fingers through her hair. She'd had highlights put in to pep up the colour, which she always thought of as boring brown. She still wore it long, often with a stretchy hair band that held it off her face and covered her ears. She put her hands on her hips and stretched her back, which was tight with tension. 'Craig, about Caroline. There's days you can go to St Catherines' House, they help you find marriage certificates and all that. I'm going to go.'

'Good.' He nodded.

'I thought last night . . . what if she's dead?'

He made a noise.

'Then we'll never know, will we?'

'We might not anyway,' he pointed out. 'There may be no epilepsy or anything else in the family.'

'I keep thinking about it, more and more, what I'll do if we find her. Things I'd like to ask her, not just health stuff. Maybe . . . I don't know . . . see her face to face.'

He looked surprised. 'Really?'

She nodded. 'Unfinished business.' She smiled ruefully.

'Would you do it if Ella was OK? If they found out what was wrong?'

She considered, stroking her hair over her left ear. 'Yes,' she said at length, 'I think so. Not like this, not immediately, I'd want to take it more slowly, but yes, I think I would now. It seems . . . inevitable — if she's still alive. If she's willing to meet me.'

'Jeez, Theresa. Been a hell of a year.'

She blew a breath out. 'You could say that.'

* * *

How on earth did you break the news to your children? She'd practised the phrases — Daddy and I aren't getting along very well, we've decided to separate — and rehearsed the responses to the inevitable questions — no particular reason, we've just drifted apart, it's mutual.

She had decided not to reveal anything of Adam's affairs. Oh, there was still a vindictive streak in her that would have relished souring his reputation for them but she didn't want to hurt them. They didn't need to know.

It had been two weeks since she'd told Adam she wanted out. And it had taken her months to find the courage to say so. He was putting away the Christmas decorations at the time. All the little bells and baubles. The figures they'd collected over the years. Thirty years. The set of robins that had been the twins' favourites. She dragged herself away from reminiscence and into the harsh reality of the present.

'Adam, I want a separation.'

He sat back on his heels, peered at her. He wore glasses now, his hair had turned a steely grey but he was still an attractive man. He always would be.

'But why?' He sounded amazed.

'The children have gone, there's no need to stay together . . .'

'But we're happy.'

She shook her head.

He sighed, started to speak and stopped. Began again. 'This is about Julie, isn't it?'

'No.'

'Yes, you're still punishing me . . . after all the . . .'

'Adam. I'm fifty years old. I've raised a family and I'm proud of that, but that part . . . I need something else . . . Not this.'

'It's a mid-life crisis . . .'

'Adam. I'm not going to change my mind.'

'Jesus, Kay. I thought we'd grow old together.'

'Don't,' she said sharply. She couldn't bear the sentiment. She had dreamed of that once. No longer.

She felt her lip quivering and fought to contain her emotion. She must be strong.

'Are you seeing someone?' His face darkened.

'Oh, Adam,' she laughed, tears in her voice. 'No. We could sell the house — too big for us now.' She couldn't imagine leaving the house. It would be as big a wrench as ending her marriage. The babies had grown up here, learnt to walk, climbed the apple tree. She knew all the neighbours, the people in the parade of shops on the main road.

She felt her composure crumbling. 'We'll need to sort things out. Not now. But I had to tell you.' And she went upstairs, away from his consternation and his wounded eyes.

And now in her daughter's London home, in the kitchen with its Aga and its pretty blue-and-white tiles, pine cupboards; with her granddaughter in her arms she prepared herself to tell Theresa.

She saw the shock ripple through her daughter's features, noted the unconscious movement of her hand to her left ear, waited for the questions to tumble and answered them as best she could. She was determined not to join in when Theresa began to cry, clenched her teeth fiercely around the inside of her cheeks and sniffed several times.

They drank tea and talked and Theresa fed and changed Ella and made more tea.

'Mum,' she said, 'there's something I need to tell you, as well. It's . . . When Ella had her fits, the doctors wanted to know our medical history.'

Kay nodded. Theresa pulled at her hair, stroking it over her ear again. Why so nervous? Was there bad news about Ella?

'It's easy for Craig, but me . . . well . . . I'm trying to trace my birth mother, to see if there's anything on my side. I've got my records, my adoption records. I wanted to tell you. And there's a letter.'

Oh, God. Kay's head swam. She closed her eyes, squeezed them tight. She swallowed. Opened them again.

Nodded. 'Yes,' she said, offered a wobbly smile. Thinking all the while, Oh Jesus, I don't think I can cope with this.

* * *

Theresa

'Is Caroline there, please? Caroline Wainwright.' She stared across the office wall to her certificates displayed on the wall opposite, the family photos alongside them.

'She's not here at the moment. Can I help? This is Paul Wainwright.'

'No . . . erm, no thanks. Thank you.'

Theresa put the phone down. Sat down. Stood up immediately. She made a curious jumping movement across the room, then clasped her hands to her mouth. 'Oh, God!' she exclaimed.

She picked up the phone again and punched in a number.

'Craig, I've found her, it's the right place. She wasn't there but her husband answered. Oh, God!' She stopped speaking.

'Good God!' Craig said.

'I can write or get Helen to, she said it's best to use an intermediary at first. Oh, God. I can't believe it. It's really her. Somerset . . . No, I'm fine. I'm going to ring Mum, let her know. Yes, see you later.'

She paced some more, her face alert with excitement, shaking her head with disbelief, and then rang her mother.

'Mum, it's me. I rang that number, it's the right one. She wasn't there though, she's away, but I spoke to her husband. Pardon? No, not like that, just to ask for her, and he said could he help, he was Paul Wainwright. Probably thought it was a customer or something, it's a nursery and garden centre.' Sudden, unexpected emotion robbed her of further speech or coherent thought. She listened to her mother's congratulations and fought to retain control. She cleared her throat. 'Talk later,' she managed. 'Bye.'

She locked the door to her office and returned to her chair, the tears already splashing down her face. Like a dam bursting, bringing relief and easing the awful pressure in her chest. She let it all go. All those hours in the records office searching, peering over microfiches and registers. The awful fear of not getting there in time.

Once she had found the marriage certificate she had to go all the way to Bristol to follow up the records. It had been hard, the family had moved. But she tried local phone directories in adjoining counties and found Wainwrights listed in both the residential and the business section in listings for Somerset. Now she had found her. Even if they never met, never spoke, she knew where she was. And she could write and ask about Ella.

She wiped her eyes and blew her nose. She had a tutorial group in fifteen minutes. She went to the ladies' and washed her face. Tried to make herself presentable. It obviously didn't work, for on the way back she passed her colleague Dan Kingsley, who looked at her with concern. 'Theresa? Bad news?'

'No.' She smiled and with alarm felt her eyes water again. 'Good. Just a bit hard to take in. Found my birth mother,' she explained. 'I'm adopted.'

'Oh,' he said, disconcerted, and his face flooded with colour.

'And now I'm late for my ethics tutorial.'

'Busman's holiday, eh? Digging up your past? Mining for information.'

'Very good, Dan.' She was grateful for his clumsy humour. 'I'd best go. First years and still keen . . .'

* * *

Caroline

The address was handwritten and the sender had printed *Private* in the top left hand corner. That alerted Caroline's curiosity but that was all.

She invariably opened her mail when she stopped for coffee halfway through the morning. Carl the postman called in about ten most days and the bulk of the mail was for the business.

She assumed the letter would be from one of the work-experience students wanting a reference or some local youngster enquiring about vacancies. Unemployment was high in the area, farms were going to the wall, and although people were moving into villages they weren't bringing jobs with them. They were commuters, happy to spend a couple of hours a day travelling into the city.

Dear Caroline Wainwright,

I am writing on behalf of Theresa Murray, who I believe you knew briefly in Manchester in May 1960. Theresa would very much like to contact you and has left a letter with me to give to you.

Would you please ring or write and let me know if I can pass this on to you?

If you have any queries I would be more than happy to talk with you, at your convenience, in complete confidence.

Yours sincerely,
Mrs Helen Fairley

She scrambled to her feet, spilling her coffee. No, it couldn't be. No. She stood by the desk, staring at the letter as though it might lash out and bite her. Theresa Murray. Theresa. The name rang in her head like a bell. The name she'd chosen. She tried to imagine her but the picture she had in her mind was of an infant, Baby Theresa. What was she going to do? How could she possibly tell Paul? Or Davey and Sean?

She made a moaning noise, sat heavily in the chair and rocked to and fro. The letter before her. Oh, my baby.

After a few minutes she got up and put the snib on the Yale lock on the office door. Her heart was hammering as she dialled the number. She could just get the letter. No one need know.

'Hello, Helen Fairley here.'

'This is Caroline Wainwright. You wrote to me,' she cleared her throat, 'about Theresa.'

'Yes, of course. Thank you so much for ringing. She will be so pleased. It must have been a terrific shock.'

'Mmm,' she mumbled, not trusting herself to speak.

'I ought to explain my part in all this. I've been helping Theresa with her search and counselling her as well. With something like this everyone needs time and space to adjust and it's not in anyone's interest to rush into things. I'm what they call an intermediary, a sort of go-between. I'll be there to support Theresa, and you as well, if you wish, with each stage of the contact process.'

'My husband doesn't know, my family. I can't . . .' She broke off.

'You haven't told anyone about Theresa?'

'No.'

'That's quite a common situation. Theresa already knows that you're married and that you have two sons, from the letter you sent. We did wonder whether they'd been told anything since. Obviously you have built up a life of your own since the 1960s and Theresa understands the need to respect your privacy and your wishes, though I know she very much hopes to meet you eventually.'

Oh, Theresa. Caroline pressed her lips tight together but there was nothing she could do to contain the tears that began to stream down her face. She sniffed loudly. 'I'm sorry,' she squeaked.

'It's a very emotional time. A rollercoaster for everybody. If at any time you'd like to talk, then we can meet up. I'm based in London but I can always get the train your way if it's difficult for you to come up to town.'

'Tomorrow, I could get there by the afternoon,' Caroline blurted out. 'Can I come then? And get the letter?'

'Yes. I can give you Theresa's letter then and tell you a bit more about her.'

'Is she . . . ?' What? Happy? Lonely? Beautiful? Gifted? Angry? 'Is she all right?'

'Yes, she's married and she has a little girl. She has a good job as a university lecturer. They have been living in America for some time but now they've moved to London.'

Caroline tried to collate all this with the events of twenty-seven years ago and failed completely.

'I have a photograph for you with the letter.'

Caroline couldn't talk.

'Let me give you directions. Will you be driving?'

Mechanically Caroline wrote down the details and agreed that she would aim to arrive after midday.

When the call was over Caroline gathered up the letter and placed it with the directions in the envelope. Her hands were shaking, thoughts helter-skeltered round her mind. She mopped up the coffee from her desk. She took the envelope with her and went up to the house. She washed her face and brushed her hair. It was a grey, cold day but she had to get out. She wasn't expecting anyone that afternoon, Paul and Davey were visiting a site for a water garden, they wouldn't be back till later. She left a note for them, saying she'd be home in time for tea. She changed into her walking boots, got her waterproof coat out and let the staff know she was going out, they could run the place for the afternoon.

She walked quickly over the footbridge and into the woods. She began to climb the hillside but she was oblivious to her surroundings. She was in a new dimension, turning the unfamiliar facts over and over in her mind like the nuggets of stone that she carried in the deep pockets of her waxed jacket. Strange as a new language. Theresa had a little girl. That made her a grandma, somehow. She thought of her own grandma, calling her Mouse and entertaining her with her daft antics. Theresa. They'd kept her original name. Theresa. Who was now Theresa Murray, married, a little girl, America, lecturer — Theresa Murray. Would like to meet you. She sifted them again and again. Drumming them into her soul.

* * *

He could sense the tension in her. Even though she returned his smiles and made small talk, asking how the site meeting had gone, he could read the signs. Eyes slightly guarded, the set of her shoulders, the extra precision with which she cut up her food. As if control was in the detail, the banal. And she had taken off this afternoon.

He wouldn't press her, she would confide in him if and when she was good and ready. Any enquiry he made would be met with a dismissive shrug followed by brighter smiles and further withdrawal. It was a game of suspense. He reminded her that Davey was taking the transit, he wanted to collect some parts for the old motorcycle he was fixing up.

'I'm going into town tomorrow,' she said. 'Dentist. This crown's bothering me again.'

Perhaps that was it. She loathed the dentist.

* * *

Kay

'It's bloody awful timing,' Kay told her friend, Faith, who was sitting beside her hospital bed. 'I want to support her, I have to. But if I'm honest I just wish . . .' she let her hands play along the edge of the sheet.

'What?'

She glanced away, uncertain whether to continue, her mouth pulling with emotion.

Theresa had rung Kay a week before after another session with the intermediary. 'I've been a secret all this time. So she said that she couldn't see me but Helen says that often changes, that if you don't push too hard they often decide to tell their family. She passed on my letter and she was really pleased to have it.'

Kay had held the phone, not trusting herself to say much. Theresa was so bound up in this business, it dominated everything. It was like she was in love or something, she couldn't think about anything else, anyone else. She was frightened of rejection but desperate to meet Caroline. Kay was expected to listen and love and support her every inch of the way when Kay wanted to explode with worry and hurt.

'I'm not going to sleep,' Theresa said, 'my mind's just full of it.'

You're not the only one, thought Kay.

'I'd better go collect Ella. Oh, Mum, what will I do if she doesn't want to see me? I couldn't bear it.'

Kay tried to sound bright. 'Given time, I'm sure she will.' She had closed her eyes and leaned her head back against the wall.

'Kay?' Faith prompted her.

'I've dreaded this. Oh, I can be rational and understanding till I'm blue in the face about her right to know and how Adam and I are the parents who raised her and loved her and . . . but I'm frightened she'll walk away, fall in love with this stranger who just happens to be her blood mother and that'll be us done with.' She tore at a paper napkin as she talked, shredding it and rolling the pieces into tight balls. 'I keep imagining them meeting and it . . . it makes me sick to the stomach. I'm jealous, Faith, I know that's ridiculous but that's what I feel. And on top of all this there's this operation and, God,' she hissed, 'I feel so bloody hateful. I keep hoping she'll turn out to be a horrible person and Theresa will never want to see her again.'

'It's only natural.' Faith reached out to touch her arm. 'Anyone in your position would feel the same. Have you said anything to Theresa?'

'A little. But how can I, really? I've talked about what an upheaval it's been and that her father and I have worries but we love her and she has to do what's best for her. Adam never says much about his feelings but then she hasn't discovered a birth father, he doesn't have a rival in that sense.'

Kay had spoken to Adam on the phone about it. It was easier than meeting. They saw each other still on family occasions, Ella's birthday had been the last time. He had a new partner, Karen, but at least he had the tact not to bring her along — yet. It hadn't taken him long to find someone. Maybe he had her lined up, ready and waiting. Kay dreaded the prospect of meeting her. And she resented the fact that even now what Adam did could still hurt her so. It was as if the scars had never healed properly. Or perhaps she still loved him.

'I never really expected this. I know I always told them they could search for their parents if they wanted to but . . . when we adopted Theresa, and the others, that was supposed to be it. Legally ours, no redress. Like it or lump it. It was a promise. Now it's all changed and it feels like that promise has been . . . dishonoured. I just wish it was all over. But I was thinking this morning, it can't be the same, whether Theresa meets her or not or sees her once and never again there'll always be that woman there . . . oh, it sounds so awful.'

'You're the ones who raised her and you and Theresa are close. I'm sure it will be all right.'

Kay stretched, winced at the pain.

In the days immediately after the operation she had found herself angry with her body. At the womb that had never held a child and then caused her such pain. Its removal felt like a symbol writ large — she had been barren before but now there could be no late miracle to affirm her womanhood. She had been surprised at such thoughts and depressed by them. What did it really matter? But in those bitter moments she counted her regrets rather than her blessings. All the things she had never had: the swelling of her stomach month by month, the twisting of a child inside her, the magic of birth, the feel of a newborn in her arms, breast feeding. Not being able to look at her children and see herself in them, her own parents in them, gestures, the way they walked.

And now Theresa was likely to meet the woman who had all that. Birth mother. Caroline. And Kay felt pierced and ugly and spent and miserable. It was truly lousy timing.

'I'd better go,' Faith said. 'They'll let you home tomorrow, yes? Shall I pick you up?'

'Theresa's offered.'

'OK. I'll call round. Let me know if you need any shopping or anything. Remember, no lifting.'

Faith turned back to her. A good friend, so important. 'What about a holiday? We could go away.'

She looked at her askance, peering over the top of her glasses.

'No, really.' She smiled. 'Do something for ourselves. You and me, free woman now. Once you're feeling better.'

She couldn't imagine feeling better.

'I've always fancied the States,' Faith said.

'Christ, Faith. I was imagining Devon.' Faith had holidayed there for years. The odd trip to Brittany. No further afield with three children.

'The States?' Kay repeated.

'Yep. Well, where would you go?'

'I don't know,' she considered, her mind flicking through continents and countries. 'Egypt.'

'Egypt!'

'Yes,' she smiled.

'OK.'

'OK, what?'

'Egypt, this year, the States the next.'

Kay grinned. Why the hell not? It wouldn't change everything else but it wouldn't make it worse. And after all it was about time she saw something of the planet.

* * *

Caroline

She had written again and Theresa had replied again. More photos. Wonderful pictures of her with her husband and Ella, the little girl. Her granddaughter. They were worried about Ella. Theresa had asked Helen to find out about the family medical history. Caroline didn't know of anything like epilepsy in her background and she didn't remember anything like that about the Colbys. There was a picture of

Ella as a newborn and she looked just like Theresa had. She had put everything with her stones, hidden away.

She had spent two hours with Helen in London. Once she started talking she couldn't stop, an avalanche. She had told her everything. About the breakdowns, about the night they caught her trying to run away with her baby. The memories so vivid they were like flashbacks and the feelings so strong she got in a right state but Helen was very good about it.

'Some things have gone forever,' she said, 'the ECT, bits that are just missing. I feel so guilty. She sounds so happy but I still feel guilty. I always have. Like carrying a big sin around. No one knew. Well, my parents, but they pretended it was all hunky-dory. I'd lost a child and there wasn't even a grave.'

I want to meet her, she realised. I want to see her.

'I'd like to meet her,' she told Helen. 'But I have to tell Paul. I don't know what he'll do.'

'What do you think he'll do?'

She shook her head. 'And the boys.' She sighed, maybe she shouldn't.

'We find that siblings are often quite pleased to find a brother or sister, especially when they're already grown up. After the first surprise it can be quite a strong relationship. Responses vary of course but it sounds like you're quite a close family anyway.'

Caroline shrugged. 'I don't know. I'm frightened of what might change. It's like blowing everything up.'

'It feels destructive?'

'Isn't it?'

'I don't think so. It's a big upheaval certainly and people feel a lot of conflicting emotions but there's the positive aspect of some sort of resolution. You must decide for yourself, take your time. If you want to talk to me just pick up the phone. And if you do decide to tell your husband and your sons I'd be very happy to see any of them if they needed some support.'

But she hadn't told them yet. And each time she thought about it she felt her skin grow cold and her stomach sink and dread seep into her, tainting the joy and the passion she felt when she looked at the pictures.

* * *

There was a small enclosed area to the side of the house that Davey and Caroline had designed to try out some ideas for the garden makeover service. It had become known as Mum's grotto. The main feature was a large still pool, with flagged paths alongside it. Its edges were fringed with marginal plants, reeds and rushes. At one end they had placed a huge slab of the local limestone, big enough to sit on. Two sides of the garden were built in dry-stone walling and dotted with alpines and creepers, a homage to Paul's Yorkshire roots. Opposite the rock an arching framework covered with honeysuckle and wisteria provided an arbour for a seat.

The grotto, or variations on it, had sold itself several times over at the upper end of the market.

Caroline was sitting on the arbour seat when she heard Paul coming, with the distinctive footfall and the tap of his stick.

'Getting late,' he observed, sitting beside her.

'Yes.'

He put his hand on her leg. She stiffened. Then covered his palm with her own. 'Paul, there's something I have to tell you.'

He turned to look at her, she stared straight ahead. She's leaving me, he thought, though the idea surprised him. Why would she want to leave him? Where would she go? With whom?

'Before I met you, when I was just sixteen, I had a baby, a girl. She was adopted.'

There was a pause. 'I know,' he said.

'What?'

'I know . . .'

'But . . .'

'One of the doctors let it slip, when you were in hospital, when you were in Collins Hill, after Davey.'

She gasped. 'Why didn't you say anything?' She was stricken.

'How could I? You'd kept it a secret, you never breathed a word, what else could I do? I thought about it but I was worried that . . . I didn't want to upset you.'

'You just carried on?' She was angry.

'Like you did, you mean?' He retorted. 'Pretending Davey was the first? Talking about how a girl might be nice? Yes, Caroline.'

'Oh, god. You must have hated me.'

'No!' he protested. 'OK, I felt deceived at first. It felt like everything was false, our marriage, Davey. I was furious, actually, but what could I do? You were ill, Davey was at my mother's. It felt like everything was coming apart but I didn't want to lose you. I wanted us to make a go of it. So I settled for second best.'

She whimpered.

'No, not like that.' He put his other hand on hers. 'I mean, because you couldn't trust me, I had to get used to the idea that you didn't love me enough to share everything. So I decided that would have to do, I'd take whatever you could give. And the kids, of course, they mean the world to me. They always have.'

'Oh, Paul!' Her eyes stung, 'I did love you, I do, completely. I was a coward. I thought I might lose you if I said anything and then as time went on . . . Was I wrong?' She began to cry, noiselessly. 'Maybe I was wrong but I didn't dare test it out. I'm so sorry.'

'Why now?' He asked her. 'Why tell me now?'

'She's been in touch. I've got photos, letters . . . she . . .' She could no longer speak and turned sobbing into his chest.

And he held her close and let his own tears slide down his face and into her hair.

* * *

Kay

'I just want today to be over,' Kay said. 'I'd like to go to sleep and wake up and find it's next week.'

'We could go out for bit,' Adam said, 'get lunch.'

Once the date had been arranged Adam had offered to visit Kay. She suspected that Theresa had put him up to it. She had almost refused, not sure she wanted to share her vulnerability with him but then he was Theresa's father. It was the two of them who had been to St Ann's to bring her home and watch her grow and read her *Winnie the Pooh*, and who had taught her to sing 'Incy Wincy Spider' and to ride a bike and make daisy chains, and who loved her. He had always loved her, just like Kay, and it seemed appropriate that they wait together for word of the reunion.

'She might ring . . .' She looked at him in anguish.

'Kay, they're not meeting till two o'clock. Why would she ring before?'

'Reassurance?'

'So we just sit here?'

'And climb the walls.'

The doorbell interrupted her. She went to open it.

'Dominic! Jacob!' She put a hand down to her grandson, still having to avoid heaving things about. 'This is a surprise! Come in.'

Dominic winked at his father. 'I need a haircut, Gill's at work. I thought if you could have Jacob for a bit . . .'

'Of course. Give me something to keep my mind occupied.'

'You sure this is all right?'

'Fine,' Kay said, 'be as long as you like. C'mon, Jacob, let's find you something to play with.'

* * *

Caroline

'Time to go,' Paul yelled up the stairs.

Caroline hung over the toilet, retching without effect. She rinsed her mouth out, took another Rennie. 'Oh, God,' she prayed. 'Help me.'

Downstairs she looked around anxiously. 'Where's my bag?'

'There, with the presents.'

She collected her coat.

'Ready?'

'No.' She blinked hard, took a breath through her nose. 'Yes.'

She followed him out.

'Paul, I'm scared.'

He rested his stick against the wall. Put his hands on her shoulders. 'It'll be all right.' She looked into his eyes, warm and loving. Nodded, *Yes.*

Heard her grandma's voice, loud and full of life, urging her on. *Go on Mouse. Go on.* Laughter.

She took a deep breath of air, full of the scents of her plants. Looked back at the house, which would never be the same after today, and turned to the car.

I'm coming, Theresa. I'm coming.

* * *

Theresa

'Is it creased?'

'It's fine.'

'Oh, Craig, I'm so nervous. It's worse than getting married.'

'It'll be all right.'

What's the time? We can't be late.'

'We're not late.'

'What if she hates me?'

'Nobody's going to hate anybody.'

'What if she doesn't come?'

'She'll come. Get in the car, for the love of God.'

'You'll wait outside, you promise?'

'Aye, until hell freezes over.'

She swallowed. 'I feel sick.'

He looked at her steadily. 'Car.'

'Hold me.'

He hugged her tight.

'I love you,' she said.

'Me too. Now get in the car.'

It was time to go. Time to discover her past. And to find her future. Time to complete the circle. She stood on the threshold and felt the world stop turning.

* * *

Outside the door, poised for flight. Her heart was bumping too fast in her chest, fingers clenched. She could just go. Turn and walk away. Cruel, yes, but not impossible. This side of the door there was still room for fantasies, for dreams of what she might be like, for scenes of happy ever after, of coming home, of finding peace. But in there, once across the threshold, there would only ever be reality: stark, unrelenting, unchangeable. No going back. No escape. Her ears were buzzing and her skull and back felt tight with tension. She couldn't breathe properly.

She closed her eyes momentarily, fighting the rising panic. Don't think. Just open the door.

She put her hand out and grasped the handle. Turned and pushed. Stepped into the room. Saw the woman on the couch rise unsteadily to her feet. Smiling. Moving towards her, mouth working with emotion. Little exclamations popping softly, *hello, oh, hello*. Arms opening, eyes drinking her in.

The two women embraced.

Theresa started to cry, noisy sobs and sucking sounds.

'Twenty-eight years,' Caroline said, her voice muffled with emotion, 'I never thought I'd see you again. Come on.'

She led her daughter to the couch and sat with one arm around her, listening to her weep, her own tears sliding down her face. She smelled Theresa's hair and felt the smooth skin of her fingers and waited for the crying to gentle and cease. There was no hurry after all. Years lost, but now they had all the time in the world. Forever.

And Theresa in her hot, damp sea of tears, felt them emptying out of her, on and on like when they change the lock gates on the canals. Made no effort to control them. Holding the hand, strong and bony like her own, hearing the drumbeat in her ears. Till she is all cried out. Feeling the wheel turn. Finding herself in a new place. Tender and bewildered and brave.

EPILOGUE

The conference reception area was lined with exhibitions from adoption charities and organisations. And there were tables laden with leaflets and booklets, petitions and contact sheets. The place was filling up with people arriving. Some came alone, others in twos or threes, some even in coach parties. All ages, and men as well as women.

Helen, the counsellor, accompanied Caroline to the registration desk. They were greeted warmly and given a room plan and timetable. Keynote speeches in the large hall at ten, one thirty and three, workshops and discussion groups in-between.

'Tea and coffee over there,' the volunteer told them, 'do help yourselves.'

Caroline felt another swirl of trepidation, doubtful about the wisdom of coming here. She hated crowds, hated talking in front of people. Heat flushed her forehead and the nape of her neck.

'I'm going outside,' she told Helen, 'get some air.'

'Fine. We don't start until half past ten, we're just in there.' She pointed to a door at one end of the foyer. It was labelled with a notice, large black letters. *Room 4 Session 1a: Birth Parents — Breaking the Silence, 10.30–12.30*

Caroline made her way through the crush and out into the damp, drizzly day, past the knots of smokers lingering on the steps. She walked slowly round the courtyard, breathing in the smell of wet stone. She studied the old walls and architectural details to avoid looking at all the people. Helen had told her there'd be people from all aspects of adoption, of the triangle as she called it, and professionals too. The whole thrust of the day was to hear from people about their own experiences and to learn from that what services should be developed in the future.

A shriek of laughter made her turn. There were three women coming through the gates, two middle-aged and one younger and heavily pregnant. Were they related? They didn't look particularly alike. Were they adoptive parents, social workers, birth parents, adoptees? Impossible to tell. Caroline wondered about the pregnant woman, did she really want to be here? Did she feel at all awkward? She didn't look it. There was a crèche too, Caroline remembered, so there'd be children here, maybe babies. Which was what it was all about: babies. Losing them, finding them.

Panic made her stomach lurch. She could not do this. She'd have to tell Helen. It had been a stupid idea. She walked quickly inside, intending to make her excuses and leave, wander round the unfamiliar town centre while the rest of them got on with it.

It was busier than ever in the building and she couldn't see Helen among the many faces. Above the hubbub someone clapped hands to quieten them and asked them to take their seats in the hall. People began to move that way.

Still no sign of Helen. Caroline was annoyed, her jaw tightened with tension. She couldn't walk out without a word, not after all Helen had done for her.

A hand touched her arm and she turned to see a diminutive old woman, frail, with wispy white hair and thick glasses. 'Would you mind,' her voice quavered, 'I need to get a seat but I'm not so steady . . . I'm so very sorry to be a bother.'

'Not at all, here . . .' Caroline offered her arm and helped the woman through the throng.

'I've never been to anything like this before,' the woman said.

'Neither have I.'

'I'd no idea there would be so many people. Just look at them all.'

Caroline nodded. 'Here we are.' She guided her into the second row.

On the dais at the front, three people sat and behind them a projected message welcomed them all.

'Thank you so much. Elsie Carr.' She held out her hand, reaching up to Caroline.

'Caroline.' She hovered in the aisle.

The people on the dais were still chatting to each other and adjusting their papers.

'Have you come far?'

'Somerset, a couple of hours.' She hesitated, the last few delegates were taking their seats. 'What about you?'

'I got the coach, from Newcastle. I had to come yesterday. The people in the booking office sorted me out with a bed and breakfast.'

'That's a long way.'

Elsie nodded. The lights began to dim. 'Ooh!' She turned her attention to the front then glanced back at Caroline, who was still standing. Elsie pulled a face, a mix of excitement and apprehension, and patted the seat beside her.

With a feeling of misgiving, Caroline slid into it and watched as the woman at the podium began by thanking them all for coming.

The half hour flew by and then people were asked to leave the hall and join their morning sessions. Caroline helped Elsie once again and when they reached the foyer she asked her which session she wanted.

Elsie ran her finger down the printed sheet. 'Room four.' She looked about.

'This way.' Caroline led her over.

'What about you, dear?' Elsie cocked her head and looked up at Caroline.

It was ridiculous, Caroline thought. If Elsie had been in any other session she could have taken her there then nipped back to explain to Helen and ducked out of the session, but she felt some stupid sense of responsibility for Elsie and she couldn't lie to her.

'Same as you.'

'Good.' Elsie patted her hand. 'Good. You can hold my hand.' And she gave Caroline's hand a squeeze.

'And you mine,' Caroline muttered.

* * *

Inside Room four a circle of twenty chairs had been set out and at the back a table with tea and coffee. Helen was there, talking to a small group of women, and she nodded hello to Caroline across the room. Caroline got teas for herself and Elsie and joined her to wait as the room gradually filled up. The tea was watery and she didn't know whether drinking it would make her feel better or worse. She fiddled with the cup and saucer. The place was hot and a rush of saliva in her mouth made her stomach heave. She put her drink down and told Elsie she was nipping out for a minute.

'I'll save your seat for you.'

* * *

In the ladies', Caroline splashed water on her face and rinsed her mouth. She felt ghastly. She stared at her face in the mirror. Daft, wasn't it. Inside, she was still fifteen, still the girl who was happiest running free up on the tops or trotting after Grandma, not this middle-aged woman with grey hair and bags under her eyes and her face the colour of putty. She found a mint in her bag and hoped it would help settle her stomach. She could just stay here, hiding in the toilet, but Elsie was expecting her back . . . and Helen. And how would she ever explain to Paul or to Theresa, who both knew she was coming.

She steeled herself and set off back. As she rejoined the corridor she almost collided with another woman who'd come hurtling from the other direction.

'I'm sorry, I'm terribly late, not sure if I'm going the right way. Are you all right? You don't know . . .' She broke off. She was staring at Caroline.

Caroline looked at her. Petite build, red hair, face sprinkled with freckles, deep lines round the mouth and the eyes. Bright eyes, vivid blue. Caroline frowned. 'It's not . . . Megan?' It couldn't be.

'Oh, Jesus!' Megan's hands flew up to her face. 'I never . . .' Her hands went out to grasp Caroline's. 'Caroline?'

'Yes.'

'Oh, my God! You'll give me a heart attack!' She shook her head, her eyes filled with tears.

'Long time.'

'A lifetime. How are you? Are you . . . Did you . . . What . . . Oh, Jesus!'

Caroline couldn't help laughing at Megan's verbal contortions.

'We'll have lunch,' Megan told her, 'we'll talk.'

'Yes.' Caroline didn't hesitate. 'Your boyfriend . . . Declan?'

'Brendan. Still together. Got married, had three more. Oh, Caroline. You?'

'I'm married. Two boys, all grown up now.'

The question they both wanted to ask hung unspoken. It was Caroline who surprised herself by breaking the pause, speaking quickly. 'I met my daughter, we had a reunion.'

'Oh, I'm so glad.' Megan's face relaxed with relief. 'So did I. Well . . . mine not yours. Turned up on the doorstep. We've had our ups and downs, but—' she smiled and nodded her head — 'I wouldn't have it any other way.'

Helen appeared at the end of the corridor. 'Caroline?'

'Sorry,' Caroline gasped.

'Sorry,' Megan added and they stepped apart guiltily. 'Remember Sister Vincent?'

'Oh, don't,' Caroline laughed.

They walked back with Helen and explained to her how they knew each other. Caroline sat with Elsie on her left and Megan on her right. Helen opened the session but Caroline found herself assailed by memories: pulling the heavy laundry cart with Megan, the porridge at breakfast, the cold bedroom they had shared, Joan comforting her after they'd told her about Grandma, the terrifying labour and that first glimpse of her baby, red and streaked, a shock of hair, overwhelming, lovely. She remembered watching as the babies in the nursery were moved round closer to the door as each was taken and the night when they pulled Theresa from her arms.

She wrenched her thoughts away and back to Helen, who was now asking them to introduce themselves and say a little about their situation. Helen asked Elsie to start.

Elsie cleared her throat. Caroline felt her nervousness, saw her misshapen knuckles whiten as she tightened her hands, which were clasped in her lap. Caroline put out her hand and rested it on Elsie's arm, gave a gentle squeeze. Elsie nodded. 'I'm Elsie, Elsie Carr. I had a baby, a little boy, back in 1943. His father was a GI.' Her voice wavered. 'I've never told anybody about it. Not until today. Thank you,' she added.

'My name is Caroline. I had a daughter when I was very young. We've had a reunion.' She stopped abruptly. What else should she say? There were a million things. She turned to Megan. Megan gave her a smile.

'I'm Megan. I was in the same mother and baby home as Caroline, a place in Manchester. I wanted to get married and keep my baby but they wouldn't let us.' She paused and pressed her lips together, swallowed. 'She traced us as soon as she reached eighteen. Her dad and I, we did get married and we had three others. That's me.'

'I'm Gloria . . .' The next person began.

* * *

'I feel all . . . I don't know, inside out,' Elsie remarked when the session was over.

Megan laughed. 'You're not wrong there.'

Caroline blew her nose again. She had been in tears several times as people recounted their stories and shared their grief and anger and hopes and despair. She hadn't been the only one either. A room full of people who knew exactly what you were talking about. She felt completely drained. And she wouldn't have missed it for the world.

Helen came over. 'Lunch?'

'We're going to have a proper catch up,' Megan told her, smiling affectionately at Caroline.

'You were at St Ann's at the same time?' Helen said.

'Had our babies on the same day. Three of us, us two and this other girl, Joan. They reckoned it was a record.'

'We all shared a room,' Caroline said.

'Shall I take you to get something to eat then, Elsie?' Helen said.

'Oh, thank you. I'm famished.'

* * *

Megan and Caroline had already learnt something of each other's lives from the workshop but there was so much more to say. They were talking furiously, the conversation jumping from memories of St Ann's and the weeks after they had left to later years. Caroline told Megan about meeting Paul, her depression, the horrors of hospitalisation, the years of waiting to hear from her daughter, marking each birthday, the fact that Paul had been told about her secret. Megan talked about the lean years when Brendan was laid off and they had lived from hand to mouth, about Aidan — 'He went right off the rails and he never came back' — and the bitterness she had harboured towards her own father for refusing them the right to marry. And they spoke about their daughters, what they were like, looks and personality, compared them to their siblings, related how they first met, the whole rollercoaster ride.

Their intense talk was interrupted by Helen. 'Sorry to butt in but there's someone who would like to meet you both.' She stepped aside.

Megan and Caroline looked up at the younger woman. Shock rippled across their features.

'Joan!' Caroline whispered. 'I mean . . .'

'You must be . . .' Megan started.

'This is Pamela,' said Helen. 'Joan's birth daughter.'

'You're so like her,' said Caroline, taking in the deep-blue eyes, the long nose, the jet-black hair, the identical features.

'Spitting image,' said Megan, 'really.' She shook her head. 'Sit down.' She pulled a chair round and Pamela joined them.

'Is Joan here?' Caroline asked her.

'No, she died. Cancer.'

'Oh, God, I'm so sorry.' Caroline said.

'Oh, no.' Megan echoed.

Pamela nodded. 'I . . . never got to meet her. Helen said you knew her, at St Ann's.'

'We shared the same room: Joan, Caroline and me,' said Megan.

'You traced her, then?'

'I was a year too late.'

Caroline's eyes watered and she blinked rapidly.

'I got photos and other things but I've not been able to find out anything about when she had me or before that. She never talked about it. If you could tell me anything . . .'

'Of course,' said Caroline.

'We thought she was the bees knees,' said Megan. 'She was older than us, she had a good job, shorthand typist.'

'She was very kind as well, not gushing or anything, just in a quiet way. My grandma died while I was there and I wasn't allowed to the funeral or anything; Joan was great, she smuggled tea up to the room for me and got me to talk about my gran, I remember that. It meant a lot.'

'She couldn't knit for toffee,' said Megan and they all laughed. 'No!' she protested, 'I did it for her. Made you a matinee jacket. White, baby mix so it was nice and soft and pearly buttons.'

'Megan knitted for everyone there.'

'Do you know what time I was born?' Pamela looked from one to the other.

'You were first,' Caroline said.

Pamela frowned.

'You were all born the same day.'

'Twenty-fourth May?'

Caroline and Megan nodded.

'I started first and finished last,' said Megan. 'Thirty-three hours. Can you imagine? And you,' she said to Caroline, 'yours was really fast.'

'You were tea-time,' said Caroline to Pamela. 'I remember Joan saying later that she was getting hungry and she didn't want to miss tea. I don't know exactly what time.'

'Five o'clock they served tea,' said Megan, 'and she had some, didn't she? So you must have been a bit before then. She called you Marion.'

'I don't know why.'

'I think she just liked the name. You are so like her.' Megan shook her head again.

'Were you looking for her long?' Caroline asked.

'No, I only found out that I was adopted when my mum died. It was an awful shock.'

'They never told you?' Megan asked.

'I think they were going to when I was older but then my dad died when I was seven and I think my mum . . . I don't know, maybe she was scared of how I'd react. I don't know.'

'What else?' Megan looked at Caroline. 'Joan was the last to arrive.'

'She had a beehive, very fashionable.'

'And suits, we called them costumes then. This lovely blue suit.'

'She could play anything on the piano.'

'And she'd make these verses up for people's birthday cards, d'you remember that?'

'She became a song writer.'

'Did she?'

'You know "Walk My Way"?'

'You're joking!' said Megan.

'Really.'

'Crikey!'

'She wanted to go to London,' said Caroline. 'She'd a friend there I think already . . . Is this the sort of thing . . .' She spread her hands wide in question.

'Oh, yes,' said Pamela, her cobalt-blue eyes hungrily searching first Caroline's then Megan's, avid for anything they could remember. 'Yes, please. Just tell me everything. I want to know it all.'

And the three heads, the trio of women, bent close together once more.

THE END

THE JOFFE BOOKS STORY

We began in 2014 when Jasper agreed to publish his mum's much-rejected romance novel and it became a bestseller.

Since then we've grown into the largest independent publisher in the UK. We're extremely proud to publish some of the very best writers in the world, including Joy Ellis, Faith Martin, Caro Ramsay, Helen Forrester, Simon Brett and Robert Goddard. Everyone at Joffe Books loves reading and we never forget that it all begins with the magic of an author telling a story.

We are proud to publish talented first-time authors, as well as established writers whose books we love introducing to a new generation of readers.

We won Trade Publisher of the Year at the Independent Publishing Awards in 2023. We have been shortlisted for Independent Publisher of the Year at the British Book Awards for the last four years, and were shortlisted for the Diversity and Inclusivity Award at the 2022 Independent Publishing Awards. In 2023 we were shortlisted for Publisher of the Year at the RNA Industry Awards.

We built this company with your help, and we love to hear from you, so please email us about absolutely anything bookish at: feedback@joffebooks.com.

If you want to receive free books every Friday and hear about all our new releases, join our mailing list: www.joffebooks.com/contact

And when you tell your friends about us, just remember: it's pronounced Joffe as in coffee or toffee!

ALSO BY CATH STAINCLIFFE

DETECTIVE JANINE LEWIS MYSTERIES
Book 1: BLUE MURDER
Book 2: HIT AND RUN
Book 3: MAKE BELIEVE
Book 4: DESPERATE MEASURES

STANDALONE
THE LOST GIRLS OF ST ANN'S

Printed in Great Britain
by Amazon

39416851R00199